HISTORICAL

Your romantic escape to the past.

Lord Lambourne's
Forbidden Debutante
Lucy Ashford

Liaison With The Champagne Count
Bronwyn Scott

MILLS & BOON

LORD LAMBOURNE'S FORBIDDEN DEBUTANTE
© 2023 by Lucy Ashford   First Published 2023
Philippine Copyright 2023   First Australian Paperback Edition 2023
Australian Copyright 2023   ISBN 978 1 867 29825 0
New Zealand Copyright 2023

LIASON WITH THE CHAMPAGNE COUNT
© 2023 by Nikki Poppen   First Published 2023
Philippine Copyright 2023   First Australian Paperback Edition 2023
Australian Copyright 2023   ISBN 978 1 867 29825 0
New Zealand Copyright 2023

MIX
Paper | Supporting
responsible forestry
FSC® C001695

Published by
Harlequin Mills & Boon
An imprint of Harlequin Enterprises (Australia) Pty Limited
(ABN 47 001 180 918), a subsidiary of HarperCollins
Publishers Australia Pty Limited
(ABN 36 009 913 517)
Level 19, 201 Elizabeth Street
SYDNEY NSW 2000 AUSTRALIA

Cover art used by arrangement with Harlequin Books S.A.. All rights reserved.

Printed and bound in Australia by McPherson's Printing Group

Lord Lambourne's Forbidden Debutante

Lucy Ashford

MILLS & BOON

Lucy Ashford studied English and history at Nottingham University, and the Regency era is her favourite period. She lives with her husband in an old stone cottage in the Derbyshire Peak District, close to beautiful Chatsworth House, and she loves to walk in the surrounding hills while letting her imagination go to work on her latest story.

DEDICATION

For Alan.
Thanks for your help, as ever.

Chapter One

London, September 1817

As the clock in the corner of the drawing room struck ten, Lady Julia Annabel Emilia Carstairs counted off the chimes on her fingers. The clock was very old and its chimes stuttered with age. But she was only eighteen and so she had no such excuse for the way her pulse was jumping all over the place.

Her father cleared his throat, which was something he always did when he was about to issue a rebuke. 'I hear from your mother, Julia,' the Earl of Carstairs pronounced, 'that there was an unfortunate incident this evening at Lord and Lady Bamford's party.' He stood with his back to the fireplace, looking every bit as tall and stately as you would expect of an eminent aristocrat. Next to him stood Julia's brother, Charles, who was gazing at her even more disapprovingly than her father.

Oh, dear.

Julia, who was sitting on the velvet sofa beside her mother, swallowed down the sudden lump in her throat.

She loved her family, truly she did—her father, her mother and her two sisters, Penelope and Lizzie, who would doubtless be upstairs waiting to sympathise with her over her latest misdemeanour. She even loved her twenty-five-year-old brother Charles, when he wasn't being a pompous ass.

Everyone was waiting for her to speak. Even her father's Labradors, Rex and Mollie, were gazing at her slightly sadly as they lay in their usual places on the hearth rug. 'I did my very best to behave at the party,' Julia said at last. 'Only, you see, I didn't really know anyone except Mama. So I was sitting in a corner, on my own.'

As usual, she silently added.

'And then, I heard Lord Bamford's son say something rude about me.'

'What, exactly, did he say?' demanded the Earl.

Julia had begun fiddling with some of the stupid bows and ribbons that adorned her yellow muslin dress. She hated it. She hated going to these 'little *soirées*', which her mother insisted she attend in order to prepare herself for her presentation to London's elite as a debutante next May. That truly would be a day of doom.

She met her father's stern gaze and said with a slight shrug, 'Tristram Bamford told his friends that I resembled a stick insect wrapped up in a frilly yellow curtain.'

Her father's frown deepened. Her brother Charles muttered an oath. Her mother moaned softly, not for the first time that night.

Charles said at last, 'I must say, Mama, that Julia's dress is a little over the top, you know.'

Her mother, who was dressed in a startling shade

of pink and who very much prided herself on her taste in fashion, visibly bristled. 'Nonsense, Charles! Julia looked perfectly delightful tonight—Lady Bamford herself said so. Besides, our dear Pen wore a gown that was almost identical when she attended Lord and Lady Bamford's autumn party last year and she surpassed everyone there with her loveliness. No wonder she succeeded in winning the heart of a viscount's son!'

'Mama,' pointed out Julia patiently, 'my sister Pen is everything a girl should be. She's blonde and beautiful. Men fall over themselves at the sight of her. But look at me! My hair is dark and straight, despite all your efforts to make it curl. I'm too thin for most men's tastes. Worst of all, I like taking long walks by myself and reading books about far-off countries. I don't like parties and I particularly dislike being insulted!'

The silence that followed was broken by her father. 'Which is doubtless why,' he said, 'you spoke as you did to Lord Bamford's son. I gather from your mother that you were not polite.'

Julia lifted her chin to meet her father's clear gaze. 'I told him he was an ignorant boor and looked like a toad. Which I'm sorry about,' she added swiftly, 'because actually I *like* toads, very much. They are exceptionally intelligent creatures.'

'And then,' put in her father softly, 'you threw a glass of champagne over him?'

'It was only a very small glass. I'm sure it will wash out of his shirt!' She looked round at them defiantly. 'After that, I went to collect my cloak and I walked home.'

'On your own?' exclaimed Charles incredulously.

'On my own, Charles, yes. After all, Lord and Lady Bamford's house is only a couple of hundred yards from ours and there were plenty of respectable people around. Besides, who is going to try to molest a stick insect dressed in a frilly yellow curtain?'

She gestured at her horrid dress and tried to laugh, but honestly, she felt more like crying. Rex the Labrador lifted his head to gaze at her mournfully, then padded over to lie by her feet. Swallowing down the lump in her throat, she reached to stroke one of his silky ears.

'Julia. You're mad,' Charles said with a sigh.

Her father, bless him, looked at her brother rather sharply. 'Charles, I don't like the way you're speaking to your sister. Don't forget, she deserves our loyalty in spite of this unfortunate incident.' He sighed, too, and turned to Julia. 'My dear, you must try to understand that we want the very best for you. We really want you to be happy, as Pen is.'

'But I'm not my sister!' cried Julia, almost in despair. 'I've told Mama over and over that I hate parties and shopping for clothes. And I hate gossiping with other girls about eligible men and how they plan to ensnare them—it is truly sad!'

At which her handsome brother, the heir to the earldom and target of female wiles from every quarter, smirked a little. Which annoyed her even more.

'Yes,' she declared, 'it's all very well for you to laugh, Charles, because you're a man. You can do as you please, spend your money as you please. Why, even after you're married, you can carry on having mistresses—'

'Julia! For pity's sake!' Her mother's cheeks were as pink as her dress and she was fanning herself in agitation. 'You shock me! You are eighteen and old enough to show the manners of a lady. You could have had your Season last year with dear Pen had you not broken your ankle riding your horse at a gallop in Richmond Park. And now—*now*, the scandal of tonight's episode will be all around town by tomorrow. You need a wise husband to teach you to control your behaviour!'

'I'm sorry, Mother,' said Julia rather desperately. 'But I don't want a husband to teach me anything. In fact, I'm not sure I want a husband at all and I doubt very much anyone would want me, even though I'm the daughter of an earl. I just want things to be as they used to be!'

Her father looked grave but kind. 'What do you mean, Julia? What used to make you happy?'

She felt the tears welling up and blinked them back furiously. 'I loved it,' she said in a small voice, 'when we lived most of the year at our house in Richmond. I loved it when Pen and Lizzie and I could go out and play all day in that big garden, or ride our ponies in the park. I don't like being here in the middle of town. I don't like the crowds and the noise and the way people talk all the time about money and marriage. I don't want to have a Season at all.' She gazed up at her father almost desperately. 'I'm sorry. But I really don't feel I can go through with it.'

Her mother was reaching for her smelling salts. Even Charles appeared a little shaken. 'Look, Ju,' he said, 'I'm sorry you have such a bad opinion of men. But I assure you, you'll find there are a lot of decent fellows who would make you a kind husband. In fact, if you like, I'll look out for a few.'

'No! I do not want to be married off! I would quite honestly rather be a—a spinster!'

'Steady on,' said Charles. 'You're not *that* bad-looking, you know.'

'Charles,' pronounced her father, 'you are not helping matters in the least.'

'No.' Charles looked a little bashful. 'I apologise.'

The Earl looked almost sorrowfully at his daughter. 'I'm afraid that your mother is correct, Julia. There will be a good deal of talk by tomorrow about tonight's unfortunate exchange with young Bamford. I think it may be as well if you stop attending these pre-Season parties, just for a while.'

Julia flinched. A scandal—that was what she'd become—and her dreaded Season hadn't even begun. 'I'm sorry, Father,' she said in a low voice. 'Really, I am.'

He shook his head. 'It's by no means the end of the world, but I do have an idea. I think that perhaps we ought to let you have a brief respite from London society.'

Julia's eyes opened wide. 'You mean—I can go to our house in Richmond?'

'No,' her father quickly said, 'not to Richmond, since neither your mother nor I could leave London to stay there with you. But I've been wondering. I believe you'll remember my elderly cousin in Somerset, Lady Harris?'

'Aunt Harris, my godmother? Of course I remember her! We used to visit her for at least two weeks every summer. It was fun.'

Her mother frowned. 'The journey there was a nightmare.'

The Earl just smiled. 'You never were fond of travel, my dear, were you? But the children always found it a great adventure and you must admit you did enjoy the odd day trip to Bath whenever we were there.'

Julia listened to all this eagerly. Lady Harris, aged around sixty or so, had a splendid old house that was surrounded by wild woodland, like something from a storybook. Lady Harris was also outspoken, self-opinionated and distinctly odd, but Julia and her sisters used to love her company, not least because she was the only person they knew who dared to tease their mother about her rigid sense of propriety.

'The last time I saw my aunt,' Julia said, 'was when she came to London for our grandmother's funeral two years ago.'

'Yes,' said the Earl, 'and she vowed she would never come to London again.'

Julia hid a smile. Lady Harris had always declared that she hated London and at the moment Julia was in complete agreement. She looked up at her father. 'I like Lady Harris,' she said, 'very much. But why have you mentioned her, Papa?'

'We correspond regularly,' he replied. 'She always asks after you, Julia, and I was wondering if perhaps you might like to go and stay with her for a while.'

Julia's mother almost leaped from the sofa. 'My dear husband!' she cried. 'Lady Harris may be your cousin, but she is surely no fit companion for Julia! She is eccentric. She shuns society.'

'My cousin is much cleverer than most people give her credit for,' said the Earl firmly, 'and she does have considerable experience of life. She's nobody's fool, believe me.'

Charles was looking as amazed as his mother. 'But

Somerset! Are you truly serious, Father, about sending Julia so far away?'

'It would be for a few weeks only, Charles. That would allow ample time for any gossip about Julia and Tristram's unfortunate altercation to be replaced by something far more exciting. As further reassurance, we will of course send one of our most reliable maids to stay with our daughter during her visit—though I imagine even Julia would be able to get up to little enough mischief in such a quiet spot.' He smiled down at her as he spoke.

Her mother still looked upset. 'Oh, Julia,' she cried. 'I do declare that after staying there, you will surely come to appreciate what is on offer in London!'

Julia wasn't at all certain about that. In fact, as her father explained his plan, she'd begun to feel a ray of hope. Yes, her godmother lived in a remote place, on her own, but she was *happy*—she'd told Julia so after the funeral two years ago. 'Take no notice,' her aunt had said, 'of those who say you must be put on the marriage mart like a prize cow. You do what you want, my girl. You live the life you want!'

The life Julia wanted was certainly not the life of a debutante. 'Papa,' Julia said, a little hesitantly this time. 'How do you know that my aunt will agree to have me?'

'I will write to her first thing tomorrow,' answered her father, 'and I would be amazed if she did not wish for your company. She once called you a girl after her own heart. So…' he looked around '…are we agreed on this?'

Charles shrugged. 'If you say so, Father. Though I

think my friends will be laying bets as to how soon Julia will be pleading to come back to London!'

Julia saw her father give his son and heir the kind of look that was guaranteed to put anyone firmly in his place. 'Charles,' he pronounced, 'I hope very much that your last comment was made in jest. If any of your so-called friends should lay bets on the futures of my daughters, I trust you will show your disapproval instantly.'

Charles flushed slightly. 'Yes, Father,' he said stiffly.

'Julia,' said the Earl, in a far milder tone, 'you may leave us now. Perhaps we can discuss my plan for you in more detail tomorrow morning.'

Julia rose and went to quickly hug him. 'Thank you, Father,' she whispered. 'I'm truly sorry I've caused a stupid scandal. And thank you for thinking of Lady Harris. I should love to go and stay with her!'

Her father smiled and touched her cheek affectionately. 'Off you go to bed, then, my dear. Sleep well.'

Julia dutifully kissed her mother goodnight, then dashed off before anything more could be said. Though as she climbed the grand staircase to her bedchamber, she guessed yet more questions awaited her—and she was right, because she found her two sisters sitting on her bed.

'Julia!' cried Pen, who was twenty years old and due to be married soon. 'What has *happened*?'

Then Lizzie, who at fourteen was the baby of the family, burst out, 'We heard Mama crying and Papa speaking sternly. Was it because of the Bamfords' party? Was it just awful?'

'Appalling,' said Julia, as she tugged off her yellow

satin shoes and sank into a nearby armchair. 'Though I survived it until I heard that horrid Tristram Bamford say that I looked like a stick insect with frills, so I threw some champagne over him.'

'You didn't!'

'I did. Though honestly, who can blame him for laughing at me?' She pointed at her now very crumpled frock. 'I hate this silly dress! Hate it!'

'Is that what you were all arguing about downstairs just now?' Pen asked with sympathy.

'Oh, the truth of it is, I'm an embarrassment to them and no doubt Tristram will tell everyone around town what I said. But Father was superb. He stayed calm when Mama was on the verge of hysterics and told me he had an idea. He suggested that I could go and stay for a while with Lady Harris in the country.'

'No!'

'Yes. He did.' Julia still couldn't quite believe it herself.

'But that's amazing.' Lizzie clapped her hands in glee. 'We used to love it, didn't we, whenever we went to visit her in that big old house of hers. She was such fun. She drove Mama wild because she encouraged us to roam in the woods and have adventures!'

'She is rather mischievous,' agreed Julia. 'But Papa likes her and so do I.'

'I wish I could come, too,' said Lizzie. 'But what does Charles think?'

'Naturally, our brother was as horrified as Mama. But he disapproves of anything I want to do—and I've decided I really, really want to stay with Aunt Harris and to put my Season off for as long as possible. Especially as I'm quite sure it's going to be a disaster.'

'Nonsense,' said Pen briskly. 'You'll have plenty of men falling for you if you only give yourself a chance! But Lizzie and I shall miss you dreadfully while you're away. Besides, won't you be lonely? I've heard that Lady Harris hardly sees a soul.'

'Being lonely would be an improvement on being insulted at parties.' Julia shuddered.

Suddenly their mother's piercing voice rose from the bottom of the grand staircase. 'Lizzie. Lizzie, darling, are you with your sisters? Your maid is looking for you. It really is time you were in bed!'

Lizzie jumped up. 'Oh, no. I'd better go. But first, can the three of us have our usual hug?' She held out her arms and the sisters embraced. 'There,' declared Lizzie happily, 'that's better. We'll stick by each other to the end, isn't that right?' She popped a kiss on Julia's cheek. 'Dear Julia, some day you will find a man who is truly amazing. I just know you will!'

After Lizzie had scurried off, Pen sat down again slowly. 'I suppose I ought to go as well. But, Julia, I just want to tell you something.'

Julia grinned. 'Secrets? Oh, good.'

Pen blushed a little. Then she said, 'Yes, it is a secret— sort of. You see, I've discovered that…well, it's rather marvellous being in love.'

'I can see that.' Julia pretended to scrutinise her. 'Pen, you positively glow with it.'

Her sister blushed even more. 'Do I?'

'Most definitely. You have a mysterious smile every time you mention Jeremy's name.' Jeremy, who was the son and heir of Viscount Dersingham, was going to marry Pen in less than two months. He was exceedingly pleasant and anyone could see that he adored his bride-to-be.

'Oh, Julia!' Pen sighed. 'I really can't help being happy. You see…' and she lowered her voice to a whisper '…whenever darling Jeremy kisses me, it makes me just long for our wedding night!'

Julia sat on the bed beside her. 'Pen, darling, I'm sure you'll be terrible happy with him. You deserve to be, you're so lovely and kind. But I'm neither and I do not want to marry the kind of man who finds himself an heiress, then goes off and grabs a mistress to have fun with, as soon as his wife has had a baby or two— Oh!' Julia clapped her hand to her mouth at the look on her sister's face. 'I'm so sorry, what a dreadful thing to say. Everyone can see that Jeremy adores you and I'm sure he'd never take some silly mistress, ever!'

Pen nodded. 'I know he won't. But I'm also quite positive that Father will never make you marry someone you detest—so please, don't give up before you've even started looking!' She glanced at the marble clock on Julia's dressing table and stood up. 'I really must go, too. No doubt one of the maids has been waiting in my room for ages to help me out of my gown. Shall I help you with yours before I go?'

'No, I'll ring for a maid myself. Though I'd rather tear this dress off piece by piece!' Julia tried to laugh as she, too, rose to her feet.

Pen studied the yellow gown sympathetically. 'When it's time for you to make your debut, I shall insist to Mama that she take you to the most fashionable dressmaker in town and I shall come with you both. There'll be no yellow, no frills—but you will look gorgeous, I promise! Goodnight, Julia dear. Sweet dreams.'

With that Pen, after blowing her sister a kiss, flew off down the passageway to her own room.

Julia went to close her bedroom door, but halted when she caught sight of herself in her mirror. Gorgeous? Never. She didn't have the feminine curves her sister had. She didn't have the angelic blue eyes either; instead, her eyes were a strange shade of pale greeny-grey—'rather like the sea on a cold day in midwinter,' an anxious man trying hard to be polite to her had once said. Distinctly unappealing, in other words.

Otherwise, Julia supposed there was nothing exactly *wrong* with her face—in fact, a noted London artist had once wanted to paint her, because of her delicate cheekbones, he'd enthused. But even he had confessed that her hair was all wrong for a portrait, because it simply refused to curl.

Mama always insisted on her having it wound tightly in rags for hours before Julia was due to attend any social event. 'Then,' her mother would promise, 'one of the maids will put it up in ringlets for you, just like Pen's!' But the attempt was futile because during the evening the curls would gradually flop, making Julia look like an over-warm spaniel with its ears drooping in the heat.

She shut her bedroom door and sat rather despondently on the bed. A moment later though, she jumped up again—because she'd just remembered that she'd left something rather embarrassing downstairs in the hallway.

She had put her beaded silk purse on the table there, the one she'd taken to Lord and Lady Bamford's horrid party, and in it was her tiny diary. Well, it was more of a private notebook really, because there wasn't room for all the engagements her mother dragged her to. But the worst thing was that she used it to keep a list of young men to avoid like the plague. She called it her *Guide to the Gentlemen of London* and it wasn't a flattering list, because beside each man's name she'd scrawled his deficiencies.

> *Sir Frederick Timms. Breathes garlic everywhere.*
> *Lord Percival Sumner. Always lets his clammy hands stray to your bottom when he dances with you.*
> *Viscount Clive Delaney. Walks like a waddling walrus.*

And so on. Good grief. If her mother were to read it, she would faint.

Hurriedly Julia descended the broad staircase and sighed with relief to see that her reticule was still there. She was about to grab it when she realised her father and Charles were still talking in the drawing room—and they were talking about her. Sidling close to the not quite shut door, she listened carefully.

'There's another thing, Father, about this plan of yours,' Charles was saying, 'to send Julia to Lady Harris. You do realise, don't you, who might be staying close by?'

There was a brief silence, in which Julia was convinced they would hear her heart thudding. At last came her father's terse reply. 'There's not much chance of him being there, Charles, since the last I heard, the fellow had no intention of leaving Vienna any time soon. So you needn't worry about him.'

Julia listened intently. Who did they know in Vienna? Why were her father and Charles worried about him? They talked on in lowered voices, though at one point her father spoke more clearly.

'I suppose,' he said, 'that like the ladies, you and I ought to retire. But there's one last thing, Charles.'

'Which is?'

'I fear there will be talk around town about Julia's behaviour tonight. So you'll do what you can to quell any malicious gossip about your sister, won't you?'

'Of course. But she really must learn to use some tact!'

'She's Julia,' said her father. 'We all love her dearly, but she's different, Charles. She wants to feel she has choices in her life. Obviously she must learn to restrain her impulsiveness, but we must all do everything we can to support her, do you understand?'

Before she could hear what her brother had to say to that, Julia, clutching her reticule, fled back up to her room.

Different. In other words, she was an oddity who would probably end up a spinster—and all she could say to *that* was that spinsterhood was a far better fate than being married to someone like Tristram Bamford. Yes, she'd written about him in her notebook, too, only the other week.

His eau-de-cologne reminds me of mothballs.

She remembered a little despairingly what Lizzie had

said to her. *'Dear Julia, some day you will find a man who is truly amazing. I just know you will!'*

Not at Lady Harris's. Julia almost laughed at the thought. Not in the wilds of Somerset.

Absolutely no chance.

Chapter Two

Two weeks later, Benedict Lambourne was chopping down some overgrown ash saplings on a wooded hillside in rural Somerset.

The saplings had sprung up around an old summer pavilion that was in sad need of repair. Slates had fallen from its roof and the stone walls were crumbling. The ash saplings had claimed his attention because soon their roots would be clawing their way into the building's foundations, so since dawn he'd been swinging his axe like a labourer, clad in an old linen shirt, corduroy breeches and scruffy leather boots.

It would, he reflected, be hard for any passer-by to believe that for several years he'd been working as a diplomat for the British government in Austria. Hard to believe also that he was the Fifth Baron Lambourne, the new owner of the historic Somerset mansion in whose lands this pavilion stood. His father, the Fourth Baron, had died three months ago, but by the time the news reached Ben he was lying in a hospital bed in Vienna with a badly broken leg.

His father's lawyer, Thomas Rudby, had travelled from London to visit Ben there, bringing countless documents for him to read and sign.

'Your Somerset estate, Lord Lambourne,' Rudby had warned, 'is not in a good way. You'll be giving up your post here, I imagine?'

Ben had nodded wearily. He was still fighting the pain from his injury and the nausea from the medicines he'd been given. 'Of course,' he said. 'But the doctors have warned me it could be weeks before I can travel.'

'With you permission, my lord,' said Rudby, 'a cousin of your father's has offered to organise the funeral and it will be a quiet affair, as your father stipulated in his recent will. As for Lambourne Hall, you probably realise it requires a considerable amount of renovation and might not be suitable for you if you are still...' he glanced at the bandages and splints encasing Ben's leg '...encumbered by your physical condition. Perhaps London would be more appropriate?'

Ben had shaken his head. As things stood, he had no desire to live in London. Instead, when he was finally well enough to travel, he'd come home to Lambourne Hall, accompanied only by his valet, Peter Gillespie, who'd been with him for years. No one else knew he was here, except Rudby.

Ben was twenty-five years old. He was lame and God knew when he'd be able to walk properly. He didn't even know if there was enough money in the estate to make the Hall fit for living in again. But he wanted to be here and nowhere else, for he knew that he should have been here during the last year of his father's life.

He should have realised the extent of his father's troubles and supported him in his adversity—

'Yoo-hoo!'

What on *earth*? He almost dropped the axe he was holding because he'd heard footsteps, followed by a most distinctive voice.

Carefully he laid the axe down, realising what—or rather who—was heading his way. It had to be Lady Harris, his one and only neighbour, whose land bordered his.

'Now, it's no use pretending,' the piercing female voice went on, 'that you're not there. Or ducking behind those trees, since you've chopped most of them down.'

Ben straightened himself up as a tiny, grey-haired lady dressed in a voluminous purple cape came along the path to where he stood. 'Lady Harris,' he said. 'And a good day to you, too. It's been a long time since we saw one another. How are you this morning?'

'A good deal better than you, I imagine,' she replied, 'because you must have had weeks of travelling and that leg of yours can't have healed up yet. Yes, I heard you broke it in some far-flung country. Whatever were you up to?'

'I was thrown from my horse in Austria,' he said. 'A sudden thunderstorm spooked the animal.'

She nodded. 'It was a bad break, too, wasn't it? No wonder you had to miss your father's funeral. But I knew you were back at Lambourne Hall, because I spotted some smoke coming from one of the chimneys up there last night.'

Ben liked Lady Harris, he really did. She was, he guessed, around sixty years old; he also knew she'd lived at Linden House, down in the valley, for almost all of her life. 'Lady Harris,' he said, 'I don't want anyone to know that I'm here. Not yet.'

'Any particular reason, young man?'

'Yes, plenty. There are things I want to do. Matters I need to sort out.'

She nodded. 'Matters concerning your father? Here's a word of advice, then. Your father was a good man, but he had his problems and it's no good ruining your own future by dwelling on them.'

'I want,' Ben said quietly, 'to restore the estate for him. I also want to clear his name.'

'And you're going to do that all by yourself? Here, at the back of beyond?' She pursed her mouth. 'Wouldn't it be easier doing all that from London? You have a property there, don't you?'

'I do, but it's rented out at present. Anyway, I wanted to come to Lambourne—and, Lady Harris, I must emphasise that I don't want anyone to know yet that I'm here.'

'But you're Lord Lambourne! People will be curious. You'll be seen when you go out and about—bound to be!'

'My manservant will get in any provisions I need. No one will recognise him—besides, I only need my privacy for a short while.'

'So you're up to something, are you?'

He shook his head, smiling. 'Very little, but I'm not really in the mood for company. So will you do me a great favour? Will you tell no one that I'm here?'

She put her head on one side, bright as a little bird. 'So you won't even come down and play chess with me, like you used to whenever you came home?'

Chess. Yes, he used to enjoy those games with her.

She was good. He smiled and said, 'Why? Are you lonely down there, Lady Harris?'

'Lonely? Ha, no chance of that! Don't forget I have my servants, who drive me to distraction as usual. Besides, I'll have a guest soon.'

He'd noticed she was looking mysterious and a moment later she was pulling a folded sheet of paper from her pocket.

'A guest?' he said.

'Indeed. I got this letter last week, from a cousin of mine in London—which, by the way, is a place I can't abide.'

'You've told me so before, I believe.' Ben grinned. 'What does this letter say?'

'My cousin says—' and she peered at the paper closely '—that he hopes I'm well and all that kind of nonsense. Of course I am! Then he asks if he may send his eighteen-year-old daughter to visit me, as soon as possible.'

'I see,' said Ben. But in fact it seemed to him a mighty strange decision to send a girl of that age out to Somerset, in the care of the eccentric Lady Harris.

'You'll be wondering why, young man.'

'I was, rather.'

'Well, as it happens, I know the girl pretty well. She's my goddaughter and I've always liked her. Why? Because she refuses to act all sweet and obedient like girls her age are supposed to. And I would guess—mind, this is only a guess—that she's been in a bit of bother, so maybe her parents think a spell of isolation is in order.'

Ben was curious. 'So you don't mind having her to stay with you?'

'Of course not. In fact, I'll look forward to seeing her again.'

'Good for you.' Ben nodded his approval. 'But why are you telling me all this?'

'Because I wouldn't be surprised if she's still just a little bit wild. Likely to go roaming, you know? And though there's not much to harm her in these parts, I thought that since you were around, it's possible you might run into her. From what you say, I imagine there's little chance of you rushing off on foreign adventures for quite a while.'

'Little chance indeed,' he acknowledged rather quietly. 'You may be sure of that.'

Lady Harris wagged her finger. 'Don't let this business over your father embitter you, young man, will you? It's the last thing he would want for you, believe me. Now, this girl could be arriving any day, so you'll know who she is if you come across her.'

'I very much hope I won't. Lady Harris, let me repeat— I do not want the news that I'm here to spread around so you won't tell this girl about me, will you?'

'Don't worry, she won't be interested in *you*. Have you looked at yourself in the mirror lately? It must be days since you shaved. As for your clothes, words fail me.'

She chuckled and Ben had to grin, too. His valet Gillespie, generally known as Gilly, had begun to despair of dressing his master like the lord he was supposed to be.

'Do you know something?' Gilly had told him only this morning. 'Unless you get that hair of yours cut soon, people will think you're some kind of mad poet, wandering the countryside for inspiration.'

A poet? Yes, that was quite likely, thought Ben, especially since he had a lame leg into the bargain—just like Lord Byron. Then he realised Lady Harris's expression had changed.

'Your father was very fond of this place, wasn't he?' She was gazing up at the pavilion now.

'I think it reminded him of my mother,' Ben replied quietly. 'He often told me that she used to adore coming here.'

'Then I'll let you carry on, young man.' She nodded, her usual brisk self. 'Help me over this pile of rubble, will you? And I'll be on my way.'

He guided her over an obstacle of fallen stones and watched as she set off along the path that led past a small lake, then down through the woods to her house in the valley. But suddenly she stopped and called out to him, 'I forgot to tell you the girl's name, didn't I? It's Julia.'

After that she carried on, until she was out of sight.

What, Ben wondered, had this Julia got up to in London? Trouble with a man was the usual problem. Perhaps sending the girl to her godmother's was a punishment for some mild flirtation? He pondered a moment, recalling his own encounters with well-born young females in London and Vienna. Quite frankly, he couldn't imagine a single one surviving more than a week here in the wilds without screaming to be sent home and he guessed this Julia might find even a week too long.

His leg had begun to ache again, so he picked up his axe and began to swing it at yet another stray sapling. Action. That was the remedy for most problems—and he certainly had plenty to keep him busy here, in all kinds of ways.

Chapter Three

'Lady Julia? My lady? Do you realise that we're almost there?' Betty leaned across to tap Julia's arm.

The gentle rocking of the Earl's luxurious travelling carriage had almost lulled Julia to sleep, but she woke with a start at the sound of her maid's voice and quickly looked out of the window. There, in the distance, was the steeple of the little church rising above Lambourne village—which meant they were less than a mile from her aunt's house.

'You'll regret this, Julia,' her brother Charles had warned her three days ago as the family gathered outside their Mayfair home to bid her farewell.

'Nonsense!' she'd replied. Then she'd hugged her two sisters, who'd both looked a little tearful. 'I'm going to have a grand adventure,' she'd whispered to them, 'and I'll write often, I promise I will!'

The journey itself had been uneventful. Toby, her father's chief coachman, was a silent fellow, but he had dealt excellently with any awkward inn owners or ostlers who weren't immediately ready to change the horses on the way. But it was in Betty's nature to talk constantly, even in the bedchambers she and Julia shared each night in the different inns. The worst of it was that she was going to stay at Lady Harris's, as Julia's maid.

'Yes. We're almost there,' Betty was saying as the carriage rolled onwards. 'Though why you wanted to leave London and go to the back of beyond, my lady, I shall never understand. All these fields and blessed trees—give me town life any time!'

Julia said nothing. She was gazing out of the window again, because now she could see the old stone bridge over the stream where she and her sisters used to paddle when they were little. Lady Harris had always encouraged them in their adventures, which had annoyed their mother extremely.

She smiled at the memory. Being with her aunt was going to be a treat, but oh, if only her maid would stop talking!

'Of course,' Betty said, 'I don't mind staying with you in Somerset, my lady, not in the least. But there's many who wouldn't like it, no, not at all— Oh, my saints!' Her voice suddenly became a squeak. 'What on earth is happening?'

For the carriage had suddenly lurched to a juddering halt and Toby could be heard cursing vociferously. Julia opened the window and called, 'Toby. Is something wrong?'

The horses were stamping and snorting. Toby had already jumped down from his seat and was trying to soothe them. 'It's a wheel come loose, my lady,' he called back. 'Might take me a while to fix it. I could walk to your aunt's house to get help—it's only half a mile—but I can't leave these horses. You see how frightened they are?'

Julia was already climbing out. 'I can go,' she said. 'I can fetch help.'

Betty was beside her now. 'You must not even think of it, my lady!' she exclaimed. 'Tramping through those woods, who knows what might happen? And besides—'

She broke off.

All three of them had seen a man up in the woods, who stood looking in their direction. Toby cupped his hands round his mouth and bellowed, 'Hey. You up there, fellow. Come and give us a hand here!'

At first, Julia thought the man was going to ignore them and move on. But then, slowly, he began descending the hill towards them. 'Oh, my,' breathed Betty as he drew nearer. 'Will you look at *that*?'

Julia, as it happened, was already looking.

He was around her brother's age, she guessed. He had thick brown hair that clearly hadn't been trimmed for some time and an unshaven jaw. He wore a loose linen shirt and breeches and walked with a noticeable limp. After scanning the scene, he said, 'I gather you have a problem?'

He was well spoken, but he didn't smile or offer to introduce himself and to Julia it was clear he would much rather not have been summoned like this. But Toby was already beckoning him bossily over to the side of the carriage.

'You see this rear wheel? That, my man, is the problem. The bolt's come loose. Now, you look a strong enough fellow, so if you put your weight just here—' he tapped the side of the carriage '—to keep it steady, then I can tighten up the bolt again. Then we'll be all right and tight.'

The man nodded and was about to put his shoulder to the carriage when Julia stepped forward. 'Toby,' she said, 'it's really very heavy. Perhaps we shouldn't be asking him to do this!'

The man looked at her steadily. His eyes were a rich brown and she noticed that they darkened as she spoke. Had she insulted his pride? Was he angry with her?

But he merely said to her, 'It's no problem at all. I assure you.' Then he proceeded to apply himself to the task Toby had set him.

Julia watched in silence, fascinated by the way the muscles of his arms and shoulders bunched beneath his shirt as he took the weight while Toby worked on the wheel. Betty was more vocal in her appreciation of the handsome stranger. 'Will you look at him?' she kept murmuring. 'Will you just look at that fine man?'

It was all over very swiftly. Soon the wheel was secure and Toby straightened himself with a nod of satisfaction. 'Thank you, my man,' he said loftily to the stranger. 'We're obliged to you, I'm sure.' He turned to Julia and Betty. 'Ladies. Shall we be on our way?'

But Julia didn't move. She wanted to do something to thank him; she felt she *had* to do something to thank him, so she reached for her purse and called out to the man before he left. 'Please. Let me offer you some money for your trouble!'

He turned to look at her, then said, 'There is no need at all, I assure you. I bid you good day.' Then he set off, walking up into the woods again, and Julia felt mortified. She knew she'd offended him with her offer of money and she was more sorry than she could say.

Soon the carriage was on its way once more and Julia tried to concentrate on the pleasures in store. No parties to attend! No pompous idiots to insult her! But somehow all she could think of was that man.

Her spirits, though, began to rise as they emerged from the woods and Linden House came into view. Built by a noted maritime explorer from Bristol, it was a rambling building that its owner had filled with reminders of his love of the sea. There were stained-glass windows portraying his various vessels, there were stone lintels carved with the dates of his most notable voyages and even the weathervane fixed to the highest roof was in the shape of a ship.

This was truly one of the most fascinating places Julia knew and its surroundings were exquisite, too. Now that autumn was here, her aunt's extensive gardens were filled with the purple and pink hues of Michaelmas daisies, while the leaves of the beech woods on the surrounding hills shone like polished bronze in the sun.

So much to explore again. It was just like old times— and indeed, there was Lady Harris standing outside her front door, looking as she always did, tiny but bold and bright in her startlingly colourful attire. As soon as Julia had emerged from the carriage her aunt strode briskly up to greet her.

'Well, my dear,' pronounced Lady Harris, 'it's about time they let you escape from that ghastly city.'

'Aunt, it's lovely to be here with you again.' Julia took her aunt's hands and smiled, though then she couldn't help but burst out, 'Did you know you have twigs in your hair?'

'Have I? That's because I've been chasing the pig boys. You'll remember what a pest they are.'

'You mean the boys from Lambourne village? Do they still bring their pigs to your oak wood for acorns?'

'They do indeed, but I'm not having it. Cheeky young things!'

Julia hid her smile. From what she remembered, it was a fine game for all, because Lady Harris enjoyed chasing the boys just as much as they enjoyed teasing her.

She realised her aunt was glancing with narrowed eyes at Betty, who was haranguing Toby over the unloading of the luggage. 'Is she your maid?' said Lady Harris. 'Is she staying?'

'She is, Aunt.'

'Hmmph. Well, let's go inside and you can get your bearings. Welcome to Linden House, my dear. It's very good to see you.'

'You, too, Aunt,' said Julia warmly. 'Oh, you, too!'

An hour later, Julia stood on the front terrace, watching Toby prepare his team of horses for the first stage of the long journey home. She'd left Betty upstairs in her bedchamber and the maid had speedily expressed her feelings as she set about unpacking Julia's clothes. 'If I were you, my lady,' she'd pronounced, 'I'd not be staying here for one night, let alone a matter of weeks. Feel free to change your mind, because Toby can always take us back to London with him!'

Back to odious noblemen like Tristram Bamford?

Julia shook her head, appalled. 'No,' she declared firmly. 'I will be fine here, Betty. Absolutely fine.'

With an audible sigh Betty went on with her work, rattling drawers and glancing with dismay at the model ship in full sail that sat on a table by the window. Julia loved the ship, which she remembered from when she was a child, but Betty shook her head. 'It does nothing but gather dust,' she said. 'As for all the boat paintings hanging everywhere, they make me feel all at sea myself.'

Ships, Julia wanted to say. *They are ships, not boats.*

She refrained, however, and decided to go downstairs, for Toby and the coach were surely almost ready to depart and she wanted to bid him farewell. As she walked through the house she passed two young maids—sisters, she guessed—who curtsied to her shyly. She smiled at them and hurried outside to Toby.

'Thank you for bringing me here safely,' she said. 'I hope you have a swift journey home.' Then she stood and watched the departing carriage until it was out of sight. *'Freedom,'* she murmured softly.

'Freedom indeed,' said her aunt, who had suddenly appeared at her side and must have heard. 'Which is exactly what you need. Now, where's that maid of yours?'

'She's still unpacking my things upstairs, Aunt.'

'Thank God she's out of the way, for a while at least. Does the blessed woman ever stop talking?'

'No,' said Julia and laughed aloud. 'Oh, Aunt. It's lovely to be here with you again!'

'Of course it is. Now, you've already seen your bedchamber, but I'll show you the rest of the house, shall

I? Just in case you've forgotten your way around. Most people do.'

Linden House was indeed a puzzling old building, for one room opened into another, then another, and if you weren't careful you could get completely, delightfully lost. Julia, though, remembered it well, for she and her sisters had taken great delight in the way that if you went through one door, it could lead to a twisting staircase or if you opened the next, you might find the library or the music room. Everywhere there was evidence of the house's first owner and his travels, in the form of lamps shaped like giant seashells and draperies embroidered with images of exotic birds.

'Nothing has changed since you were last here,' said Lady Harris as they finally reached the hallway once more. 'Though my staff can be most irritating. I have my work cut out keeping them in order.'

Julia smiled. Lady Harris always grumbled about the variety of servants who had passed through her doors. 'Do you still have Miss Twigg?' Miss Twigg was unforgettable: she had been her aunt's companion and housekeeper for many years.

'Yes. I put up with her and she puts up with me, somehow. My last butler left long ago, but since I've so few visitors, I don't really care. A couple of lads come from Lambourne village two or three days a week to tidy around outside, then there are the two girls who come every day to do the washing and cleaning. They'll be in the kitchen. Grace! Dottie!' she called in her piercing voice. 'Come and meet Lady Julia!'

The two maids she'd seen earlier, both wearing huge

white aprons and white caps, hurried from the kitchen and curtsied. 'Welcome, my lady,' they chorused.

Julia smiled. 'Thank you.' They looked friendly. They looked fun.

'Twigg tries to push them around,' said Lady Harris to Julia. She turned back to the maids. 'But you put up with her. Don't you, you flighty pair?'

'Yes, Lady Harris!' they spoke in cheerful unison again.

'Off you go, then.' Lady Harris turned to Julia. 'They take very little notice of Twigg in fact. Can't say I blame them. And of course, there's Sowerby—you remember him, I'm sure.'

'He's your handyman, isn't he? And he was your groom, but do you still keep horses, Aunt?'

'I still have Nell. Do you remember her?'

'I do.' Julia hesitated. 'But looking after Nell is hardly a full-time job, is it? And surely Mr Sowerby is—'

'Getting rather ancient? Yes, he is.' She led Julia outside and along the side of the house, where some hens clucked at their approach. 'He and Twigg are forever arguing, but they do enjoy their battles. Talking of battles, I often find Sowerby skulking in the barn here and playing at soldiers.'

'I remember!' exclaimed Julia. 'He used to make tiny figures from copper wire, then put them on painted boards and pretend they were at war.'

'Exactly. He still does.' Lady Harris walked towards the barn and bellowed, 'Sowerby. Are you in there?'

A rather elderly man emerged. 'My lady?'

'Sowerby,' said Lady Harris very loudly, 'you remember Lady Julia, don't you? She's staying with us for a while—yes, staying—so don't go boring her to death with your endless soldierly talk, do you hear?'

'I'm sure I'd never be bored,' Julia said quickly.

'It's a pleasure to have you here again, my lady.' Sowerby bowed. 'You'll doubtless remember that your aunt is one of the best people one could meet.'

'Stuff and nonsense,' declared Lady Harris. 'Now, you get back to your battles, Sowerby.' She waved him away, then led Julia to the stables. 'Here's Nell—she's still going strong. There's an ancient gig round the back which Sowerby sometimes drives down to the village on errands for me and that gives her some exercise.'

As Julia stroked Nell's velvety nose, Lady Harris inspected the large old watch she kept on a chain at her waist. 'Now,' she said, 'it's just gone two o'clock. Are you hungry?'

'No,' said Julia honestly. 'I had a huge breakfast this morning, at the last inn.'

Lady Harris nodded. 'Then we'll have afternoon tea at four, shall we? Twigg's made some chocolate cake. But before your chatterbox of a maid finds you again, I'd like to know exactly why you've been packed off here. Well?'

Julia hesitated, not knowing how much her father had told her aunt in his letter. 'I'm afraid I was rude to a man at a party, Aunt.'

'Did he deserve it?'

'Oh, yes.' Julia was emphatic. 'Most definitely.'

'Then good for you.' Lady Harris grinned.

Julia had to smile back, but then her spirits sank anew. 'Yes, but it's my Season coming up soon and I shall have to behave myself! Though I detest the prospect of being paraded before ogling suitors and so far I've not met one I can abide.'

'Hmm.' Lady Harris pulled a thoughtful face. 'There are ways to put men off, you know. Maybe I can give you a few hints that will send them scuttling for the door.'

'Can you? Really?'

'Of course. Express your own opinions and if you know they're wrong about something, then tell them so. Make them aware, too, that you're full of oddities, like going off and roaming the countryside whenever the fancy takes you. Which reminds me—I think you should go off and take a long walk.'

Julia's eyes opened wide. 'Now? By myself?'

'Why not? You've been travelling in that blessed coach for days and it's a lovely afternoon, so make the most of it. Oh, and there's something useful you can do. I need you to gather some burdock leaves, for my rheumatism.'

'I didn't know you had rheumatism!' Julia was surprised, since her aunt seemed to her to be extremely sprightly.

But Lady Harris groaned a little and put one hand to her hip. 'Sometimes it's really bad. So I make a concoction with burdock, but I've nearly run out.' She pointed towards the woods. 'There's often some growing by the lake up there. It's close to the pavilion—do you remember it?'

'The old stone pavilion? I've seen it from a distance. But—is it yours?'

'Oh, nobody cares what belongs to anyone around here. There are no walls, no fences. Besides, you know what I always say. Property is theft!'

Julia couldn't help but remember her aunt's aversion to the pig boys on her land. But Lady Harris had already changed tack because she'd caught sight of Miss Twigg, who was hanging out some washing in the side yard.

'Twigg! Twigg, you remember Lady Julia, don't you? She's escaped from London for a while—isn't she the lucky one? Now tell me, Twigg, where on earth have you put that book I was reading about herbal medicines? Really,' she muttered in an aside to Julia, 'can't the woman leave anything where it was?'

Off Lady Harris set to harangue her housekeeper and Julia glanced down at herself. As soon as they arrived, she had changed out of her travelling habit into a pink, long-sleeved cotton dress and light shoes, but she definitely needed some more suitable footwear if she was going exploring. She went upstairs cautiously.

There was no sign of Betty, but the maid had been allotted a small bedchamber next to hers and from there Julia heard the sound of snoring. She peeped in through the half-open door to see Betty lying fast asleep on the bed.

Quickly she changed into a pair of laced walking shoes, slipped on a simple blue jacket, then pushed her diary and a pencil into a pocket, just in case she was inspired to write something. The path through the woods beckoned. Freedom beckoned.

How absolutely wonderful.

Chapter Four

Ben had finished his tree work and was up on the pavilion roof, fitting in a new corner-stone to replace one that had crumbled with age. He knew that Gilly would tear a strip off him if he saw him. 'Are you mad?' Gilly would say. 'Scrambling about up there with no help?'

He'd certainly been mad to let himself be seen by that coach driver earlier, especially as he'd guessed immediately that the girl in the coach was Lady Harris's new guest. With luck, he'd never see her again. She had fine clothes and haughty manners, and no doubt she'd remain indoors at Linden House, doing a little watercolour painting or gossipy letter-writing to alleviate her boredom.

He doubted she would even mention their meeting to her aunt. She had assumed he was a labourer and such men were quickly forgotten by the likes of her.

After climbing carefully back down the ladder, Ben stood and looked up at his work. He'd noted already that his white linen shirt was speckled with lichen from the stones he'd been heaving around earlier, as were his boots and breeches. When he got back to the Hall Gilly would issue a stern rebuke, but then he would grin and say, 'I can see you've been having a fine time of it, my lord!'

Which he certainly had. There was still plenty to be done, but the pavilion was just starting to look something like his childhood retreat of old, the place he used to pretend was a castle or whatever took his fancy long, long ago.

Brushing the lichen from himself as if trying to banish old memories, he put the chisels away in his toolbox and set off towards the lake to rinse his hands and face. But all of a sudden he stopped—because something had caught his eye. There had definitely been a flash of movement down by the water's edge and he would swear he'd seen something that was pink. Pink? What on earth…?

All was still now, but he didn't move a muscle.

There it was again, that burst of colour. Some birch trees partly blocked his view, so he moved silently between them until the lake's edge was only yards away. That was when he saw her—a girl with long dark hair, sitting on a slab of rock down by the water and writing something in a small notebook she'd rested on her knees. Her pink dress and white petticoat were pulled up well above her ankles, while her stockings, shoes and jacket lay discarded some yards away. She was dabbling her bare feet in the shallows and he could hear her humming softly as she wrote.

It was the girl from the coach. Lady Harris's young relative, Julia. Damn it all, what was she doing up here, on his land? Obviously his best tactic was to promptly retreat and leave her to it, but he was too late because some-

how she'd sensed his arrival and was looking around.
On seeing him, she jumped to her feet with a gasp. Already she was tugging her skirt down, although Ben had
been offered a very fine view indeed of her slender yet
shapely calves.

She looked confused. She blurted out, 'How long
have you been there?'

He frowned, wondering if maybe she feared he'd
been staring at her for ages from the undergrowth. He
raised his hands in a gesture of both protest and apology. 'I've only just arrived,' he said. 'I was working up
there on the pavilion, then I headed down here to wash
the dust off my hands. I didn't mean to frighten you.'

'No. You didn't, not really.' He saw her draw a deep
breath. 'As it happens, meeting you like this gives me
the chance to thank you properly for helping my coachman this morning. It was very good of you. I fear that
Toby imposed upon you.'

When he saw her glance at his leg, he felt a familiar
spasm of anger, which he swiftly quelled. But he hated
receiving anyone's pity.

He said rather coolly, 'It was no trouble, I assure you.
I might be lame, but I'm still capable of most physical
tasks.'

'Yes,' she said. 'Obviously. And I'm sorry that I offered you money; it was thoughtless of me. But you see,
I'm from London, and there—well, there such things
are expected.'

'You're a long way from London now.'

'Indeed.' Her tone softened. 'I've come here to stay
with my aunt, Lady Harris. She lives at Linden House,
just down in the valley—and she's not my aunt, ex-

actly, but a cousin of my father's.' Suddenly a little smile brought life to her face. 'When people talk of my aunt,' she added, 'they use the expression "Once met, never forgotten".' She gazed up at him. 'My name is Julia. And I would be most obliged if you could tell me who you are, Mr...?'

She was actually quite pleasant, thought Ben. Rather pretty, too—her figure was slim, her features delicate. And he knew exactly what he should do. He should tell her right now that he was Lord Lambourne, owner of these woods, many acres of farmland, the mansion nearby and a large house in London.

But he didn't. He needed a few weeks of complete privacy here and he could only pray that Lady Harris would never mention him to anyone, especially this girl. So he said at last, 'My name is Smith. Ben Smith.'

'I see. And who is your employer, Mr Smith?'

Damn, that was a tricky one, but she was bound to discover who owned this land sooner or later. 'Why, Lord Lambourne, of course.' He spread out his arms to indicate the woodland. 'All this is his.'

He saw fresh dismay ripple through her. 'So I'm trespassing?'

'He won't care,' said Ben quickly. 'Trust me.'

She shook her head. 'Nevertheless,' she said firmly, 'I would be much obliged, Mr Smith, if you would say nothing to either my aunt or your employer about finding me here like this.'

He said softly, 'Did you really think that I would?'

That veiled rebuke made her look thoroughly miserable. 'No,' she whispered. 'Of course not. And I truly did not mean to insult you.' She was casting glances now at her discarded items of clothing nearby, but no doubt she was horrified at the thought of having to dress herself with him in the vicinity.

'Mr Smith?' she said at last.

'Yes?'

'Would you mind… I mean, I wonder if you would leave me now, so that I can, er, put on my things before I return to Lady Harris's house?' She gave an awkward laugh. 'Oh, dear. This is so very different from my life in London, you wouldn't believe it.'

'I suppose you have servants there,' he said. 'Maids everywhere, rushing to do your bidding.'

'Well, yes.' She hesitated. 'Though I love it here, I really do. But you see, I decided I needed a rest from town life. Dear me, there are so many parties to attend in London, and trips to the theatre, and outings with friends—' She took a delicate step forward and slipped. 'Oh, bother,' she muttered.

'I'm afraid,' said Ben, 'that you have mud on your feet and on the hem of your dress.'

She blushed madly. Her attempt at sophistication had vanished and she gazed up at him almost pleadingly. 'I wonder, would you grant me a little privacy, Mr Smith?'

He would rather have liked to watch her pulling on those silk stockings, but her discomfiture was almost painful. 'I'm going,' he said. 'But if you're cleaning yourself up, watch out for the frogs. There are dozens of them around here.'

He'd said it in downright mischief, expecting her to scream or shudder at least—but instead she just nodded and said, 'I like frogs.'

That was very much not what he was expecting. Feeling

almost as though he'd been put in his place, he nodded his farewell and began to head back up towards the pavilion.

As Julia watched him walk away, she realised her heart was pounding. She'd been alone with a strange man half a mile from her aunt's house—and he had seen her bare legs. Perhaps he didn't see them, she desperately tried to tell herself. Perhaps he wasn't looking…

Of course he was looking. He must have noticed everything, just as she'd noticed a good deal about him.

Betty's admiration of him had been ridiculous, for he was clearly just a workman. His thick brown hair was untrimmed, he hadn't shaved for a while and his clothes were grimy from his labours. But he intrigued her, more than she cared to admit. She'd noticed again how he limped, though he did his best to hide it. He spoke far too well for a labourer and his manners were… well, his manners were lacking in the sense that she felt he was gently teasing her. But she did not feel in any way unsafe with him.

She sighed. Clearly he was not impressed by her, but few men were. She began pulling on her stockings, knowing she would have to keep completely quiet about this encounter, because if her parents were to hear of it, she would be hauled back to London immediately. But unfortunately there was yet more trouble to come, because just as she was lacing up her shoes, she was forced to utter a moan of exasperation.

Mr Smith, who hadn't gone far, was still within hearing distance for he turned round and called, 'Is something the matter?'

'Yes,' said Julia miserably, rising to her feet and facing him. 'I've completely forgotten that my aunt sent me up here on an errand.'

He returned to where she sat and she saw him frown. 'What did she ask you to do?'

Julia rose to her feet. 'She said there was a patch of burdock growing near the lake. She asked me to pick some leaves—oh!' She put her hands to her cheeks and gazed up at him, now thoroughly confused. 'But surely she realised that the lake was on Lord Lambourne's land?'

A corner of his mouth lifted in amusement. 'I believe she doesn't approve of fences or boundary walls. She likes to declare that property is theft, so, as far as she's concerned, there's nothing wrong with trespassing.'

'Except,' she murmured, 'in the case of the pig boys.'

'I beg your pardon?'

'The pig boys,' she explained. 'She doesn't like them bringing their pigs on to her land. But you're right—it wouldn't occur to her that I was doing wrong. Though even so...'

'I'll tell you what,' said the man. 'I happen to know where the burdock grows. I'll fetch some for you. I won't be long.' He picked up her little basket and off he went.

Slowly Julia fastened her boots and pulled on her blue jacket, feeling more confused than ever. He seemed to know a fair amount about her aunt and maybe that wasn't so very odd if he'd been working here a while. Probably her aunt had come across him in her wanderings. Yes, that must be it. Her aunt would talk to anyone.

By the time she had buttoned her jacket and brushed down her skirt, the man was returning with a basket full of leaves.

'Here you are,' he said.

She took her basket carefully, suddenly feeling shy again. 'Thank you. And I really am truly sorry if I insulted you earlier by offering you money for your help, Mr Smith.'

'Think nothing of it.' He smiled and, though it was only a brief smile, it did something rather odd to her, because all of a sudden she felt breathless and a little dizzy.

There was just something rather disturbing about Mr Smith, with his over-long hair and his brown eyes that always seemed to be teasing her. For some reason he made her senses swim quite confusingly.

He was also clearly waiting for her to go. She blurted out, 'I hope you don't mind me asking, but how did you injure your leg?'

His expression grew instantly cooler. 'I broke it months ago, in a fall from a horse. It's taking a while to heal, that's all.'

'I'm sorry. That must have been a blow for you.'

'It was, but life goes on.' He looked around. 'It really is time for me to get on while the light lasts and I'm sure your aunt will be expecting you back.'

'Of course. But what kind of work are you doing here, exactly?'

'Do you see that pavilion behind the trees? Well, I'm repairing it.'

'Are you a stonemason, then?'

'Julia,' her mother was always saying, *'young ladies of good birth do not ask questions, especially of men. Young ladies should be mysterious and aloof.'*

She saw him hesitate, but then he nodded. 'Yes,' he said, 'I am a stonemason. Among other things.'

'And of course, you can't wait to get back to your work.' She gave a little laugh. 'How very different this is from London life and how utterly refreshing! Thank you for helping me find the burdock, Mr Smith.'

'It's no trouble,' he said politely. 'No trouble at all.'

She did her best to walk off down the path with dignity, like the well-brought-up young lady she was supposed to be. But unfortunately she'd not got far before she tripped over a shoelace that had come undone.

She didn't quite fall flat on her face, but it was a near thing. Muttering under her breath, she knelt to retie the lace, absolutely refusing to look back in case the man was still watching her. Her cheeks, she was sure, were crimson with embarrassment.

After that, she walked very carefully and, she hoped, very calmly. But as she approached her aunt's property she stopped abruptly. Her afternoon of disasters wasn't yet over, for she had forgotten her blessed notebook. She'd been writing in it as she sat by the edge of the lake, so she must have left it there—and of course at the back of it was her *Guide to the Gentlemen of London*.

What if Mr Smith were to find it? To read it, even? She burned with mortification. It was too late now to return for it, but she resolved to sneak up there tomorrow, somehow. She could only pray it would still be there.

Ben watched until her pink dress quite disappeared from view.

Dear God, that meeting had been unfortunate, to put it mildly. Besides, he was puzzled. He'd already guessed the girl had come to stay here because she'd got herself into a little bit of trouble in London and her parents had decided to send her away until the tattle died down. But why had Lady Harris told her to come up here for burdock? Didn't she realise they might meet?

He needed time alone. He needed space and privacy. He knew London society would welcome him back even if he was on crutches—his title ensured that. But before he returned to the life expected of a peer of the realm, he had to fulfil his obligations both to the estate and to his dead father's memory.

The Hall had been the home of the Lambournes for generations, but Ben was an only child whose mother had died when he was six. His life had followed the expected pattern; he went to Eton, then Oxford, and when Ben was offered a diplomatic post abroad, his father had supported him wholeheartedly. Often Ben had not come home for months on end, so he'd known nothing about the fact that around a year and a half ago his father, who was passionate about his fine stables here at Lambourne, had sold a promising young gelding to a friend of his, a fellow aristocrat.

The horse's name was Silver Cloud. Ben had seen the beautiful dapple-grey thoroughbred only once and his memories were vague; however, there were many paintings of his father's horses hanging still in the main hall and the one of Silver Cloud took pride of place. But the gelding had proved to have a serious flaw; Ben's father had been accused of making a fraudulent sale and the feud that followed had blighted the remainder of his life.

Ben's father had isolated himself here in Somerset, renting out his London house while Lambourne Hall sank into decline. Now most of its rooms were closed off, while the furniture—what was left of it—was covered in dust sheets. The whole magnificent building spoke of neglect and dereliction. If during his infrequent visits Ben had noticed a similar decline in his father's well-being, he'd done nothing about it.

He knew, though, that his father would never have sold a damaged horse, so how had this happened? Why hadn't his father realised that Ben would have abandoned everything to help him in his time of crisis?

But he hadn't known anything about the horse sale. He hadn't even been in the country. Nevertheless, he was going to clear his father's name now, whatever it took, and to achieve that he wanted no visitors, no distractions. He felt confident he would see no more of Lady Harris's young guest, for she believed him to be a stonemason and girls of her kind were not even supposed to look at men of trade, let alone talk with them.

It was time to go, so he picked up his heavy tool box, intending to head back to the Hall. But as he cast one last glance at the lake, something caught his eye, right down by the edge of the lake where the girl had been sitting. He headed down there and picked it up. It was a small notebook—a diary, he guessed. Hers.

He shook his head in sheer exasperation. Damn. What should he do with it? He could just leave it here, but the night-time dews were heavy and it would be ruined by the damp. Maybe he could tell Gilly to deliver it to Lady Harris's house in the morning? Certainly the last thing he wanted was for the girl to call here again.

While he pondered the matter he flipped idly through the notebook, but found nothing of interest until his glance strayed to the final pages. *Guide to the Gentlemen of London*, he read.

His eyes widened.

*Sir Frederick Timms. Breathes garlic everywhere.
Viscount Clive Delaney. Walks like a waddling
walrus...*

Stifling a chuckle, he pushed the book in his pocket.
He knew Delaney and she was absolutely right. It appeared there was rather more to this girl than he'd realised.

On returning to Lambourne Hall he headed straight
for the large kitchen, which was one of the few rooms
in this building that was usable. Gilly looked up from
the pan of stew he was cooking for their supper. 'I take
it you've been busy, my lord?'

Ben poured himself some ale from the jug on the
table. 'I met someone,' he said. 'A girl. She's staying
with Lady Harris.'

'Is she, now? And there was I, my lord, thinking
you'd said you were giving yourself a rest from the fairer
sex—from everyone, in fact—while you were here.'

Ben shook his head. 'She has no idea who I am. And
actually—' he thought of the diary '—she appears dis-
enchanted with all men, me included.' He sat at the table
and swallowed a welcome draught of ale.

'She's staying with that old lady, is she?' Gilly
plonked down both plates of food and drew up a chair
for himself. 'Then good luck to her.'

'I rather like Lady Harris,' said Ben thoughtfully.

'Ha! You're starved of proper company, that's your
trouble. You should go back to London and live in com-

fort. There'd be good doctors, too, to help that leg of yours to heal. You'd also have the women queuing up— they all love a wounded hero, especially if he's got a title. Maybe this place should be locked up and left to the spiders and the mice.' Gilly suddenly reached up to shove aside a particularly lively spider dangling on a thread just over his head.

They ate for a while in silence. Then Gilly cleared his throat and said, 'The girl you mentioned.'

'Yes?'

'What are you going to do, my lord, if she finds out from Lady Harris who you are? She'll be up here again and again, because she won't be able to resist a prize like you!'

'I don't think for a minute,' said Ben, 'that Lady Harris will break her word to me and tell her who I am.'

Gilly was still curious. 'Is the girl very plain?'

Ben shrugged. 'No. No, I suppose she's not.'

Gilly interpreted that instantly and chuckled. 'Pretty, is she? Then I'm telling you, my lord, beware.'

'She thinks I'm a stonemason, Gilly!'

'Maybe. But she'll have noted a thing or two, like the way you speak, and no doubt she'll want to find out more. You'll have another visit from her soon, I reckon.'

Ben shook his head. 'This fine weather won't last for ever and she's not going to come marching up to the pavilion in the rain.'

'You think so? If she's taken a fancy to you, she'll probably hide in there and wait to pounce on you.'

Ben was about to laugh, but all of a sudden he had a most wicked vision of himself and Julia in the pavilion with the rain pouring down outside, curled up together under a cosy blanket with a fire blazing in the hearth… My God. Gilly was right. He was starved of female company—and for the time being at least, he needed to keep it that way.

Gilly was watching him with that particular look in his eye. 'Gilly,' Ben said, 'whatever you're thinking, you're a rogue.'

Gilly just smirked.

With a sigh, Ben carried on eating in silence. When he'd finished he rose and said, 'I'll perhaps spend an hour or two in my father's study.'

Gilly started gathering the plates. 'I suppose you're still wanting to find out exactly what happened over the business of the horse?'

'I want to know why my father's name was blackened. Wouldn't anyone?'

'Just make sure you don't waste too much of your own life doing so, my lord. After all, you might never discover the truth.'

'I will,' said Ben softly. 'Trust me, I will.'

But once in the study, the first thing he did was to pull out the girl's little book from his pocket and flick through it once more. This time, he saw something he'd missed earlier. Something she must have written today, with neat precision.

Our coach had a slight accident as we neared Linden House and a stranger came to help us.

There were some indecipherable squiggles and Ben guessed that Julia must have been crossed out several words. Then:

I wish that I had met someone like him in London.

He slammed it down in astonishment. 'No,' he muttered. 'No, this will not do!'

It would not do at all. The girl was most definitely a distraction he didn't need.

Pushing her book aside along with his memory of her, he unlocked the drawer where his father kept his most private correspondence and pulled out the letter he'd found in there after making the long journey from Austria to England, lame and travel-weary.

I am not a vindictive person, Lord Lambourne. I will not take the matter to the courts. But this was an act of fraud, not worthy of a man of your rank, and if the world gets to hear of this affair, then so be it.

Ben knew the man who'd written it. He held a high rank in society, his good reputation was indisputable. But Ben was not going to rest until he had proved his father's innocence—and forced this man, his accuser, to proclaim it also.

Chapter Five

Lady Harris was in her vegetable garden inspecting a row of leeks when Julia returned to Linden House. 'Sowerby,' her aunt pronounced, 'is not earthing these leeks up properly. Do you know what "earthing up" means, Julia?'

'No, Aunt,' said Julia politely. 'I've never had the opportunity to learn about growing vegetables. But I have brought you some burdock. I'll put it in the kitchen, shall I? Then I really must go and change my dress.'

'I should think so.' Lady Harris was scrutinising her. 'You look as though you've been fighting your way through a bramble patch.'

Julia laughed a little weakly before going inside to deliver the burdock to the kitchen. Then she scurried up to her room, where Betty was rearranging some of her clothes in the wardrobe.

'My goodness,' Betty exclaimed as Julia entered. 'You look as though you've been—'

'Fighting my way through a bramble patch,' said Julia. 'Yes, I'm afraid the path I chose was a little overgrown.'

Betty sighed. 'You shouldn't be going anywhere without me, my lady! You never know who you might meet. Now, let me help you out of that dress—dear me, the hem is all muddy. I'll try to clean it later, *if* I can get some hot water from that dragon of a woman your aunt employs.'

'You mean Miss Twigg? But she's a dear!'

'Not in my eyes she isn't,' said Betty darkly. 'I had a good talk with her earlier, telling her what you were used to eating, what time you usually took your bath and all the rest of it. Do you know what she said? She said she was the housekeeper here, so I was to mind my own business!'

Oh, dear.

'Betty,' said Julia, 'I shall be very happy with the way things are run here, I'm sure.'

'But you're the daughter of an earl, my lady, and don't you forget it! Now, I'm going to tidy your hair.'

Silently Julia submitted and reflected on her disasters so far.

Of course, she'd said nothing at all to her aunt about the encounter with Ben Smith the stonemason. How could she? She'd been sent here because she'd misbehaved in London and now she'd wandered off, dabbled her bare legs in a lake, then engaged in conversation with an unknown man who'd informed her that she was trespassing on a neighbouring landowner's territory. As for her diary, she shuddered at the thought that it might have been found—and possibly read—by Mr Smith.

At least Betty's mood improved as she helped Julia into a clean dress and restored her hair to order. Then Betty set off downstairs to clean Julia's muddy shoes and shortly afterwards Julia descended also, to be informed by one of the maids that Lady Harris was taking tea in the sitting room.

As soon as Julia appeared, her aunt began pouring out a cup for her. 'Well?' she enquired as Julia sat down. 'Have you recovered?'

'It was only a short walk.' Julia tried to laugh. 'I'm not tired in the least.'

'You can't fool me,' said Lady Harris. 'I know something happened while you were out there.'

It was no good. She had to confess. 'Aunt,' she said, 'I'm afraid I was caught trespassing this afternoon.'

'Trespassing? Good heavens.' Lady Harris peered at her over her cup of tea. 'How far did you wander, for goodness sake?'

'I only went as far as the lake, as you suggested. But apparently it belongs to your neighbour, Lord Lambourne. I truly didn't realise I had crossed into his land.'

Her aunt, far from looking dismayed, made a dismissive gesture. 'Pah, take no notice of that. Property is theft, after all, and most of the land was stolen from the people anyway.' She peered at Julia even more closely. 'Who told you this? Was it that young fellow who's hell-bent on rebuilding the pavilion? You'd remember him if you met him. He has brown hair and walks with a limp.'

'Yes.' Julia steadied herself. 'Yes, I did meet him as it happens.'

Lady Harris was nodding. 'I believe he was quite badly injured, but he seems determined to fix that pavilion all the same.'

'And the pavilion belongs to Lord Lambourne?'

'I suppose so, though like I say, all property is theft.'

She looked around. 'Wherever is Twigg with that chocolate cake? I imagine you'll be hungry after your walk.'

Hungry? Not really.

Lady Harris was staring at her. 'Well? You seem a little lost for words. What did you think of the fellow?'

Julia attempted a smile. 'He appeared rather startled to find me wandering around.'

'I guess he'd expect you to be in London, being paraded in front of a bunch of foolish young suitors.' Lady Harris was vigorously stirring extra sugar into her tea, as if she was attacking the young suitors with her spoon. 'But what, Julia, did you think of *him*?'

Julia took a moment to sip her own tea. She said at last, 'I must say, Aunt, that I was a little surprised by him.'

'Why is that?'

'He seemed well spoken. Well educated. It also appears rather strange for him to be working so hard when he has an injured leg. I can only hope that Lord Lambourne is paying him well.'

Lady Harris had cupped her hand round one ear. 'What? What's that you're saying?'

Julia spoke a little louder. 'I said, "I hope Lord Lambourne is paying him well for his work on the pavilion!"'

'No good. I still can't hear you. It's all that clatter from the kitchen that Twigg's making. I suspect she's pointing out to us that she's hard at work while you and I natter.'

At that very moment Miss Twigg brought in a plate of chocolate cake and for a few moments she and Lady Harris argued over whether or not the tea was too strong. Then Lady Harris suddenly chuckled. 'I enjoy a good battle. Just think of the pig boys! Though I rather like pigs, as it happens,' she added thoughtfully. 'They are intelligent creatures. But will I let those boys trespass? I will not!'

She drank her tea and grinned. 'I am quite firm on the issue. Aren't I, Twigg?'

'You are indeed,' said Miss Twigg, slicing the cake for them with great precision. 'You're a terror, in fact. How I put up with you, I do not know.'

Lady Harris chuckled, then leaned across to Julia. 'You're maybe thinking my staff should call me "my lady". I can't stop people doing that if they wish, but I've no time for titles and all that flummery. I'm quite the revolutionary, you see.' She pointed to the cake. 'Help yourself, Julia. Generally Twigg's a pretty hopeless cook, but her chocolate cake, I must say, is not bad.'

Miss Twigg was on her way out, but she paused to raise her eyebrows at Julia as if to say, *You see what I have to put up with?* Julia, smiling at her, took a slice, then her aunt took one, too, and for a while there was a contented silence.

'Tonight,' said her aunt when there was nothing left on her plate but crumbs, 'once we've had our supper, maybe you'll play chess with me, Julia. Yes?'

'Yes,' said Julia. 'Most definitely.' She loved chess, but rarely had the chance for a game. Her sisters said that chess was dull beyond words, while Charles, who'd taught her in the first place, refused to play with her when she began beating him just a little too often.

Chess. And chocolate cake. She gave a little sigh of pleasure.

This really is a grand adventure.

But—Mr Smith. And her diary. Her optimism was dispelled. How ever was she going to get it back, without running the risk of bumping into the man again?

That evening Julia had won the chess game easily, much, she suspected, to her aunt's delight. But afterwards she went upstairs to see Betty, feeling a little guilty because earlier Betty had moaned to her, 'There's nothing for me to do here. No one for me to talk to either!'

She found her maid sitting on her bed, nursing a swollen wrist. 'Betty! Whatever have you done?'

'It's this house,' exclaimed her maid. 'Everything's so *old*. So full of twists and turns. I was exploring, that's all.'

'Why?'

'Well, I like to know where everything is. So I'd gone up some narrow stairs to the attic rooms and I heard that woman calling out from below. "Who's up there?" she was shouting in her ratty way.'

'You mean Miss Twigg?'

'Yes. I do. Anyway, I hid from her and she went away. But when I was coming back down those stairs, I slipped and hurt my wrist.'

'You poor thing. It isn't broken, is it? Here, let me see.'

Gently Julia examined it.

'I can move it,' Betty was muttering, 'so it's definitely not broken, but it will take days and days to get better.'

'I'll fetch you a cold compress,' said Julia decisively. 'I'll also see if my aunt has a soothing remedy.'

'No!' groaned Betty. 'I don't want any of her concoctions! And don't send that Twigg woman to look after me, or I'll bolt my door!'

Lady Harris looked up when Julia came downstairs again. 'What's happened?'

'It's Betty. I'm afraid she's sprained her wrist.'

'Send her home,' said her aunt decisively.

'What?'

'Send the woman home. She's neither use nor ornament. There's a carriage for hire in Lambourne village and Matthew—Dottie and Grace's brother—drives it. Matthew can take her to Bath tomorrow, for the next London-bound coach.'

'Are you sure, Aunt?'

'Absolutely.'

Feeling a little guilty at not raising more opposition, Julia went back upstairs—but the look of relief on Betty's face when Julia told her the news was almost laughable. Betty did manage to express some concern about Julia's dire fate in having to manage without her, but Julia quickly soothed her. 'Betty,' she said, 'I shall be fine. My aunt's servants will attend to me. You will tell my parents so, won't you?'

That night, as she lay in her bed, listening to the sound of the breeze softly brushing the branches of an old lilac tree against her window, she was thinking hard. If her mother knew that, in fact, Julia intended to call on her aunt's staff as little as possible, she would be horrified. If her mother knew Julia had been alone for an hour in the woods with Mr Smith, she would most likely faint.

Mr Smith. If Julia closed her eyes, she could still see the look of surprise on his remarkably handsome face as he caught sight of her sitting by the lake and writing in her book—

She opened her eyes abruptly. Her book. She had to get it back before he read it. She would have to go up there once more to get it back and, if she met him, she absolutely must refuse to talk to him, as was proper for a young lady of her rank. Yes, it was just not right for her to be on speaking terms with the man.

But the trouble was, she could still picture his smile as she finally drifted off to sleep.

The next morning Julia was woken by a great clattering sound outside in the yard. Scurrying to her window, she saw that a rather ancient coach had drawn up there and a man in a big caped coat was attending to the harness of two horses. This, she realised, must be Matthew, brother to Dottie and Grace. Dottie had explained to her last night that the coach belonged to the village inn, the George, where Matthew did various jobs and driving the carriage was one of them. Betty was out there already in her cloak and bonnet, with her packed valise at her side. Clearly she couldn't wait to be gone.

Julia dressed hastily. She took one look at her usual stays and corsets before thrusting them back in the chest of drawers with a shudder. Instead she put on her chemise and a blue cotton frock, tied back her hair and pulled on her stockings and shoes. Then she went downstairs and Betty saw her as soon as she emerged from the house.

'Oh, my lady,' she exclaimed. 'Why don't you come back to London with me?'

Julia shook her head, appalled. 'No,' she declared

firmly. 'I will be fine here, Betty. Truly, I will. Tell my parents that I will write, very soon!'

She stood and waved to the departing carriage until it was out of sight. The morning was crisp and fresh, the sun was shining and the whole day lay before her. The only shadow on the horizon was the business of her blessed notebook. She prayed it might be buried by falling leaves by now, or may even have slipped into the lake. He wouldn't have found it yet, surely? Even if he did, he surely wouldn't waste his time reading it. Or would he?

'Thank God she's gone,' said Lady Harris, who'd appeared at her side. 'Does the blessed woman ever stop talking?'

'No,' said Julia and laughed aloud. 'Oh, Aunt. It's lovely to be here with you again!'

'Of course it is,' said her aunt, with considerable satisfaction.

The morning held further surprises for her. After they'd both taken their breakfast, her aunt led her out to one of the barns to show her the two-seater gig she kept in there. 'Now,' said Lady Harris. 'What do you think of this?'

It was so unlike the elegant carriages in which the fashionable set toured Hyde Park each afternoon that Julia smothered a gasp. 'I think it's quite extraordinary, Aunt! Do you drive it yourself?'

'I used to. But now I have to get Sowerby to drive me and he just doesn't go fast enough.' She looked sharply at Julia. 'Do you fancy having a go?'

Julia didn't hesitate. 'Oh, yes!'

'Then grab yourself a coat and gloves. I'll tell Sowerby to harness up my mare, Nell, and we'll be off.'

Julia took scarcely ten minutes to pull on her jacket and leather gloves and then they were on their way, along an ancient farm track that threaded between mown corn fields. She'd driven a gig once before at their house in Richmond, when she'd begged the grooms to let her take it around the grounds while her parents were out. But when her parents got home, her mother had declared her a hoyden and the grooms had resisted every one of her pleas to repeat the experience.

The trouble was, she loved being a hoyden—and her aunt encouraged her avidly. 'That's the spirit, Julia my girl! Bit of a hill here, so Nell will slacken up. But then you can let her loose again. She's loving it as much as I am. Hoorah!'

Occasionally Julia thought of Betty and she felt a twinge of unease, picturing the surprise with which the maid would be received when she finally reached London. Would her parents send someone instantly to fetch Julia back home?

No, she told herself firmly. Her father would reassure her mother that even Julia could not get into trouble in Lady Harris's remote dwelling. No, no trouble at all. Apart from meeting with Mr Smith yesterday, which of course, would not happen again.

Except that she had to find her diary. That blessed diary—she really must retrieve it. She had to think of some excuse to go up there again, somehow…

She jumped as her aunt tapped her arm. 'You're daydreaming, girl. Nell thinks you've fallen asleep. Tighten the reins!'

* * *

Later, once they'd had a hearty lunch back at the house, Julia wondered briefly if she might be able to hurry up to the lake and back without her aunt noticing, but Lady Harris dashed her hopes by asking Julia to read to her. 'Let's have *Gulliver's Travels*,' her aunt declared. 'I do not want anything pious in the afternoons—sermons would send me to sleep.'

Julia resigned herself to the task, but she had scarcely read for ten minutes when her aunt broke in to say, 'Right. That's enough. Now, I've a feeling you would enjoy taking that gig out again while the light's good, wouldn't you?'

Julia, a little surprised, said, 'Yes, I would. But are you suggesting I drive it on my own?'

'Of course I am. You're competent enough, so you may as well make the most of this lovely afternoon. Why don't you go and find that young fellow you met and ask him if he'll play chess with me tonight? There's a good track up there that Nell can cope with.'

What?

Julia felt slightly stunned. At last she said, 'Do you mean Mr Smith, the stonemason, Aunt? But does he play chess?'

'Most certainly he does and very well, too. He's been over here for a game several times.'

Julia was floundering. 'What if he's not working there today?'

'Oh, he'll be around somewhere. He's living up at the Hall at present, I believe.'

'He's actually living in Lord Lambourne's house?'

'Yes. It's been badly neglected, so I guess he gets on with other jobs while he's there. He's a handy fellow.'

Julia's heart was bumping rather hard. 'Aunt,' she said, 'do you really think I should be going to see him on my own?'

'You're in the country now, my girl. No need to worry over all that silly chaperoning business here. I've got to know the fellow and you can trust him not to do anything he shouldn't.'

Yes, Julia thought, a little deflated. Of course. She was not one to tempt any man to distraction; in fact, she already knew how to put them straight off her, since all she had to do was speak her mind. Besides, this might give her the ideal chance to look for her diary. 'Very well,' she said. 'I'll go.' But Lady Harris didn't even answer, because she had fallen asleep in her chair and was snoring gently.

Chapter Six

It was around four in the afternoon and the warmth of the sun was dwindling, but Ben was still working at the pavilion. He'd brought a jug of ale and a pasty to keep him going till supper time and he was just finishing his food when he noticed a slight movement among the birch trees beyond the clearing. He stayed very still.

It was a young fox, he realised; nothing unusual about that, for these woodlands teemed with wildlife. But it was no wonder this particular creature had caught his eye, because its coat was spotted with patches of pure white.

Ben knew what happened to these rarities out in the wild. Their parents shunned them and they usually died young, prey to hunger, disease or predators. Indeed, this one had done well to survive for so long. Already it was vanishing into the undergrowth and Ben began to rise from the low wall he'd sat on, cursing slightly because his leg had stiffened up again.

That was when he realised that a gig was being driven up the lane that led from the valley. And driving it was a

slim, dark-haired girl in a blue frock and light jacket—
Julia. He rubbed his forehead. What now?

As soon as she spotted him, she drew the gig to a halt.
'Mr Smith?' she called out. 'There you are. I hoped you
might still be here.'

Her greeting was cheerful. Lady Harris must have
offered her the gig, but this really did break all the rules
of propriety. Reluctantly he went to help her down, making sure the physical contact was as brief as possible,
but even so he couldn't avoid inhaling the delicate scent
of her as he put his hands to her waist. He said, 'Julia.
This is a surprise.'

'Yes,' she answered lightly, brushing down her skirt.
'Yes, here I am again.'

He stepped back, shaking his head in disapproval.
'What,' he said, 'would your parents think, if they realised you were coming out alone to meet a man you
barely knew? They would be horrified, surely. You could
be taking a huge risk.'

His rebuke hit home, he could see that. 'What do you
mean?' she whispered.

He sighed then remembered he'd undone the top buttons of his shirt as he worked. Swiftly he reached to
fasten them. 'Your parents,' he said, 'must have warned
you often that if you were found alone with any man in
an unchaperoned situation, then your reputation might
be in danger.'

'But my aunt trusts you, Mr Smith. She sent me to
you.'

Devil take it, what was Lady Harris playing at? Why
hadn't she told the girl who he was? Because he'd told

her he wanted his identity kept a secret, he supposed, but then why was she sending the girl to him like this?

The silence hung heavily. He realised she was looking around, especially at the lake, and he thought he knew why. He said at last, 'I gather you've told Lady Harris that we came across each other yesterday?'

She met his gaze again. 'I suppose I felt I had to. But she just nodded and said I was safe with you.'

'Your aunt,' he said, 'is a fine woman in many ways, but she is not noted for her observance of society's rules. Surely you realise that?'

He broke off because at that moment he'd noticed her hands. She wasn't wearing gloves and he could see that her palms were chafed and stained by the leather reins. With a suppressed exclamation, he reached to touch them. 'Your hands! Why on *earth* didn't you put on driving gloves?'

She whispered, 'I don't know. I suppose I forgot.'

'No maidservant to remind you. Is that it?'

He saw her colour rise and he sighed, letting go of her hands. 'At least the skin isn't broken, but you do need to bathe them. I have fresh water and cloths by the pavilion—you can wash them there. Then I'll lend you some gloves to drive back.'

She followed him and sat where he'd indicated, on the low stone bench. He went inside and came out with a bowl of water and a muslin cloth and silently she began to wash her hands.

Then she looked up and said, 'You think I'm a fool. Don't you?'

Ben sighed again. 'No. I don't. But I'm certain your

parents would not be happy about you being here. They would be concerned about your future prospects.'

'You mean my marriage? Oh,' she said airily, 'lining up some suitors for me won't be a problem, believe me. Besides,' she added quickly, 'no one needs to know about this. Do they?'

'No. Except your aunt. Speaking of whom, why did she send you to find me?'

'My aunt wishes to know, Mr Smith, if you will come and play chess with her tonight.'

Once more Ben was completely thrown. Was this Lady Harris's idea of a joke? If so, it wasn't funny. He said, 'Chess? Is she serious?' He was suddenly suspicious. 'This wasn't your idea, was it?'

'No, indeed not!' she cried. 'How could I even have known you played?'

That was heated, most definitely. She rose to her feet and said, 'I told my aunt I ought not to come here. I knew this was a bad mistake.'

She was already heading for the gig, but he caught up with her. 'Julia. Wait. I'm sorry. Tell Lady Harris that, yes, I'll come—'

Suddenly he grimaced with pain. Damn, his leg had almost given way again and of course she'd noticed.

'What is wrong?' she breathed. 'Is it your leg? Is it troubling you?'

'Really,' he assured her, 'I'm fine.' He pointed to her hands. 'I promised to lend you gloves, didn't I? Don't go without them. And by the way, yesterday I found something of yours.' He pulled the notebook from the pocket of his breeches.

She looked frozen with embarrassment, so he pointed

to the bench and said, as gently as he could, 'Perhaps you'd better sit down again.'

As he gave it to her he expected her to snatch it from him, or maybe to question him fiercely. Instead she said very quietly, 'Did you read it?'

He suddenly realised that he very much wanted to spare this girl yet more embarrassment. He said lightly, 'Only to check that it was yours. It's for all your appointments, I gather. Reminders of your hectic London life.'

She took it back in silence, not even looking at it before slipping it into her pocket. Then she gazed around at the woods, which were tinted with gold by the setting sun, and she said softly, 'I love it here. It's so beautiful that I think I could live somewhere like this for ever.'

He said quietly, 'I think it's beautiful, too.' He was silent a moment, then sat down also, but kept his distance. He said, 'Julia. I wonder if you have maybe had one or two unpleasant experiences with London's gentry?'

She shrugged. 'Oh, most girls tend to get pestered from time to time. Insulted even. I'm told it's my own fault.'

He said sharply, 'Have your family told you that?'

'Not really. They're actually very kind to me.' She tried to smile. 'But I'm afraid I did say some foolish things recently, to a man at a party.'

'Did he deserve them?'

This time her eyes gleamed with humour. 'Oh, yes. Most definitely. I also spilled some champagne over his shirt.'

'Deliberately?'

'Of course. So my parents decided that until the fuss dies down, I should come here to stay with my aunt.

I've known her since I was small. When I was younger we used to visit her often and I'm very fond of her. You see, she's different. Like me.'

'What do you mean, different?'

He saw her screw up her eyes a moment in thought. 'Different in that I don't enjoy the things my sisters love, like shopping for clothes, or having dancing lessons. My older sister Pen is perfectly lovely and she's getting married very soon, while as for my younger sister, she already dreams of her wedding even though she's only fourteen! But I'm not as pretty as them, though when I try to say marriage may not be for me, everyone thinks I'm mad.' She looked up at him with challenge in her eyes. 'No doubt you do, too.'

Ben considered his next words carefully. 'Marriage is a huge commitment and I believe it's your right and yours alone to make that decision. No one should be forced into a lifelong relationship because it's what society expects. If you feel it's not for you, then stick to your beliefs.'

'Indeed,' she said in a lighter tone, 'that should prove very easy, because so far no man has shown the slightest interest and I really do not care. My aunt has offered me some advice on how to drive men away, but I think I have plenty of ideas of my own. As you'll have noticed, I find it easy to appear positively eccentric!'

Ben pointed to her feet. 'At least you've remembered to lace up your shoes properly this time.'

He'd meant it as a joke, but she looked mortified and he felt a sharp pang of regret. Something about this girl was puzzling him, badly. She'd declared she wasn't pretty—well, he had to disagree with that. She had a most attractive face, with sparkling grey-green eyes and high cheekbones. Her slender figure gave her a look of fragility that was outrageously deceptive, for she clearly loved the outdoors. Why on earth did she have such a low opinion of herself? What had people *done* to her?

He realised she was rising from the bench and preparing to return to the gig.

'You need gloves,' he said firmly. He went into the pavilion, calling back to her, 'I'm afraid they'll be huge on your small hands, but they'll do the job. You can give them to me tonight, at your aunt's house—'

He broke off, because he realised she had followed him in.

'Oh,' she said. She was looking round, amazed. 'Mr Smith, this is wonderful. It's like a miniature palace! Who painted all this?'

He had to smile at her enthusiasm. 'It was built and decorated decades ago.' He pointed. 'I believe the wall paintings were done by an artist from Bath.'

She was still gazing raptly round the room. But surely, for a girl of her upbringing, there was nothing much to admire? The furniture consisted only of two wooden chairs, a table and an old sofa. There was a fireplace, which he'd had to clear of the ancient debris left by nesting birds. But the octagonal interior was full of light, thanks to the south-west-facing windows. The scenes on the walls were exquisitely done in shades of ochre and cobalt blue, while framing them all were stencilled friezes in exactly the same colours.

'This is truly exquisite,' she murmured.

He nodded. 'I certainly intend to restore it fully, if I can.'

She looked up at him. 'For Lord Lambourne?'

He hesitated only briefly. 'For Lord Lambourne, yes. And now, it really is time for you to go.'

She was gazing at the stone lintel above the door, in which was etched the Lambourne crest of a phoenix. Then she pulled on the leather gloves he'd handed her, laughing a little at the size of them, and followed him outside.

She was really rather beautiful, Ben thought suddenly. All the more so since she was unaware of it.

He helped her up into the gig. 'You can tell Lady Harris,' he said, 'that I'll come down to Linden House later.' He added, 'Your aunt, I must warn you, loves nothing better than to tackle me at chess and she's rather a fine player.'

She chuckled as she gathered up the reins. 'I beat her, though. Last night.'

'You did?' He was astonished. 'Good for you.' He patted Nell's neck and stood watching until the gig was out of sight. Once again he recalled what she'd written about him in her little book.

I wish that I'd met someone like him in London.

He shook his head and returned to his work. She had better forget any thoughts like that as soon as possible, but he would be seeing her again, tonight! What was Lady Harris thinking of? More to the point, what on earth was *he* thinking of, in agreeing to go?

As Julia drove into the yard, old Mr Sowerby looked up from the logs he was sawing and came over to take

Nell's bridle. 'You've got an eye for this, my lady,' he said approvingly. 'Good to see a young lady taking the reins so well.'

Julia smiled as she hopped down. 'Nell's a dear.' She quickly removed the outsize gloves and stroked the horse's velvety nose. 'So easy to handle.'

'Aye, but you're a natural,' said Sowerby. 'Oh, and Lady Harris is out in the orchard picking damsons, if you want to find her.'

Goodness. Did her aunt ever stop? 'Thank you, Sowerby. I'll join her soon.' But first, Julia went up to her room, where she put the gloves and her notebook in the back of a drawer, then sat on the bed and tried to make sense of this latest encounter with Mr Smith.

Clearly he was trusted by Lord Lambourne, since he was working for the nobleman in his absence and even living in a part of his house. He spoke well and appeared well educated. But he was right—her mother would swoon away if she knew her daughter had been talking to him, let alone if she'd seen how her daughter's wandering gaze had strayed instantly to where Ben's shirt was unbuttoned at the neck. He'd quickly fastened it, but she still couldn't erase the memory of his bare chest, which was smooth, muscular, tanned…

Julia, she scolded herself, *the man must think you a complete idiot.*

Indeed, he'd looked positively horrified when he saw her approaching. She should be used to that, for most young men in London did find her a nuisance. But Mr Smith was definitely different to the men she met in town, because she felt quite odd whenever he was near. In fact, she could not help staring at his handsome face, especially his mouth, which curled up quite delightfully at the edges whenever he smiled.

Her diary, though! She was hot with embarrassment. How much had he actually read of it? Quite honestly, she couldn't bear to know.

After rolling over on her bed so she could prop her chin in her hands, she gazed out of the window and up into the woods. The light was fading fast and she couldn't see the pavilion, but she could picture it. She could picture Mr Smith, too, trying to hide his limp in a way that somehow twisted her heart. When he'd put his hands on her waist to help her down from the gig, she had not wanted him to let go.

Oh, dear. She'd always teased her older sister whenever Pen rambled on about her fiancé, Jeremy. But the stonemason was disturbing her mightily, which just would not do, especially as tonight he was visiting her aunt's house. There was only one answer—she would have to make sure that she stayed out of his way and didn't embarrass him or herself any further.

'Julia!' Her aunt's voice pierced the silence. 'Are you up there? Whatever are you doing? Did you manage to ask the young man to play chess with me tonight?'

Julia leaped to her feet and hurried out to the top of the stairs. 'Yes, Aunt. He's agreed.'

'Good. Come down and have your tea with me.'

A command from Lady Harris was enough to banish any girl's vaguely romantic notions. Quickly Julia went downstairs to the dining room where Grace bustled about serving the food while Lady Harris once more extolled the virtues of living in the countryside. No more mention was made of Mr Smith. Even when Julia rose from the table and explained she was going upstairs to write letters to her family, her aunt just looked at her a little curiously.

'Letters? Very well,' she said.

But once in her room, Julia didn't write a thing. Yes, she did sit at the little writing desk in the corner, but for heaven's sake, she had neither paper to write on, nor ink and a pen. Though a few moments later there was a knock at her door and Miss Twigg marched in bearing a tray, on which were all the writing implements Julia required.

'Lady Harris,' Miss Twigg announced, 'said you might need these if you're writing letters.' She set the tray down on the desk.

'Yes.' Julia was blushing to the roots of her hair. 'Yes, of course. Thank you.'

She hesitated a moment. She'd never had the chance to speak to Miss Twigg without her aunt being present. 'Miss Twigg,' she said, 'you've known my aunt for a long time, haven't you? Do you wonder if sometimes she gets lonely here?'

'Lonely? Heavens, no. She has me and Sowerby, of course, and the maids, and sometimes Matthew from the village drives her into Bath to do some shopping and take the waters.'

'Does she ever go to church? I know she didn't when we used to stay here.'

'Church? Not her. Her husband was a churchgoing man, but that didn't stop him having women galore.'

'No!'

Miss Twigg eyed her carefully. 'Yes. Didn't you know? Though I suppose it's not the kind of thing your parents would mention in front of you. But the rogue married her for her money, then after a year or two he headed off to Europe with some floozy or other. You can imagine how the experience of that man's so-called virtue put paid to any notion of religiosity on Lady Harris's part.'

'Yes,' said Julia, a little dismayed. 'I suppose it would, rather. But, Miss Twigg, my aunt is very independent, isn't she?—and perhaps just a little eccentric. For example, don't you think it's odd that she's befriended that man who's coming to play chess tonight? The stonemason working on the Lambourne estate?'

Miss Twigg's expression became guarded. 'I don't know him myself. But I do know your aunt is a good judge of character and she is particularly partial to a game of chess.' She took a step towards the door. 'Listen, I think that's her calling. Yes, indeed. I must be off.'

So Julia was left alone in her room, supposedly writing letters ,but instead sitting there thinking, *The life of an elderly single lady. No family, no children.*

Was that really what she wanted for herself? She certainly wanted freedom and the chance to make choices for herself…

She jumped up as she heard the sound of a horse's hooves clattering into the yard. Dashing over to her window, she carefully parted the curtains an inch and saw Mr Smith, on a rather good bay mare—he'd borrowed one of Lord Lambourne's horses, she guessed. She also noticed that he had smartened himself up for the occasion. He had taken the trouble to shave and his buff coat and buckskin breeches were quite respectable. But those locks of hair falling over his forehead made him looked quite wickedly handsome. Oh, dear. She dashed back to her desk and sat down, her pulse racing. It was as well she'd been sensible enough to isolate herself up here in her room. She began to write her letter.

Dear Mama and Papa...

What could she say? She could tell them about the journey. She could try to explain why she'd sent Betty home. Or—

'Julia?' That was her aunt's shrill voice coming from the bottom of the stairs, causing her to drop the pen and splatter her letter with ink. 'Julia,' her aunt called again, 'I'd like you to come down here, now!'

Chapter Seven

As Ben handed the reins of his horse over to Sowerby, the old fellow greeted him cheerfully. 'Evening, sir!'

Sir. That was just fine, for it appeared the man didn't recognise him in the slightest. Miss Twigg was a different matter, for she was as sharp as a new pin, but if Lady Harris was true to her promise, she would have made Twigg swear to keep his identity secret as well. Any other staff, he believed, came here by day only. But surely Lady Harris would have to tell the girl at some point who he was? He'd been wondering all the way here if Her Ladyship was maybe planning something for tonight, other than chess.

He soon found out. She was planning to have a headache, that was what.

Miss Twigg greeted him at the front door. 'Mr Smith. Good evening. Her Ladyship is expecting you in the drawing room.'

Mr Smith, she'd called him. That was it, then. Lady Harris was clearly intent on keeping his secret for now. He looked around as Miss Twigg led him into the drawing room, noting that a decanter of sherry and two glasses were on the sideboard, but there was no sign of Julia. Lady Harris was on her feet and raising a hand in greeting. 'Thank you, Mr Smith, for coming here to oblige an old lady! Twigg, you may go.'

Already his hostess was waving him towards the chessboard set upon a table, but there were matters to be discussed first. He waited until she sat down, then he said, 'Lady Harris. Why did you send your young guest with your invitation? You know I wanted no one to realise I was here.'

'Of course I know,' she retorted. 'I haven't told her who you are, young man, and I don't intend to. Now, do sit down. You make me feel quite uncomfortable, looking at me like that.'

He sat with a sigh. 'Yes, but don't you see? She is being misled and this is very awkward—'

He broke off as Lady Harris suddenly put her hand to her head. 'Goodness,' she exclaimed. 'I am the victim of an almighty headache. It must be Twigg's fault. That cake we ate earlier was far too rich for me and she should have known it!' She rose from her chair, marched through the open door to the foot of the stairs and called, 'Julia? Julia, I'd like you to come down here, now!'

Ben had followed her. 'Lady Harris,' he hissed. 'Why in God's name are you *doing* this?'

She said, 'Because the girl needs you.'

What? Ben was speechless. Whatever was she talking about? But it was too late for him to say or do anything more because moments later Julia was coming slowly down the stairs, rather unwillingly, he felt. But damn it, she looked so pretty that he almost forgot how awkward all this was.

Her dark, silky hair was pulled up into a loose top-knot, but most of it had fallen out from its ribbon and was fascinatingly untidy. Her lips looked pink and full and, whether she realised it or not, the simple dress she wore emphasised her delicate curves to perfection. But she was *not* pleased to see him, for she merely nodded to him and said tightly, 'Good evening, Mr Smith.'

He murmured a polite reply and wondered what came next, but Lady Harris did not hesitate.

'Julia,' she announced, leading the way back into the drawing room, 'Mr Smith would like a game of chess with you.'

'What?' This time Ben said it aloud.

'You heard me, both of you. As for me,' Her Lady-ship continued, 'I must retire upstairs, since I feel distinctly unwell. Come to think of it, I've been poorly all afternoon. I really do not know why Twigg insists on serving such elaborate food; I am beginning to believe she does it to deliberately annoy me.'

Off she went—and Ben could see that Julia did not know what to say or where to put herself.

Heaving an internal sigh, he pulled out a chair and gestured for her to sit down. 'I'm sorry,' he said. 'Your aunt seems determined to push us together and this is rather awkward for you. But here we are. So how do you feel about a game with me?' He added quietly, 'You know, if you prefer it, I can always go.'

For a moment she stood very still and he realised he truly had no idea what thoughts were racing through her mind. At last she said, 'No. Don't go.'

That was when Ben realised that he shouldn't even have asked her. He should have come to his senses, made a polite farewell and marched—no, limped— straight out of her life. This was the start of a slippery slope and didn't he know it. But he nodded and they both sat down at the chessboard.

The game was absorbing, for he was an experienced player and so, he swiftly realised, was she. At first Julia made her moves primly, showing no emotion, and he, too, said hardly a word. But the game swiftly developed into one of intense concentration on both sides, giving him the chance to study her face and the fleeting expressions that crossed it: success, self-rebuke, pleasure in a particularly clever ruse.

When the end finally came and he had to submit, he leaned back in his chair and applauded. 'Julia,' he exclaimed, 'you are really rather good at this. Aren't you?'

He saw her almost glow in pleasure at his compliment. Rising to his feet, he went over to the sideboard to pour them each a small glass of sherry. 'I think we should drink a toast. To you, Julia, and your campaign for independence. As for chess, I acknowledge you as my better, absolutely.'

But as he placed the glasses on the table, he leaned too heavily on his injured leg and stumbled slightly. God damn it, he didn't want the girl seeing his weakness yet again. He strove to cover up the moment of agony, but Julia must have seen the pain etched on his face because she, too, was on her feet.

'Mr Smith. I'm so sorry. Does your leg hurt *very* much?'

'Only now and then,' he lied.

'And will it get better soon?'

He sat down again and tried to smile. 'I'll probably always have a limp. But the doctor tells me the stiffness should gradually ease, if I keep exercising it.'

'It must be horrid for you,' she blurted out, 'when you're clearly used to being active. If you don't mind me asking, how did it happen?'

'It's simple really.' He lifted his shoulders in a shrug. 'I fell off my horse and, in doing so, I managed to break my leg in three places.'

He saw her gasp. 'How awful! I broke my ankle last year in Richmond Park, because I fell off my horse when I was galloping—which I wasn't supposed to do. My mother was very cross. But at least it healed quickly and I was looked after, whereas you—haven't you any friends or family to help you?'

That was when he should have cast his resolve aside and told her who he was, in precise detail. But he didn't, and why? Because he was being a selfish idiot, that was why. He was enjoying her company more than he'd enjoyed anything in a long while and the way she was looking at him so earnestly, so compassionately, disarmed him completely.

How could he avoid being fascinated by those wide eyes of hers that were fringed by lashes as intensely dark as her hair? All those stray locks tumbling around her face gave her an appearance that was sufficiently déshabillée to set any red-blooded man's pulse racing. It was certainly dangerous for his peace of mind and his body.

He said at last, 'I'm absolutely fine on my own. I was well cared for after the accident, even though it occurred when I was abroad.'

'Did you enjoy your travels, Mr Smith?'

'Most of the time, yes.' He smiled. 'In fact, until I fell off my horse I found foreign cities quite fascinating.'

Her face brightened. 'I would adore,' she exclaimed, 'to travel. My older sister is getting married very soon and afterwards her husband is taking her to the south of France, then Rome.'

'Is she happy about it? The wedding, I mean?'

'She is ecstatic. And I do envy her just a little, because I would love to go to the places I imagine you must have been. But not with a husband telling me what to do. I wish I'd been born a man. I do. I do!'

'Instead,' he said, 'you're intent on keeping men, or suitors at least, out of your life. Haven't you thought that you might some day find a husband who would sympathise with your longing for adventure and travel?'

She shook her head. 'He would still expect me to spend most of my time in London. Have you worked for rich gentlemen there, Mr Smith?'

'I've spent a fair bit of time in London, yes. But it's not my favourite place, I suppose because of the crowded streets, the smoke, the people… Well, some of them, anyway.' He pointed to her glass. 'Don't forget your sherry. Let's drink a toast. May you some day find exactly what—or whom—you are looking for.'

'I'm not on any kind of hunt!' she cried. 'I am quite happy as I am, thank you!'

'I'm glad to hear it,' he said gravely. He lifted his glass. 'Long may you remain content with your life.'

Julia raised her glass too but sipped only a little of the over-sweet sherry. Was she content? No. She wasn't.

She'd declared she was happy, yes, but she suspected he was mocking her. He'd seen right through her and she was troubled, because she knew she must sound ungrateful. She had loving parents and a beautiful home—how could she complain?

'I really should not grumble about London,' she said slowly. 'But there are some people I meet there whom I find detestable. They can be foolish and conceited and—'

She broke off, because she had suddenly remembered her notebook. Oh, heavens, how she prayed he'd not read her *Guide to the Gentlemen of London.*

But he still looked quite calm as he said, 'You are fond of your family, though, aren't you?'

She answered swiftly, 'Oh, yes. Very fond. But I wish my mother and father would listen to me when I tell them that I do not want a Season in the slightest. How on earth would I cope with it?'

'Like all the other debutantes?' he suggested mildly. 'I have heard that most girls enjoy it.'

She bit her lip and frowned.

Yes, she wanted to say. *Yes, they do.*

But not her, for she attracted trouble wherever she went. Her parents had assumed Somerset would be safe, but look at what an utter disaster her first day here had been—trespassing on private property, being caught by a stranger dangling her bare feet in a lake, and now here she was, talking about completely improper subjects with a man who—it was no use denying it—made her feel quite dizzy whenever he smiled.

He was still watching her when he said, with just a hint of that fatal smile, 'I take it that you're determined not to marry?'

'I am!' she cried, 'But how can I avoid it, when I'm soon going to be forced into this wretched Season?'

'But your parents will consult you on your choice of husband, surely? And hasn't the idea of romance ever entered your head?'

'I'm sure my parents would never force me to marry a man I loathed, but in my world, Mr Smith, marriage is a business arrangement. My older sister Pen is suitably betrothed, but my father still has two daughters to marry off and he will be assessing every proposal very carefully.' She looked at him. 'I cannot blame him. But I do need more ideas to put men off me!'

'Wear the most hideous gowns you can?' he suggested. 'Eat garlic?'

She felt herself cringe.

Sir Frederick Timms. Breathes garlic everywhere.

Oh, no. She'd written that in her notebook. *Had* he read it? She really could not bear to ask so instead she laughed a little weakly. 'My mother wouldn't let me make myself unpresentable. She would scrub my mouth out if I ate garlic and burn any hideous clothes or bonnets I tried to wear. But maybe—' and she was sounding, she knew, a little desperate '—maybe I could think of a topic so dreadfully tedious that I could bore them to death when they tried to court me.'

'Such as…?' he prompted.

'Chess!' she cried out in triumph. She pointed to the board in front of them. 'I could recount, step by step, some of the cleverest moves made by the chess masters. I've read lots of books about chess, you see.'

'That doesn't surprise me,' he murmured.

'Or I could talk about obscure literature. I remember that when my sister Pen came out, there was another debutante who had an obsession with medieval poetry. She used to go round parties reciting *Piers Plowman* and Pen said she could empty a room in five minutes.'

Ben looked intrigued. 'Is this literary lady still single?'

'I'm glad to say she married a man who is a professor of history and they are very happy travelling around Europe in search of obscure old manuscripts.' She sighed, feeling a little crestfallen again. 'I think I might enjoy that kind of life, too. But I don't think I'm likely to find another professor of history at a London society ball, do you?'

'I should think it's highly improbable,' he agreed.

'So,' she said with an air of resignation, 'I shall make the most of my freedom here while it lasts. After all, I could never have talked with you like this in London. It's funny, though, isn't it, how my aunt wanted you to come here to play chess with her, then said she'd been feeling poorly all afternoon? But she does seem a little absent-minded at times. How, may I ask, did you come to meet her?'

She was surprised to see him choke slightly on his sherry. At last he said, 'Oh, I've come across her a time or two chasing off those boys and their pigs.'

'Ah, yes.' Julia had to smile. 'I believe the boys only do it to annoy her. But I am truly sorry about her disappearing and you having to play with me.'

'It's been a pleasure,' he said politely.

'You are very kind to say so, Mr Smith. And you

will, won't you, tell me if you think of any other ways in which I can repel any suitors? Oh, dear me. I seem to have spilled a little of this wretched sherry on my dress!'

Ben waited patiently as she sprang to her feet, turned her back on him and fetched out her handkerchief to rub at her skirt. The material, though, was flimsy and he realised that as she bent over to deal with the stain, the view he got of her pert bottom was startlingly delectable. That, he thought, was definitely not the way for her to repel suitors. Why Julia was so convinced of her own unattractiveness was a mystery to him. Maybe it was because her older sister, Pen, was forever outshining her?

Yes, Julia was different. Unconventional. But the funny thing was, he couldn't remember ever having enjoyed a conversation with a girl so much.

She didn't want to get married. Well, neither did he, at least not yet, so that was another thing they had in common—though he certainly couldn't see her surviving her Season without a multitude of proposals. Damn it, as she wriggled around, sorting out her dress, he longed to pull her in his arms and kiss her right now…

That was the moment when he heard the rattling of pots and pans out in the kitchen. Julia heard it, too. 'That will be Miss Twigg,' she said. 'My aunt's housekeeper.'

Ben nodded. Miss Twigg's nearby presence reminded him that he really ought not to be here alone with Julia and probably Miss Twigg thought it, too.

'I think,' he said, 'that it's time for me to go.' It was also, he warned himself, time for him to make a firm resolution not to see her again.

But as Julia was leading him to the door she suddenly said, 'I envy you your ride through the woods at night. Sometimes, when my sisters and I used to stay here, we would creep out of the house in the dark and walk up into the woods. It was wonderfully alive. We saw owls, badgers, foxes…'

That was the moment when he made his biggest mistake yet. For he began to tell her about the young fox he'd seen, alone and undernourished.

She was clearly upset. 'Why is the poor thing in such a state?'

'Because he's rather unusual. His coat is patched with white, which sometimes happens, and those markings mean he'll always be spotted by predators. He'll have spent most of his short life in hiding.'

'What will happen to him?'

Ben hesitated. 'He's done well to survive so far. But he'll find it difficult once winter arrives and he'll probably die, I'm afraid.'

'Oh, no!' She clasped her hands tightly together. 'Surely you can do something to help the poor creature?'

'I've left out some food for him, by the pavilion. But really, it's almost impossible.'

'Please!'

He was already shrugging on his coat, but he hesitated again. Often interfering with the course of nature merely prolonged a creature's sufferings, but her eyes were so pleading that once more an unfamiliar feeling tugged at his heart. 'I'll carry on putting out some food for him by the pavilion,' he said. 'The little fellow seems to like it there. You could maybe come to see him, too.'

Now, that was unbelievably foolish of him, but the words were out before he could stop them.

'I would love that.' Her eyes positively shone. 'What can I do to help?'

'Bring a little food,' he suggested, 'Scraps of bacon, some bread perhaps. I'll put out water, too. But, Julia, I'm afraid the young fox still might die. He's clearly been in a bad way for months.'

'I'll come tomorrow with food…' She stopped, suddenly looking anxious again. 'That is, if you don't mind me foisting myself on you?'

He shook his head. 'Not at all.' How could he have said otherwise?

'Thank you,' she whispered.

Then she jumped, because there were loud footsteps in the hallway behind them and Lady Harris's familiar voice boomed out, 'So, have you thrashed him at chess yet, young lady?'

'I did win our game.' Julia smiled at her. 'But Mr Smith is rather good.'

Lady Harris looked sternly at Ben. 'I hope you played properly? No deferring to the fairer sex or any of that kind of nonsense?'

'I assure you,' said Ben, 'that I would not insult her skill.' He nodded politely to them both. 'I really must be off. I sincerely hope your headache is better by tomorrow, Lady Harris.'

'My what? Oh, yes. The headache. Dratted nuisance. But at my age, what can one expect?'

Outside, Sowerby fetched his horse and Ben set off into the night. The moon was full and as he rode up the woodland track towards Lambourne Hall he was aware of the faint rustlings in the undergrowth that indicated the scurrying of small creatures, while from overhead came the eerie cries of the owls.

Lady Harris had invented that headache, he was quite sure of it. What was her game?

Ben needed to have it out with Her Ladyship at some point, but she would probably be awkward as hell.

'She pretends to be an eccentric old lady,' he murmured to himself. 'But her wits are as sharp as a new carving knife. What can she be up to? Why is she pushing the girl and me together like this?'

He was not interested in any kind of courtship, not yet. He was well aware it was his duty at some point in the future to look for a suitable bride and to provide the estate with an heir, but his priorities for the moment were to secure the family fortunes, give his leg time to heal and, above all, to clear his father's name. As for Julia, he could rest assured she wasn't fixated on men and marriage like most girls of her age and class.

But he hated the fact that Julia was being deceived— and the worst of it was that the girl seemed to trust him. As for him, seeing her so often was doing very little for his peace of mind.

Back at Linden House, Julia said goodnight to her aunt, then went upstairs to her room, where she lay on her bed fully dressed and sighed aloud. She'd placed her solitary candle so it illuminated the model sailing ship and now she remembered how that same little ship had made her dream of adventures whenever she stayed here as a child.

Meeting the stonemason, Mr Smith, was her biggest adventure yet—and quite possibly the most foolish. She told herself she was being extremely sensible about him. She was fortunate to have found a man with whom she could hold a friendly conversation, without worrying if he was imagining her as a possible bride. But the trouble was that she felt warm and unsettled in a most disturbing way whenever he was near.

At first she'd been horrified when her aunt left her alone with him tonight; embarrassed, too, because surely he hadn't expected to be landed with her yet again? But he'd been kind. He'd been considerate. During the chess game he had taken her seriously as an opponent from the beginning and he'd shown no vanity, made no brazen flourishes as he'd moved his pieces. Instead he'd made her feel they were silent equals in a situation where rank and wealth did not matter.

As for the moment when he'd applauded her victory, she'd felt the thrill of that compliment tingle all the way down to her toes. For a moment she'd been quite unable to speak.

Back in London, she had resigned herself to the fact that she just wasn't interested in the things other girls relished, like courtship and flirtation and stolen kisses. She truly thought she was indifferent to all that—but with Ben, she felt less certain. It happened every time she saw him and was struck anew by his handsome face, or noticed without meaning to how his arm muscles tightened beneath his shirt as he casually went about his work at the pavilion. He made her feel hot and awkward and not like an earl's daughter at all.

Maybe it was being in the country and free of society's rules that caused her to act and think so foolishly.

But tonight, during the chess game, she'd had difficulty pulling her gaze away from his brown eyes and his rare but delightful smile. It was a wonder, actually, that she'd managed to move her pieces, let alone win.

She also loved the way he wasn't conceited about his appearance. Yes, he'd smartened himself up a little for tonight's visit, but his hair was still tantalisingly unkempt and he obviously couldn't care less that his clothes were old. But the odd thing was that he sounded and behaved like a well-bred gentleman, so why was he a stonemason? Had something tragic happened in his past, maybe? A financial calamity, perhaps? She had already guessed he must have secrets, because sometimes he looked sad, though often he looked as if he might be laughing at her, just a little.

She sighed aloud. Who could blame him? She was rather ridiculous, after all. Who had ever heard of a girl who dreaded her Season and wanted to drive her suitors away?

'Why on earth do you not wish for a husband?' an objectionable acquaintance of Pen's had once said to Julia at a tea party. Her name was Georgina Sheldon. 'Do you really wish, Julia, to be on your own, for ever? No husband, no children, just a sad old lady?'

A sad old lady. Like her aunt?

But Lady Harris wasn't sad. Her marriage had been a disaster, but now she was very happy, ordering around the servants who clearly thought the world of her, condemning society in very round terms while actually loving to read the latest scandal sheets that Sowerby picked up for her from the village. Her aunt acted like a lady who owned the world, because she was free and independent—just as Julia intended to be.

But she couldn't wait to see Mr Smith again tomorrow. The thought rose in her chest like a bubble of excitement. Meanwhile, it was clear she wouldn't get to sleep, so perhaps she should try to write a letter to Pen. She hopped up from her bed and sat at the little desk on which Miss Twigg had earlier laid out fresh ink and paper.

Dear Pen... she began.

I am here at last. It is quite delightful to be with Aunt Harris again. By the time you receive this letter, Betty will no doubt have arrived in London and I hope Mama is not too cross, but poor Betty hurt her wrist and was of no use to me at all.

I am being well looked after here by my aunt's staff...

Oh, dear. That was Lie Number One, for as a matter of fact she was being allowed to do whatever she pleased. She ploughed on.

My aunt is most welcoming. The countryside is beautiful, as you will remember, and Linden House is as pretty as ever.

Her thoughts wandered. She sat with the pen dangling in her hand, then wrote on.

While I was walking in the woods, I met a man. Tonight I played chess with him. He is a stonemason and I like to think he is my friend...

Oh, no. She slammed down her pen. She could not possibly send that! But then again, why not? Mr Smith worked for his living, but he wasn't what everyone would assume. He was a man of the world, he had travelled and no doubt been employed by rich men throughout Europe. And oh, she did love the way his brown hair strayed so wilfully across his forehead and the look of approval in his eyes as they'd played chess tonight! If she wasn't careful, she'd be thinking yet again of what Pen whispered to her, about the things young women weren't supposed to think about until they were safely married.

She added to her letter.

Do not, on any account, tell Mama and Papa about Mr Smith.

She could trust Pen, she knew she could. Tomorrow, Mr Sowerby would take her letter to the post, but now it was time to get changed into her nightdress. As she did so, she couldn't help but glance at herself in the full-length mirror. Maybe she was just a little pretty? She sighed. What did it matter? Mr Smith wasn't interested in what she looked like, she was sure. He was just being kind to her.

She buttoned up her nightgown, blew out the candle, climbed into her bed and was soon fast asleep.

Chapter Eight

The next morning Julia woke to find the sun pouring through her window. She knew she should have rung for Dottie or Grace to help her dress, but instead she chose a comfortable brown frock that she could easily button up herself, then she brushed her hair and tied it back loosely. It was truly a blissful relief not to have a maid fussing around, telling her she must look like a lady before even getting out of bed.

During breakfast, her aunt alternated between reading one of her news-sheets and grumbling to Miss Twigg about the dire state of the world. 'It's truly dreadful, Twigg, what goes on these days! Dreadful!'

For a while nothing could be heard but the rustle of paper and Lady Harris's mutterings. But as soon as Miss Twigg departed to the kitchen to tell Dottie to make more toast, Lady Harris turned her beady gaze on Julia and said, 'I forgot to ask you last night—did you challenge that young fellow to another game of chess?'

Startled, Julia put down her cup of tea. 'No, I didn't. I really don't think that men like to lose at anything, especially to females. My brother certainly doesn't.'

'Mr Smith,' declared her aunt, 'is not like Charles, thank God. What an almighty fuss your brother makes about his blessed cravats. How long does it take him to get them right, do you think?'

Julia smothered a smile. 'Often an hour, I believe.'

'Hmph. I guessed as much.' Suddenly Lady Harris turned towards the kitchen. 'Twigg! Twigg, where's the sugar for my tea? Really, do I have to do everything for myself?'

Julia said swiftly, 'I'll get the sugar, Aunt.' She rose and fetched the sugar bowl from the sideboard, then settled in her seat again and drew a deep breath. 'Aunt,' she said, 'I was just wondering. No one seems to talk at all about your neighbour, Lord Lambourne.'

Lady Harris looked up swiftly. 'Eh? What was that?'

'Lord Lambourne,' Julia repeated patiently. 'Mr Smith works for him, doesn't he? Have you ever met Lord Lambourne? I don't recall you ever mentioning him.'

Lady Harris cupped her ear. 'What did you say? I didn't quite catch that.'

'I was asking about your neighbour, Lord—'

'Pah, I never see any neighbours. Would I live in this God-forsaken place if I wanted to be bumping into people every time I left my front door, like you do in London? I visit Bath to see my doctor and take the waters, and that is quite enough for me.

'Anyway, you know I've no time for titled men, be they viscounts, earls or whatever—meaning no disrespect to your father, of course.' She turned impatiently towards the kitchen door. 'Twigg, get a move on with that toast, then come and read me this piece about whatever the Prince Regent is up to, will you?'

Miss Twigg appeared moments later with a plate of toast and a pot of fresh tea. She winked at Julia as she sat down and said, 'Here you are, my lady. Now, where's this article? Is it the one about the latest squabble between Prince George and his wife?'

'That's the one—nice and loud now. I'm feeling particularly deaf this morning.' She pointed at Julia. 'It looks like a lovely morning, so why don't you go for a nice walk? While you're out, I'd like you find me some blackberries. Yes, blackberries—there should be plenty of them up in the woods. I use them to make a cure for winter colds. Off you go, now!'

Julia didn't need any more encouragement. She went to fetch her jacket, then after saying a cheerful 'good morning' to Grace, who was sweeping the tiled hallway, she sneaked into the well-stocked larder to cut a couple of slices of bread. Carefully she wrapped the slices in a napkin and put them into a small basket together with some scraps of cold bacon, then she called goodbye to her aunt and set off for the path up the hill.

'This is all perfectly correct,' she told herself. 'I'm going to find blackberries for my aunt. But I also promised Mr Smith I would bring some food for the fox cub and I am doing so. I will, of course, speak to him calmly and decorously, as is proper.'

The sun shone down from a perfect blue sky and crisp leaves crunched beneath her feet as Julia climbed steadily through the woods. She stopped when she heard the rhythmic chink-chink of a hammer and chisel—and there was Mr Smith in the clearing, chipping away at a block of stone. His white shirt was loose at the neck, he'd rolled up his sleeves to display his muscular forearms and for a moment she was transfixed.

He hadn't seen her, so she stood very still at the edge of the clearing and felt her heart tighten in that peculiar way again. She also felt a little breathless, even though the walk hadn't tired her in the least. Oh, my. His obvious strength together with the skill he used in shaping the stone fascinated her exceedingly. Then he saw her and straightened up.

'Good morning, Julia.'

It was time to act with decorum. 'Mr Smith. Good morning,' she said very politely. 'I've brought some food for the young fox. Have you seen him this morning?'

'Not yet.' He looked around, then smiled at her. 'I'm afraid the noise I've been making here probably made him wary, but I wouldn't be surprised if he's lurking nearby. Foxes are intelligent creatures and he'll have realised I'm not his enemy. Why don't you put your food out at the edge of the clearing there?' He pointed. 'Then we can sit here by the pavilion and see if he appears.'

She hesitated. 'Are you quite sure I'm not holding you up in your work?'

'No. Oh, no. I'm ready for a break.'

She set out the food as he suggested, then sat on the stone bench. She said, 'I wish I knew more about wild animals. I suppose you've learned a good deal on your travels?'

He laid his hammer and chisel carefully in his toolbox, then settled himself on the bench also, at a respectful distance. He said, 'I suppose I learned most of what I know about animals from my father. He was especially good with horses. He used to talk to them and, believe it or not, I really think they understood him.'

He spoke calmly, but something in his voice made Julia ask, 'Is your father dead?'

This time he looked at her directly. 'He is.'

'But he can't have been terribly old! Was he ill?'

'He was fifty.' He looked at her and his eyes were suddenly dark. 'He died earlier this year—and I think he died of despair.'

For a moment she couldn't speak. Then she whispered, 'Oh, no. Whatever happened?'

Ben had never spoken about his father's disgrace to anyone except Gilly and he'd certainly never intended to tell this innocent girl about it. Why should he? But incredibly, as she gazed up at him, he found himself revealing more. 'My father,' he said, 'was accused of selling a horse that was unsound—for a large sum of money.'

'That is a dreadful accusation.' She said it very softly. 'I can imagine how hurtful such a thing would be to a man of honour.'

He nodded. 'My father was indeed an honourable man,' he said tightly. 'But he was accused of fraud by a man of considerable power. My father could not prove his innocence, nor could his accuser truly prove his guilt, but my father's life was ruined.'

He realised that she had reached out to put her small hand on his. 'I'm sorry,' she whispered. 'Really, I am.'

'Yes.' He could hear that his voice was still bitter. 'So am I, especially as I wasn't there for him when he passed away.'

'What about your mother?'

'She died when I was six.'

'Oh, *no*.' She was looking up at him and her expressive eyes were wide with distress. She shook her head. 'I really should not grumble about my family. I'm so lucky to have them.'

Gently he eased his hand away from under hers. 'They will know that you love them,' he said. 'Trust me.' Suddenly his attention was caught by a movement nearby and he pointed. 'Look, Julia. Over there. I can see the fox.'

Indeed, gazing at them from the edge of the clearing where she'd put the food was the white-spotted fox, who had seen them and was wary. But after a moment he began eating very quickly and once he'd finished he stood very still, his eyes fixed on Ben. Then he turned and trotted away.

Ben realised he'd been holding his breath. He saw that Julia, too, was still gazing at the place where the fox had been, then she said to Ben, very quietly, 'Thank you. I'm truly grateful for all of this. Being able to come up here on my own has been wonderful. But I mustn't keep you from your work any longer. I really ought to go.'

She'd risen to her feet and he rose also. 'Do you want to go, Julia?'

'Not really.' She smiled a little shyly. 'I love it here.'

Once more he found that his common sense—his instinct for propriety and society's rules—had vanished. Because he said, 'Then stay. Why not?'

He saw the hope in her eyes. 'May I? Really?'

He was already pointing at the pavilion. 'Do you want to look inside again at those paintings? I've brought the original stencils and the paints from the Hall and some day I mean to have a go at restoring them.'

Julia followed him inside and was gazing raptly at the faded frescoes. 'Would you let me help you? Please?'

How could he say no?

He continued to repair the outside of the building while Julia worked inside for over an hour. Whenever he looked through the windows he could see her, mixing the paints and applying them with the utmost care. She looked, he thought, as happy as he'd yet seen her. She concentrated so hard that she hadn't even noticed she had a large splodge of blue on her cheek and maybe she'd almost forgotten he was there, because she jumped as he entered the pavilion.

He said, 'You've done this kind of thing before. Haven't you?'

'Oh, you startled me! No, I've never actually worked with stencils, but I always used to love painting.' Her expressive face fell a little. 'My sisters and I once had an art tutor, but he was dismissed after two months because he fell in love with Pen. Everyone falls in love with her.'

He was curious. 'Are you jealous?'

'No!' She laughed. 'How could I be? Pen is perfectly lovely.'

And so are you, he thought silently.

He pointed to the door. 'Come and sit outside for a while. I have a flask of lemonade I brought from the Hall.'

He was fascinated by that splodge of blue paint on her cheek. He knew it was wicked of him, but it made her look so delightful that he didn't want to tell her about it. He waited for her to follow him outside to the stone bench that caught the afternoon sun, then decided his conscience would allow him no rest until he mentioned it.

He pointed to her face. 'You have some blue paint on your left cheek,' he said. 'Just a little. It should come off with a damp cloth.'

Her hand flew up to her face in horror. 'Oh, no. And I would never have known!' Her happiness had vanished. 'I'm ridiculous, aren't I?' she said in a low voice. 'Truly ridiculous!'

'Of course not.' He rose and fetched a clean cloth which he dipped in the fresh water barrel nearby. 'Here. You can wipe it off with this.'

She did so, but she still looked utterly despondent, so he took the cloth from her and put it down. 'Julia,' he said, 'I do not find you ridiculous. But I do think it a pity that you think so little of yourself. You are different, perhaps, but is that so dreadful?'

'It is if you're about to be put on the marriage market,' she said glumly. 'My brother keeps introducing me to his friends, but they usually back away as soon as possible.'

He poured her some lemonade. 'That marriage market again. It really worries you, doesn't it? Have you ever wondered if the fault maybe lies with your brother and his friends?'

'I would be foolish to say or even think so, since they are considered very eligible by most other girls!'

Ben hid a smile as he remembered her comments on various men in that notebook.

Waddles like a walrus.
Breathes garlic at you.

Instead he said, 'That's because they're rich, presumably. Heirs to peerages. But I wonder, have you confided in your mother about your worries? She might give you a little more time to grow used to the idea of a Season.'

She picked up her lemonade and laughed. 'My mother? She's very sweet, but she's the worst of them all, believe me! I am a tremendous worry to her, I'm afraid, since she finds the idea of a dedicated spinster in the family truly appalling.'

His mouth quirked a little. 'A dedicated spinster? You're sure about that? How old are you?'

She looked defiant. 'I'm eighteen!'

'Ah,' he said with mock solemnity. 'Then your fate is sealed. Clearly you will spend the rest of your life knitting by the fireside and tending a multitude of cats.'

She'd been sipping her drink, but she gave a splutter of laughter. 'I don't think I'm ready for that!'

'Of course you're not,' he said briskly. 'And let me tell you this, Julia. If those men in London have any sense at all, when your Season begins they'll be fighting over you.'

This time, Julia almost dropped her drink entirely. What? *Fighting* over her? She really didn't know what to say—as a matter of fact, she suddenly felt very odd indeed. Of course, she'd met lots of young men, but all in all she had found them a complete nuisance with their noisy talk and their efforts to impress everyone around them.

Ben was different. She supposed it was because he wasn't rich, which meant, of course, that he had no airs or affectations. But there was something else—something that made her feel a little breathless whenever he was near, because she thought he was, well, *nice.*

That was it, she told herself firmly. *Nice.* He probably still thought she was slightly mad, just as her brother's friends did, but he was at least trying to be kind about it.

The trouble was that she found him exceedingly attractive, too. She couldn't stop herself sneaking sideways glances at him whenever he wasn't looking, admiring his profile and his stubbled jaw. She was doing it *now*, for heaven's sake. She dragged her gaze away and pretended to be looking at the surrounding scenery instead.

'Julia.' Ben's voice was touched, she noted, with more than a hint of amusement. 'May I ask, are you practising some new idea to put men off you?'

'What?' That shook her back into looking at him.

'You were,' he announced, 'staring into the distance—somewhere over there, in fact.' He pointed to the horizon. 'Are you trying to tell me that I'm boring you rigid and you'd rather I was anywhere else?'

'Oh, no, no!' she cried in dismay. 'I was just thinking that I really should not be here at all. It's not that I don't trust you. Of course I do! But I'm afraid my mother would be appalled.'

He nodded gravely. 'Do you think she would worry that I might take advantage of you?'

She jutted her chin. 'Well, I don't think you would for one minute.'

'Good. And besides, you can probably run much faster than I can.'

Smiling, he pointed to his lame leg. He was brave, she thought, to joke about it, because she guessed he was often in pain.

She said, 'I'm sorry, I didn't mean—'

'I know you didn't,' he broke in gently. 'And please believe me when I tell you I have no intention whatsoever of taking advantage of your trust.'

Of course. He was tactfully trying to indicate that he didn't find her tempting in the least. Besides, her parents would never, ever permit her to be courted by a stonemason, but even so she felt suddenly desolate at the thought that soon he would be gone from her life completely.

She rose to her feet, picked up her basket and spoke as brightly as she could. 'Dear me, how foolish I am. Do you know, I'd almost forgotten that my aunt asked me if I would find some blackberries for her.'

'Blackberries?' He rose, too. 'What is she making this time?'

Julia laughed. 'She's concocting a medicinal syrup, I believe, for the winter months. She said there would be some blackberries in the woods, but I really don't know where to start.' She hesitated. 'I don't suppose you…?'

Ben smiled. 'There are plenty of blackberries along the path just above the lake.' He pointed. 'Shall we go and look together?'

Ben found he was rather sorry that Julia was back to being her prim and proper self. As they walked, her gaze never met his but was firmly fixed on the path ahead. She'd withdrawn once more into her tight little shell of formality.

She must, of course, come from a wealthy family, quite possibly a very distinguished one. He'd always been aware that Lady Harris had many aristocratic relations, but Ben wasn't going to ask any more questions on the topic because he'd decided that he didn't want to know the answers.

But he felt angry with her parents. He feared she'd been brought up as many well-bred daughters were, to be decorative, polite and subservient to her parents' and her future husband's wishes—which was all *wrong*. Here she was, active and independent and curious, yet she felt that the only way she could be her true self was to remain unmarried. What a criminal waste.

By now, she was some way ahead of him on the path and was looking all around for blackberries. He knew where there was a bramble patch bursting with ripe fruit and he could have guided her there immediately, but he was deliberately dragging it out. Yes, he was being wicked because, damn it, he was enjoying her company. Enjoying also her complete unawareness of the way her print dress—which she probably thought the epitome of modesty—clung to her pert hips as she walked along the path before him.

She was so graceful and slender that he guessed she would be a delight to dance with. Even more of a delight to hold and kiss…

Just then he realised she'd found the blackberries for herself because she turned to call back, 'Look, Mr Smith! Here's a fine patch of blackberries. Gorgeous ones.'

She was already gathering them avidly so he joined her as she started to fill her little basket. 'They are delicious,' she breathed as he drew nearer. 'Try one.'

Her expression brimmed with delight. Her lips were stained dark red and, when she licked them and gave a little sigh of pleasure, his pulse thumped. He said quietly, 'My name is Ben. Please call me Ben.'

Then he reached out and brushed away a bit of blackberry that clung to the corner of her mouth. He could have sworn a slight tremor ran through her as his finger touched her skin, then she gazed up at him and whispered, 'Ben.'

His hand still hovered. He felt an overwhelming urge to haul her against his body and kiss her senseless. His pulse was pounding and his loins throbbed warningly. She would never, he hoped, guess at the willpower it took him to step away. He said, in a voice that was harsher than he intended, 'It's time, I think, for you to go home.'

Time, too, for him to come to his senses. Time to remind himself why he'd come to Lambourne Hall in the first place. Why he'd intended to keep himself isolated from company while he concentrated on finding out exactly why the sale of his father's fine horse had gone so wrong.

Every day since he'd arrived, he'd spent hours each morning and evening, combing through his father's papers, especially those relating to his father's stables. He came to the pavilion in the afternoons because he found the physical work a way of making reparation for his neglect of his duties in the past.

But his prime concern was to find something that would clear his father's name. Anything else—anyone else—was a distraction, especially this lovely girl.

Ben guessed she was deeply wounded by his apparent dismissal, even though she nodded and said lightly, 'Of course I should go.' But as she pulled on her jacket, she

added, almost in a whisper, 'Ben. Please tell me. Have
I done something wrong again?'

'Wrong?' he said sharply. 'How do you mean?'

'You know. Something odd. Something to add to my
list of how to put men off me—like being good at chess.'

Damn it. She'd done nothing wrong—he was the one
at fault, he was the one who was totally to blame! 'You
haven't,' he said at last. 'Not at all.'

She still looked a little anxious, but she nodded.
'Good. I've enjoyed this so much,' she said, more
steadily now. 'Please may I come and paint again? Of
course, I'd hate to stop you working and get you into
trouble with your employer, Lord Lambourne. But it's
so lovely here, and in London I hadn't quite realised—'
She broke off.

'What?' he said. 'What, Julia?'

'I hadn't realised,' she said quietly, 'that I could be
so very happy.'

Christ. That really did almost fell him. He was getting in deep, far too deep. 'I'll walk you home,' he said.

Not another word was spoken on the way and he
told himself, *This is it. I must not see her again, and
it's for the best.*

But as they approached Linden House, she turned
to him and said, 'You didn't give me an answer. May
I visit you again?'

What could he say but *Yes*?

Chapter Nine

After that, each day after lunch Julia said to her aunt, 'I think I'll just go for a stroll.'

Every time, she expected Lady Harris to say *No*, or *Why?* or *Where are you going, exactly?* But she didn't. She mostly said things like, 'Hmm. You may as well enjoy this fine weather while it lasts', or 'Do what you like. You're only young once.'

Lady Harris never mentioned Ben; in fact, only Dottie and Grace showed any curiosity concerning Julia's wanderings. Julia enjoyed her chats with the two sisters, who never ceased to ask her about London. 'We've heard such stories, my lady, about what a wonderful place it is! They say there are palaces on every street and fine ladies and gentlemen parading everywhere!'

Dottie particularly enjoyed brushing Julia's long hair. 'I would love to put it up for you, my lady, with fancy pins and ribbons, as if you were going to a grand ball.'

Julia smiled, but shook her head. 'No, Dottie. Just tie it back plainly with a ribbon, if you please. Do you know, I find it amazing that here I can be ready to go out in ten minutes, while in London it can take hours.'

'But that's because in London you'll be making your-self beautiful to catch the eye of some fine gentleman,' exclaimed Dottie, securing the ribbon with a neat bow. 'It's a pity that there's no one for you here. Such a shame that the new Lord Lambourne hasn't arrived at the Hall yet.'

Julia felt her pulse jump. 'The *new* Lord Lambourne? Why do you call him that?'

'Because the old Lord, his father, died only recently. No one saw him very much, but he was good to every-one around here and he really loved the horses he kept at the Hall's stables. Didn't you realise?'

Julia said slowly, 'No. I didn't.'

Dottie sighed. 'He died suddenly in the summer and his heir still hasn't come back. This new Lord will be a catch, though, when he does come home—I've heard he's lovely and handsome, but it's wicked to leave that huge old place lying empty. There now, I'm letting my tongue run away with me.' She gave a last tweak to Julia's hair, then stood back. 'How pretty you are, my lady. I'm sure you have plenty of admirers in London.'

Julia felt her breath catch in her throat.

Not really, she thought. *Besides, there's no one that I want as much as Ben.*

She sighed. She was also doing as much as possible to put him off her, whether she intended it or not. Trip-ping over her own feet. Going around with blue paint on her face. Letting him find her embarrassing book— *had* he read it?

Oh, dear. There was no doubt that kind as he was, he must think her ridiculous.

Every afternoon though, as she walked up to the pavilion, Ben always greeted her with courtesy. He continued to repair the pavilion's crumbling stonework, while she did her best to complete the faded stencilling. Always, at around three, they would settle on the bench overlooking the valley to share the bottle of lemonade that Ben had brought with him.

He often brought scraps of food, too, to place close to the undergrowth that surrounded the clearing and the young fox would appear to swiftly eat Ben's offerings before vanishing into the woods again.

She found herself telling Ben more about the happy times she'd spent as a child here at Lady Harris's, while he spoke of the cities and countries he'd visited in his travels. But he never told her about himself, she realised. He never told her any more about his father, or his mother who had died when he was a child—and she was careful not to ask too much. Not to pry.

It was as if there was an unspoken pact between them—*we know we each have secrets.*

She did not want him to know her father was an earl and guessed his silence about his own background was because of the gulf between them. Often she was aware that what she said or did betrayed her naivety—for instance when she asked him to explain exactly what one of the faded wall paintings was about.

'Is it a party?' she asked, eagerly pointing at the wall. 'Or perhaps a Greek or Roman bath house? These people don't seem to have many clothes on...'

Her voice trailed away, for suddenly she'd realised they were all enjoying themselves very much and very intimately. 'Oh,' she murmured, blushing a fiery red. 'How foolish of me.'

Ben didn't bat an eyelid. He said politely, 'Not to worry. After all, the painting is so faded that the details are far from clear.' Then he added, 'And perhaps they had better remain so.'

Julia turned back hurriedly to her stencilling, but she could hear Ben at work outside whistling cheerfully and suddenly thought, *I am going to miss him terribly when it's time to go home.*

Something even worse occurred to her. She didn't really want to go home—because it meant she would never see him again.

Almost a week had passed by swiftly and the October weather stayed fine. Each afternoon Julia went up to the pavilion and Ben kept his distance, continuing to repair the exterior of the pavilion. But just knowing that he was near filled her with a kind of quiet contentment.

Then one afternoon, as she was preparing to put away her painting things, she remembered that her aunt had asked her to look for more blackberries.

'You're usually heading back for your tea by now,' warned Ben. 'Will you really have time?'

'I'm sure I have.' She was putting on her jacket and picking up her basket. 'It's not far, is it? I can remember the way.'

So off they set, a little reluctantly on Ben's part because his leg ached from all the work he'd done that day, which slowed him considerably. Julia was well ahead when she turned and called back to him over her shoulder, 'I think I need the path to the left, Ben. Don't I?'

Then she was off again, walking briskly.

Damn it, muttered Ben. She'd come to the place where the track divided into three and already she was heading up an overgrown path that hardly anyone used these days. 'Julia,' he called. 'That's the wrong way. Wait.'

But she didn't hear him. 'Julia,' he called again. 'Julia—*no*.' He cursed himself for letting her outpace him. 'Not that way. For Christ's sake...'

Somehow he managed to catch up with her just before she reached the edge of the old stone quarry. Here, the builders had carved out quantities of stone in order to construct Lambourne Hall a century or more ago, but the great, excavated hollow still gaped like a deep wound in the hillside and the drop to the bottom was sixty feet or more. The place was lethal and didn't he know it—for this was where, earlier in the year, they had found the body of his father.

Ben clutched Julia's shoulders and almost shook her, so overwhelmed was he by the mingled fury and powerlessness that had seized him. At last he ground out, 'You could have been killed.'

She was very pale. 'I'm sorry. I—I didn't know.' She glanced in disbelief at the quarry's edge. 'I never guessed that it was here.'

'I told you to wait for me,' he said between gritted teeth. 'You should never have gone rushing off on your own, do you hear me? Don't *ever* do that again.' He was furious. He was also holding her as if he would never let her go and he was frightened by the power of the emotions that coursed through him.

She was searching his face, as if trying to comprehend his rage. 'I'm sorry, Ben,' she repeated. 'But I would have seen it in time—the quarry, I mean.'

'I didn't know that, though, did I? All I could see was you, dashing onwards into a situation where you might have been killed!' He shook his head, trying to calm himself. Then he added more quietly, 'You shouldn't be wandering in these woods anyway. Lady Harris shouldn't be sending you up here and I'm a fool for letting you do so.'

'You're angry with me,' she said. He saw now that her wide, wonderful eyes were glistening with unshed tears. 'And you're hurting me, Ben. Just a little.'

He knew that he was still holding her far too tightly, knew, too, that he was putting her in another kind of danger entirely and he released her so suddenly that she almost stumbled. It was as if he had no control over his own body. This place had terrible memories for him, but the helplessness he'd felt when he feared he might lose this precious girl was shattering.

She was safe from tumbling to her death in the quarry. But maybe—just maybe—she wasn't safe from *him*.

The problem was that she looked so damned lovely. Her eyes were wide and vulnerable, and when she moistened her parted lips with the tip of her tongue, he wanted to kiss her—or so he told himself, though to be honest, he wanted a good deal more.

'Should we go back now?' she whispered.

He realised she was still stunned by his anger, shocked and even a little frightened. So he attempted to quell his raging thoughts and the fierce arousal that had come about when he held her tender body next to his and he said, in a voice that was still gritty with tension, 'You came here, didn't you, to collect some blackberries?'

She nodded, still looking crestfallen.

'Then follow me,' he said.

At last they reached the copse where the blackberries grew. There weren't many left, for the birds had eaten most of them. But he helped her gather what remained, then said, 'Right. It's growing dark, so I'd better walk with you back to your aunt's house.'

'But your leg!'

Damn. She'd noticed his limp was worse. He shrugged. 'I can manage.'

They walked back together in silence, but as soon as Linden House came into view she stopped and said to him in a low but clear voice, 'What was it, Ben, about the quarry? You were so angry. I've never seen you like that. It wasn't just because of me, was it?'

'Someone I once knew died there,' he said.

For a moment she shut her eyes. 'Oh, *no*. I'm so sorry. I was an idiot to have dragged you there.'

He made a gesture of dismissal. 'You shouldn't blame yourself—after all, how were you to know? I'll leave you now. Your aunt will be wondering where you are.'

He turned to go and walked—no, get it right, man, he *limped*—back to Lambourne Hall. Once there, he called out to Gilly that he'd be with him shortly. Then he went straight to his father's study and began hunting once more through all the documents his father had kept about his beloved horses. He was almost desperate now. He had thought he'd found everything there was to be found about every horse he'd owned: their sires and dams, their age and health and indeed the details of their sale if indeed they'd left his father's stables.

He'd found nothing at all about Silver Cloud's ill-fated departure. But this time, as he leafed through the same old files yet again, a loose sheet of paper fell from the rest of the documents.

He picked it up and read it with growing wonder. It was the final bill from the man who had been hired to transport Silver Cloud from Somerset to Richmond, in Surrey. There was little enough about him: he was simply referred to as 'Francis Molloy of London'.

Ben had always known it would be hard to prove any wrongdoing on the part of the horse's buyer, for he was an eminent man of high reputation. But could this fellow Molloy have had a hand in the deception?

Ben tapped his finger on the paper, thinking hard. The conveyance of valuable thoroughbreds was an expensive business, requiring the use of wagons that were fitted inside with barriers and slings to keep the animals secure. Frequent stops had to be made on the way to exercise and water them. There would be records, surely, of the men who organised these transports—and Mr Molloy of London could well be worthy of investigation.

That night Julia was challenged by her aunt to a game of chess, but she played atrociously. At first Lady Harris made no comment, but when Julia dropped her knight on the floor, her aunt finally said, 'I think, young lady, that you could do with a change of scene.'

Oh, no. Was Lady Harris going to send her home? That would mean she would never see Ben again. But would she dare now to visit him anyway? This afternoon she'd done something awful by going near that quarry and he'd been terribly angry with her. It almost broke her heart because when he'd held her in his arms, she'd wanted to stay there for ever.

She said, as she put her knight back on the board, 'Are you thinking of sending me back to London, Aunt?'

'Good grief, not yet.' Lady Harris chuckled. 'Nothing as dire as that. You've only been here a couple of weeks. But I intend to go into Bath tomorrow, to see my doctor.'

Julia looked up quickly. 'I do hope you're not ill?'

'Of course not. I'm never ill, but the wretched man insists that I see him every so often and insists, too, that I take some of those dreadful spring waters. You'll come with me, won't you?'

Julia was no stranger to Bath, for when her family visited Lady Harris in the old days, her mother often took her daughters there. Julia had always thought it was a beautiful city, with its elegant buildings and glorious parks. Lately London's fashionable set had taken to visiting Brighton instead, but Bath still fared well, especially with elderly visitors.

'I would love to come with you,' she said.

Early the next morning Grace and Dottie's brother Matthew arrived with the carriage from the George Inn nearby. Of course the conveyance was nothing like her father's magnificent carriage and its lack of springs meant that it bounced and rattled all the way to Bath. But they arrived there with an hour and a half to spare before Lady Harris's appointment with her doctor, so there was time to stroll among the shops and to drink mineral water in the Pump Room.

'This is quite foul stuff,' declared Lady Harris loudly.

Nevertheless, the room was packed with genteel visitors who'd come to take the waters, converse with friends and generally ignore the small string orchestra that played valiantly in the background.

When the time came for her aunt to visit her physician, Julia decided to remain there and listen properly to the music. But it wasn't long before she became aware of a young woman with a determined expression heading her way.

Oh, no. It was Miss Georgina Sheldon from London, known by Julia's sisters as The Gorgon. She was due to have her come-out next year, just like Julia. Some said she was nearly as pretty as Pen, but she had a tongue like acid. Julia pretended to be concentrating intensely on the rather dirge-like piece the string players were wading through, but within moments she felt a tap on her shoulder.

'Lady Julia Carstairs,' pronounced Georgina. 'Fancy seeing you here—though now I think of it, you did make rather a fool of yourself at Lord Bamford's party, so doubtless your parents thought it best to get you out of the way for a while. Dear Tristram found the incident most amusing, I can tell you. He's been telling everyone.'

She sat on the chair next to Julia's. 'I wonder if you're going to brave the Season next spring? Personally, I cannot wait. There's Christmas first, of course, with all the country house parties—I've had so many invitations! Then when I make my debut, there will be such a choice of eligible men—with your brother Charles being one of the foremost, of course.'

Julia almost gagged. Georgina and Charles? The thought of Georgina Sheldon as her sister-in-law was appalling. No. Please, just *no*.

She said, 'I'm surprised to see you here, Georgina. I thought you would be in London.'

Georgina looked around, pursing her lips. 'Yes, Bath is quite dreary nowadays, isn't it? So many old people. But my older brother Henry has a house on the Royal Crescent—you'll remember Henry, of course?'

Julia nodded. Henry was one of Charles's friends.

'Mama,' continued Georgina, 'really wished to visit Henry and his wife to take the waters.' She pretended to yawn as if bored, then suddenly said, 'Your aunt's house lies close to Lambourne Hall, doesn't it? I wonder, have you heard any news of when the new baron will return?'

Lord Lambourne—*again*. Julia shrugged, realising that the proximity of any new heir was bound to cause speculation with girls like Georgina. 'I've heard nothing at all of the man,' she said.

'Of course,' mused Georgina, 'he will be quite a catch. I was hoping to meet him while we were here in Somerset, but my brother has no news of him either. Which is most peculiar—'

Just at that moment Lady Harris sailed into view and Georgina broke off to giggle behind her hand. 'Such an oddity, your relation,' she murmured. 'Everyone laughs at her. How you stand her, I don't know—ouch!'

Georgina's giggle changed into a shriek of pain because Julia, on rising, had managed to stand on Georgina's foot.

'I'm sorry,' said Julia airily. 'How dreadfully clumsy of me.'

'You might have broken my toe!'

'I doubt it. But I do hope you weren't going dancing tonight.' She smiled sweetly and went to meet her aunt.

'Is everything all right?' asked Lady Harris, glancing sharply over at Georgina.

'Absolutely fine, Aunt.'

'I saw that Sheldon girl talking with you. Georgina's like a dose of poison. Shall we go home now? Have you had enough of Bath?'

'Yes,' said Julia, linking arms with Lady Harris. 'I've had enough of Bath. Let's go home.'

The sun shone from a clear blue sky all the way back to Linden House, making the autumn colours of the fields and woodlands quite glorious. At the slightest breath of wind, more leaves would come fluttering down from the trees and Julia remembered how, when they stayed here as children, she and her sisters used to run around laughing as they tried to catch them.

'You'll have one lucky day for every leaf you catch,' Lady Harris had told them.

Had they believed her, the three of them? Maybe. But that was years ago, and she knew now that no amount of lucky leaves could save her from her fate next spring, when she would face balls, parties and people like Georgina Sheldon and Tristram Bamford.

As for Ben Smith, he'd had enough of her. His harsh words to her at the quarry had made that all too clear.

Chapter Ten

The next morning, it began to rain. In fact, the showers continued for five days and the skies were heavy and grey. Julia browsed the books in her aunt's library, as she did when she was a child. She wrote letters to her parents and Lizzie, telling them about the trip to Bath. She also wrote again to Pen.

> *I have met with my stonemason quite often, Pen. I have grown to truly like him. He is kind and respectful, but I'm afraid I have made him angry and I might not see him again. I know you won't say a word of this to anyone else, but I miss him.*

She gazed out of the window at the pouring rain, then gave her letters to Sowerby so he could post them in Lambourne village.

One afternoon the sun came out at last and as they sat in the drawing room after lunch, Lady Harris took Julia completely by surprise.

'Now,' said her aunt in her decisive way. 'Since that infernal rain has decided to stop, I think I'd like you to help me collect some frogs.' She rang the bell. 'Twigg! Are you there? Or Dottie, or Grace! Please come and remove this tea tray!'

As Dottie hurried in, then out again with the tray, Julia's eyes were wide with astonishment. 'Did you actually say "frogs", Aunt?'

'Indeed. I usually see plenty of them in the two ponds in my woodland garden, but this year there aren't any. I would guess they've migrated to conduct their reproductive rituals up by that lake in the woods, so I thought you and I could take a stroll in that direction and bring some down here in time for their winter hibernation. A fine idea, don't you think? It's no use asking Twigg to accompany me. The woman faints at anything that wriggles.'

'But the lake...'

'I know. It's on Lambourne's land, but it's not as if the frogs belong to the man, is it? All wild creatures are meant to be as free as the air around us. They are owned by no one.'

The lake. The pavilion. *Ben.*

'Aunt,' Julia said, 'I'm actually a little tired. I was thinking of taking a rest.'

But Lady Harris was already heading for the door. 'Come along. Put your boots on, because it will be muddy around the lake after all that rain. We'll tempt the frogs with some titbits. Let's be off!'

With a feeling of acute apprehension, Julia climbed with her aunt up the familiar path to the lake, armed with a large mixing bowl from the kitchen and a bag of breadcrumbs. If Ben was here, what would he say? He might think this was her doing. She decided she could probably start filling another notebook with ways to deter admirers.

Men will not be attracted to girls who do eccentric things like attempting to move frogs from one lake to another...

'There'll be frogs here,' hissed Lady Harris in a dramatic whisper as they approached the lake's edge. 'Look, Julia. They adore the sunshine.'

True enough, Julia could see a dozen or more frogs basking sleepily on some low, flat stones that were half-submerged. 'Throw a few breadcrumbs,' whispered her aunt. There was no sign of Ben so Julia, feeling a surge of relief, swiftly obeyed and the two of them ventured closer.

'Now,' instructed her aunt, 'pick a frog up, very gently, and pop it in the bowl with more crumbs. It will be quite happy.'

Julia reached for the nearest one, but goodness, it was too quick for her! Immediately it jumped into the water and swam off, while the others stayed where they were, gazing up at her. She could swear they were finding all this highly amusing. Sighing, she prepared to try once more to coax the frogs a little nearer. 'Here you are,' she whispered. 'Breadcrumbs. Don't you like breadcrumbs? Do you prefer worms? Because if so—'

But one by one they dived into the lake and she nearly toppled into the water herself when she heard

Lady Harris calling out, 'Mr Smith! Yoo-hoo! Julia and I are over here!'

Oh, no.

'Hello, Lady Harris. Good afternoon, Julia.' It was Ben, looking effortlessly handsome as usual.

Julia's heart bumped to a stop at his husky familiar voice. Then she glanced back at the lake in horror, because she realised she had let her bowl roll into the water. Still kneeling at the edge of the lake, she tried to retrieve the dratted bowl and failed, while getting her gown wet into the bargain. How *could* she keep doing such unutterably stupid things whenever Ben was around?

Lady Harris, meanwhile, was greeting Ben warmly and explaining in great detail about the frog mission. Ben was nodding politely, but she guessed he was highly amused. Then he came over to her, crouched down beside her, rolled up his shirt sleeve and reached to pull in the bowl, giving her an awe-inspiring view of his bare forearm that was corded with muscle. She swallowed hard.

'In trouble again?' he said, rising and helping her to her feet. Then he added with a smile, 'How are you, Julia? I've missed your visits these last few days. I suppose the rain was a problem?'

Oh, no. He was being nice to her. It would have been so, so much easier if he wasn't. She had to make a huge effort to summon her normal voice. 'Of course the rain kept me mostly inside,' she said. 'I've also been rather busy. I've been helping my aunt and writing letters home, that kind of thing.'

Just at that moment Lady Harris called out, 'Julia! I must return to the house now!'

Julia was flustered again. 'Very well, Aunt. I'll join you,' she called back. 'I can do this another time.'

But Lady Harris raised her hand in a most definite gesture of refusal. 'No, you jolly well won't join me. You'll get some of those frogs for me—I'm sure Ben will help you. But I'm going home. I need to check that Twigg isn't making a hash of telling those maids of mine how to clean my precious silverware. I'll see you at the house later.'

She marched off.

Julia, hugely embarrassed, turned back to Ben. 'I know this sounds, ridiculous, but the fact is, my aunt asked me to help her collect some frogs to put in her two garden ponds. I explained we'd be trespassing, but she took no notice.'

Ben nodded, looking serious. 'She has little heed for the law, I'm afraid. Normally it doesn't matter, but as for stealing frogs from a lake—well, maybe the magistrates should be informed.'

'The magistrates? Oh, no.' Julia put one hand to her cheek. Then she gasped. 'Ben! You're teasing me, aren't you?'

He grinned. 'Of course I am. Shall I help you continue with your villainous theft? By the way,' he added, 'frogs don't eat breadcrumbs.'

She was forgiven. They were still friends. She felt such an enormous surge of relief that she couldn't stop smiling, and neither could she stop looking at his lovely strong hands as he set the bowl on its side, then managed to guide some inquisitive frogs into it.

Yes, she couldn't help but imagine his fingers warm on her bare skin, but that was quite enough of such nonsense. She ought to be practical. She ought to be sensible, for heaven's sake. She said, 'I must apologise again for causing you such anxiety the last time we met, by wandering off to that quarry.'

He leaned back a little to look straight at her. 'I should apologise, too. I overreacted.'

'Because somebody died there?'

'Yes,' he said very quietly. 'Yes. Because of that.' Suddenly he smiled and once more her heart inexplicably soared. 'Anyway, let's put all that behind us. You know, our little fox has really missed you and I see him looking for you, every afternoon.'

She laughed. 'Oh, Ben. Now you're teasing me again.'

He shook his head. 'I am not. I swear, he's been positively pining. In fact—' and he looked beyond her, then pointed '—he's already noticed you. You see?'

She could indeed see the white-spotted fox watching them from behind a tree. She clasped her hands together in delight. 'He's looking very much better. Do you still put food out for him?'

'Just a little, though soon I'll stop, because he'll be able to fend perfectly well for himself.'

Julia was quiet for a moment. Then she said slowly, 'I absolutely love it here. I do not want to go back to London.'

'No one is unkind to you there, are they?'

'No. Oh, no!' she exclaimed. 'My parents only want me to be happy! But they would not approve of all *this*. After all, just look at me. Collecting frogs for my aunt's ponds, for heaven's sake!' She tried to say it breezily.

But he was looking at her and she knew what the real problem was.

Quite disastrously, she had fallen in love.

Ben waited for her to say something else, but she didn't. Silently he bent to pick up the glass bowl in which several frogs now sat, looking comfortable but also rather puzzled. Julia was peering at them, too.

'I think they're perhaps worried,' she said, 'that this tiny world is going to be all they'll see. I wish I could explain that they will be perfectly content in their new home.'

'Just as you might find yourself happy to enter London society next spring,' Ben said quietly.

Her face fell once more and she whispered, 'If only.'

Ben's heart ached for her. 'You're quite young, you know,' he said gently. 'And a good deal can change in a few months. Most girls, I've heard, love their come-out. Surely you want to have a little fun? Enjoy a few flirtations?'

He saw her shake her head almost fiercely. 'That kind of thing is not for me! Besides, I'm no good at it, I've told you that. You've seen it for yourself!'

He felt a desperate impulse to help her. To comfort her. She was different, but she was beautiful—and someone needed to tell her so. He put his hand on her bare wrist, where the blue of her veins could be seen beneath her delicate skin, and he felt her trembling. He said, 'If I can help you to think differently, I will. And, Julia—'

He halted, because he'd seen that two fat tears were

forming in her lovely eyes. Oh, no. She was crying. 'Please,' he said. 'Julia, don't do that. Please stop.'

'I'll stop,' she promised, 'yes, of course I will.' But still the tears rolled down her cheeks. 'Oh, Ben, I'm such a fool. Only I truly love being here, with you and— and—'

She was pulling out a neatly folded little handkerchief and pressing it to her face. He touched her on the shoulder. 'You will be all right,' he urged. 'And you are not foolish. Believe me.'

But *he* was. And suddenly he couldn't bear it any longer.

This was crazy of him. This was *wrong* of him. This girl had grown to trust him and he was deceiving her badly. He had to tell her who he was—but not now. Not when she was upset and vulnerable.

Soon, though, he ordered himself. *It must be soon.*

'I'll take you back to your aunt's house,' he said quietly. Carefully he picked up the bowl of frogs.

They walked in silence down the path, but as they reached Lady Harris's extensive and rather wild gardens, he realised the lady herself was out there with her aged manservant, Sowerby. She was busy clearing a large pond of weed with a net fastened to a pole, while Sowerby's job was to untangle the soggy mass of greenery from the net each time she lifted it.

Lady Harris looked up when she saw them approach. 'You've got some frogs for me,' she said, pointing her net at them with a flourish. 'Excellent.' She put down the net and came marching forward to collect the bowl, which she lowered to the edge of the water. 'Here you go, my beauties,' she crooned, tilting the bowl on its side so several of them could clamber out.

Then she rose, peering into the bowl she still held. 'That's six of them left. Now, I've another pond up behind that clump of willow trees. Take the rest of them there, will you? And, Sowerby, you can spread all that slimy stuff on my vegetable plot. It will be excellent for the beans next spring. As for me, I'm going inside to clean myself up.'

Ben and Julia looked at each other as she marched off, then both burst into laughter. 'Oh, dear,' said Julia, as they walked to the other pond and watched the rest of the frogs crawl happily in. 'I feel this is a dreadful imposition, Ben. You don't deserve it.'

He was still smiling. 'Why?' he said.

For a moment she hesitated. Then she said, 'I fear my aunt has been thrusting me into your presence ever since I arrived. I don't know why—I really don't understand. It must be very awkward for you.'

He was shaken yet again. Awkward for him? She was so sweet. So modest. 'It's no hardship to be in your company, believe me.'

'That's just what I mean!' she exclaimed. 'Whatever I say, however foolish I am—you are just so very kind to me!'

She spoke as if he'd just offered her the best present in the world—merely by being kind to her. But then, she completely took his breath away because she stood on her tiptoes and kissed his cheek.

It was a mere butterfly touch of her sweet lips, but it stunned him. It broke down his defences against the raging desire that had been simmering inside him for days and his whole body tightened with raw male need. He stepped back from her and tried to fight it down, saying almost harshly, 'Be careful, Julia. How can you be sure that I'm trustworthy?'

The sudden change in his voice must have shaken her because he saw how those wondrous grey-green eyes widened in surprise. She said, haltingly, 'You are my friend, aren't you?'

Her friend?

Good God. This lovely girl had just kissed him and, light though the caress was, the warmth of her, the sweet scent of her was sending the blood pounding to his loins, heating him and hardening him down *there*. Didn't she realise what she was doing? Probably not. He said at last, aware that his voice was sharp with the effort to control his desire, 'Julia. I think you are very innocent, aren't you?'

A faint blush rose in her cheeks. 'I do know what happens between a man and a woman, if that's what you mean.'

'Have you ever been kissed?'

She met his gaze steadily now. 'Of course not. In London, I'm guarded night and day.'

'Yet your parents,' he almost growled, 'sent you here without a chaperon. They made a big mistake. And Lady Harris should be protecting you better.'

Now she had gone rather pale. 'My father did his best! He sent a maid with me, but she…she…'

Her voice trailed away. He said, 'What did she do?'

'Betty never stopped talking,' she replied defiantly. 'Then she sprained her wrist, so I sent her back to London.'

He wanted to laugh. He wanted to scold her. Damn,

most of all he wanted to make love to her, though it appeared that she did not regard him as a threat in the least.

He rubbed his hand across his temples, then looked again at the girl. Who was she, exactly? She was clearly from a wealthy family and she was beautiful, too, with her silk-soft dark hair and delicate features. She had also somehow worked her way past his defences and into the dangerous territory of his heart—dangerous because he was in no position to take anything further. He had sworn to clear his father's dishonoured name before he thought even remotely of settling down.

Every day, he'd been seeking new ways to discover anything more about Francis Molloy. He'd been scouring his father's bills and records, writing to friends in London and soon he knew he would have to go there himself, to follow up various leads. Maybe he should tell her this now, but not just yet, for he couldn't bear this countryside idyll to be broken.

But she must have mistaken his silence for disapproval, because she said at last, in a very quiet voice, 'Ben. Please tell me if I've done something wrong again. We are still friends, aren't we?'

His heart—yes, his damned heart again—twisted within him. Dear God. Her friend? He didn't want to be her bloody *friend*. He felt himself reaching out for her, he couldn't stop himself, because his hands weren't his to control any more and he was grasping her shoulders, pulling her towards him while her eyes, her beautiful grey-green eyes were raised to his in surprise and something else. Longing. Desire even.

So he kissed her. He held her closely, until her slender body fitted intimately against his powerful one; his arms tightened around her and he kissed her. He heard her give a faint sound of shock and he moved back, just a little, though his arms still clasped her.

He saw that her eyes were asking a thousand silent questions, so he answered in the only way he knew, by pulling her close again and letting his lips brush hers before caressing them more firmly. When he realised her mouth was beginning instinctively to open to him he let the tip of his tongue tease and lick her until her tentative but sweet response drove his body into the full madness of male desire.

Ben was losing control. Cupping the back of her head with just one hand, he used the other to clasp her tiny waist, pressing her against his hard frame until all he was conscious of was the overwhelming need to make love to her—here. *Now.*

'Julia,' he whispered. 'Dear God. Julia…'

She muttered something incoherent, then her hands were on his shoulders and she was kissing him back, driving him even wilder. When she paused for breath he let his lips trail hungrily down along her jaw to her neck, licking and nibbling, and now he could feel the exquisite softness of her small breasts as she nestled against his chest. Hell, the urge to hold those breasts in his hands was all but overwhelming…

No. No, you brute. Ben pulled away abruptly. She stood there, looking confused and uncertain.

Well, he was certain of quite a few things. She was gorgeous. She was passionate and sensual. Her parents thought she would be safe, out here in the country; her parents were very, very wrong. Doubtless she was ignorant of the very physical and very risky response she'd aroused in him, although she still had a soft glow in her eyes that told him she, too, had forgotten her self-control. This must not happen again. She did not know what she was doing and he, Ben, was badly in the wrong to take advantage.

He was aware of her gazing up at him. Her eyes looked wounded. 'That was a mistake, wasn't it?' she said quietly.

He hadn't thought so at the time. His body still didn't think so; the hardness at his loins still throbbed. But she was right. Talk about heaping fiery coals on his head. He dragged his fingers across his stubbled jaw. 'Yes,' he said. 'Yes. I'm sorry. It was.'

This girl deserved far more than what he could offer her. He was damaged, both physically by his accident and mentally by the bitterness he harboured over his father's tragic end. She deserved to have her Season, she deserved to enter London society and to realise her own true worth. He'd been a blundering fool to befriend her and a fiend for kissing her like that. The problem was that he could not bear the thought of another man taking her in his arms and making her his.

She whispered at last, 'Will I see you again?'

'Julia,' he said abruptly, 'how long are you staying here?'

'At my aunt's? Maybe for another two weeks.'

He nodded. 'Then it isn't goodbye yet.' He ground the words out. 'But now, you had better go.'

Yes, he needed her to go before he kissed her again. Before he made sweet, glorious love to her, which his whole body was aching to do.

'I'll leave,' she said. 'But please remember this. I don't care who you are, or how other people judge you. And I never will care, I swear it.'

Julia walked very slowly back to Linden House, thinking. Ben had kissed her. Really, truly kissed her. It had only lasted a few moments, but she was still reeling from it. When his mouth had caressed hers she'd felt herself trembling with wanting him. All of him. Everything.

She knew now what Pen and her friends whispered about. When Ben pulled her close, there had been that hardness pressing against the softness of her abdomen which betrayed his physical need and stirred her, too, filling her with a sweet yet almost unbearable kind of ache. She'd wanted him to touch her lips, her breasts, she'd wanted him to touch her *everywhere*, even in her most secret place.

Of course he'd had the sense to end it quickly. She knew she ought to be burning with embarrassment because she'd kissed him first, so it was her fault. Her shame, because he'd had to almost push her away. Well, that gave her something else to add to her list of ways to put men off.

Make yourself appear far too eager for their attentions—even to the point of kissing them first.

The trouble was, she didn't care. Yes, he was a stonemason, but she didn't care about that either, because his kiss had made her feel so warm and wonderful that if he'd asked her to, she would have agreed to run away with him tomorrow and live anywhere.

As if he would ever do such a thing. She shook her head and tried to smile instead of crying.

You fool, Julia. You fool.

When she reached Linden House her aunt was dozing in the sitting room with *Gulliver's Travels* in her lap, but she sat up with a start when Julia came in.

'Well?' she said. 'Did the two of you get those frogs nicely settled?'

Julia nodded. 'They seem very happy.' She sat down in another chair.

Take deep breaths. Calm yourself.

'Aunt,' she said, 'I asked you soon after I arrived about Lord Lambourne. But I hadn't realised that the former Lord had died and there's now a new heir. Do you know anything about him?'

For a moment her aunt went very still. But then she waved her hand in the air and said, 'You know me, Julia. Titles and all that are nothing but nonsensical privilege. I'm quite the revolutionary, you know.'

Just at that moment Miss Twigg entered with the tea tray, which she set down on a table at Lady Harris's side. Julia could have sworn she winked at her before departing once more.

'But, Aunt,' said Julia, once the door had closed again. 'My father is an aristocrat and you always appear very fond of him.'

'Well, yes! That's partly because he's family and also because your father is a decent man.'

'What about the new Lord Lambourne, though?'

Julia persisted. 'Have you heard if he is what you would call a decent man?'

Lady Harris had reached for the teapot and was lifting the lid to poke at the contents with her spoon. 'I believe he travels often, which means he spends hardly any time here.' She gave an exclamation of disgust. 'Twigg has made this tea far too weak. We need a fresh pot and I will tell the woman so.'

She rose and went towards the bell pull, but as she did so she happened to glance out of the window and stopped abruptly. 'Bless me,' she cried, 'if I don't spy those wretched boys with their pigs again, up in my woods and after my acorns! Come along, Julia! Let's be after them!' Within moments she was at the front door, where she grabbed her purple cloak and was off.

Julia managed to keep up with her, but of course by the time they arrived the boys were already scurrying away, laughing. Once again, she'd got nowhere with her questions, but Lady Harris wasn't telling her everything, of that she was quite sure.

That evening she made her way to the library at the back of the house, for she'd remembered that in there she had spotted a volume called *Notable Families of Somerset*.

Laying it on the table and pulling up a chair, she sat and searched the book's index—where under the letter *L* she found 'Lambourne'.

Among the most distinguished landowners of our region are the Barons of Lambourne Hall, who can date their ancestry back to the time of King

Charles II. They have played a prominent part in Lambourne's history and in London society also. The Fourth Baron, Robert, born in 1767, has emulated his ancestors in his duty to the responsibilities of the title. In addition, he keeps a stable of fine horses. His wife, Lady Sophia Lambourne, is a younger daughter of the Viscount Huntingdon. There are no children as yet...

No children. Julia looked swiftly for the date the book was published—it was 1789. So the book was printed almost thirty years ago and of course there would be nothing about the heir who'd recently inherited the title. She went slowly up to her room and looked again at the letter she'd received this morning from Pen.

How is your handsome stonemason? I do hope, darling Julia, that you are not getting yourself into trouble.

Oh, but she was. Deep, deep trouble. She settled at her little desk and tried to write back, but she struggled to say a word. She was thinking, *I kissed him. He kissed me and it was wonderful.* And how could she possibly write *that*?

Ben had returned to Lambourne Hall, knowing what he ought to do. He could not go on lying to Julia like this, so he should go to her tomorrow and tell her exactly who he was, together with the problems he faced ahead. Soon, within weeks maybe, he would be re-entering London society, where they were bound to meet. So wasn't it the right, the only thing to do?

Gilly met him at the door; he must have been watching for him, which was unusual. But Gilly was blunt, as always. He put his hands on his hips and said without preamble, 'I guess you've been seeing that girl again?'

'Yes.' Ben walked into the kitchen with Gilly close behind and poured himself some ale. 'Don't read me the riot act, Gilly. I mean Julia no harm.' He sat on a wooden chair and began pulling off his boots.

Gilly, however, wouldn't be deterred. 'My lord,' Gilly said.

Ben looked up sharply. His valet didn't often use that tone.

'There's something you ought to know,' went on Gilly. He folded his arms. 'I think you should be calling this new friend of yours *Lady* Julia.'

Ben sat very still, with one boot off, the other half on. He said, 'Lady Julia?'

'That is correct. My lord—she is the Earl of Carstairs's daughter.'

Ben thought that if the world could spin and change utterly, this was what it would feel like. He stared at Gilly in disbelief. 'If this is a joke, I must tell you that I'm not finding it amusing in the least.'

Gilly shook his head. 'It's true, I'm afraid. I learned it when I went to the village this morning for your post.'

Ben closed his eyes. His leg was hurting again, really hurting. *Damn.* The terrible row over the horse. The slur on his father's integrity that had ruined his father's final years.

The man responsible for that was none other than Julia's father.

Gilly said quietly, 'Brandy, my lord?'

'Yes.' Ben grated the words out. 'A large one.'

Gilly brought the drink, then picked up Ben's boots from the floor. 'I'll take these outside and give them a clean,' he said. It was an action performed, Ben guessed, to give him time to absorb exactly what Gilly had just said.

Ben knew that the Earl of Carstairs and his father had been friends, meeting often at the races in Brighton and Newmarket. Yes, friends—until around a year and a half ago, the Earl had made an offer for a promising young gelding that was the pride of the Lambourne stables: Silver Cloud.

The rest was a story that Ben had gone over and over in his mind. When Ben had visited his father for the very last time here at Lambourne, his father had told him everything. He'd told him how the valuable gelding, on delivery to the Earl, was inspected by the Earl's veterinary surgeon and was found to have a twisted tendon and could never race. The animal had been like that, the vet said, from birth.

Ben's father could not understand it, for he'd had the animal thoroughly inspected before it left his stables. He felt he'd been unendurably maligned and after despairing of ever proving his innocence, he'd sold nearly all of his horses and started to neglect the Hall badly. The quarry fall in which he died was pronounced by the justices as an accident, but Ben believed it was an act of utter despair. His father had quite simply lost the will to live.

Ben knew that life could be cruel, but this news about Julia's father was something he could never have imagined. It seemed that Julia was ignorant of the bitter rift, but if Ben showed his face to her family, she would learn about it swiftly enough.

Did Lady Harris know of the feud? She was no fool and surely she'd heard about it. Perhaps that was why she hadn't told Julia who Ben was—she wanted to keep from her the fact that their fathers had been enemies. But Julia would find out some time soon and it would be all the worse.

Gilly had come back into the kitchen and was silently placing a platter of sliced ham and bread on the table, but Ben didn't want food. He wanted Julia. He felt as if she had brought light into his life with her innocent trust in him. They'd shared their love of the countryside, they'd shared tender moments, then there had been that kiss—that wonderful kiss that made him ache for so much more.

But to fantasise about any kind of future together was impossible, because Julia's father was involved in destroying his own father's life.

Gilly was eyeing him in that way of his. 'I get the feeling I've given you bad news about your new friend.'

'Yes. You have.' No more. He couldn't say another word.

Gilly gave a sympathetic grunt but added, 'Then it's as well you found out sooner rather than later, isn't it? Best eat up your supper, my lord. Going without food will mend nothing. By the way, there's a letter for you.'

Ben opened it to find that it was from a friend of his, in London.

You wrote asking me about a man called Molloy, who had a finger in many aspects of the world of horses. I've found no trace of his whereabouts, but I do believe that Tattersall's may have records of the man.

Ben drew a deep breath. Of course. Tattersall's auction house close by Hyde Park was known not only for its sales of fine horses, but as a fount of information regarding every consequence of those sales: contract negotiations, funding, even the transport of valuable thoroughbreds all around England.

This, then, was the next stage of his quest. He would go to London in search of Francis Molloy—and he had to tell Julia he was leaving.

Chapter Eleven

As Julia walked up to the pavilion the next day, she clutched the note she'd received that morning from Ben.

Please come. We need to talk properly.

He must have called at the house very early to push it under the door. He'd sealed it, then written her name on the outside—*Julia*—and Miss Twigg had handed it to her without a word.

She felt sick with apprehension. For days, she'd been telling herself that she and Ben were just friends, until that kiss yesterday. But from the curtness of his note, it seemed they were not even friends now.

She could see him up by the pavilion, carefully smoothing in fresh mortar between the stones where it had crumbled away. He must have heard her footsteps because he turned to face her, but there was no lovely warm smile for her. Instead he said, 'You got my note, then?'

Julia nodded. She lifted her head almost proudly. 'I can guess what you want to say. You don't want me here. Do you?'

She saw his hesitation and, oh, that was hard to bear, for she wanted him to hold her as he had yesterday, with his eyes full of desire. She wanted him to kiss her again; yes, even now she felt the longing unfurl deep inside her. She'd never thought she could feel like that about any man, ever. Yet now her stonemason, who'd awakened her heart in a way she'd not thought possible, was saying wearily, 'I'm sorry. But it's just not appropriate that we meet like this—Lady Julia.'

She felt his words fall on her like hammer blows. Shakily she took a step back. 'You've heard, then? That I'm an earl's daughter?'

'I have. Oh, Julia. Why didn't you *tell* me?'

She tried to lift her chin defiantly. 'Does it matter?'

'Yes.' He'd put down his pail of mortar and seemed to speak with a great effort. 'Of course it matters and you and I should not have been meeting like this anyway. I blame myself for that, very much.' He was silent a moment. Then he added quietly, 'All the same, I wish you'd explained to me from the beginning who you were.'

Julia felt a great lump rising in her throat. She realised she'd crumpled his curt note into a tight ball in her hand.

I want you, Ben, she said silently to herself. *Only you.*

'Can we pretend,' she whispered. 'just for a day or two more, that I'm not an earl's daughter?'

She saw Ben bracing himself. He said, 'I've told you, it's not possible. Besides, I have to go to London now, for several days. So it seems an appropriate time to say goodbye.'

This was the end. He was telling her she would not see him again. Of course, he was right. But she had been so happy during her days here with him and she'd thought he'd been happy, too; she'd even thought that perhaps he was beginning to care for her. One by one she tried to think of all the arguments she could present, all the words she could say, but it was like preparing to fight a battle that she had already lost.

She said, in rather a choked voice, 'May I stay just for a while? I could maybe do some more painting.'

He sighed. 'If you wish. But really, Julia…'

'It's all right,' she said. She smiled, even though she was fighting back the tears. 'I'll just finish what I was doing yesterday and then I'll be on my way.'

Damn. *Damn*, thought Ben. Julia looked utterly forlorn, but it really, really was no good. He remembered again the letter that the Earl, her father, had sent to his father.

> *I am not a vindictive person, Lord Lambourne. I will not take the matter to the courts. But this was an act of fraud, not worthy of a man of your rank, and if the world gets to hear of this affair, then so be it.*

It was likely that the Earl's bitterness over the affair would poison any hope of reconciliation, even if Ben succeeded in proving his father's innocence. He watched, riven with conflicting emotions, as Julia went into the pavilion to collect her paints, then came out again to mix them in the sunlight. She loved her family dearly. He could not force her to choose between them and him.

Suddenly she lifted her head and said, 'I've heard that your employer, Lord Lambourne, is unmarried. Is he looking for a wife, do you think?'

He said, *'What?'*

She began again. 'You must know him a little, through your work here. I was just wondering—do you think that maybe he wants a wife?'

He was astounded. He said curtly, 'Doubtless he'll marry some day. It's the duty of all aristocrats, after all. Why are you interested in him all of a sudden?'

'Because I've been thinking. I've told you that soon I'll be thrust into my London Season and, as you say, I must resign myself to it. I will have a large dowry when I marry so men are never going to leave me alone. So perhaps I should get the business over with.'

He was stunned. 'What business? What are you talking about?'

'Why, getting married, of course.'

He could hardly speak. 'But who to?'

'I'm trying to suggest,' she said, tossing her head a little, 'that maybe I could marry your employer. Lord Lambourne.'

Hell. That nearly floored him and it must have shown, because she looked even more defiant. 'You'll think I'm ridiculous. People often do. I suppose there's some problem, is there? Perhaps you've heard that he has a mistress to whom he is utterly devoted?'

'Julia! I mean, *Lady* Julia…'

She held up her hand to silence him. 'All right. I realise you think I shouldn't understand about men's mistresses, let alone talk about them, but you see, I wouldn't care if he did have a mistress. In fact, I would be very glad, because I don't think I would like that side of marriage at all, I don't think I would be any earthly good at it—' She broke off. 'Ben! What *is* it?'

He was trying to point, subtly, at the bodice of her dress. He'd realised that she must have fastened the buttons up wrongly when she put it on and some of them had come undone, revealing the delicate swell of her bosom.

As she glanced downwards her expression changed to one of absolute horror. 'Oh, no. My buttons. I am utterly mortified!' Desperately she tried to fasten them, but her fingers fumbled and her cheeks were turning a fiery red. 'I really think I must go—'

He grabbed her as she turned. 'Julia. Lady Julia. Stop.'

She did. She was gazing up at him, her eyes wide and wounded. He should have released his grip instantly but he didn't, because something had robbed him of his willpower. As the low autumn sun lit her face with touches of gold, he had to fight the longing to pull her into his arms, wind his fingers through her long dark hair and kiss her senseless.

He thought, *This intelligent, unusual girl sees herself as an outcast. What has society done to her, to let her think that her only way to lead a fulfilled life is to sacrifice herself to marriage with a man she's never met?*

And what kind of a man was he, not to have told her straight away that *he* was Lord Lambourne? Why didn't he tell her *now*?

Because any action on his part was far too late. For

her father had been his own father's worst enemy, that was why.

She was young and very innocent. She needed to return to her family, who would surely help her to enjoy her Season and give her a fair choice in who she could marry. Plenty of men would find her as irresistible as he did, God help him. When he finally re-entered London society and saw her surrounded by suitors, he would feel like punching them—but bear it he must. For her sake. Her happiness.

He let her go at last. She said in a low voice, 'You think I'm foolish. Don't you?'

Ben was appalled for her. 'You're not—' He stopped, gathered himself, then carried on. 'Julia. Let me assure you that you deserve every kind of happiness.'

There was a long silence. Then she looked around and said, 'I could be happy here. I suppose that's why I had my stupid idea of marrying Lord Lambourne. At least I would have his gardens and this countryside to enjoy and, from what you say, he would probably be away most of the time. A marriage of convenience, that's all I'd be after. Whoever I marry, I shall be an extremely tolerant wife and I shall be very happy if my husband spends time in London with his friends.'

He burned with frustration of all kinds. 'I do not understand why you expect so little for yourself. Don't you think you deserve a man who respects you? A man who loves you?'

She lifted her head proudly. 'Oh, no doubt I'll attract a good number of offers. As I said, my dowry, I believe, is substantial.'

He exploded. 'For God's sake, Julia! London's bachelors won't just be after you for your money. You're beautiful, don't you realise? Many men will desire you!'

She met his gaze steadily. 'But not you. I'm right, aren't I?'

What could he say? Some day he hoped she might understand, but at the moment he could say absolutely nothing, because he had to distance himself; he had to push her away, before he was tempted beyond endurance to kiss her again.

'Julia,' he said at last. 'There are many reasons why we cannot be together.'

'Then I'll spare you the trouble of having to think up any more of them,' she said softly.

'Julia. Listen—'

'Goodbye, Ben.'

He watched her as she set off down the path without a backward glance.

'You're exceptionally silent tonight, Julia,' said Lady Harris.

They were playing chess again in the drawing room and Julia forced a smile. 'Am I? I'm sorry, Aunt.'

'No need to apologise. Thinking about your family, are you? They'll be missing you.'

'Yes,' she said. 'I must write to them again soon.'

But she wasn't thinking about her family. She was thinking about Ben's warm brown eyes and the way his mouth curled up a little at one end when he was trying his best not to smile at something she'd said. She was remembering the way he'd kissed her, only yesterday…

'Julia! Are you daydreaming, girl?'

She realised her aunt had just taken her bishop. 'I

wasn't concentrating,' she said quickly. 'How foolish of me.'

She was trying to force Ben from her mind, for she guessed she would never see him again. He must always have known she was wealthy, but the discovery that she was an earl's daughter had shocked him badly. He'd been so very angry, too, when she suggested she might set her cap at Lord Lambourne. She knew it was stupid, of course she did, but she'd half done it to provoke him into…what? Another kiss?

Thus, you stupid creature, prolonging your misery.

'Julia!' chided her aunt. 'Don't you realise I'm about to capture your king? What's wrong with you, girl?'

'I'm sorry, Aunt.' She smiled. 'I congratulate you on your victory.' But she was still miles away. She was in love, she realised, and how it hurt.

Oh, Ben, she thought silently. *I wish I was just a serving maid or a farmer's daughter. You wouldn't turn me away then, would you?*

For the next two days Julia was kept busy helping her aunt and Miss Twigg to make jams and chutneys with the autumn harvest. But when she put a ladleful of flour instead of sugar into a pan of apples, her aunt said, 'For heaven's sake, girl. Your heart's not in this, is it? Why don't you go off into my library and find yourself something to read?'

So Julia headed once more to the library and went inevitably to the book called *Notable Families of Somerset*. She turned the pages until she reached the chapter about the Lambourne family and realised that there was also a section describing the Hall.

*Lambourne Hall is a fine example of late Stuart
architecture and the gardens were designed by a
follower of Capability Brown. Everywhere, even
in the gardens, the family crest of a phoenix rising from the flames can be found.*

She frowned. She'd seen the phoenix carved into the
lintel above the pavilion door, but she'd also seen it somewhere else, on something she couldn't quite remember…

Yes, she could. It was on the tool box Ben used. The
box's mahogany lid had a bronze panel on which the
phoenix symbol was etched. She put the book down,
pondering. Of course, the tool box would belong to the
Hall, so it was natural that Ben would use it while he
worked here.

Suddenly she rose and put the book firmly back in
its place. Whatever happened at Lambourne was none
of her business. Soon she would be going home, where
she would do what was expected of her. She would brace
herself for her Season and maybe soon she would be
planning her wedding, just like Pen.

But she guessed she would never meet anyone like
Ben. Never.

Chapter Twelve

Ben had begun his journey to London the very next day. Gilly drove him to Cheltenham in the light chaise stored in the Hall's coach house and from Cheltenham Ben travelled by mail coach, stopping twice overnight at posting inns. On reaching London, he hired a cab to take him to the Pulteney Hotel in Piccadilly, where he gave his name as Ben Smith.

The family did have a town house in Clarges Street, but his father had let it out several years ago and the family lawyer, Thomas Rudby, managed the tenancy. Ben found himself comfortable enough at the Pulteney, where the staff were discreet and his bedchamber luxurious. Indeed, often in the past when he'd returned briefly to England from Vienna, he'd chosen to stay at the Pulteney instead of making the journey to visit his father.

He remembered with bitter regret how his father never complained about his son's rare visits, but on the occasions when Ben did make it to Lambourne Hall he would welcome him warmly. 'You're busy, Ben. Enjoy yourself. I'm fine.'

Always, he said that. Always.

That evening Ben knew he could have gone to dine at his club, where there would be old friends to meet. Instead he ate alone at the hotel, thinking of three people: his father, the Earl of Carstairs and Francis Molloy.

The next morning he went to Tattersall's sale yard at Hyde Park Corner, where there were daily auctions of fine horses. As ever, the place was crowded and the familiar scents of horses and hay brought back powerful memories for Ben of his father's stables at Lambourne, where the grooms had once cared for all his fine animals.

He straightened his coat and entered the office, where he approached a clerk. 'I'm looking for a man called Francis Molloy,' he said. 'He used to transport valuable horses around the country. I think you sometimes recommended him to your clients?'

'Just a moment, sir.' The clerk went over to a large register and brought it to the desk, but after a few moments of scrutinising the pages he looked up, frowning slightly. 'It appears, sir, that Francis Molloy is no longer on our list of recommendations.'

Ben snapped to attention. 'Why?'

The clerk hesitated. 'There were certain doubts raised about him. Nothing was proved, you understand. But we decided we no longer wished to be associated with Mr Molloy.'

'An address,' Ben said. 'Have you his address?'

'Sir, we are not allowed—'

At that moment a man in expensive clothes bustled through the door and spoke loudly to the clerk. 'Hey.

You there. I need to speak to someone about a horse. Am I going to be kept waiting for ever?'

Ben said to the clerk, 'You'd better see to him.'

The clerk followed the man out of the room, but the register still lay open and by the time the clerk returned to his desk Ben had memorised Molloy's address and departed.

Fernley's Lodgings, Goslett Yard. Ben vaguely knew the name, knew also that Goslett Yard was in St Giles, one of the roughest areas in town. He hired a cab outside Tattersall's and paid off the driver in Soho Square, then walked onwards, noting that though it was still daylight the sun was blocked out by high tenement buildings. Ragged children played in the street and outside a nearby drinking house, several men with ale mugs in their hands watched him with narrowed eyes.

A faded sign hung above a door: *Fernley's Lodgings*. He rapped until the door was opened by a woman in a patched dress and shawl.

'I'm looking for Francis Molloy,' Ben said. 'Can you tell me if he lives here?'

She looked him up and down. 'He left last winter without paying his debts. Are you going to pay them for him?'

'I wasn't—'

She slammed the door in his face.

He looked around, realising that those men outside the drinking house were still watching him. He walked up to them. 'Do any of you know a man called Francis Molloy?'

They looked first at each other, then at him, saying nothing. But just as he was turning to go, one of them spoke up. 'Listen, mister. We don't like strangers asking questions and usually we deal with them in our own way. But we reckon you're either brave or mad, nosing around these streets when you've a crocked leg. So as long as you leave sharpish, we'll not harm you.'

Ben met the man's gaze steadily. 'I believe Molloy may have wronged my father,' he said.

The man laughed. 'For God's sake, most of us here don't even know who our damned father is. Now, we'll give you five minutes to get out of here—no, make that ten, since you hobble so.'

Ben walked on to Soho Square. He felt sure those people knew Molloy, but where was the man now? He hailed a cab to take him to the office of his lawyer, Rudby, who ushered him to a chair with a broad smile on his face.

'My lord! I was about to write to you. I have excellent news about your London house. The long-term tenant was a problem to us with payments, but we've taken action on your behalf and he is finally leaving. From next week, you can take up occupation of it whenever you wish.' Rudby rooted among the papers on his desk. 'I fear the interior might be somewhat neglected, but I'm delighted to say I've made considerable progress in recovering further sums of money for you.'

Ben frowned. 'How?'

'I believe I warned you that your father was rather remiss in his handling of his affairs. However, I've now discovered large sums owed to him by various people and I've already retrieved many of these debts. Here you are.' He passed some financial documents across to Ben. 'Believe me, my lord, there will soon be enough money in the estate for you to fully refurbish both your town house and Lambourne Hall! Let me explain some of the figures to you…'

Ben was there for over two hours. He was rich, he realised. He had wealth which, together with his title, gave him the status to live among the elite.

He dined that night at one of his clubs and would have been content to remain alone, but some old friends spotted him and eagerly invited him to join them. They sympathised over both his bereavement and his injury, but soon enough the invitations were pouring in, to parties in London and to house gatherings in the country. He resisted them all, telling his friends he had much to do yet to sort out his affairs. But he didn't tell a single one of them that his overriding mission was to clear his father's name.

The next morning he visited his bank, then in the afternoon Rudby came with him to inspect the Lambourne town house in Clarges Street.

'As I said, some rooms need repair and renovation, my lord,' said the lawyer apologetically. 'But it really could be very fine.'

Ben nodded, gazing around the spacious drawing room in which they stood. 'I have to go to Somerset first,' he said. 'But after that I'll be back here to make plans. No doubt I'll be hiring builders, decorators, whomever I need.'

They returned to Rudby's office to finalise some paperwork, but the lawyer hadn't quite finished with him yet. 'There is something else, my lord. We hold various

documents for your father, as you know. But I've found
an old file relating to your father's purchases and sales
of horses. Would you like to see it?'

Ben looked through the papers swiftly. There did indeed appear to be details of buyers and sellers for the
last twenty years or more, but he guessed there was
nothing he'd not already found at Lambourne Hall. He
replaced the papers in the file. 'I'll take it with me,' he
said, 'back to Somerset, to add to the records in my father's study. But, Rudby, there is something else. See if
you can find out for me, will you, where a man called
Francis Molloy might be living? He was a well-known
transporter of fine horses, but he was struck off Tattersall's lists a while ago and appears to have vanished.'

Rudby nodded. 'I'll do my very best, my lord.'

Ben spent one more night in London, catching up
with old friends and their news. But the following day
he rose early, for he had decided it was time to return
home.

He reached Lambourne Hall at around three, after
two days of travelling. Gilly served him a cold meal,
then Ben decided to walk through the beech woods
to the pavilion, just as his father always did whenever
he had been away. Even during his brief absence, the
days appeared to have grown shorter and there was a
chill in the air. More of the trees had lost their leaves
and already the distant horizon was streaked with pink.

As he approached the pavilion he saw that a family
of squirrels were scurrying around after beech nuts. So
absorbed was he in watching them that he didn't notice

until he was almost there that the pavilion's windows flickered with light.

Slowly he drew closer, but he somehow knew exactly what to expect. Julia was in there.

The doorway was wide open so he could see that she was working with absolute precision on the wall stencils, using her brush to dab paint on to the wall plaster. She wore an apron that was far too big for her over her gown and every so often she stepped back to assess her progress. It hit him like a hammer blow that she looked unbelievably lovely in that ridiculous apron with her long hair falling, as usual, out of its ribbon.

He steadied himself and went inside. 'Julia,' he said. 'Julia, what are you doing?' It was an utterly foolish question, of course, when he could see the answer for himself.

'Ben!' She whipped round, almost dropping her brush and stencil. 'I—I started working up here again on the day after you left.' He saw her hesitate. 'I suppose I just wanted to do something to thank you for your kindness to me while I've been here.' She put down her things and added anxiously, 'You don't mind, do you?'

She was glancing back at her work, hesitant, vulnerable. Briefly Ben closed his eyes. He had money enough now to have this pavilion rebuilt and fully decorated by the finest craftsmen in the country, but the thought gave him no pleasure.

She was the daughter of the man who had accused his father of fraud. Oh, God, he wanted her, but it could never, ever work. He said, fighting back the longing to take her in his arms and kiss her senseless, 'How could I mind? But you must have been working on this for days.'

She nodded. 'Ever since you left! Though I came up here only for an hour this afternoon and soon I must go. The problem is, you see, that my aunt is unwell.'

'Your aunt? What is wrong with her?'

'I truly don't know. She tells me not to fuss; in fact, she practically ordered me to come up here and, of course, she has Miss Twigg with her. But she is just not herself, though she refuses to let me send for the doctor from the village. She is hardly eating and she seems tired all the time.'

Ben, trying to lighten her mood, said, 'Whatever it is that bothers her, I guess she won't be ailing for long. She'll soon be after those boys and their pigs again.'

'True,' she said, allowing a brief smile to illuminate her face. But she still looked anxious.

'You're worried, aren't you, Julia?'

'Yes,' she admitted. 'Yes, I am.'

'Then I shall come and see her. Right now, if you like.'

'But you must have only just returned from London!'

'That's no problem,' he said. 'Let's go.'

Julia had made one resolution after another while Ben had been away. She'd vowed not to bother him in any way again and she knew that now she should tell him it was none of his business if her aunt was ill.

But she couldn't. She didn't even try. He waited while she removed her apron and pulled on her jacket, then they walked down together to Linden House. By the time they got there it was dark and beginning to rain—and her aunt was worse, Julia realised. Much worse. Julia had left her sitting in a comfortable armchair by the fire in her bedchamber, but now she was lying on her bed with her eyes half-closed while Miss Twigg hovered anxiously nearby.

Julia hurried to her aunt's side. 'Aunt, I've brought Ben. He has come to see how you are. Can I do anything at all for you? Would you like a drink of your honey and chamomile tea, perhaps?'

'Stuff and nonsense,' muttered her aunt, 'all this fussing. And why have you brought young fellow-my-lad here? I thought he was in London. Do you think I want *him* seeing me like this?'

But when Ben drew closer and took her hand in his, Lady Harris let him. She trusted him, Julia realised. She, like Julia, was glad he was here.

'Lady Harris,' Ben said. 'I can see you're being as stubborn as a mule, as ever. You appear to have a raging temperature and you're driving poor Julia and Miss Twigg mad with worry. I am fetching a doctor from the village right now.'

Julia drew him aside to murmur, 'I believe the only physician there is Dr Barnes. My aunt says he'll never move from his fireside after sunset. It's almost dark now.'

'I'll manage something,' Ben said. 'Miss Twigg, would you find Sowerby and ask him to saddle up Lady Harris's horse?'

As Miss Twigg hurried off he said to Julia, 'I'll be back very soon. Keep Lady Harris warm and try to get her to drink something, will you? Even if it's only a little tea.'

'Oh, Ben…' Julia's voice broke a little. 'I should never have left her, even for a minute!'

'Nonsense.' He touched her cheek lightly. 'You came to the pavilion and you met me, remember? Which is fortunate, because I'm going to help.'

Julia went to the front door to watch him ride off into the darkness. She hadn't expected him for days. She'd even guessed that she herself might have been summoned back to London by the time he returned. But when he'd arrived at the pavilion, her heart had been filled with both relief and despair. *I love him*, she'd realised. She could not bear to think of life without him—and that was disastrous.

She went slowly back upstairs, where Lady Harris, that indomitable source of humour and energy, was looking more and more frail while Miss Twigg did nothing but fuss and fret. Julia asked her to make some chamomile tea.

But while Miss Twigg was down in the kitchen, Lady Harris began to grow restless and started muttering to herself. *'I should have done something about the two of them sooner.' Yes, much sooner...'*

Julia took her hand. 'Dear Aunt, whatever are you talking about?'

Lady Harris opened her eyes, suddenly alert. 'Me, talking? Nonsense, I've been asleep.'

'But you said—'

'Must be all this being treated like an invalid. It makes me thoroughly confused.' She tried to haul herself up. 'There's a great deal to do. Remind Twigg to keep a lookout for those dratted pig boys, will you? She always forgets!'

Julia shook her head. 'It's dark outside, Aunt, and

starting to rain. They won't be coming to your woods at this hour.'

'Rubbish. They're bound to come if they know I'm confined to my bed in this ridiculous way.' She sighed and lay back against her pillows. 'Where's that fellow Ben? I could have sworn he was here a minute ago.'

'He was, Aunt. But he's gone for the doctor.'

'Hmm. Interfering, is he? I cannot bear people interfering!' But her aunt seemed soothed, because soon she was sleeping again.

Julia went downstairs to listen anxiously for the sound of Ben returning.

When she heard hooves clattering in the courtyard, she ran to open the front door and saw that Ben had a companion with him, also on horseback. Sowerby had already come to hold both horses' reins.

'This is Dr Barnes,' Ben said as the two men dismounted.

'Thank you,' Julia said. 'Doctor, my aunt—'

'It's all right, Julia,' Ben told her as he led the way in. 'I've explained everything.'

'I'll go up and see her now,' said Dr Barnes. He was taking off his riding coat, which was soaked with the rain. 'Then hopefully I can prescribe a course of treatment.'

Miss Twigg had come to join them and he gave her a nod of recognition. 'Miss Twigg, come with me, will you?' He added cautiously, 'Just in case Lady Harris is a little awkward, as I confess I've found in the past.'

They went upstairs and Ben smiled at Julia. 'There,' he said softly. 'You can relax a little now.'

Her heart shook. His smile always did that to her—always. She was such a fool. 'Tea,' she muttered. 'I shall make you some tea.'

Just for a moment Ben rested his hands on her shoulders. 'Julia. Listen to me. Your aunt is going to be all right. Do you understand?'

She nodded. But what about *her*?

Ben took off his damp coat, then followed Julia into the kitchen and watched her busying herself over the tea things. He had to smile to himself again. As an earl's daughter, she surely wasn't used to such mundane tasks and when she struggled to open the tea caddy, he tactfully took over. 'Allow me,' he said. 'In fact, let me do it all, will you? I hardly suppose you've made many pots of tea in your life. And don't worry too much about your aunt. Doctor Barnes is a good man and he'll be used to dealing with her.'

He realised his mistake immediately, even before she said, 'Ben. How do you know so much about the doctor and my aunt?'

He cursed himself silently. 'Oh, one learns things.' He spoke in what he hoped was a reassuring tone. 'Your aunt is, after all, a well-known character around here. As for Dr Barnes, I've heard from several sources that he's very kind. He'll probably tell her she's been over-doing her home-made remedies.'

In fact, Ben had known the doctor for many years and when Ben had explained as they rode here that for the time being he wanted his identity kept a secret from Lady Harris's guest, the doctor had agreed, though he'd added, 'I trust you have sound motives, my lord?'

'I do,' said Ben. 'Believe me, it's for the best.'

Now Ben saw a hint of a smile on Julia's face at the mention of her aunt's unusual remedies, though it quickly faded. 'Sometimes,' she said, 'I worry it's because of me being here that she's ill. She's been doing far too much lately.'

He shook his head. 'She always does too much—just ask Miss Twigg. As for it being your fault that she's ill, that's nonsense. She's very fortunate to have you here with her, though you're looking tired yourself. Sit down, will you?'

He pointed to one of the chairs at the kitchen table and she slowly sat. Suddenly she blurted out, 'She's lucky—*I'm* lucky—that you arrived back today. Did you manage to do everything you needed to do in London?'

'Yes.' He sat also. 'I had a few business matters to attend to, that was all.'

She suddenly rose again, walked to the window, then turned round. 'You're not going to tell me any more, are you? Ben, I know nothing about you. Your family, your childhood—you've told me so little and there are too many things I don't understand!'

He tried to appear calm. 'Such as?'

She sat down once more and briefly put her hand to her forehead. 'You are living—actually *living*—in Lambourne Hall. You're employed in physical work, which seems utterly wrong when you're hampered by your injured leg. I'm sorry, but it's true! You ride to fetch a doctor who is notorious for not coming out after dark, yet he comes, immediately. Who exactly are you, Ben? Why haven't you told me more about yourself?'

'Perhaps because the details of my life are not important,' he said quietly. 'Certainly not to you. Your life lies in London, with your family. You're only here for a very short while, after all.'

He saw her shake her head. 'I've realised from the start that you're eager for me to return and face my fate. But I hate the thought of what lies in store for me.'

'Julia.' He leaned forward. 'You deserve a wonderful time in London. You will positively shine among the other girls when you are presented at court—and you are bound to obtain vouchers for Almack's without any problem whatsoever!'

She stared at him. She looked disturbed almost. At last she said, 'So you are an expert on the Season, are you?'

Hell. He'd made yet another blunder. He said lightly, 'Oh, everyone knows that only the most privileged young women are admitted to Almack's. I've travelled, you see. I hear things. Perhaps I'm only trying to tell you I'd guess you are as pretty as anyone else who will have their come-out soon.'

Far prettier, he thought. Adorably so.

She still frowned a little. 'Oh, flattery is wasted on me,' she said dismissively. 'Anyway, I've decided to stay here until I'm quite sure that my aunt has recovered. But after that, I shall go home.'

Ben nodded. 'An excellent idea.' She deserved the life and the opportunities she'd been raised to expect. She would surely find a decent man to marry.

And whoever that man was, Ben felt like punching him.

Just then the doctor came down. 'I'm afraid I'm unable to identify her exact ailment,' he said. 'But I'll give you some powders for her.' He was reaching into his bag for a packet which he handed to Julia. 'Hopefully they'll soothe her and, of course, I'll call again tomorrow morning. I gather you're here for a little while yet?'

'Yes,' she said. 'Of course. I will be here for as long as my aunt needs me.'

Doctor Barnes turned next to Ben. 'By the way, Mr Smith, Her Ladyship was most insistent that she wanted a word with you.'

Ben nodded and headed for the stairs. Lady Harris appeared to be sleeping, but as he entered she shifted a little on her pillows and murmured weakly, 'Ben. I'm very glad you're here, you rascal.'

She reached out for his hand, which he gave to her. 'You,' she said, 'remind me of your father, do you know that?' She was watching him intently now. 'He missed his wife dreadfully, but he found great consolation in you.'

The guilt that always lurked returned with full force. 'Even though I was hardly ever here?' he said.

'Young man, he wouldn't have wanted you to be here! He wanted you to see the world, which you did—and he was immensely proud of you!'

He pressed her hand, finding that for a moment he couldn't speak. Then he said lightly, 'I believe you were always a good friend to my father. But why are you calling me a rascal?'

'Because the girl... The girl...' Her voice faded. She licked her dry lips and Ben, quickly reaching for a glass of cordial nearby, offered it to her. She swallowed most of it, pulled a face then leaned back against her pillows. 'The girl has fallen for you,' she whispered at last. 'Can't you see, you fool, that the two of you were made for each other?'

He drew a deep breath and sat down on the chair beside her bed. 'Lady Harris,' he said at last. 'You've been pushing us together from the start. Haven't you?'

She thrust the near-empty cup back into his hands. 'Well, of course I have!' She was almost her old brusque self. 'You have to marry some time, surely, and the match is obviously ideal.'

'You talk of my *marriage*? I've only been back in England for two months! My leg is a wreck and the estate requires a good deal of work. Obviously Julia is charming, but really, we barely know each other and her father and mine were enemies. Julia would have nothing to do with me if she knew about it.' Ben looked at her sharply. 'You've not spoken to her, have you? About who I am?'

'Of course not. But do you think she would actually care?' She tried to heave herself up a little. 'The girl has missed you dreadfully while you were away.'

'I'm sorry to hear it. But she loves her family very much—I'm sure of that. You know all about the feud— the anger her father felt towards mine, the accusations he made. I cannot forget any of it easily. And how do you think Julia would feel, if she had to choose between us? Because that's what it would mean if I asked for her hand!'

Lady Harris looked suddenly weary. 'You men and your grudges. I'm not sure how you'll do it, but you must find a way. Yes, the girl loves her family, but she also has a fierce sense of justice and might want to know your side of the story. She'll know they're not perfect—which of us is?—so show some sense and take action! The girl's been pining desperately for you while you were away. She would deny it, of course. But she's a lovely little thing and, believe me, someone else will snap her up double quick when her Season begins if you don't get in there first.'

Ben closed his eyes briefly. Then he said, 'You don't what know my feelings are for her.'

'Of course I do!' she snapped. 'I may be old, but I'm neither blind nor deaf. I've watched the two of you together. I've heard you, laughing and talking. Get on with it, man.' She rested back against her pillows again and waved her hand irritably. 'Now, send Twigg back to me, will you? I'm still an invalid, you know.'

'I do know,' he said. 'Lady Harris, you'll follow the doctor's instructions, won't you? Or I'll be back to scold you.'

She made a tutting sound. 'Of course I will. Off you go, young man—and do something, for heaven's sake, to comfort the girl.'

He found Miss Twigg waiting at the foot of the stairs and she needed no bidding to return to Lady Harris's side. Ben headed onwards, to where Julia was.

She looked up quickly when Ben came back into the kitchen. He appeared tired, she thought. She'd been searching the pantry, wondering whether he was hungry, but she guessed that all he really needed was to return to the Hall and get some sleep.

'How is my aunt?' she asked quickly.

'She is no worse.' He smiled then and his smile warmed her, as always. 'She's also actually agreed to take the powders the doctor left for her.'

'Thank goodness,' said Julia with feeling. 'But I hope she was suitably grateful to you, for fetching the doctor?'

'That? It was nothing.'

Julia put her hands on her hips. 'Nothing?' she exclaimed. 'But you rode all the way to Lambourne village, in the dark and the rain. I don't call it nothing!' She pointed to a glass of wine she'd poured for him and said in a quieter voice, 'I wondered if you might like some refreshment before you leave.'

'Thank you. That's thoughtful.'

He sat down and she waited until he had tasted the wine, then she sat, too, and said, 'Why are you being so very good to my aunt, Ben?'

'Maybe,' he said, 'because she has been good to me, in the past. I'm not going to go into details, but our paths have crossed, several times. I also feel that, in just a very small way, I'm perhaps making amends for some bad mistakes in my life.'

'We've all made mistakes,' she said softly. 'What exactly do you mean?'

At first he didn't answer and she found that her heart was thumping almost painfully. But then he sipped a little more of the wine and said at last, 'Julia. I wasn't with my father when he died. I wasn't even able to attend his funeral.'

His voice, she realised, was almost bitter with self-contempt and she struggled to find a reply. At last she said, 'Maybe it was impossible for you to be there, Ben!'

He held up his hand to silence her. 'My father suffered a great injustice towards the end of his life and never recovered, but I ignored it. I travelled abroad, enjoying myself—I'd convinced myself it was what my father wanted. But I should have realised how desperate he had become. I should have been there for him.'

Julia realised she could not bear to see him like this. He looked haggard. Distraught. 'Ben. Listen to me,' she said steadily. 'Your father would have been glad that you made your own, successful life and turned into such a fine person—'

He rose to his feet and shook his head. 'You're wrong, Julia. So wrong. You don't understand the half of it. I am not a fine person!'

She longed to hold him. To smooth his hair back from his forehead and to tell him—what?

That she wanted him so badly that her whole body ached with need?

He cared for her, she was sure of it. Maybe miracles just might happen. Maybe she could defy all society's foolish rules and marry Ben the stonemason, then they could live as her aunt did, far away from London and heedless of its whims and fashions.

But Ben would never accept that. She knew it without asking, because he had his own kind of pride. But the thought of losing him dug as deep as any wound to her heart.

She rose to her feet. 'Ben,' she whispered. 'Oh, Ben. I'm going to miss you.'

He came to take her in his strong arms then. He held her so close that she could feel his heart steadily beating, but there were no words. After all, she thought sadly, what could he say?

He let her go at last. 'I'm sorry,' he said. 'I think we both realise this is impossible.'

She did her very best. She swallowed down that great lump in her throat, looked around and said almost lightly, 'Of course. I am being utterly foolish and I'm quite confirmed in my resolve that I shall never marry, ever! Now, the doctor recommended weak tea for my aunt as well as those powders, so I'll take some up to her. And, Ben, thank you. I don't know how I'll ever repay you for your help tonight.'

He went to look out of the window, then said quietly, 'It's nothing. But it's probably time I returned to Lambourne Hall. It seems to have stopped raining and the sky is clear, so may I borrow Nell again, to ride up there?'

She nodded as brightly as she could. 'Of course. Sowerby will saddle her up for you.' She hesitated, then said more quietly, 'Will you come here tomorrow?'

'I will,' he said. He was already pulling on his coat. 'I'll have to bring Nell back, after all. I'm sure that the doctor will visit, too.'

Julia bolted the front door after he'd gone, then leaned against it, feeling cold and empty. He could have kissed her, then—kissed her and more. But he was wiser than she and no doubt it was as well that he didn't.

For the next three days, Ben visited Linden House and Julia found his presence both a joy and a torment. He was wonderful with Lady Harris, telling her stories that made her laugh, and as she rapidly grew stronger, he helped her downstairs so she could roam the house looking for dust or chiding Dottie and Grace if the kitchen wasn't spotless.

'We're glad to see you back in good spirits, my lady!' Grace said to her, making Lady Harris chuckle.

Ben kept his distance from Julia and she accepted it because she had to face reality. Any day now she expected a letter from London to tell her that a carriage was being sent to bring her home and she felt as if she was about to lose something infinitely precious. She wanted Ben, but it was impossible and she knew she shouldn't torture herself so.

'That Ben,' her aunt said as Julia was reading to her in the sitting room. 'I'm disappointed in him.'

Julia put aside the book, which was the inevitable *Gulliver's Travels*. Goodness, she felt she knew the first chapter by heart now. Ben had called earlier to check all was well and she couldn't see a single reason for her aunt's criticism. She said, 'What exactly do you mean, you're disappointed?'

Lady Harris stared at her. 'Well, knowing him as I do, I expected more of him.'

'But he's been here every day to help you. I don't know how we'd have managed without him! It was amazing how he persuaded the doctor to come out so swiftly.'

Her aunt murmured, 'If the doctor won't come out for him, I swear I don't know who he *would* come out for.'

'For Ben? But surely the doctor won't have met him before? After all, Ben's only been working here for a while.'

'Hmmph. Shows how little you know.'

Julia said slowly, 'Aunt, what exactly do you know about him?'

'Well,' huffed her aunt, 'he is a good man, whatever they say about his father.'

'His father? Did you know Ben's father? But how—'

Lady Harris waved her hand dismissively. 'Now, where had you got to with poor Gulliver? Please carry on before I lose the thread entirely. Later, perhaps, we can play chess. How glad I am that you're here, for you have a far better brain than most females of my acquaintance.'

And much good has it done me, thought Julia rather sadly.

Ben had arrived home from his latest visit to Linden House to find Gilly standing in the kitchen looking rather stern. He also noticed there was an array of documents laid out on the nearby table.

'I suppose,' Gilly said, 'you've been to Linden House to see that girl, yet again. But for the life of me, I cannot understand why you're taking such a risk.'

Ben pulled off his coat. 'I've been visiting Lady Harris,' he said. 'Someone needs to help her out. She is my neighbour, after all.'

'While that girl is a guest there?' Gilly was not impressed. 'You'll be getting yourself into real trouble if you're not careful.'

'I hope I have enough sense to behave myself with Julia, if that's what you mean.'

Gilly raised an eyebrow. '*Lady* Julia. Just remember who her father is.'

As if he could forget. Today he'd walked back home up the hill with his head full of wild dreams. For several deluded minutes he'd even wondered if he might visit the Earl, her father, to apologise for what had happened in the past and to ask for Julia's hand.

My lord, I love your enchanting daughter. I am wealthy and have a good position in society, so can we forget the past? Will you permit me to marry her?

But what if her father refused to accept that Ben's father was not guilty of deceit? Where would that leave Julia? She would be forced to make an impossible choice between her family and him. Even if Ben found positive proof that his father was innocent in the business of the horse, would the proud Earl be willing to accept that proof?

Suddenly he realised that Gilly was pointing to those papers on the kitchen table. 'There's something there you ought to look at, my lord,' said Gilly quietly.

Before leaving the house this morning, Ben had remembered the documents Rudby had given him in London last week, about the sales and purchases of his father's horses over the years. Truly he'd expected nothing new, but he'd asked his valet to check them and now Gilly's words brought him sharply to attention.

Ben sat down and pulled the papers towards him.

'I took a look at them,' Gilly was saying, 'like you asked me to. The sheet I've left on top is the one you want.'

Ben scanned it and realised instantly that this was a report written by a veterinary surgeon, a familiar enough document to Ben, for he knew his father always had one done whenever he purchased a new horse. Only this time, the report was about Silver Cloud—and it was drawn up by the surgeon employed by the Earl of Carstairs.

It was a copy, Ben saw, maybe sent by the Earl to

Ben's father in protest at the transaction. Ben had never seen it before.

'There are the usual illustrations over the page,' said Gilly. 'You need to look at them.'

Ben looked. As usual, there were some detailed line drawings of the horse viewed from all angles, with notes at the side listing height, colour and other details. Ben read the notes with care and said, 'What have you spotted, Gilly? This describes Silver Cloud pretty well, doesn't it?'

'That's what I thought, at first. But come and take a look, my lord, at the painting of the horse in the hallway.'

Ben followed him and they both gazed up at the painting. Ben was still holding the report and as he looked down once more at the written description, he suddenly felt his pulse rate quickening. 'Silver Cloud,' he said, 'had a dappled grey coat and a silver mane. The report agrees. But according to the painting, there is a distinctive patch of darker grey, *here*.' He pointed to the picture and the horse's left hindquarter. 'It's shaped almost like a heart.'

Gilly nodded. 'Exactly, my lord. Now, look at the surgeon's report. Is there any mention of it? No. None whatsoever, even though reports like this are meant to be accurate in every detail.'

Ben felt a slow but steady sense of growing hope. Still holding that vital paper, he looked again at the painting. 'There can be only one explanation. My father hired Molloy to take Silver Cloud to the Earl's stables in Richmond—and Molloy delivered a different horse. Somewhere on the way, Silver Cloud was substituted with a horse that looked similar, but was fatally flawed. The question is—have we enough proof?'

Gilly said, 'I know someone who might help. When I rode into Claverton the other day for supplies, I spotted an old groom of your father's, Jem Thornberry. Do you remember him?'

'I do. He was a good man.'

'He's working now at the saddler's in Claverton. He would remember your father's horse, in every detail.'

Ben glanced at the picture again, then at the report. 'I'll go there tomorrow.'

He rode to Claverton the next morning, and found Jem Thornberry working outside the saddler's. 'My lord!' Jem was effusive in his greetings, effusive, too, in his description of the horse when Ben questioned him. 'Silver Cloud? Yes, he was the finest animal I ever did see. Perfect almost in everything—in fact, the only fault you could claim in him was that he had a darker patch of grey, almost heart-shaped, on his left hindquarter. But that horse was quality, my lord. Yes, real quality.'

'You'd swear to the magistrates about the flaw in his colouring, Jem? The darker patch?'

'I would, my lord.'

Ben shook his hand. 'Thank you, Jem. I'll be in touch.'

Ben rode homewards. He knew that the time had come for the truth to be exposed—which meant that he must return to London and confront the Earl of Carstairs.

Chapter Thirteen

The next day, Lady Harris seemed downcast as they settled down to lunch. 'This morning,' she announced, 'I received a letter from your bossy father. He wants you back home. Apparently he's sending your brother Charles for you.'

Of course, Julia knew this had to happen. She had been expecting the news daily, but even so her heart quailed within her. 'How soon is Charles setting off?' she asked her aunt. 'Does my father say?'

Lady Harris was adjusting her spectacles and peering at the letter again. 'I can't see anything about dates. It's a downright pity, though, that your family are intent on dragging you back to London, which is a place—'

'You cannot abide,' filled in Julia, smiling in spite of herself. 'Yes, you have told me that, several times.'

'I can't say it too often, in my opinion. Oh, and I almost forgot. There's a letter for you too.'

Julia opened it. It was from Pen and she read it with growing dismay.

Julia.

Absolute horrors. Charles has somehow got hold of your letters to me and realises you've met someone special. He's not going to tell our mother and father, but he says the man you've been seeing will regret it if he's laid a single finger on you!

Charles is setting off very soon to bring you home. I'm afraid our brother is very angry with you.

Slowly Julia folded the letter up again. She realised her aunt was watching her and frowning a little.

'Well, my girl,' said Lady Harris, 'you've been making a big fuss over my health, but you're looking quite peaky yourself. Do you want me to tell that family of yours that you're not fit to travel?'

Julia attempted a smile. 'Of course not. I must have been here over four weeks and I always knew I'd have to go home. But truly, I've had a marvellous time!'

'Hmmph,' said Lady Harris. 'I'm going to miss you.'

Julia suddenly realised her aunt was dabbing a tear from her eye. 'Oh, Aunt! I'm going to miss you, too.' She rose and went swiftly to take her hand and Lady Harris nodded.

'That's enough sentimentality.' She sniffed. 'You're a good girl, Julia, that's for sure. Now, it's my opinion that you need to go and find young Ben.'

'Aunt, I really don't think…'

'What? You don't think he deserves to know you're leaving? That's up to you. But I would like you to tell him that I'm finished with any mollycoddling and I know he's got better things to do than come here and fuss over an old lady! Now, I'm going to sit by the fire in the sitting room and go through the household accounts with Twigg.'

Once she had gone, Julia looked again at her sister's letter and those words of doom. Then she went upstairs to put on her jacket and her walking shoes, because her aunt was right. It was time for her to go and say goodbye to Ben.

As Julia climbed the path to the pavilion she noticed that in the distance the sky was heavy with rain clouds. Would Ben be working there today? He might have finished for good because as far as Julia could see, there was little more to be done. If he was at the pavilion, he might not be pleased to see her. Yes, he'd made daily visits to her aunt, but since that night when he'd fetched the doctor, he'd made sure he was never alone with Julia.

She pressed on, but the rain was starting to fall and as she neared the pavilion, it began to hammer down. How foolish she was, to have set off here at all! But it was too late to go back so she speeded up her steps, hoping to take shelter in the pavilion. Ben would never be there, not on an afternoon like this.

She reached the pavilion and ran inside. Her flimsy clothes were already soaked through; indeed, she had to brush the rain from her face and her eyelashes to see anything at all in the dark interior. 'Oh, my,' she muttered to herself. 'I am such a fool...'

Her voice trailed away—because she'd seen that Ben was there.

He, too, had clearly been caught in the downpour, because he had taken off his shirt and was preparing to put on another dry one. 'Julia,' he said. 'What on *earth*—?'

For a moment she couldn't speak. She thought that his tanned and muscled chest was perhaps the most glorious sight she had ever seen. But what she felt for him was far more than merely physical. In fact, he'd come to mean just about everything to her during this short time, but now her brother knew about him and that brutal fact reminded her how anything there might have been between them was over.

She had prepared herself to tell him that she was leaving for good, but for a moment the pain clutched so deep that she couldn't breathe. Couldn't move.

Ben broke the silence. 'Julia. Are you all right? For God's sake, why are you here?' He'd pulled the dry shirt over his head. 'Is your aunt unwell again?'

'She is fine,' she replied. To her relief, her voice was steady. 'We are all grateful,' she added, 'for everything you've done.'

'There's no need for thanks. It was no trouble at all.' He looked at her searchingly. 'But there's something else, isn't there?'

'Oh,' she said, shrugging, 'it's nothing I wasn't expecting. I've come to tell you that I'll be leaving soon.'

'For London?'

'Of course.' She tried to say it lightly. 'I'm returning to my family.'

He was silent a moment. Then he said in a quiet voice, 'Back to where you belong.'

With that, Julia's heart felt as if it was sliced in two.

No, she wanted to cry. *I belong here. I belong anywhere, as long as I'm with you, Ben.*

She couldn't believe he didn't see that. She couldn't believe, after all that had happened between them, that he could accept her departure so calmly.

But clearly he did accept it and, dear God, it hurt. She drew a deep breath, deciding that her only option was to act as she should have done from the very beginning, so she echoed his words firmly and brightly. 'Back to where I belong. That's exactly it, of course.'

He was keeping his distance, with his arms folded across his chest as if to deter her. But his shirt was still unbuttoned at the neck and his breeches clung tightly to his lean hips; his brown hair was tousled as usual and his jaw unshaven. He was her Ben, her stonemason, and she couldn't forget the way his lips had kissed her to distraction.

She lifted her chin to meet his gaze. She reminded herself that it was all over, of course it was, especially now that Charles knew. But wasn't Ben even going to fight for her? Her throat ached with unshed tears. She remembered his kiss and the strange things it had done to parts of her body she'd never even thought about.

Love of that kind—physical passion, physical intimacy—was not for her, she'd always told herself. But he'd proved her wrong, for everything about him made her long to know more of those strange feelings he could arouse in her with just one touch. At this very moment, her heart was thumping wildly and even when she lowered her gaze she was hardly able to breathe. Quickly she looked up again, but that was even worse because his eyes were glinting, his cheekbones were tanned and taut and his mouth reminded her of his kiss…

Too late. All far, far too late. She felt cold in her

heart, as cold as the rain clouds that were blotting out the sun. But she could not forget the intimate moments they'd shared, could not forget his smiles or his caresses. From the beginning, everything had seemed so *right* with Ben. But he regretted it, that was clear, and she had to agree that anything further between them was impossible. Pen's letter and her brother's fury had reminded her of the depth of antagonism her family would feel if a workman presented himself as her suitor.

She looked at Ben defiantly. 'I have to face reality sooner or later. Perhaps it's time I came to my senses and accepted who I really am. That's all I came to say— and you needn't wish me luck in my hunt for a husband, for I am never going to marry, ever.'

Lifting her head high, she began to walk towards the door. But as she stepped outside she stopped with a gasp—because of course the rain was still pouring down and at that moment lightning flashed across the dark sky. She stood there, shaking, while thunder rumbled overhead, unable to move until she felt Ben's strong arms around her and he was pulling her back inside.

'Oh, Julia,' he was murmuring, 'what am I going to do with you?'

And all of a sudden she realised exactly what she wanted him to do.

As for Ben, he knew he should have sent her home to Linden House the minute she appeared. Yes, it was pouring down, but he could have perhaps wrapped his large coat around her and hustled her back down that muddy path in the rain whether she liked it or not.

Now, though, it was too late. She was totally drenched.

She was shivering, she was distressed and what could he do but put his arms round her and cradle her against his warm body and kiss the top of her damp hair until she was nestling into him, clinging to him as if she would never let him go?

She needed his protection. But how could he even think about offering her his, when all he wanted to do even now was make love to her? The raging desire he felt was pounding through his blood this very minute. She'd declared she had no intention of marrying, but he had guessed already that there were depths of passion lying beneath her purity and the man who gained access to her heart and her body would be lucky indeed.

He longed for that man to be him. He longed to be the one to caress her lips and her sweet breasts with the ardour they deserved and to awaken her to the heights of bliss, but it would be wicked of him. For even if she hadn't already declared she would not marry, he knew that when he finally came face to face with her father— a meeting that must come soon—the bitterness between their two families might grow even worse.

But he couldn't send her out in this! The rain was still hammering down, so he let her go and went swiftly to light the fire in the hearth, fanning the low flames until the room lost a little of its chill. But when he looked up, he realised she was still shivering badly. Her hair and dress were soaked; she had her arms folded across her breasts and what he'd thought were raindrops trickling down her pale cheeks were in fact tears, even though she made no sound.

She looked so lost and lonely that he wanted to take her in his arms to comfort her—and more.

Be honest with yourself.

Much, much more.

'Dear God, Julia,' he breathed, 'I cannot bear to see you like this.'

She tried then to smile and he found it even more heartbreaking than her tears. 'You can rest assured,' she said, 'that you won't have to put up with me for much longer. I really was rather foolish to come up here like this, wasn't I?' She stopped and added in a quieter voice, 'Foolish—and rather scared, too.'

'Scared?'

'Yes.' She gazed up at him, her eyes brimming with emotion. 'You see, I realised that I'm very inexperienced. Very innocent. I know that I don't want to marry, but my parents won't take any notice. Soon I shall be flung on London's marriage mart and I'm afraid of what I'll face, Ben.'

'Oh, Julia.' He took her in his arms. 'What can I do to help?'

'Just hold me,' she whispered. 'Hold me, Ben. I'm truly dreading being paraded in front of rows of suitors. But when you kissed me, it was wonderful. Please tell me— could other men's kisses be like that? And what would they want from me in return?'

'You,' Ben said hoarsely. 'That's all, Julia. They'll want *you*.' His self-control was in pieces. He pulled her close—and he kissed her.

He was still trying to tell himself that this must be merely a gentle meeting of their lips, a gesture of comfort, no more, for surely this was wrong in every way. But then she flung her arms around his neck and the sweetness of her answering kiss took over his body, his mind and his senses.

* * *

The rain poured down outside and the fire in the hearth cast flickering shadows around the room, making the figures on the walls appear to dance like the Greek nymphs of old. Julia caught just a glimpse of their knowing smiles before Ben's kiss tore away the foundations of her world.

She would not have guessed that a man of such strength could also convey such tenderness. His powerfully muscled arms held her close and that was her last rational thought, because when his lips met hers she forgot who she was. Who she was supposed to be. Lady Julia Annabel Emilia Carstairs was no more; instead she was just Julia, she was in love with this man and, as his kisses cherished her lips, her face, her throat, she felt all the strength and heat of his body.

Her heart pounded like the thunder overhead. Could there be more? Yes. Definitely, yes, for his hands were wickedly at work, too. While one stayed tight around her waist, the other was moving down to clasp her bottom and draw her so close that she could feel the hardness of him through her scant clothing. *Oh, my.* She might be innocent, but she knew very well what it meant. He wanted her, badly. He wanted to make love to her, now.

She felt her senses swimming, along with a delicious hunger for more. Lifting her face to his to invite more kisses, she let her own hand stray to the opening of his shirt, allowing her fingers to brazenly explore the temptation of his smooth golden skin. When she heard his soft groan of pleasure, the sound set a pulse throbbing low in her own body. 'Ben,' she whispered. 'Ben.'

It was a plea and he answered it, because she felt his hand cupping her small breast, teasing and caressing its peak through the thin cotton of her dress. She felt herself melting into a hot puddle of desire. She knew that all her senses were under assault, for even the scent of his skin—heady, male, intoxicating—had robbed her of reason.

She lifted her hand to run her fingers through his hair, just as she'd always longed to do. He was beautiful, there was no other word for it, and if he let go of her now she thought she might die. But suddenly he was pulling away and gazing at her with anguish in his eyes.

'No,' he said in a low voice. 'Julia, this is not right.'

She met his gaze proudly—boldly even, for what had she to lose, when she had already lost her heart to him and knew she would never love anyone else? For answer she undid the top buttons of her damp dress. 'I'm cold,' she whispered. 'Please warm me, Ben.'

Then she reached up to lay her palms on either side of his face and stood on tiptoe to kiss him, shyly at first, but with growing courage, teasing his lips with her tongue as he had done to her, probing and exploring until she was shivering not with delight, but with new-found power.

For he was hers. Maybe just for this moment, maybe never again; but for now he was hers and she wanted to remember this for all of her life. Once more he was pulling her close, his body hot and hard against hers. Had she really undone so many of her buttons? It appeared so, for his hands were everywhere, cupping her breasts, stroking her nipples.

The next thing she knew, he was carrying her to the

sofa, where he held her and kissed her again as she fell back against the cushions. After that he lowered his head to her bosom and…oh, my…she felt his mouth on her breasts.

He was using his tongue to tease and caress first one nipple, then the other. *'Ben.'* It was a whisper of disbelief at the unbelievable pleasure, for as his lips were licking and sucking, she felt that secret place between her thighs hungering for him in a way she wouldn't have believed possible.

Down there she was tight with yearning and he must have known it, for now his strong hand was reaching down, pulling up her skirt and moving higher and higher until her trembling thighs fell apart and he was stroking the slick flesh of her most intimate place.

She gasped as his fingers teased her there, again and again. She was physically shaking with tension until he kissed her gently on her mouth, 'Julia,' he whispered. 'Julia. You're so beautiful.'

'Don't stop.' Her voice was urgent. 'Ben. I cannot bear for you to stop.'

She felt his hands steadying her for a moment. Then she gasped as he began once more to caress her. She clutched at him, her fingers digging into his back as the incredible sensations mounted. More? Surely there couldn't be more—she couldn't bear it, could she? Already, she could hardly breathe; but then, then she heard herself gasping aloud as he caressed her one last time.

'Please,' she cried, 'please, I can't…'

'You can,' he whispered back. 'Darling Julia, you can.'

At that very moment an exquisite torment gripped her entire body and she shook in his arms as wave after wave of delight rolled through her. He continued to hold her, murmuring words of passion to her, kissing her breasts, her forehead, her lips.

'Ben,' she whispered at last. She lay sated in his arms. 'Ben, I had no idea.' She was pulling his head down, trying to kiss him back. She loved this man and she wanted all of him. But carefully he was easing himself away. She felt cold when she heard the rain still pounding on the roof, colder still without his arms around her.

She drew herself up a little. 'Surely,' she said, 'there must be something I can do for you? What I mean is…'

She was confused, Embarrassed. She knew that he must be aroused, too, and must be in a state of torment.

'No.' His voice was harsh and he'd drawn a deep breath as if deciding what to say next. 'What I mean, Julia, is that what you suggest is *not* a good idea. Believe me.' He shook his head to emphasise his words. 'No more. Do you understand?'

She nodded because, yes, she did understand. She watched in silence as he went to pick up a folded blanket from a chair and came back to wrap it carefully around her shoulders, before going to put more logs on the fire.

The room heated up, but she was still cold inside. She had begged for this intimacy. She had begged for *him*. She knew that after she returned to London, everything would be as it was before. She would once again be the Earl of Carstairs' daughter, to be offered in marriage to the highest bidder. But there would never, ever be anyone like Ben.

Ben was still struggling to get much heat from the fire, but God help him, his body was in flames and his erection still pounded. He had self-control, yes, but it had its limits. He glanced back at her. She was sitting on the sofa trying to straighten her disordered clothes, but her eyes were still wide with the aftermath of desire and her lips were still swollen from the power of their kisses. He could see her small breasts heaving as she fought to recapture her breath. As for him, he was in a state of mental and physical torture.

It had been a dangerous mistake on his part to ever lay hands on this sweet girl who tasted of honey and wine. Didn't she realise what she was doing to him? She'd thrown any caution to the winds and clearly she'd longed to go further, longed perhaps for him to ruin her, which was what it would amount to.

He added some fresh kindling sticks to the fire, then gazed through a window at the rain pouring down outside. He had awakened her heart and it was completely wrong of him to have done so, for clearly she had no idea of how even her lightest caresses could fill a man with raging desire, even if the man in question—himself—knew it would be desperately wrong to take advantage of her. He should have put an end to all this at the very beginning. She should be back in London, with her family standing guard over her whenever she set foot outside her house.

He should have waited until he could speak with her father about the feud and only then, when and if peace was made between their families, should he have considered courting her with the delicacy and respect she deserved. Instead, he'd almost seduced her. Yes, she was sure she wanted him, but what would happen when she realised his deception? She might hate him then.

Perhaps she would meet someone else she could love. Perhaps she would change her mind about marriage and find herself an eminently suitable husband who would be welcomed into the heart of her family. But the trouble was that Ben couldn't bear the thought of it.

He realised she was speaking at last. She said in a low voice, 'I've made a fool of myself. Haven't I?'

He joined her swiftly and put his hands on her shoulders. 'No. Not in the least. But what happened between us just now must be kept between us, do you understand?'

'Of course.' She tried to smile. 'After all, my parents could never allow anything like this to happen, could they?'

'No,' he said. No, they couldn't, for reasons she didn't yet understand.

But he saw the heart-wrenching sadness in her eyes before she looked around and said, 'Well, I suppose I had better be off. It sounds as if the rain has almost stopped. But, Ben—do you remember how you found my rather foolish notebook, that I'd left by the lake? Did you read it?'

He couldn't deny it, for he'd told her too many lies already. 'Yes,' he said. 'I did.'

'Then you'll know,' she said softly, 'what I wrote about you.'

How could he forget it?

I wish that I had met someone like him in London.

Just for a moment, he allowed himself the cruelty of hope. If he could quickly resolve the issues with her father, could he approach her then? He would never trap her into a commitment she declared she loathed. But he would give her as much freedom as she wanted and he would give her love. So much love…

She was walking to the door of the pavilion, where she looked out. The rain had indeed stopped and a watery sun was gleaming on the trees and the lake. He followed her.

'Borrow my coat,' he said. 'You'll catch a nasty chill if you walk home just in those wet clothes. You can leave it by the gateway to your aunt's gardens. I shall collect it later.'

'Thank you,' she said. She spoke politely, as if they were strangers. 'So this is goodbye, Ben. Truly, I wish you well.'

Without another word, she pulled on his coat and it hung almost to the ground on her slender frame. But God help him, he found that she looked adorable even in that outsize thing. He wanted to run after her and hold her tight, to tell her who he was and why he'd lied to her. But might she not hate him for it? She might feel tricked, betrayed even. So what could he do, but stand there and watch her go?

Julia left Ben's coat by the gate as he'd instructed, though just for a moment she held it to her face, breathing in Ben's scent, Ben's warmth, and her heart ached as if it would break. After that, in her wet dress and boots, she hurried on towards the house, hoping desperately to get up to her room so she could have a few private moments to get changed and compose herself. But as soon as she opened the front door, she heard her aunt calling out, 'Is that you, Julia?'

Then Miss Twigg appeared in the hallway. 'You'd better go to her,' she said. 'She's sitting in the drawing room and she's in a bit of a tizzy.'

Indeed, as Julia went to find her, Lady Harris looked quite agitated. 'I've had another look at that letter from your father,' she announced. 'I do wish he would write more clearly. Apparently your domineering brother could arrive as early as tomorrow to take you home. I was not expecting him so soon.'

Julia sat down. Charles. Tomorrow. And he'd read her private letters to Pen, about her and Ben.

Lady Harris was looking at her sharply. 'Are you quite all right, Julia?'

'Yes,' she lied. 'Yes, of course.'

'Well, you don't look it.' Her aunt sighed. 'Do you know, I'm feeling rather weary with the world so I'd like you to read to me for a while. *Gulliver's Travels* will do—the bit where he finds he's captured by all those little people called the—the—'

'The Lilliputians? But, Aunt, I've read that to you several times already!'

'I know, but I like it. It's funny. Makes me chuckle, a big strong fellow like him pegged to the ground.' She pointed at a nearby table. 'The book's over there. See?'

So Julia settled down to read it aloud and her aunt shook with silent mirth, but her own heart still ached unbearably. She had told Ben she would never marry, but there was one man she would say yes to—him. She couldn't stop thinking about Ben's last kiss and the look in his eyes as he'd drawn away. He'd taught her to know desire and she had encouraged him, every step of the way. It was what she had longed for. It was something she would never forget.

But Charles was coming to take her home. Her brother, she was sure, would be watching her like a hawk once she re-entered the social life of London, ready to pounce if any other unsuitable stranger tried to steal her heart. But there was no need for him to worry in the least about that, thought Julia sadly. Because Ben had already stolen it.

Ben had walked back to the Hall from the pavilion and Gilly immediately detected he was in an awful mood. 'Is it your leg?' Gilly said.

Ben nodded. 'Yes.' It was true; his leg was hurting him, but he was in no mood for Gilly's sympathy. Instead he went straight to his study. He re-read the bill for transporting his father's valuable horse, carried out by the firm of Francis Molloy, who had vanished without trace. Then he once more studied the veterinarian's report, filled in when the horse arrived at the Earl's stables in Richmond. Superficially, all looked perfectly correct.

There was just one problem: the horse the Earl received was not Silver Cloud.

The watercolour painting of the horse proved it, as did the evidence of his father's old groom, Jem Thornberry. But Ben was going to try another tactic first. He had given his lawyer Rudby instructions to find out, if he could, the whereabouts of Francis Molloy and this morning, Ben had received Rudby's answer.

My lord.
On making enquiries, I have discovered that Molloy was committed to Newgate nine months ago.

He was convicted of various crimes, including horse thieving.

Ben's course was obvious. He needed to go to London again, because it was time for him to enter society as Lord Lambourne and to proceed with the business of clearing his father's name.

Chapter Fourteen

The next day Charles arrived at Linden House just before noon. Lady Harris had gone out with Miss Twigg to feed the chickens, so Julia was on her own, drinking tea in the sitting room, when he arrived. A very nervous Dottie showed him in and immediately Julia could see her brother was in a furious mood.

Her heart was sinking, but she looked up and said, 'Charles. How pleasant to see you. I hope you had a good journey?'

He slammed down his hat and gloves on a nearby side table. 'I trust, Julia, that you will be able to pack immediately, because I'm taking you home straight away.'

She rose to her feet. 'Surely you're in need of a brief rest. And wouldn't it be polite for you to spend a little time with our aunt, who has taken good care of me?'

'Are you joking, Julia? From what I gather, you have been unchaperoned for almost five weeks. You sent Betty home so you were without a maid and since then you've been wandering around the countryside all on your own. It is truly unbelievable!'

'Lady Harris does have staff, Charles!'

'But have any of them looked after you as they should have done? No! Neither, I gather, has Lady Harris!'

Julia bit her lip. It was clear that Charles truly had read every word of her letters to Pen. How wrong of him. How disastrous for her. She said quietly, 'You read the letters I wrote to Pen. Don't you think that's rather unforgivable?'

Charles showed no sign of softening his tone. 'I think,' he said grimly, 'that it's your behaviour that's disgraceful, not mine. I warned our father before you even left London that he was making a grave mistake sending you to our absurdly eccentric aunt. I did hope that since she lives at the back of beyond, there wouldn't be much mischief you could fall into. But you managed to find someone to make foolish eyes at, didn't you? Do you know who your stonemason really is?'

Julia was beginning to feel as if the air in this room had become difficult to breathe. She tried to speak, but couldn't, because already Charles's next words were washing over her like a cold grey tide.

'Your so-called stonemason,' he said, 'is none other than Lord Lambourne. I realised it straight away, because you told Pen, didn't you, about his work abroad and his broken leg? You also told her he was living at Lambourne Hall, yet unbelievably, you never guessed, never even suspected who he truly was! But I can see by your expression that you understand the enormity of it now. You've been cavorting with Lambourne, unchaperoned and unprincipled. How could you?'

Julia somehow stood her ground, but inside she was shaking. She was remembering suddenly the conversation she'd overheard between her father and Charles, on the night it was decided to send her to Somerset.

'You do realise, don't you,' Charles had warned her father, *'who might be staying close by?'*

Her father had dismissed Charles's concerns, saying that the man in question was still abroad. 'You needn't worry about him,' he'd said. But her father was wrong, because Ben, Lord Lambourne, was indeed back home.

There had been very many things about Ben that she'd found odd. For example, despite his workman's garb his manners were those of one used to living in the highest echelons of society. He knew this entire district for miles around; he knew her aunt, he even knew the doctor in the village—and was living at the Hall, for heaven's sake!

How could she not have realised his identity? She had visited her aunt often as a child and Ben must have lived close by. But he was seven years older than her. He would have been away at school, or at his father's London property. Besides, her aunt rarely talked about any neighbours; she wasn't one for formal socialising, though she must have known who Ben was, and she should, she really should have told Julia…

But Julia herself ought to have known. Instead, she had deliberately blinded herself to reality—because she had fallen hopelessly in love.

Now she lifted her head proudly. 'So he's Lord Lambourne. Isn't that good news, Charles? I would have thought you would be relieved that I wasn't meeting with a mere stonemason.'

'But this is *Lambourne*!' cried her brother. 'Did he tell you about his father's fraudulent deception of our own father? The bitter argument they had, when Lord Lambourne—your Ben's father—refused to apologise?'

She couldn't help it. Her hand flew to her mouth in shock.

'He didn't tell you, did he?' Charles spoke with grim satisfaction. 'I'm not surprised. He'll know full well that his own father's behaviour was disgraceful.'

'Charles, I knew there was some trouble, but Ben believed his father was innocent of any wilful deceit. There must have been a terrible mistake!'

'Oh, Julia.' Her brother shook his head. 'Don't you see that the man has been playing you for a fool? Let me tell you what really happened. Our father and Lambourne's were once friends, linked by their passion for fine horses. Lambourne agreed to sell a young gelding of his to our father, but when it arrived, it was unfit to be ridden, let alone to race. Father had paid Lambourne a high price for it—and it was worthless! Are you truly saying you believe that our father lied about this?'

She shook her head and said heatedly, 'No! Of course not! Papa would never do such a thing!'

'You are absolutely right. Why should he? The sum of money he paid for that horse, large though it was, would be nothing to him. What angered our father most was Lambourne's adamant refusal to admit to his deception.'

'But Ben swore that his father had deceived no one—and he told me that his father was broken by this, his life was ruined!'

Charles lifted one eyebrow in scorn. 'And Lambourne explained all this while he was pursuing you under a false name? Do you call that kind of behaviour either trustworthy or innocent?'

She could find no words to answer him.

'Has it occurred to you,' Charles went on relentlessly, 'why Benedict Lambourne might have decided to latch on to you?'

She was beginning to feel quite sick, but she answered clearly, 'He did not "latch on" to me, as you so crudely put it. For goodness sake, he didn't even know who I was. When we met—purely by chance!—he was kind to me.'

'You truly believe you met by chance? You call it "kind" of him to pursue you and let him kiss you? Yes, I know about that from your letters. What other liberties did you allow him, I wonder? Sit down, Julia.'

'No! I won't!'

'I think you'd better, because you're not going to like what I'm about to say. When his father died, Benedict Lambourne was abroad and in hospital. But when he returned, he stopped briefly in London before going on to Somerset—and he was heard to vow revenge on our father, for supposedly driving his own father to an early grave. I thought little of it at the time. I believed that he could do our powerful family no harm. But Lambourne's a cunning fellow, there's no doubt about it—because he's found a way through our defences, hasn't he?'

Julia sat down on the sofa, for she had begun to tremble inside. Charles watched her closely.

'Yes,' he said at last. 'He's sworn revenge on us and his strategy is to seduce you, I'm afraid. Julia, you've been taken for a fool—' He stopped, perhaps because he'd realised that tears were welling in her eyes, no matter how hard she tried to blink them back.

He came to sit beside her then, her big brother Charles, who used to play silly games with her when she was small and let her ride on his shoulders. He put his arm around her. 'Oh, Julia. You haven't fallen in love with him, my dear—have you?'

When she gave him no answer, he shook his head and held her tight. 'I will kill him,' he muttered. 'I will kill him for this.'

'No!' She pulled away and shook her head fiercely. 'No, Charles. I cannot allow you to even *think* something like that!'

His face darkened. 'You do believe what I'm telling you, don't you?'

Still she could not speak, but Charles must have seen her expression, for he hesitated a moment, then said, 'I'm sorry, Julia. I blame our aunt, Lady Harris, for this. She badly neglected her duty to you in allowing you the freedom to meet this rogue.'

With a great effort, Julia pulled herself away from him. 'No, Charles. You will not put the blame on her— or on Ben either! He has been completely honourable towards me from the start; indeed, when he realised who I was, he told me that we must stop seeing one another immediately. But I took no notice!' She shook her head emphatically. 'What happened between us was all my fault.'

Charles looked at her, amazed. 'What on earth do you mean?'

Her voice was steady now, even though her heart was aching with pain. 'I encouraged him,' she said, 'at every step. I told all the family before leaving London that I wanted a taste of freedom and I found it. Ben was working on his estate, close to Lady Harris's property, and I pursued him. Day after day, I went to find him and talk to him. I encouraged our intimacy, Charles. Let me make it quite clear: this was not his fault.'

Her brother was on his feet. He began to pace the room, then he swung round to face her. 'Julia,' he said at last. 'Do you realise that if you go around spreading this story, you will be utterly disgraced?'

She shrugged. 'I'm not going to be spreading the story. But if you try to blame Ben…well, I've told you the truth of it and I shall defend him if necessary. Please make no mistake about that. I believe, even if you don't, that he is totally honourable.

'If you try to raise the matter in public, then he could lay the blame for what happened entirely on me and I swear to you that I would not deny my behaviour. In fact, I would tell everyone what I've said to you—that I did my best to seduce him.' She still spoke clearly, but found she was feeling a little breathless, a little faint. 'Is that all, Charles? Shouldn't I go upstairs now and pack?'

Her brother stood there, looking both bewildered and angry. At last he said, 'Very well. Very well. But as soon as you're ready, I intend to start our journey. I've no wish for you to spend any more time with Lady Harris who, in my opinion, has let you down quite abominably. I'm hoping that you might have time to reflect on the problems you've caused yourself and, for the sake of our family, I shall mention none of this once we are in London. I also hope you've remembered that it's Pen's wedding in a matter of weeks. It's best if both of us aim to forget that any of this unpleasantness has happened.'

It was at that moment that Lady Harris marched in. She took one look at Julia's brother. 'Hello, Charles,' she said, untying her bonnet. 'Throwing your weight around as usual, are you?'

Charles was tight-lipped. 'Lady Harris. I'm sorry to have to say this, but I hope you realise that you've let Julia down?'

'Really? Have I?' She plonked her hat on a side table. 'Funny, but I thought it was her family who did that. Trying to squash this delightful girl's spirits, just because she didn't fit the accepted mode. Hah!'

'Aunt,' said Julia.

But Lady Harris was still glaring at Charles with her hands on her hips. 'Well, young man? I've known you since you were a boy. I guess you mean well, but sometimes you can be a pompous ass, did you know that? What have you to say for yourself, hey?'

To describe her brother as annoyed would be putting it mildly. For a moment Charles looked about to explode, but then he merely straightened his exquisitely knotted cravat and replied haughtily, 'I have nothing further to say to you, Lady Harris—except that I warned our father you were not to be trusted with a single member of our family.'

He turned to his sister and spoke more quietly. 'Julia,' he said. 'You mustn't ever think that we don't care for you. We do, very much—which means that we want the best for you.'

He examined his pocket watch. 'I must go and check that the horses have been properly fed and watered by the grooms. Julia, we shall set off in half an hour and I trust you will be ready by then. We can dine when we stop to change the horses.'

He gave a curt bow to Lady Harris and left the room.

'Pompous twit,' muttered her aunt.

Julia sat down again on the sofa, feeling exhausted. Her aunt came over to sit at her side. 'Chin up, my dear. Your brother's a fool and some day he'll meet a woman who'll teach him some sense. I don't believe he intends to be so hard on you—he thinks he's helping, that's all, and he really does care for you. So you go back to London with him—and who knows what lies in store?'

'I'm afraid,' Julia said, 'that my brother is determined to take me in hand, Aunt. But I want you to know that I've loved my time with you. Really I have!'

Her aunt patted her shoulder. 'Be true to yourself,' she whispered. 'That's my advice to you, my dear.'

Julia wanted to ask if her aunt guessed that meeting Ben and losing him had broken her heart. But what was the use? Yes, Lady Harris had contrived the first meetings between the pair, but her aunt had not ordered her to fall in love. As for what happened in the pavilion yesterday, she really could blame no one but herself.

She met her aunt's enquiring gaze. 'You knew, didn't you, who Ben was? Did you also know about the bitterness between his father and mine?'

'I heard something of the sort, yes.' Lady Harris sighed. 'But take my advice and trust the young man—he knows what he's doing. So be patient and have hope. Sometimes we must wait for what we most desire. Now, it's time for you to pack your things.'

With a heavy heart Julia went up to her room, where

Grace was already waiting to help her. It was almost, thought Julia, as if the maid guessed her despair, for Grace said very little as she quietly began emptying the chest of drawers and folding Julia's clothes on the bed. Julia tried to be of some use, but in the end Grace said, 'You leave all this to me, my lady.' She pointed to some books Julia had borrowed from her aunt's library. 'Why don't you take them back where they belong?'

Julia nodded and carried them downstairs, finding seclusion of a sort in the book-lined room. Her aunt spoke of trust and hope. But how could she hope for any kind of future with Ben when, as well as the fact that he would be totally unacceptable to her family, she had told him she was not interested in marriage, ever?

Of course, Ben would not have proposed anyway, despite her sad attempts to lure him. He would have realised, as soon as he discovered who she was, that even something as simple as friendship between them could affect his efforts to clear his father's name. But would Ben use her for revenge? Never!

She could see she would make an easy target for an unscrupulous rogue. But Ben wasn't unscrupulous. Ben was a man of integrity, of that she was completely sure. When he'd learned who she was, he had been genuinely horrified and had told her they must on no account meet again.

Julia believed in Ben. She loved him. But now, for his sake, she must never see him again, although they were bound to meet some time, at one of those society events in London that she hated. Slowly she returned upstairs, where Grace was packing her frocks into a leather-bound trunk. 'Are you all right, my lady?'

Julia forced a smile. 'I'm fine, thank you, Grace. But I'm sorry to be leaving you all.'

'We shall miss you, too, my lady. But you're going back to London, aren't you? How exciting!'

Yes, Julia was returning home. But she knew she would never meet anyone else like Ben, not ever. And when some day their paths did inevitably cross—how, oh, how could she bear it?

Chapter Fifteen

Three days later, Julia and Charles arrived back in London on a grey and misty afternoon. Throughout the journey it rained as only English rain knew how, making the roads muddy and enforcing a slow pace. But her brother had made sure there were always heated bricks in the carriage to warm Julia's feet and rugs to wrap around her. He was his usual commanding self at the inns where they made their overnight stops, swiftly securing the very best rooms and service.

When they finally reached London and drew up outside Carstairs House in Mayfair, all the family were there to welcome her—her father, mother, Pen, Lizzie and even her father's two Labradors. Her mother hugged and kissed her, then led them all into the drawing room, where dozens of candles were lit and a large fire blazed.

'Oh, my darling Julia,' Lady Carstairs exclaimed. 'It's such a relief to see you back safely! It was a mistake to send you so far away, I knew it!'

Charles intervened. 'Mother. Father. I've spoken with Julia and I gather that her stay in Somerset was quite an adventure. But she is back with us now and has come to no harm whatsoever.'

He smiled at Julia, a smile that she felt was more than a little forced.

She guessed he was really saying, *Your turn now, Julia. Put our parents' minds at rest, for heaven's sake, or there will be the devil to pay.*

So she spoke in the lightest of tones. 'Oh, I've had a lovely time! Of course it was very quiet at Linden House, although one day we had a delightful trip to Bath. But really, nothing of exceptional interest occurred, and it is wonderful to be back with you all!'

Pen and Lizzie were watching her anxiously. Pen, she guessed, would have told Lizzie about her letters and what she'd written about Ben. Pen would have told her, too, that Charles had read them. No doubt they would be questioning her soon and she dreaded it, even though she loved them dearly.

She smiled round at them all once more, but really she was exhausted and Charles must have noticed, for when her mother declared that they would all have tea and scones straight away and hear every detail of her stay in the country, it was Charles who said, 'I think Julia is tired after her journey, Mother. Perhaps we should allow her to go to her room and at least get changed out of her travelling clothes.'

'You are right, Charles!' cried her mother. 'Julia, I shall send one of the maids up to you—Betty, I think.'

'No!' burst out Julia. Then she spoke more calmly. 'Thank you, Mama. But may I have a little time to be on my own?'

Charles escorted her to the foot of the stairs, where for

just a moment he held her arm and murmured, 'I will say nothing whatsoever about Lambourne to our parents and neither, I hope, will you. It's our secret for ever. Yes?'

'Yes,' she whispered.

He looked at her searchingly and not unkindly. 'Is it really all over between you and him?'

She nodded. 'Indeed. It's all over, Charles.'

When she entered her bedroom it seemed desolate. Elegant, yes, beautifully furnished, yes, but there was no model ship to make her smile, no lilac tree brushing its twigs against her window in the light breeze. No distant view of the woods and the pavilion. No Ben.

Wearily she sat on the bed with her heart aching so badly that she wasn't sure how she would get over it. She rose again and had just begun to pace her room in despair when the door flew open and her sisters came in.

They took one look at her, then they came silently over to hug her, Lizzie first, then Pen. After that they drew her back to the big bed and they all sat down, with Julia in the middle.

'Oh, Julia,' said Lizzie, wriggling a little closer so she could place her hand on hers. 'Are you quite, quite sure you're all right? You look so sad.'

Pen said, 'You're still thinking about *him*, Julia, aren't you? That lovely man you told us about. The stonemason.'

'He sounds really nice,' said Lizzie with a sigh. 'Julia, did he kiss you *properly*?'

Pen reached across to poke her sister in the ribs. 'Lizzie! Don't be so inquisitive! And even if he did,' she added, 'it really is as well that you and I do not know, in case our mother decides to question us.'

'But, Julia, maybe you can tell us just a little about him?' pleaded Lizzie.

Julia tried to swallow down the huge lump in her throat. 'He is called Ben,' she whispered. 'He has brown hair and a lovely smile. He broke his leg badly in the summer and still walks with a limp, but he likes nothing better than to be outside, working in the sunshine. I met him almost every day.'

'No wonder you're missing him,' said Pen sympathetically. 'Poor you. But you must have known our father and mother could never approve of you marrying a stonemason.'

'I knew it, of course. But then I found out more.' Julia drew a deep breath. 'You see, I discovered that he's not a stonemason—he's a baron, Pen! His real name is Benedict, Lord Lambourne.'

Her sisters gasped in delight. 'Why, that's perfect!' cried Pen, 'Why on earth can't you be married? Unless...' she hesitated '...unless he's married already? Or a fraudster, or a terrible gambler?'

Julia almost smiled. 'Believe me, he's none of those. But the trouble is that his father was our father's enemy.'

Pen looked puzzled again. 'Why would our father bear a grudge against your Ben, for something his father did? Surely the argument, whatever it was, has been long forgotten?'

Julia shook her head. 'Charles says that it hasn't. I think the matter was very serious.' She was blinking back a tear now. 'Charles also says that during the weeks I was at our aunt's, Ben was using me to get revenge on our father.'

'Using you for revenge?' Lizzie gasped. 'How awful. Do you think it's true?'

'Not for a moment! Oh, Lizzie! I really liked him, so very much!' She had to stop and pull out her handkerchief because her tears were flowing fast.

Pen began stroking her hair gently. 'Darling Julia. You must have trusted Ben. You must have believed he cared for you. So are you positive there's absolutely no hope?'

Julia mopped up her tears and tried to speak calmly. 'I realised, I suppose, that even though we spent a lot of time together, Ben was trying to keep his distance. I thought at the time it was because he was a stonemason, though I understand the true reason now. He was afraid I would have to choose between him and my family, because of the feud, and I think he didn't want me to have to make such an awful decision. But I don't want anyone except him and I'm already missing him, so much!'

She felt her tears well up again. Ben. Oh, Ben.

Her sisters were silent. At last Lizzie said, 'We are sisters. Remember? And we shall stick by each other *always.*'

They held hands for a moment, then Pen said thoughtfully, 'Julia. You are a good judge of character and you've never been impressed by anyone's fancy words or boasting. I agree with you that Charles must be wrong about this "revenge" business. If you really like Ben and you know he likes you, then there must be some way the two of you can be together.'

Julia shook her head. 'I told him,' she whispered, 'that I never wanted to marry, ever, and it's true that I didn't—until I met him. Though I still carried on pretending. I was always saying, "Heaven forbid that I should lose my independence!" Of course, he believed me. So it's over. I've ruined everything.'

For a moment there was silence, then Lizzie said suddenly, 'You can't have ruined everything. There must be a way. Why not ask Papa *now* to tell you all about this horrid argument with Ben's father? You never know, you might find out it wasn't as bad as you think!'

Julia gave a faint smile, but shook her head. 'I know it was bad, Lizzie.'

'But you can at least hope!'

'I don't think so. Everything has gone wrong.'

There was silence. Her poor sisters were clearly at a loss as to how to offer any further comfort, so it was up to her to summon a smile.

'Now,' she said to them, 'that's enough about me. So please tell me all of your news. What's been happening in London? What have I missed? How are your wedding plans, darling Pen?'

'Oh, yes. The wedding!' exclaimed Lizzie. 'Julia, you wouldn't believe the fuss Mama is making about it. It's not far off and she is already in a state of panic about the church, about Pen's wedding gown and the extra servants we'll need—everything!'

Pen joined in eagerly, largely, Julia guessed, to stop her thinking about Ben. As if she ever could. As if the great void in her heart could ever be filled by anyone else.

Over the next few days she was swiftly drawn again into her former life as the Earl of Carstairs's daughter. Although she had not yet been formally presented at court, her mother was eager to take her to private balls or parties and Pen, of course, joined them, often with her fiancé, Jeremy.

Julia made the best of it, for Pen's sake. She smiled and made light conversation with the other guests, as was expected. Gradually, it started to occur to her that some of the men who were present at these affairs were actually noticing her. Admiring her, even.

She responded politely to their pleasantries, but why was this happening? It could, of course, be her exquisite attire, because her mother, after a lecture from Pen, had taken Julia to a stylish modiste who provided her with some wonderful gowns. She had expected the gossips might still be muttering over her sudden disappearance from London, after she'd emptied that glass of champagne over Tristram Bamford. But, no, her brother's high-living friends were looking at her with something she wasn't used to—admiration.

When she found herself trapped in a corner by a tedious baronet who was eagerly telling her about his homes and his wealth, she caught sight of her image in one of the many gilded mirrors and realised that, yes, she did look different, somehow. It was hard to pin down. But maybe her lips looked fuller and her eyes, whose colour had once been compared to the sea on a cold day in midwinter, were more vivid. More expressive.

Her mother was thrilled. 'Julia, my dear, we might be planning a wedding for you before too long! I believe your trip to the country has done you a world of good. You have acquired an air of elegance, an air of mystery even, which all young men adore.'

Julia was in despair. She knew she ought to be flattered, but she wasn't. She missed Ben dreadfully. Would he be missing her? She doubted it. Even worse, he was bound to return to London soon, to take his place in society. Would he be looking for a wife?

Of course he would. All men of his rank had to have an heir. But how would she bear it?

Then one day, as she and Pen and their mother returned to the house after yet another shopping trip, Charles beckoned her quietly to one side.

'Julia,' he said. 'I've heard that Lambourne's in town.'

For a moment she could hardly breathe.

'If,' Charles continued, 'you should come across him anywhere, I trust you will act as if the two of you have never met. Do you understand?'

Her heart still hammered. But she nodded and somehow said coolly, 'Of course, Charles.'

She said it for Ben's sake. She knew he would not want Charles stirring up fresh trouble and she owed him this, at least.

But— *Ben*, she thought. *I miss you, so very badly.*

Their meeting happened even sooner than she'd feared. Less than two weeks after her return home, some friends of her parents, the Duke of Danby and his wife, held a twenty-first birthday party for their oldest son in their magnificent house in Grosvenor Square. Julia went with Charles, Pen and their mother. Their father, who tended to avoid these large social affairs when he could, had made his excuses.

There was dancing, of course, in the ballroom. The

whole house was crowded, yet Julia had not been there for ten minutes when she saw Ben. He was dressed in the usual evening finery of gentlemen of quality, a black tailcoat and skin-tight buff breeches. He looked heart-breakingly handsome. He also looked completely at home in this aristocratic *milieu*, surrounded as he was by the fashionable elite: men who were clearly friends of his and of course young women, too, girls who gazed at him and fluttered their fans flirtatiously.

All around her she could hear people talking about him. 'Have you seen that Lambourne's back? They say he'll soon have his father's estate put to rights, then no doubt he'll find a wife. One of the Duke's daughters would make an excellent match for the man...'

Julia wanted to ask her mother to take her home, but Lady Carstairs was nowhere to be seen. She thought of hiding, but she felt as if she could not move. And then—then, she saw that Ben was coming towards her, a little slowly because of his limp. People were watching, but he didn't seem to care.

'Julia,' he said. 'I've only just arrived in London. No doubt you've realised by now who I am. I know you must be hurt and furious over my deception—'

She held up her hand. 'Please,' she said in a low voice, 'don't make this worse for both of us. I understand that what happened between us was a bad mistake and nearly all of it was my fault.' Her heart was pounding painfully. 'I think you and I ought to forget everything about our time together in Somerset.'

He looked at her. He was pale, but his gaze was steady. 'I don't want to forget it,' he said. 'It's not over as far as I'm concerned. But if that's the way you feel—'

He broke off because at that moment, the musicians struck up a brisk waltz and a girl in a green satin gown and emeralds came eagerly towards them. She was Lady Eleanor, one of the Duke of Danby's daughters. Julia knew her because for a while they'd had dancing lessons together.

'Lord Lambourne,' Lady Eleanor exclaimed, putting her gloved hand on his arm. 'I know you are unable to dance, which is such a shame! But my father and mother are wondering if you will join us in the dining salon for a glass of champagne and some refreshments. We really must celebrate your return to London.' She glanced at Julia. 'Lady Julia. We haven't seen you for a few weeks, have we? Though of course we all know about your distaste for fashionable society. Come, Lord Lambourne. Let me take you to my parents.'

She led Ben away, chatting to him eagerly. Moments later Charles, looking furious, came to stand by Julia's side. 'Was Lambourne actually talking to you? I can't believe he had the audacity to approach you. I swear, if he said anything to upset you, I will not be responsible for my actions.'

'He will not speak to me again, I'm sure,' said Julia. 'Whatever there was between us is over, Charles—and now, I really want to go home.'

She couldn't hide the tell-tale break in her voice and Charles must have heard it. After making his apologies to their hosts, he led her to the front door and went to find a footman to summon their carriage. In the meantime Pen came hurrying up.

'Julia,' she whispered. 'Darling, are you all right? Why are you leaving?'

'Ben is here,' Julia said.

'Oh, no!'

'Pen, he came to speak to me. But it's no good. I know there's absolutely no hope. I realise I'll have to get used to seeing him everywhere, but I can't, not yet. Charles is summoning our carriage to take me home.'

Pen looked hugely concerned. 'Where is Ben? Is he still here?'

'Yes. He was led away by Lady Eleanor to the dining salon. She was clutching his arm as if she'd won a prize.'

Pen gasped. 'Is he the tall man with brown hair and the slight limp?'

'That's him.'

'Julia, he looks lovely. He looks kind—and you say that he came to talk to you? Are you quite sure that there's no hope?'

'This feud between our father and his will never be forgotten, Pen. Never. Charles is absolutely furious that he even approached me.'

'Oh, Charles can be so bad-tempered. Have you thought of speaking to our father about it all?'

Julia looked at her sadly. 'How can I do that, exactly? Can I tell him that I fell in love with Ben while I was supposed to be isolated in the countryside to preserve my good name?'

'Of course.' Pen frowned. 'I'd forgotten. You were already in trouble over that stupid Tristram Bamford, weren't you? Thank goodness he isn't here. But our father just might understand...'

'Pen, it's impossible. I can't allow myself to think that there's any chance of us being together, because it hurts too much, don't you see?'

Just then Charles returned. 'The carriage is waiting outside, Julia,' he announced. 'I'll come home with you. Pen, explain to our mother that Julia is a little overtired, will you?'

Chapter Sixteen

Ben had seen her leave with her brother and he felt close to despair. She was no longer his Julia. She was someone else entirely: she was Lady Julia, the highly eligible daughter of the Earl of Carstairs. She'd looked exquisite in her gown of pale pink, but he had preferred the simple frocks she'd worn in the country. He had loved the determination with which she'd walked along rough paths to gather blackberries and he'd loved the way she had laughed with him.

They had become so close. This could not be the end for them, it couldn't.

He had arrived in London just two days ago with Gilly and, after collecting the keys from Rudby, he'd gone to unlock the family's town house in Clarges Street, Mayfair. The previous tenant had left weeks ago, but the spacious interior had clearly been neglected for far longer. He could see dust and cobwebs everywhere.

There were also heaps of letters to be read and his first task was to skim swiftly through them. Some were from old friends in the diplomatic service. Others were gilt-edged invitations to various social events at the houses of London's aristocracy, making it clear that Lord Lambourne's return was widely known and widely welcomed in most of the *ton*'s drawing rooms. That was why he'd come to the Duke of Danby's ball tonight, for it was part of his duty to re-establish his connections with other members of the aristocracy. He knew it was his duty also to marry before too long. But seeing Julia arrive in that ballroom tonight had all but knocked the breath from his body.

Until meeting her, he'd told himself that nothing, absolutely nothing, could be more important than making it clear to the Earl of Carstairs that his own father had committed no fraud. But now his life was in turmoil. He loved Julia. But how could he ever overcome her family's hostility?

He looked at his pocket watch and groaned because it was scarcely half-past nine. He'd escaped from the Duke of Danby's daughter, but she would find him again soon. Did he really have to stay to the end? The answer came unexpectedly, in the form of a folded letter brought to him by one of the Duke's footmen.

'A messenger came with this for you, my lord,' he said.

Ben opened it quickly. It was from Gilly and it was about Molloy.

On the very first day of his return to London, after Rudby had written that Molloy was in Newgate, Ben had begun the process of finding out what exactly had happened to the man, so he'd gone there—only to be told that Molloy was no longer there.

'Was he set free?' Ben had asked sharply.

'No.' The surly gaoler shook his head. 'He was sent somewhere else. Don't know where, though.'

Ben had offered more money with no result, but the ever-loyal Gilly had taken it upon himself to make further enquiries. Ben knew he'd gone out again this evening and now he'd sent a message to the Duke's ball, telling Ben to meet him at a drinking house in Holborn on Fetter Lane.

Immediately Ben made his excuses to his hosts and hired a cab to take him there. He was thankful that his long, dark greatcoat covered his evening finery, for the inn was filled with working men: dockers and market traders, he guessed. Gilly hailed him over to the beer-stained table in the corner where he'd been sitting.

'I've been to the Fleet Prison,' he said. 'It's close by, as you'll know. A gaoler told me Francis Molloy was transferred there from Newgate earlier this year, but he died in August of the prison fever. Apparently the man was guilty of any crime you can think of involving horses. God alone knows how he got away with it all for so long. Here. I've written down what the gaoler said.'

Ben was already reading Gilly's notes. Clearly Molloy got up to all kinds of trickery for years—altering records, bribing grooms to put horses out of action before big races. He looked up at Gilly. 'Molloy must have been a cunning man. I would guess that when my father hired him to take Silver Cloud to the Earl of Carstairs, Molloy remembered seeing another horse that was almost identical in looks, but valueless because of its defects.'

Gilly was listening closely. 'So you're wondering if somewhere along the way, Molloy replaced your father's horse with another?'

'I'm sure of it,' said Ben softly. 'And no one realised until you and I did—thanks to that vet's report and the painting.'

Gilly sighed. 'I wonder where your father's fine horse ended up? Ah, well. There's no use dwelling on that. Besides, I'd guess you've got all the information you need now, my lord, to prove your father's innocence. I deserve another pint of ale for what I've discovered to-night, don't I? And you owe me money! I had to fork out a guinea to get the information.'

Ben beckoned the barman and ordered more drinks. 'I owe you a good deal more than a guinea and a pint, Gilly. But you probably know that.' He folded the sheet of notes and put it deep in his pocket.

Gilly was still watching him. 'What are you going to do next? Will you visit the girl's father to tell him what you suspect?'

Ben hesitated. The answer, he knew, was obvious. Molloy was a convicted fraudster and Ben should confront the Earl of Carstairs and tell him everything. Surely he had enough evidence to persuade anyone that his father was innocent? But the Earl, he'd heard, was a proud man and would still, surely, bear a grudge. He would hardly fling the past aside; he was unlikely to ever welcome Ben through his door as a visitor, let alone as a prospective son-in-law. Again Ben had to fight down the old bitterness as he recalled the Earl's letter to his father.

This was an act of fraud, not worthy of a man of your rank.

Their drinks had arrived and Gilly raised his tankard. 'To the memory of your father, my lord. And remember that whatever you do next, he would have wanted you to be happy.'

Ben lifted his drink also. 'To my father.'

They talked then of times gone by, of Ben's travels in Europe with Gilly always faithfully by his side. Some other men in there came to join them; they were old soldiers who'd noticed Ben's lameness and asked if maybe he'd been injured in battle. For an hour or so he was able to forget his title and his wealth as they told one another of the countries they'd been in and the people they'd met.

Ben drank his pint, then another and another, until Gilly said, 'Time to go home, my lord.'

He had realised that just for a while, he'd not thought of Julia. Maybe some day, if things didn't work out, he would get over her. But as he unlocked the door to his house, the silence of it enveloped him. He remembered again how very beautiful she'd looked at the ball tonight and how he'd loathed all the men who surrounded her.

'Please,' she'd said, *'don't make this worse for both of us. I understand that what happened between us was a bad mistake and nearly all of it was my fault.'*

It was a mistake, yes, but not her fault because he had behaved in an unforgivable way by deceiving her and quite possibly convincing her to stay away from men and marriage for good. The problem was that he realised his whole life would be quite empty without her, so he was not giving up. No, not until he heard her say she didn't love him, because he would swear that she did.

* * *

Ben woke the next morning with a well-deserved headache. At around eight Gilly brought him some coffee and the latest mail, in which were several more invitations, including one to the home of Lord and Lady Sheldon in Kensington for a musical soirée tonight.

'Never,' he muttered to himself.

Dear God, he remembered—how could he forget?— the Sheldons' daughter Georgina, who'd used to chase him with grim determination whenever he was back in London from abroad. Would she still be after him? No doubt.

He rose and began dressing himself. On their arrival in London Gilly had hired some housemaids and footmen, and on his way downstairs he saw they were already hard at work, sweeping and cleaning, opening shutters and polishing the big windows so the sunlight could pour in. Gilly was giving instructions to a pair of footmen as Ben entered the breakfast room, but Gilly sent them away and began to reproach his master instead.

'You should have allowed me to dress you, my lord. You ought to start living in a way that's appropriate to your rank.'

Ben had to grin. 'You can't wait to turn me into a fine lord, can you? It will be quite a while before I get used to all that again.'

'You can't deny you're enjoying the food.' Gilly looked on in satisfaction as the two footmen came back bearing a selection of hot dishes which they placed on the sideboard. One of them served Ben a plateful of ham, kidneys and eggs while the other poured him some coffee. Ben drank it with relish, feeling the rich and fragrant liquid restore his spirits.

Today marked the start of his new life. He had substantial evidence that his father was completely innocent of any wrongdoing. He was going to confront the Earl, even if it meant…

Losing Julia? *No.* He would do his damnedest to make things right between them. He would never forgive himself if he gave up on winning her love.

Later that morning he visited his bank to discuss the estate's financial affairs. 'You have considerable assets, my lord,' said his banker, 'together with income from rented property and various investments.' Enough, he was assured, to maintain his town house in some style and at the same time to completely repair and refurbish the Somerset estate.

Yes. He could open up Lambourne Hall. He could marry and have children, he could take them to watch the wild creatures in the beech woods and learn the joys of nature…

He stopped, because when he thought of the children's mother, he could picture no one but Julia. He saw her face vividly every night, before he went to sleep; he remembered her smiles and her shy laughter. Most of all he remembered her kisses. It was time, whatever the consequences, to visit the Earl of Carstairs and tell him about the crook Molloy. The Earl might be furious to have his word doubted, but the truth had to be known. He gave Gilly a letter to deliver to the Earl's house.

Lord Lambourne would welcome a meeting at a place of your choosing.

And Gilly returned soon afterwards.

'I was told,' he said, 'that the Earl is at his estate in Richmond for the day, but he's due back in town later this afternoon. I left your message with his butler.'

Ben was restless. He attended to more letters and invitations, then started to make notes about the work to be done on this house, but soon realised there was no peace to be found in any of the rooms, since there were servants everywhere. In the end he decided to go for a walk in nearby Hyde Park.

He had forgotten just how crowded the park could be on a fine afternoon such as this. The autumn air was cool, but the sun shone, and it seemed as if all the *ton* had decided to come here, whether on horseback, on foot or in elegant open carriages. He was dressed plainly and kept to the quieter paths, but more than a few of the passers-by glanced at him, then looked harder before coming towards him to say, 'It's Lambourne, isn't it? How good to see you back in town!'

They all, of course, noticed his halting walk and he knew he would have to accustom himself to giving the same explanations, over and over. 'Yes, I broke my leg in a riding accident in Austria, but it should get better in time. Yes, I'm back in London for a while and I'll try to get to your party next week…'

Or ball. Or dinner. Or—whatever.

Very soon he'd had enough of the interrogations, some of which were insistent. Besides, his leg was beginning to ache so he decided to set off home. He had just managed to extract himself from a noisy group of former Oxford friends when he noticed two well-dressed girls—sisters, he guessed—walking towards him on the main path.

He noticed them because he was aware that they were casting curious glances in his direction. They must be well born, for a maid was following at a discreet distance. He was slightly annoyed because now they were staring at him openly.

'Good afternoon, ladies,' he said, touching the brim of his hat and attempting to carry on.

But one of them, the older one, spoke up hesitantly, 'Excuse me, sir. But aren't you Lord Lambourne? I saw you last night, at the Duke of Danby's ball.'

He frowned. 'Who are you, may I ask?'

The girl replied swiftly. 'I'm sorry. You must think my sister and I are dreadful for intruding like this. But you see, I am Lady Penelope Carstairs—'

'And I'm Lady Lizzie!' broke in the younger one. 'Julia is our dear sister and she has just returned home from Somerset, where she stayed with our aunt Lady Harris. Julia told us that, there, she met someone called Ben and she—'

'Lizzie!' Her older sister nudged her with her elbow. 'Lizzie, not so fast.'

Ben took a steadying breath. Julia must have told them all about him. 'I am Lord Lambourne, yes,' he said.

Pen nodded. 'I thought so. Why did you tell my sister you were a stonemason, Lord Lambourne?'

That was direct. They obviously knew a good deal. 'Ladies,' he said. 'It was never, ever my intention to deceive your sister. As a matter of fact, I had no idea for quite a while who *she* was. We met unexpectedly because, to be quite honest, she had trespassed on my land and I didn't wish to embarrass her by telling her so. Then...' he hesitated again '...then we became friends.'

Lizzie clapped in delight. 'Julia was trespassing on your land? Oh, isn't that just like her! And you became friends—perfect.' Then she frowned. 'Lord Lambourne. Are you married?'

The girl asked it so suspiciously that he had to laugh. 'No,' he answered at last, 'I am not.'

'Or betrothed, maybe?'

'Most definitely not.'

'Thank goodness,' said Lizzie. 'Our sister likes you very much, you know. She has been positively brokenhearted since returning home and Pen and I simply cannot cheer her up.'

'Lizzie,' exclaimed her sister, 'you really are saying far too much, as usual.' She turned to Ben. 'I gather, my lord, that you and Julia had some kind of disagreement and parted badly. Is that true?'

Ben made his decision. He had to trust these two girls. He knew Julia loved them and they clearly had her confidence. Their maid, he noticed, had settled herself on a bench, still watching, but too far away to hear a word. Julia's sisters were waiting wide-eyed for him to tell them more.

He said, 'It's a long story. To put it briefly, there was a bad argument some time ago, between your father and mine. I feared your father might be very angry with Julia if he knew she'd met me.'

The girls were looking at one another with growing

amazement. 'Our father?' said Pen. 'Angry with *Julia*? Oh, never! Papa can be stern with other people, but really he is the softest, sweetest father imaginable. In fact he's lovely, as you'll realise as soon as you meet him…'

He realised Pen must have seen his reaction to that, for she drew a deep breath and said, 'Lord Lambourne, our sister Julia is pining away for you. Truly she is! So unless you've done something truly awful, like robbing a bank or gambling away your inheritance—'

'Or drinking like a fish. Like some of our brother Charles's friends,' added Lizzie.

Ben had to smile. 'I can assure you,' he said, 'that I'm not guilty of any of those heinous sins.'

Lizzie clasped her hands together. 'Lord Lambourne, tell us honestly. Do you really, really like my sister?'

'Lizzie,' scolded Pen. 'For heaven's sake!'

But Ben said quietly, 'I shall answer your question, Lizzie. Yes, I think the world of her.'

'Then you must do something,' Pen said decisively. 'You must call on our father, straight away.'

By now Ben was feeling a little dazed by this joint onslaught. 'That is my intention. I did send a message to him earlier today, but I was told he was not at home.'

'Oh, Papa drove out this morning to our house in Richmond, where he keeps all his horses. But he'll be back soon, although he'll probably go first to his club in St James's Street.' Pen screwed up her brow in thought. 'Lord Lambourne, now that you're in London you must be sent a good number of invitations. Have you received one to the musical soirée tonight, at Lord Sheldon's house in Kensington?'

'I have,' he said. 'Although I was not planning on attending.'

'But you must!' cried Pen. 'Mustn't he, Lizzie? We are all going, Papa, too.'

Lizzie nodded. 'Even though the Gorgon is awful.'

'The Gorgon?'

'That's what we call Georgina Sheldon. I suppose some might call her pretty, but she's also rather a monster and our father thinks so as well.'

'Hush your tattle, Lizzie,' rebuked Pen. 'This is a very serious conversation. Lord Lambourne, if you promise you'll be there tonight, then Lizzie and I will contrive to arrange matters so that you can see Julia on your own, just for a short time. Then you can tell her...' she went a little pink '...well, you can tell her anything you want. Anything *at all*.'

'It will be exceedingly romantic,' said Lizzie breathlessly. 'You can make everything all right with Julia, then you can tackle Papa, but don't worry because Pen and I will have him all sweetened up. He gets a little grumpy at musical evenings because he detests them, but we'll make sure that Mama lets him retreat into the card room, where he and his friends drink champagne and the music can't be heard. So he will hopefully be in a very good mood and we shall let you know exactly the right time to approach him. Won't we, Pen?'

'I agree. That really sounds like a good idea,' Pen said. 'Don't you think so, my lord?'

Ben still felt rather dazed. 'So I'm to speak with Julia and then your father. But do you really think this will work? It sounds complicated.'

'Maybe,' suggested Lizzie, 'we need a secret sign to

help us communicate with each other. A special wave, or a wink, or something.'

'No.' Pen was clearly growing impatient with her sister. 'We shall just go up to Lord Lambourne and tell him what to do.' She turned to Ben. 'You absolutely must be there, my lord! We shall not breathe a word to Julia and it will be a wonderful surprise for her.

'Now, I think we had better go, since I imagine our maid is getting fretful because we've been talking to you for so long. I shall tell her you are a nobleman and most respectable, but I shall also tell her she is *not* to mention this meeting to our parents. We'll see you tonight.' She wagged her finger. 'And you had better turn up, for Julia is quite heartbroken. She fears she has lost you *for ever*!'

Ben watched the sisters leave arm in arm, both still talking eagerly over their plan. He hadn't said yes. He hadn't said no either. But they'd told him that Julia loved him and he felt both the exhilaration and hope—a hope that was kindled further when he returned to his house to find a message from the Earl of Carstairs himself.

Had his daughters spoken to him already? Impossible. This message would have been sent long before the girls arrived home.

He read it.

Lambourne, I received your note. Kindly meet me at White's in St James's Street at five, if you are free.

Shortly before five he set off to White's club, where he, of course, was a member, like his father before him. He entered the lounge and realised the Earl of Carstairs was sitting in there already, talking with some distinguished-looking colleagues. The Earl rose to his feet as Ben approached.

'Lambourne,' he said.

'Lord Carstairs.' Ben nodded slightly. 'Thank you for agreeing to see me.'

The Earl looked around the busy room, then pointed to another door. 'I believe we can find ourselves a little more privacy through there.'

He led the way and Ben followed, noting that the room in which they arrived was furnished with only a few comfortable chairs set around the fire. A footman brought them claret and, as soon as he'd gone, the Earl sighed a little and said, 'I imagine that you wish to speak to me about your father. You were absent from his funeral, I believe? The last I heard, you were somewhere abroad, working for our government.'

'That is correct,' replied Ben. 'I was in Austria, on diplomatic business. But I injured my leg and I've only recently returned.'

The Earl lifted his glass and took a sip of the wine. Then he said, 'I wish I'd known you were back, Lambourne. You see, I've been hoping to speak with you for some time, about that rather awkward affair between your father and me.'

Ben's pulse raced but he drank a little wine also and waited to hear more.

'Well, young man,' the Earl continued, 'the argument between your father and myself has always troubled me. We were once friends, you see, but the matter of that horse I bought from him was the cause of some bitterness. So lately I've started looking into it all and I found that the dealer employed to convey the horse to my stables in Richmond has been struck from Tattersall's books. His name, I think, was Molloy, but unfortunately I don't know where he is.'

'I do,' said Ben. 'Francis Molloy was imprisoned for multiple crimes of fraud. He died in the Fleet a short while ago—and I've discovered that all his crimes were linked to his dealings with valuable horses.'

He drew a deep breath. 'Sir, I have good reason to believe that the horse delivered to you was not the one my father handed over to Molloy at his stables in Somerset. Somewhere on that journey, Molloy must have replaced my father's horse with the one you received—one that was valueless. Molloy was a clever criminal who got away with his tricks for many years.'

The Earl looked at him sharply. 'You're quite sure about this?'

'Indeed, my lord. I have physical proof in the form of a painting. I've also seen a copy of your vet's report making it plain that the horse you received was most definitely *not* Silver Cloud. There is also a former groom of my father's, who is willing to give evidence about the horse in court, if necessary. But I hope you'll agree that Molloy's name being struck from Tattersall's books speaks for itself.'

The Earl had been sipping his wine throughout, but Ben could tell he was listening carefully. Now he put his glass down. 'As I said, I've grown to regret this whole business, especially since your father's death. Unfortunately I have another appointment shortly, so I'll have to leave you now. But I promise I shall consider carefully what you've just said.' He rose, as did Ben, and the two men shook hands. 'Will you give me a little time?' said the Earl. 'I'll be in touch.'

Ben watched him depart. Nothing was yet settled, but he had to press on. Tonight, he would attend the Sheldons' party and see if it might be possible to talk to Julia properly, on her own. The evening might turn out to be a disaster, but he could not wait any longer.

He drank the last of his wine and set off for home.

Chapter Seventeen

The Carstairs family had mixed reactions to the invitation they'd received to the musical soirée.

'We must all go,' Lady Carstairs had said to her family over breakfast. 'The Sheldons have a number of distinguished friends—though not as many as us, of course—and it will be yet another formal outing for Julia, after her long absence from society!'

Her enthusiasm had not been shared by the rest of them. The Earl had spoken up hastily, saying that after a trip to Richmond he planned to dine at his club and might not be back in time. As for Charles, he was as blunt as ever. 'Mother, you know I hate musical soirées. Besides, Georgina Sheldon is quite intolerable.'

'The Gorgon,' Lizzie chuckled in an aside to Julia.

Her mother had heard and looked at her sternly. 'Lizzie!'

'I'm sorry, Mama.'

'Well, I hope, Lizzie, that you remember your manners tonight, because we are all going. Charles, since your father might be a little late, I would like you to escort us, if you please!'

* * *

By seven o'clock that evening, Julia was close to despair. She was in her bedroom, where she was supposed, like her sisters, to be preparing herself for the outing. But she did not want to go. In fact, she was dreading it.

She had slept badly after the Duke of Danby's ball last night. Seeing Ben there—talking to Ben there—had been unbearable because she still loved him, so much. But why would he bother with her, when he clearly had his pick of the *ton*'s debutantes? Why would he want to marry her, and be reminded for ever of what his father had suffered because of the dispute with her own father?

She understood now why he'd come to Lambourne Hall wanting time alone to grieve in private. Why he'd become so cold to her when he found out exactly who she was. She'd even wondered in these last few days if she could speak to her father herself about it, but, no— it was best to accept it was all over. *Least said, soonest mended*, her mother would briskly say.

The trouble was, Julia believed her heart would never mend. Worst of all, she would have to get used to seeing Ben at all the main society events. Would have to face the fact that, some day, he would get married. Meanwhile, there was tonight to be endured.

Betty, who was helping her to dress, was trying her hardest to instil some enthusiasm in her. 'My lady, you look lovely in your new gown. Really lovely. Look at yourself in the mirror—you are so very pretty!'

Julia looked. She barely recognised herself these days. Tonight, the pale blue silk gown she wore shimmered like silver when she moved, while Betty had pinned up her hair with skill. She was an earl's daughter with her whole, privileged future ahead of her and she guessed that once more tonight she would attract many admirers. She had changed beyond recognition because she knew now what it was like to be desired and to desire someone in return. But how many of her admirers would notice the sadness in her eyes?

Poor Betty had gone to such trouble over her and her mother had employed the most fashionable modiste in town to make her gown. But what was the point, when she missed Ben so dreadfully?

Charles had reminded her this morning that she just might see Ben again tonight. 'The Sheldons have several daughters to marry off,' he said, 'and Lambourne's a catch they won't be able to resist. If he is there this evening, you must treat him with the disdain he deserves.'

She had drawn herself up to her full height, which admittedly wasn't great. 'Charles, I hope you'll remember what I told you. If anyone has to be blamed for what happened between Ben and myself, then you must blame me.'

'Julia, you are being ridiculous!'

'I am not,' she'd said proudly. 'Charles, do I need to give you the actual details?'

Her brother had stalked off.

She still did not believe that Ben had decided to use her for his revenge against her father; indeed, Ben had positively tried to dissuade her from making her frequent visits to the pavilion, but she had taken no notice.

I encouraged him to make love to me! she reminded herself. *I did, I did—but I do not for one minute regret it!*

She would never forget the memory of his wonderful kisses and caresses in the pavilion as the rain beat down. She would have allowed him to go even further, but he was honourable, he was the one with the will-power to hold back. She knew he had been right to do so. But the trouble was, she couldn't bear being without him. She really couldn't.

Nor could she bear the thought of attending the soirée this evening, where she would doubtless have to listen to Georgina boasting about her skill on the piano and how half the gentlemen in London were in love with her.

Turning back to her poor maid, she suddenly said, 'I'm extremely sorry, Betty. But I'm not going to the Sheldons' house tonight.' She started pulling the pins from her hair. 'I shall tell Mama that I'm unwell.'

Betty moaned softly in despair, but then they both looked at the door, for they could hear approaching footsteps. Julia braced herself. Was it her mother? Or—worst of all—Charles, coming to read her the riot act again? Please, *no*…

The door was flung open and Pen and Lizzie burst in. They were both dressed in their finery, for Lizzie was coming to the Sheldons' house, too, a rare treat for the fourteen-year-old.

Lizzie pirouetted around Julia's bedroom. 'Look, Julia, look, Betty. What do you think of my new gown? Isn't it perfect?' Then she broke off. 'But, Julia, you aren't ready! What's happened to your hair? Whatever is the matter?'

Julia said quietly, 'I'm not going tonight. I shall tell Mother to give the Sheldons my apologies.'

Pen and Lizzie looked at each other in dismay. 'Julia,' said Pen firmly, 'you must attend. You really must.'

Why? Julia wondered. Why should it matter so much to them? 'Pen,' she said, 'I didn't expect you to force me! I really do not want to go and it's not even as if it's anything important.' Normally her sisters were on her side in everything, but this time they looked utterly dismayed.

Pen looked at Betty, who was listening with interest. 'Betty, would you leave us for a few moments, please?'

Betty curtsied and reluctantly headed for the door. After it had closed, Pen turned back to Julia. 'Now, my dear sister,' she said. 'Lizzie and I are going to make you really beautiful for tonight.'

Julia was mystified. 'Why? I've said I don't want to go, so why don't you take my side as you usually do? What mischief are you up to?'

Instead of providing an answer, Pen started looking for some face powder and Lizzie explored Julia's jewellery casket. 'No mischief,' said Pen firmly. 'But, Julia, we want you to do exactly what we say.'

Julia sighed. She knew there was no fighting them when they were in this mood, so she let her sisters set to work.

They tweaked her hair again, decorating it with two delicate diamond-studded silver combs. They powdered her face a little, adding also a touch of rouge to her lips and cheeks—and then, Pen tugged the bodice of her muslin gown just a tiny bit lower.

'No!' exclaimed Julia, looking down at herself in horror. 'I do not want to be put on display!'

'Nonsense. You will look very modest compared to the other girls there,' promised Pen. 'Georgina will have her bosom puffed up with cotton-wool padding as usual, but you don't need it and you'll look gorgeous. Now, let me put on your earrings and necklace—the pearl ones Father gave you for your eighteenth birthday. Lizzie, fetch Julia's blue silk shoes, will you? There now, Julia darling. You look wonderful and we love you very much.'

'But…why?' Julia was still mystified. 'Why all this fuss over a silly musical evening?'

Pen looked at Lizzie, then said, 'You've been away for quite some time. You'll be making a fresh start.'

Lizzie added, 'Just imagine Georgina's face when all the men crowd around you. Georgina and her mother will be livid!'

'I don't want to go,' Julia repeated. How often did she have to say it? Because if Ben was there, she really didn't think she would be able to bear it. Yes, some day soon she would have to get used to his constant presence in London. But…

Please, she silently begged her sisters. *I need time for my heart to heal first.*

Her sisters, however, clearly had no intention of changing their minds. 'Now,' said Pen briskly, 'I think our carriage should be waiting. The Sheldons live out in Kensington, so Charles has ordered it early. You'll remember that Papa has been at Richmond all day and since he intended dining at one of his clubs, he's promised to arrive at the soirée later. We'll be going with Mama and Charles, so come along, Julia! No time to lose!'

Julia sighed. No doubt Jeremy, Pen's fiancé, would be there and that was why she was in such a hurry. Without another word she allowed her sisters to drape her blue velvet cloak over her shoulders, then she followed them down the grand staircase.

Charles, who was already in the hallway and dressed as immaculately as ever, nodded approvingly when he saw Julia. 'You look very nice,' he said. He took her arm and led her out to the carriage while her sisters and mother followed, chattering away. But as Charles handed her in he took the opportunity to quietly say, 'We'll let bygones be bygones, shall we? I hope, Julia, that you have a wonderful time tonight.'

On their arrival at the Sheldons' magnificent house, they were greeted effusively by their hosts. The Sheldons expressed regret that the Earl himself was not with them, but Lady Carstairs answered promptly.

'My husband will arrive soon,' she declared.

'He better had,' whispered Pen to Julia. 'Or Mama will truly have something to say to him.' Already Pen and Lizzie were looking eagerly around the ornate hall to examine the gathered guests and Julia was surprised by their obvious curiosity, which was on the verge of appearing ill mannered. 'Are you looking for someone?' she asked at last. 'Didn't you tell me in the carriage, Pen, that Jeremy might not arrive for a while?'

'I did,' said Pen quickly. 'We are merely interested in seeing who's here already, that's all.'

At least there was no sign yet of Georgina. Julia, too, started looking around, preparing herself out of habit for the usual snubs from the ranks of eligible young men her mother would love her to marry.

But once again, just like last night, she was forced to acknowledge that something had definitely changed.

As her brother introduced her to the guests one by one, Julia noticed that the ladies nodded coolly, but the men bowed and murmured effusive greetings. Some even pressed light kisses to her hand.

'Enchanted, Lady Julia,' they said, or 'How truly delightful to meet you.' One voluble fellow said to Charles at her side, 'Where on earth have you been hiding this beauty, you rogue?'

Yes. The young men who only ever used to sigh over Pen were taking considerable interest in her. She remembered something Pen had once said, soon after she'd fallen for her Jeremy. 'It's strange, but being in love somehow makes other men notice you. It's as if you have some kind of aura about you.'

Ben had done this to her. Suddenly she felt a great and unbearable emptiness as she thought of how very wrong everything had gone between them. He was right to distance himself, of course. Right to be firm with her last night. She would have given everything up for Ben, but it was impossible.

She allowed herself to be introduced to more people whose names she forgot instantly. She talked to young men whose faces she barely registered. Jeremy had finally arrived, so he and Pen found a quiet corner where they could gaze into each other's eyes and whisper endearments. Julia's mother, with Lizzie rather reluctantly at her side, had joined a group of women who were eagerly discussing the latest fashions.

But Charles was continuing to keep a keen eye on Julia—an approving eye, as it turned out. 'Do you realise,' he said as he brought her a glass of lemonade, 'that you've become quite a talking point?'

Julia flinched. She did not want to be a 'talking point'.

Her brother was still smiling. 'You're a success, Julia. You always were quite pretty, you know, but something about you has changed. You've acquired an air of mystery. You don't appear terribly interested in any of the men who talk to you; in fact, you almost snubbed the Duke of Bristol's younger son just now.'

She was dismayed to hear that, but the Duke of Bristol's son had been so bashful that she truly hadn't been able to think of a thing to say to him. 'I'm sorry, Charles. I didn't mean to be rude to the poor man!'

Her brother patted her on the shoulder. 'Don't worry. In fact, it's rather clever of you, because you're driving all the young men wild with your lack of interest in them. Keep it up. A little aloofness on your part will land you a spectacular marriage, I promise. Who knows? You might attract a decent proposal or two before your Season even begins. Wouldn't our father be delighted? As for Mama, I think she might faint with joy.'

Julia couldn't speak.

He means well, she told herself.

Besides, it was no good arguing with him, it never was. He cared greatly for their family and she knew that if any of them were in trouble, he would defend them to the hilt. But she wanted to tear off her wildly expensive silk gown and jewels and instead put on the plain cotton dresses she'd worn in Somerset. She wanted to tug the silver combs from her carefully arranged hair, she wanted to scrub off her face powder and lip rouge and run—all the way back to Ben.

Except that he wasn't in Somerset, he was in Lon-

don. He wasn't Ben, her stonemason, he was Lord
Lambourne, and she'd told him she was never going to
marry—but that was just an attempt to hide from him
the agony in her heart. Somehow she kept a smile fixed
to her face. She was polite, she talked pleasantly to the
men who crowded around her and the time passed—
until disaster struck.

A group of latecomers had walked in and among
them was Tristram Bamford. His eyes widened in surprise when he saw her across the crowded room. Then
he positively leered.

For Julia, this was the final straw. She'd had enough.
She needed to get out, before this absolute horror of a
man got anywhere near her. She looked rather wildly
around. Charles, as it happened, had left her in order
to talk about horse racing with some friends on the far
side of the room and there was no sign of her mother.

Could she leave now and walk home? No, that was
ridiculous—they were in Kensington, for heaven's sake!
'Such a desolate place. Why, it's positively out in the
wilds,' her mother had moaned on the way here.

What could she do? Where could she hide?

Suddenly she caught sight of Pen beckoning to her
furiously. The guests were starting to move around now
because the Sheldons' oldest daughter, Miranda, was
about to play her flute and people were either occupy-
ing the rows of chairs or—as was the case with quite
a number of men—they were retreating swiftly to the
card room. Julia made her way between them all to
reach her sister.

'Julia,' instructed Pen, 'you must go to the orangery,
quickly, before that awful music starts. Or believe me,

I shall drag you there myself! Oh, there's Mother beck-oning us over. I shall go and keep her quiet. Please, just do as I say.' Pen moved off, before Julia could ask any more.

Julia was puzzled, but at least this gave her a chance to evade Tristram, so she headed for the orangery. She knew it well, for she and her mother and sisters had spent many a tedious afternoon in here sipping tea with Lady Sheldon and her daughters. Inside the glass-domed, candlelit room the delicate scent of citrus plants filled the air, while at the far end a bronze foun-tain trickled water into an ornamental pool. She stood there for a moment in bewilderment. Why on earth had Pen sent her here?

Suddenly she heard speedy footsteps followed by a very masculine shout of triumph. 'So that's where you've got to, you little tease!'

Julia whirled round to see Tristram Bamford bearing down on her. He slammed the door shut behind him; his strides were unsteady and his face was flushed. With a stab of fresh dismay, she realised he'd been drinking heavily and now he was coming closer, his arms out-stretched to block her escape.

'I spotted you back there in the hall,' he said, 'though at first I couldn't believe it. Charles, the rogue, never told me you would be here.' He chuckled. 'Maybe he wanted to surprise me and he's succeeded. What's happened to the skinny little wallflower in the awful dresses, eh? Come here, you tantalising creature, and stop looking so cross. I know you threw champagne over me last time we met, but I like a bit of passion.

Maybe it's time to get to know one another better. What do you say?'

'Get away from me, you drunken oaf!' cried Julia. She tried to slip past him and head for the door, but Tristram caught her by her shoulders and pulled her round to face him. He stank of spirits and in his eyes was a look that chilled her, for it was a dangerous mixture of desire and anger. He was much stronger than she and he was still holding her tightly.

Desperately she pummelled at his chest. 'My brother will call you out for this!'

'But your brother's nowhere near. Is he?' He was using one burly hand to tilt up her chin while gazing hotly down at her. 'Calm down, sweetheart. And don't make too much noise, because if we're caught together in here—well, you know what people will say. So let's be nice to each other, shall we? Because I think it might be rather a good idea, since there's already been gossip about the two of us, if I persuaded you to marry me.'

She kicked him on the shin. It wasn't terribly effective, but it annoyed him badly and she saw pure rage glitter in his eyes. Then he smiled again, a deadly smile.

'Oh, dear,' he said softly, shaking his head. 'Oh, dear me. Now, that was not a good idea, Lady Julia. Was it?'

Earlier that evening, Gilly had been unable to hide his amazement when Ben told him where he was going. 'The Sheldons? I warn you, Georgina will pounce on you, my lord. There'll be no escape.'

Gilly was right as usual, because as soon as Ben was announced by the pompous butler he was approached with great delight by Lady Sheldon, with Georgina by her side.

'So kind of you, my lord,' gushed Her Ladyship, 'to show such interest in my family's musical talents!'

Georgina, who wore an extraordinary gown which displayed most of her thrust-up bosom, simpered up at him from behind her fan. 'You will not, I trust, judge my little performance on the pianoforte too harshly, my lord?'

'Of course not,' said Ben with some confidence, since he very much hoped to be as far from the piano as possible.

But Lady Sheldon had thought of that. 'You will need a comfortable chair to sit on, Lord Lambourne,' she pronounced. 'Since I imagine your poor leg causes you pain if you have to stand for too long. Georgina, dearest, why don't you sit with His Lordship over there—do you see?—and I will order champagne to be brought to you immediately.'

She was pointing to an alcove in which were a small table and two chairs.

Ben felt angry and frustrated. So far this evening he'd seen no sign of Julia or her family and now he found himself being led by Georgina into a half-curtained alcove where he half listened to the girl's babble, he drank three glasses of champagne and tried all the time to keep an eye on the room for new arrivals. When he finally saw Julia enter on her brother Charles's arm, he put his glass down abruptly.

Georgina had clearly seen them, too, for she said with a profound sigh, 'Do you know, I feel dreadfully sorry for Lady Julia Carstairs.'

Ben spoke sharply. 'Why?'

'Because, poor thing, she's totally unlike her sister Pen. Sadly, Julia has not got her sister's looks and she is of a rather awkward disposition. Many of us fear she will have great difficulty finding a husband and—' She broke off and peered in another direction. 'Oh, my goodness. I see that my mother is beckoning me to the piano!' Georgina was already on her feet. 'My sister Miranda is about to play her flute and I am to accompany her. I cannot believe how many people are eagerly awaiting our performance! So I fear, Lord Lambourne, that I must leave you for a while in order to entertain our audience. I do hope that after all your illustrious travels to the capitals of Europe, you do not find my family's offerings too pitiable!'

As soon as Georgina had gone Ben rose, too. Julia was here and it was time to find her—to speak to her in private, if possible. But unlike Georgina, who had merrily pushed her way through everyone even if it meant forcing them to move their chairs, he was trapped unless he wanted to make a public spectacle of himself. Yes, trapped, with just a bottle of champagne for company, while at any minute that awful music was about to start—

He suddenly jumped up because he'd realised that someone was underneath his chair.

Highly puzzled, he bent to investigate and saw Lizzie Carstairs gazing up at him. 'Lord Lambourne!' she hissed.

'Lizzie. What on earth are you doing down there?'

'I had to wriggle under the curtains.' She tapped the

draperies that formed a half-circle around this alcove. 'It was the only way to reach you.'

He'd assumed those curtains were purely ornamental but now, as Lizzie tugged one aside an inch or two, he glimpsed an open doorway to a corridor beyond.

'You must,' Lizzie was hissing, still on her knees, 'go to Julia now! We've sent her to the orangery and she needs to speak to you urgently. Well, perhaps she doesn't realise it yet, but trust me, she does!'

This time he asked no questions. Instead he rose and eased himself silently through that doorway while Lizzie, after whispering an excited 'Good luck!', waved him on his way. But as soon as he reached the entrance to the orangery he realised something was badly wrong. He'd noticed Tristram Bamford arriving a short while ago and Ben always avoided the man because he loathed him—but now he saw that as well as Julia, Bamford was in there, too, and the wretch had his hands on her.

Revulsion together with absolute fury rose like bile in his throat. Somehow Lizzie and Pen's plan had gone badly wrong. He strode in, noting that Bamford had his back to him so he hadn't seen him yet, but Julia had and she was deathly white. 'Ben,' she whispered. 'Ben, thank God you're here.'

Bamford turned round when he heard her, letting his hands drop to his sides. Of course, his reaction was the opposite. He exclaimed, 'Lambourne. What the *hell*?'

Ben squared up to the other man. 'You bastard, Bamford,' Ben said. 'How dare you lay one filthy finger on Lady Julia Carstairs?'

Bamford puffed out his chest. 'How is it you're taking it on yourself to interfere in what Lady Julia gets up to? You've been out of London for quite a while and so has she. Do I sense a whiff of scandal here?' He smirked and glanced at Julia, then back at Ben. 'Tell me, Lambourne, you rogue. Have you taken advantage of her?'

Ben clenched his right hand into a fist, aimed it at Bamford's chin and felled him.

It was not, he was well aware, a good idea. It wouldn't silence the bastard for good. But damn, it was satisfying. As Bamford started to heave himself up, Ben stood over him and waited till he was on his feet. Then he said, 'I think you'd better go home. Your nose is bleeding and some of it's on your ridiculous cravat.'

Bamford put his handkerchief to his nose. 'I'll get you for this,' he muttered. 'You and her. Something's been going on between you two, hasn't it?' He was looking at Julia. 'You, my lady, have always looked so damned innocent. But now, I'm beginning to wonder. Her brother will definitely be interested in this—'

He broke off because Ben had grasped the lapels of his very expensive coat. 'If I were you, I'd think hard before saying anything about what's happened here, You might have to explain your own actions, because when I arrived, it looked very much as though you were assaulting Lady Julia. You'd best remember that before you open your big mouth, because I would rather enjoy shutting it again for you. Do you understand?'

'If you think you can silence me with threats—'

'I certainly hope so. But there are other ways.'

With one unceremonious shove, Ben pushed him towards the ornamental pond and Bamford toppled into the water with an ungainly splash. The fountain continued to trickle merrily away as he slowly and soggily hauled himself out.

'Well, Bamford?' said Ben, folding his arms across his chest. 'Are you still going to speak with Julia's brother? Go on, then. Off you go. He'll be in the card room, I'd guess. But I don't think he'll listen to a word you say and neither will anyone else. They'll be too busy laughing at you, because you resemble a drowned rat.'

'I'll get you for this, Lambourne,' Bamford muttered. 'Don't you worry.'

'You can try, I suppose. But I warn you, it won't be easy and if I were you I'd head for home now, before anyone sees how ridiculous you look.'

Bamford scowled and glanced briefly at Julia. Then he opened the door that led out into the gardens and disappeared into the darkness.

Silence enveloped the orangery except for the steady tinkling of the fountain. For a moment Ben stood very still, feeling as if his future lay on a knife edge. Then Julia looked up at him and said, 'You know, you really did hit him rather hard.'

She was stifling a smile and his heart soared. He said, 'I know I did. Julia, I'm sorry if my actions offended you.'

'He deserved it,' she said. 'I could have cheered. Oh, Ben.' She was coming slowly towards him. 'Ben, I have missed you so badly.'

He felt as though all the tension that had gripped his body was being steadily released. Hope began to stir in his heart, making him almost dizzy with joy. He put his arms around her and held her as if he would never let her go.

'My God, Julia,' he whispered. 'My God, I've missed you too. You don't know how much.'

To hell with waiting for her father to come to some decision. He loved this girl. He needed her to make his life in any way meaningful and from the look that was in her gorgeous eyes, she felt exactly the same.

She nestled into his embrace and laid her head against his chest as if she'd found where she wanted to be for the rest of her life and he thought, *She is everything to me. Never will I let her go again.*

Chapter Eighteen

Tristram Bamford's assault had shocked Julia. Indeed, he had terrified her, but when Ben had entered the room her heart had leaped because—oh, my—he looked so very fine in his black evening coat, with his white cravat tied so perfectly that Charles would be madly jealous. She had to smile, though, when she saw that his wayward brown hair was as tousled as ever, reminding her of the precious hours they had spent together and those kisses they had shared.

Her heart was full of emotion. She looked up at him and said, 'After last night, I thought you might not speak to me again.'

He was still holding her as he answered softly, 'I was never going to give up on you, though I guessed it might take me a while to make everything right between us. I certainly wasn't going to come here tonight, because I hate musical evenings.' He smiled, a smile that warmed her. 'But then, your sisters took a hand in the matter.'

'My *sisters*? Ben, how on earth…?'

He chuckled, that lovely, husky sound she loved so

much. 'They accosted me in the park this afternoon. Pen had recognised me from the ball last night. I gather you and your sisters have very few secrets?' Ben looked at her with one eyebrow slightly raised.

She blushed, but smiled, too. 'I love my sisters very much. I trust them, too. But oh dear, how extremely forward of them to approach you like that in the park! I gather Mama wasn't with them?'

'No, only a maid, who kept well out of the way. Anyway, they assured me that you were missing me badly.'

'Yes. Oh, yes! Ben, I felt that last night was a disaster, wasn't it? I hated seeing you with all those other girls and I didn't know how I could possibly compete. Then Lady Eleanor came for you, so I tried to act as if I didn't care.'

He was listening intently. 'I felt the same. You looked lovely, as lovely as you do tonight, and I thought I'd made such a mess of everything. I had resolved I would never give you up, but I wondered if maybe I should leave you alone for a while. Then I met your sisters in the park today and they told me that I absolutely had to come to this awful affair tonight and speak to you.'

'So Pen and Lizzie took a part in this,' she said softly. 'But how did you know, that I was in here—' she gestured around the room with one hand '—and in such trouble?'

'I did not know about Bamford,' he said grimly, 'and clearly your sisters didn't either. The man's a despicable wretch. I was looking for you, of course, from the moment I arrived, but there was no sign of you anywhere and I was collared by Georgina Sheldon. But then your sister Lizzie found me and whispered that I must come here, to the orangery. She said you needed to speak to me.'

'My sisters are mischief-makers, there's no doubt about it! Pen sent me here to the orangery and I had no idea why, but I see it all now. They wanted the two of us to meet in private. But of course they couldn't have known about Tristram. He must have been watching me. Following me.'

'I only wish,' he said, 'that I'd hit him harder. It's as well there weren't any fishes in that pond. He'd likely have poisoned the water.'

Julia almost laughed, but stopped herself. *No.* This wasn't funny. This was awful. Bamford would talk, she was sure, and Ben might be feeling that he had to offer marriage to her without really, truly wanting to, so she drew a deep breath and looked up at him.

'Ben,' she said, 'I realise you've been manipulated into a very awkward situation, for which I hope you'll forgive my sisters. They really had no business interfering, so I'll quite understand if you feel you must leave—'

He halted her by putting one finger under her chin and turning her face up to his. 'My darling Julia,' he said in that husky voice that was almost a sensual onslaught in itself. 'Do you really think that I've been *manipulated* into doing anything in my life? Do you think for one moment I would let you leave my life for good? If your sisters hadn't suggested I come here tonight, I would have watched out for you every day, thinking of your welfare, your happiness. You see, I was prepared to be patient.'

Oh. Suddenly the blood rushed to her head. What was he saying? Was he saying that he truly loved her?

She whispered, 'Do you remember what I wrote in my foolish notebook? You *did* read it, didn't you?'

He smiled. 'I'm afraid I did.' His brown eyes were full of laughter.

'I wrote,' she said softly, 'that I wished I had met someone like you earlier and I meant it. But oh, Ben! Why didn't you tell me who you were? Didn't you trust me? Did you think me a fool?'

'Never,' he said fiercely. 'Never have I thought you a fool. I'm the one who's stupid, not to explain everything from the beginning.'

Ben had his arms around her now and, thank God, she didn't move away. Instead she leaned back a little and gazed up at him. 'I suspected from the beginning you were well-born, you know,' she said.

He smiled a little. 'You kept your suspicions well hidden.'

'I did, yes.' She nodded. 'There were so many things that seemed odd, like you living at the Hall and that doctor coming out at night when you went for him. I wondered about your story of your poor father dying alone and the terrible guilt you felt. It was because of the feud between our fathers, wasn't it?'

His chest tightened. 'You know, then? About the horse your father bought from mine?'

'My brother told me when he came to take me home. Well, his version of it anyway.' Julia sighed. 'I'm afraid he is angry about it still. But it is truly unfair of him. Why should you be held responsible for your father's actions?'

Ben felt the shadows of the past clustering around them. This was it. This was the crux of the problem. He said, unable to keep the harshness from his words, 'But it was not my father's fault, Julia. He was blamed for a crime he did not commit and after that he allowed the estate to go to rack and ruin. He stopped taking care of himself. His life had lost its value to him—and I wasn't there to help.' He drew a deep breath. 'Do you remember me telling you about the man who died in the quarry?'

Julia recoiled in shock. 'Oh, no. Ben. You're not saying...'

'Yes. It was my father. Did he kill himself? There's no way of knowing for sure. His body was found at the bottom of the quarry by his valet, who'd been expecting him back hours before. He often went out to walk in the woods, so he may well have slipped and tumbled into the quarry by accident.' He added, in a voice she could barely hear, 'I should have been with my father. Defending his name. Giving him some kind of hope for the future.'

Julia shook her head. 'Ben, please don't do this to yourself. Your father must have loved you very much. Your success would have been a true comfort to him.'

'I hope that's true. But do you understand now why I felt my first priority, once I was back on my feet again, was to clear his name?'

'I do! Of course I do!' she cried. 'Have you succeeded in finding out yet what really happened?'

'I have and there's much more to the story than your brother knows. You see, there was a crook, a middle-man who stole that horse while it was being transported to your father's Richmond stables and replaced it with another that was worthless.'

'Have you proof? Can you convince my father about all this?'

'I hope so. In the meantime—' and Ben found he was smiling at last '—your sisters gave me a direct warning. They told me that I had to turn up tonight, or face the direst consequences.'

She smothered a laugh, then went to sit on one of the chintz-covered sofas in there. 'I really must apologise again for them!'

She looked so sweet that he wanted to pick her up in his arms and run off with her. Instead he went to sit next to her and took her hand. 'There's no need at all for apologies,' he said. 'Julia, I hope you can believe me when I say that I've never stopped thinking about you. Never stopped missing you. But this business with your father—I knew I had to settle it before I could do anything else.'

He stroked back a stray lock of hair from her cheek. He'd already decided he was not leaving here tonight without seeing the Earl, if indeed he arrived, which Julia's sisters had assured him would happen. He said, 'It might be sooner than you think.'

She listened. 'What,' she said quietly, 'can I do to help?'

He reached to pull her close to his heart. 'Be there for me, when all this is over. Will you promise?'

'Of course I promise! But I'm afraid my brother found out that I'd been seeing you during my stay at Lady Harris's and he was furious about it. He told me that…'

'What, Julia? What did Charles tell you?'

He sounded different now, she realised. Fierce, almost. She said, in a low voice, 'Charles told me that you must have decided to use me for your revenge. Revenge against my father, because of the trouble over the horse.' She saw his expression darken and her heart sank.

But Ben held her even closer. 'Julia,' he said, 'oh, my love, how could your brother fill your mind with such poison?'

She shook her head a little. 'He was trying to protect me, I suppose. But, Ben, I've believed in you always and I told Charles so! When he said that you must have been trying to seduce me to get your own back on our father, I told him he was wrong.' She hesitated, watching his expression. 'In fact, I told him it was the other way round—because I was the one trying to seduce *you*!'

She saw his eyes widen. 'You told him *that*?'

'Yes, I did, because it was true! You were honourable towards me, always. You tried to keep your distance, but I was the one chasing you, just like the Gorgon.'

'The Gorgon!' He laughed. 'I've been hearing that name quite often. You mean Georgina Sheldon?'

'Indeed. She told me she is determined to marry you and I loathe that girl. But I truly am worse than her, because now you've been trapped in here alone with me and, if anyone sees us, if Tristram talks, I have put you in a quite impossible situation!'

'I don't find it impossible at all,' he said. 'I find it quite wonderful. For weeks now I've lain awake at night, thinking of you. When I sleep, I dream of you. I remember the way you kissed me and what happened between us in the pavilion that last afternoon.'

'Me, too,' she whispered. 'I shall never forget it.' She laid her cheek against his chest and Ben held her even closer.

'My darling Julia,' he said. 'When I first met you, I thought you were like no one I'd ever met—you were beautiful, original and independent. But when I realised you were the Earl of Carstairs's daughter, I decided I must stop seeing you, because I guessed your father would never allow me even to speak with you, let alone dream of marrying you. Do you understand?'

'Yes,' she whispered. 'Yes, I do. But we didn't manage to stay apart for long, did we?'

Tenderly he brushed a wayward lock of hair back from her forehead. 'No. I think I would always have had to find some way to be with you again, because I've missed you very badly.'

'But what can we do?' She spoke a little shakily. 'My brother is here tonight and I'm afraid that, if he sees us like this, he will be very angry. He will tell my father that I fell in love with you in Somerset—and surely there could not be a worse way for him to learn of it.'

'I'm hopeful that your father and I can reconcile our differences soon,' said Ben. 'Because I want to ask him for your hand in marriage. Julia—will you marry me?'

Her heart was full. Who would have believed, two months ago, that the word 'marriage' could be the most wonderful one she had ever heard? How she had dreaded this ultimate commitment, but now her love for this man had melted away all her fears. 'Ben. Oh, Ben—do you mean it?'

'Of course I do.' He smiled. 'Lady Julia Carstairs, I love you very much—in fact, I adore you, so I'll ask you again. Will you be my wife?'

'Yes. Of course I will.' She could not keep the smile

from her face, and after a moment she glanced up at him almost mischievously. 'Charles might not be happy.'

'Oh, Charles.' He shrugged. 'If your brother should object, it's no problem because I'm handier with my fists than him by far, even if I have got a lame leg.'

Julia gasped. 'You mean you'd fight him?'

He laughed. 'Preferably not. My God, what a way to propose, by suggesting I could demolish your brother! I should be presenting you with flowers and romantic music and a diamond ring. But, Julia, please believe me when I say I shall do everything in my power to make you happy.'

For a moment she couldn't speak. True, there was no ring, no champagne—but there were those fragrant citrus trees and the music of the fountain to make the moment as magical as anything she could have dreamed of.

She felt like a princess in a fairy tale. No longer was she the girl lingering alone at parties, desperate to escape from the elaborate rituals of London society. She was Julia and Ben, her stonemason, loved her. Come what may, she was not letting go of this man.

She took his hands and whispered, 'You've already made me happier than I thought was possible, darling Ben.'

He pressed his lips to her fingers, causing tantalising shivers to ripple through her entire body. 'You know,' he said softly, 'if I've made mistakes—and I have, I know—it's because I never expected anything like this to happen to me. I went to Lambourne Hall to be alone while I tried to hunt for a way to clear my father's name. But then I met you—and, God help me, I fell in love.'

She smiled mischievously. 'I've told you that I fell in

love with you the moment I saw you. It was when you came to help us with the carriage.'

He pretended to look puzzled. 'I thought it was your maid who couldn't tear her eyes from me.'

'Yes, poor Betty was smitten—I remember! Afterwards, Ben, she would not stop talking about you!'

He said wickedly, 'But you were taking note of me, too, weren't you? Despite those rough clothes I was wearing.'

This time she flung her arms around his neck, wanting him so much that her blood ran hot and fast in her veins. 'You *know* I did. Didn't I tell you I would run away with you if you asked me to?'

'To live in a cottage?' he teased.

'Yes! A cottage! I truly meant it!' She added more seriously, 'Perhaps I was trying to say that I would give up everything for you if I had to.'

'But you won't have to give everything up,' he said. 'I swear it. I will never trap you into the kind of life I know you'd loathe, a life consisting of nothing but balls and parties.'

'Don't forget the musical soirées,' she said, her eyes shining with laughter as the distant sound of a warbling Sheldon daughter penetrated the peace of the orangery. 'Please, can we ensure we never have to attend another one?'

'Not a single one,' he said emphatically. 'Though I'm afraid I will have responsibilities to the estate that mean I won't always be able to live as freely as I'd wish. Do you think you can bear that, Julia?'

'Of course,' she said. 'You've changed me, in all kinds

of ways. You've made me feel free to be the person I want to be, whether I'm living in a cottage or a palace.'

'So you're quite sure you'll marry me?'

'Of course I am.' Her eyes glowed with love. 'Only can it be very soon? *Please?* And, Ben—will you kiss me again?'

Ben realised she was touching his cheek with her finger. It was only a light touch, but the caress held so much sensual promise that his blood pounded. She looked enchanting in her silk dress and her lips were full with longing. What could he do, but agree? He gathered her in his arms and her low gasp of pleasure set his blood racing all over again.

He let his lips brush hers gently at first, giving himself time to relish their velvety softness. He told himself he had the strength of mind to go no further, not here, not yet, but just as he managed to pull away, Julia took his hand in hers, lifted his fingers to her lips and kissed them one by one. When she raised her eyes to his he could see the mischief sparkling in their depths.

'I suppose, until we are formally betrothed, I should be calling you "Lord Lambourne",' she said. 'Shouldn't I?'

That did it. His restraint was demolished by her delicious smile.

'Call me Ben,' he grated out. 'My name is *Ben.*'

Then his arms were round her and he let one hand slip down her back to pull her even closer so that her small breasts were compressed against his ribs. He groaned aloud, for his loins were throbbing with need. She was Julia and she was all he could ever want.

He kissed her passionately and she opened to him,

welcoming him. He slid his tongue between her lips and her growing boldness as she responded with hers thrilled him to his core.

He felt himself losing whatever was left of his self-control, forgetting all the warnings that had been ringing through his brain—*someone might come in. Someone might see us.*

If he and Julia were discovered like this, it would be the talk of the town. He should have spoken to her father first. But whatever happened, he could not give this girl up. It was impossible—

Suddenly he heard her give a cry of alarm. He sprang to his feet to see that the door had flown open and someone was charging in—her brother. Charles slammed the door shut, shaking the leaves on the citrus trees and making all the candles quiver. He looked almost rigid with fury.

'Lambourne!' he cried. 'I *knew* you'd been trying to seduce my sister as revenge, you bastard. And, Julia, I thought you'd promised me this was all over!'

Ben had raised his hands in a gesture of peace, but Charles was squaring up to him, his fists clenched. Ben said, 'I think you've got things rather in a muddle, Carstairs. Can't we talk this over?'

'I'll do what I damned well like,' declared Charles, 'when it's a matter of defending Julia's honour. Put your fists up!'

'Ben,' cried Julia, 'please don't fight! And, Charles, you are being completely ridiculous. Ben has always behaved towards me with the utmost honour, I've told you that! And you mustn't threaten him, because surely you can see he has an injured leg?'

* * *

Julia realised instantly that she'd made a mistake, for on hearing her words Ben raised his fists as fiercely as Charles. 'Damn my leg,' he growled. 'I will not stand for these insults from you, Carstairs!'

Oh, no. They were going to fight. Julia rushed in front of Ben to protect him, but that, too, was a mistake, for Ben, her dear, beloved Ben, was clearly worried about her safety in the face of her brother's fury, so he took his eyes off Charles and pushed her to one side. At the same moment Charles let fly with a blow that landed full on Ben's jaw, forcing him to stumble to the ground.

Julia uttered a cry of distress and crouched at his side. 'Oh, my darling. Are you hurt?' She shouted up at her brother, 'You are a fool, Charles! Ben is good and kind and honourable—and haven't I already told you that it was actually *me* who tried to seduce *him*? Tonight he's asked me to marry him and I'm going to, even if we have to do it without my father's permission! Anyway, we must marry now, because you've caught us in here alone. Would you rather I was the wife of that idiot Tristram Bamford? Do you know that tonight he tried to force himself on me in here, until Ben arrived and thumped him?'

Ben was scrambling to his feet now, so she flung her arms around him and kissed him. 'Ben. I love you so very much.' She kissed him again and, in fact, was still doing so when the door to the orangery opened once more and this time her father, the Earl, came in, with Pen and Lizzie close behind. At first her sisters gasped with shock when they saw what was going on, then they looked absolutely delighted.

Ben was having trouble extricating himself from Julia's kiss. 'Papa!' Julia exclaimed. 'And Pen. And Lizzie. Oh, my goodness…'

Her voice trailed away as she realised exactly what they had all seen. But she didn't care, she truly didn't. She took Ben's hand.

The Earl gazed around at the various expressions on the faces of his offspring, then he addressed Ben. 'Lord Lambourne,' he pronounced, in the voice he used when he had something very important to say. Julia found she could hardly breathe, but still she held Ben's hand and stayed close by his side.

'I know, Lambourne,' the Earl continued, 'that you and I have unsettled business to conclude. I must confess I'd hoped to arrange somewhere more private for us to talk, but it appears that you and my daughter have been making decisions of your own. So perhaps we'd best get on with the matter now.' The Earl looked round at his family, including the still-scowling Charles. 'If the rest of you would leave us? Just for a few moments?'

'Not me, Papa,' said Julia swiftly. 'I am staying.'

The Earl hesitated, then said, 'I guessed as much. Very well.' He escorted the others to the door.

'You see, my love?' Julia whispered to Ben. 'I think there is hope for us. If not—' and she stood on tiptoe to kiss him again '—I swear, I am running away with you.'

'Rebel,' he replied. He smiled down at her. 'What *am* I letting myself in for?'

The Earl had closed the door and now he came back to face them. 'I've been checking, Lambourne,' he said, 'on everything you told me earlier this evening.'

Julia looked up at Ben with wide eyes.

'Yes, Julia,' her father continued, 'Lord Lambourne and I held a brief but enlightening discussion together and, after considering what he said, I've decided that I owe both him and his father a heartfelt apology.' He turned to Ben. 'I regret not having investigated the matter earlier myself, but...well, I hope you will forgive me? As for my daughter, I gather that you and she have formed a strong attachment.'

'We have,' said Ben. 'And I would like to assure you that your daughter is extremely precious to me.'

'I can see that,' said the Earl. Suddenly he smiled. 'Any fool can see it. Even me.' He came forward to shake Ben's hand. 'I've made mistakes, Lambourne, I see that now, and I'm sorry, so very sorry about the slur on your father's reputation. You must have felt considerable bitterness on his behalf.'

'I would be lying if I said the whole business hadn't affected me, my lord. But now that I know the truth, I realise you were tricked every bit as much as my father.' Ben looked the Earl straight in the eye. 'In some ways, I've always blamed myself for my father's unhappiness. If I'd been there for him, I might have solved Molloy's crime myself, in time to prevent the feud between the two of you.'

The Earl shook his head. 'My good fellow, you must not reproach yourself, ever. I remember that your father was extremely proud of you and your vital work for our country; in fact, I've heard nothing but good reports about you from various friends in government departments.

'As I said to you earlier, I've come to greatly regret the unpleasantness between our families. Besides, it seems—' and he glanced with wry humour at his daughter '—that Julia has already made up her mind about you. Believe me, I know from long experience that there is no shifting her opinion once her mind is made up!'

'Lord Carstairs,' said Ben, 'I realise that I've only known your daughter for a short while. But I love and respect Julia very much and I would like you to consider allowing me her hand in marriage.'

'Oh,' said the Earl, waving his hand, 'I don't need time to consider it, young man. I see quite clearly how I can make amends for the past, by allowing you to court her. Besides, it's obvious from the looks on both your faces that the matter is as good as settled, so I am extremely happy to give the pair of you my blessing.'

He stepped forward to put his hands lightly on Julia's shoulders. 'My dear, your mother will be delighted. Although I fear she'll be a little disappointed that she won't have the pleasure of your Season!'

Julia couldn't help but smile. 'Thank you, dear Papa. I always knew you were the kindest and best father in the world!'

She turned to Ben, who looked so handsome and so wonderful that she wanted to pour out all her words of love and all her hope for their future together. But not here. Not now.

There will be time, she promised herself. *All the time in the world to tell this man how much he means to me.*

So in the end, all she did was to give him a little smile and whisper, 'You see? Everything has turned out quite, quite wonderfully!'

Ben touched his jaw where Charles had hit him and

grinned a little ruefully. 'Just about,' he said. 'Although I'm not sure your brother would agree.'

The Earl was frowning. 'I gather you and my son had a disagreement in here before I arrived?'

'A slight misunderstanding,' said Ben.

'Hmm. Well, I shall have a word with Charles. He can be somewhat arrogant, so I shall be sure to take him down a peg or two.' He pointed his finger at Ben. 'But on one condition. You make sure you take good care of my precious daughter. Do you promise?'

'Of course,' said Ben quietly. 'She is precious to me, too, so with all my heart, I promise.'

The Earl was about to say more, but instead he turned towards the door—in fact, they all did, because even though it was closed they could hear the sound of more awful singing from the Sheldon sisters, accompanied this time by an out-of-tune harp.

'I think,' pronounced the Earl of Carstairs, 'that it's time I gathered up my family and we all set off home.'

Epilogue

Because Pen's much-anticipated wedding to Jeremy was to take place very soon, Lady Carstairs declared that Julia and Ben's wedding had to wait until spring. 'The month of May would be ideal!' she declared one afternoon when all the family were gathered in the sitting room. 'A wedding in the earlier months of the year would be hideously unfashionable and besides, almost all of the *ton* would be at their winter residences and unable to attend.'

'Mama,' said Julia, 'Ben and I hoped it would be sooner. I thought you might be relieved if we wanted a quiet ceremony with less preparation. After all, Pen and Jeremy's wedding is taking up a good deal of your time and rightly so!' She reached to squeeze the hand of her sister, who sat next to her on the sofa. 'Pen is your oldest daughter, so she deserves a grand affair. But Ben and I would be happy to… I don't know.' She shrugged and smiled. 'We could be married at the church in Richmond, perhaps, and hold a small party at our house there.'

Lizzie chuckled. Her mother gave a faint whimper of dismay, while Charles, who stood with his back to the fire, gave a sigh as if nothing Julia said surprised him any more. But then, much to Julia's surprise, Charles spoke up for her. 'It's Julia's wedding, Mother,' he said. 'Shouldn't she be able to say what she prefers? As it happens, I've also spoken to Ben Lambourne on the matter.'

Julia's mouth opened in amazement. 'You *have*?'

'Indeed,' said Charles. He looked faintly embarrassed by his confession, but after a moment he nodded firmly. 'I must say, I've been pleasantly surprised by the fellow. We talked about plans for the wedding and he said he'll be happy with whatever Julia and our family prefer.'

Their father, who appeared to be hiding a slight smile at this unexpected contribution from Charles, was listening in approval. 'My dear,' he said to his wife, 'I feel that keeping Julia and Ben apart for several months might be seen as a sign of unhappiness on our part, which is certainly not the case. Wouldn't you agree?'

Poor Lady Carstairs was clearly in a dilemma. 'Go on, Mama,' encouraged Lizzie. 'Do agree with Papa, please.'

'Well,' said their mother at last, 'I suppose I must. An early wedding it shall be.'

'Hooray!' said Lizzie. The three sisters looked at each other and smiled.

'In that case,' said the Earl, 'I suggest that we hold the wedding in February, here in London. In fact, I wouldn't be surprised if we have a considerable number of guests, since the countryside at that time of year can be very dull.'

'And you know, Mama,' put in Pen, 'how very good you are at arranging parties. You've had such fun over-seeing my wedding celebrations and just think—once mine is over, you'll be able to start on Julia's! You will absolutely be the talk of the town!'

'That is true,' said their mother, somewhat mollified. Then she stifled a burst of laughter. 'I've had a sudden thought. Lady Sheldon has four daughters to marry off and I've heard not a whisper of a single proposal—whereas my Pen is to be married to a viscount's heir and dear Julia is marrying a baron, no less!' She smirked. 'Poor Lady Sheldon will hardly be able to face me when next we meet.'

Charles patted his mother's shoulder. 'There you are, then. I believe it's all decided.' He looked at his sister. 'Julia, I wish you every happiness in the world with Ben Lambourne. I really do.'

Julia had feared that the next few weeks would have dragged interminably, but in fact the time flew by. Pen and Jeremy's wedding in November took up much of the family's attention and was an event of great joy, while the Christmas season, too, was filled with out-ings and parties.

Meanwhile, the Earl had given Julia his permission to meet with Ben almost every day, supposedly with a chaperon in place. But quite often when Ben visited the house Lizzie, who was Julia's one true ally now that Pen had gone travelling to France with her husband, contrived all kinds of ways to distract Lady Carstairs from keeping a close eye on the couple. So Ben and Julia were often able to spend precious moments together in the sitting room, dreaming up plans for their future. Julia, though, found it hard to keep to society's strict rules, as did Ben.

'I hate having to be apart,' he murmured one evening as he was about to leave the family's house.

'I know,' she whispered. 'It won't be for long.'

But it seemed an eternity and she worried, too, because now that Pen was away there was no one she could really talk to about what would happen on her wedding night. Shortly after the announcement of their betrothal her mother had given her a hurried and embarrassed lecture about how babies were made and Julia listened carefully. But nothing of what her mother said tied in with how she had actually felt during those moments at the pavilion, when Ben's kisses and his intimate caresses had thrilled her.

Could she bring the same pleasure to him? Would she know what to do? Might she be a disappointment to him? Even when Pen and Jeremy returned to London, Pen was hard to reach because she was either busy shopping for furnishings for her new home or wanting to spend time alone with her husband.

Meanwhile the preparations for Julia and Ben's wedding had grown more frantic. When the day actually arrived, Julia could hardly speak for nerves while she was being dressed in her wedding gown. She even felt herself trembling a little as she walked up the aisle of the church at her father's side to where Ben stood.

But when Ben turned to her and said softly, 'You look wonderful. I love you,' she knew that everything would be all right.

After the ceremony, the house was packed with guests—including Lady Harris, who had travelled all the way from Somerset. 'Of course, I loathe London,' she told everyone happily as she drank yet another glass of expensive champagne. Then she whispered to Ben and Julia, 'But you'll know why I'm here. I had to come, to make sure that the two of you were safely together at last.'

It had been arranged that the couple would spend their wedding night at Ben's house in Clarges Street. Ben had spent weeks arranging for it to be refurbished and redecorated, and when the day of the wedding finally arrived he'd instructed all his household staff, Gilly included, to be there to greet his bride and then to disappear, which they all promptly did—although Ben did suspect that a couple of the young maids might have peeked a little as he swept Julia, still in her bridal gown, into his arms and carried her up two flights of stairs to their bedchamber.

Once there he set her tenderly down on the huge bed and asked softly, 'Is there anything at all you need?'

She smiled shyly up at him. 'Just you,' she whispered.

Until now, he had been restrained in all their meetings. For weeks he had been patient, trying to suppress all intimate thoughts of this lovely girl who had taken possession of his heart and his soul. But now, at last, the time had come.

She looked like a vision in her wedding dress—ethereal, untouchable almost. Of course he realised already what passion lay hidden beneath that shy façade and he wanted to own her, every inch of her. But he also knew he had to be patient, knew he had to take his time, even though his own body was already raging with desire.

'Should I summon a maid to help you undress?' he asked. He could hear that his voice was almost harsh, such was his effort to control himself.

She shook her head and reached to pull away her headdress, setting her hair free of its pins as she did so. She said, 'Will you undress me, Ben? Please?'

He made rather a ham-fisted job of it. Dear God, he could have laughed at himself as some buttons popped off one after another and ended up scattered around the room. As for her underwear, it was fiendish, but the effort was well worth it because of the delight he felt when she began helping him with it, in the end mischievously pushing his clumsy hands aside to roll down her silk stockings. Then—*then* she began to pull her chemise over her head.

She was naked now except for her glorious hair, which fell silkily past her shoulders. He stood very still, taking in the beauty of her coral-tipped breasts, her narrow waist and gently swelling hips. She met his gaze steadily, then she said, 'Isn't it *your* turn now?'

So he began to undress, a substantially easier business for him. When he'd finished, she did not move or avert her gaze, but he could see that she was shaken by the sight of his outright desire, so he moved closer and lifted her to lay her on the bed, tenderly kissing her and lying down beside her, to put one arm around her. 'I shall be as gentle as I can,' he warned. 'But, Julia, do you know what to expect?'

She smiled. 'I trust you, Ben,' she whispered. 'And I want you, so very much!'

So his caresses began.

Julia had already tasted something of the pleasures this man could bestow. What she had not known was that there was so much more, for as well as his fingers, teasing and coaxing, there were his lips—on her mouth, her breasts, everywhere. At first she was uncertain what to do, as well as being shaken by the low insistent ache that was blooming between her thighs and making her tremble with need.

But Ben was wonderful. He calmed her, he coaxed her, he told her she was beautiful; then, as he stroked her down *there* and slid his fingers between her silky folds, she felt the beginnings of that exquisite rush of pleasure he'd given her before. This time she wanted the same, but more, and he was surely ready to offer it, for hadn't she seen the physical evidence of his need?

It scared her a little, but it delighted her, too, and she knew this was what she wanted, yes, *this*. She gasped aloud as she felt his manhood easing itself a little way inside her. She'd had no idea what this could feel like, or what it would do to her, but as the bone-deep longing for more surged through her, she clutched at him and cried out his name.

He stopped. 'Am I hurting you?' he asked swiftly.

'No,' she whispered. 'No. Oh, Ben…' She smiled. 'It's wonderful. Please don't stop.'

He thrust deeper, but was still careful; she could tell that he was restraining himself by the tension in his face. She realised how very much he wanted her and the thought thrilled her. Yes, he was taking possession of her, filling her with his male power, but then he held still and began caressing her again, down there at the heart of all her sensation.

Suddenly, she felt a molten heat swirling through her blood, inflaming her, creating in her such tension that she cried out, 'Ben. I can't. Ben, please…'

He kissed her tenderly on her lips and her breasts, each in turn. Then he began moving inside her again, hard and hot. She found herself clutching desperately at his back and his shoulders, arching her hips to greedily take more of him, and as his strokes deepened she was gasping aloud until suddenly she could not hold back any more.

Sharp yet exquisite shafts of pleasure were beginning to roll through her. She stopped breathing. She couldn't think, couldn't speak, but somehow her world flew apart and she was shaken by wave after wave of bliss as he steadily pleasured her. Then his movements grew stronger, greedier, until she felt his hips shuddering as he cried out her name.

With a sigh he fell against her, his head on her naked breast, and she could feel his heart thudding. Tenderly she stroked his tousled hair, smiling softly to herself. This was fulfilment. This was joy. This was peace.

After a moment he lifted himself on one elbow to gaze down at her. 'My love,' he said. 'My wife. Are you happy?'

What could she say? He was her husband…he was her life. 'Darling Ben. I am very happy,' she whispered. 'Unbelievably so.'

He stroked her flushed cheek. 'I wonder,' he said

softly, 'are you going to write any more about me in that notebook of yours?'

She pretended to think about it. 'Perhaps not. After all, it might make you too conceited.'

'Minx,' he said, tickling her nose. 'I'll take that as a compliment and allow you to change the subject, because I can tell there's something else you're longing to say.'

She hesitated a moment. 'Ben. You know you said that we could go to Paris or Rome or anywhere I pleased for our honeymoon?'

'Yes, minx? Where have you thought of? Do you want to go adventuring?'

She eased herself up a little. 'You told me, didn't you, that you've made Lambourne Hall fit to live in again? Please, could we go there?'

He sat up, clearly startled. 'At this time of the year? It will be cold. We'll need log fires, There might well be snow and we could be cut off for days!'

She nestled comfortably against his shoulder and positively sighed with happiness. 'Mmm… Snow. Cut off for days. That sounds absolutely *perfect*.'

He put his arm around her. 'You really love it there, don't you?'

'I do.' She twisted a little so she could look at him. 'I know, of course, that we'll have to spend months at a time in London, but Lambourne will always be my favourite place of all. Especially…' she gave a shy smile '…in a year or so, perhaps. When there might not be just the two of us.'

'You mean when we have children?'

'Yes. Of course.' She wriggled a little so she fitted

comfortably in his arms. 'Two or three children or more, maybe. I cannot imagine a more perfect place or a more perfect father for them! They can have adventures in the woods and climb trees there, the girls as well as the boys. We could perhaps have a rowing boat on the lake for them and we can have picnics there in the summer and—'

He touched her lips gently. 'Enough, sweetheart. You've convinced me.'

Her eyes were alight with joy. 'So we really can go to Lambourne Hall and make it our true home?'

'Yes, of course we can. You've also convinced me that I've found the most wonderful bride in the world.' He kissed her and she kissed him back, sliding down the bed and pulling him with her. She was smiling a little—a secret, sensual smile. 'Ben,' she murmured, 'would you think me very greedy if I asked for some more of what we just did?'

'As a matter of fact, Lady Lambourne,' he answered softly, 'I would think it absolutely inevitable. Can't you tell? But this time, we are going to take things more slowly.' He took her hand and kissed it. 'There's no need to rush. Remember, we have all the time in the world.'

Julia gave a sigh of complete happiness. He was right. All the time in the world to share her life with the man she loved.

* * * * *

Liaison With
The Champagne Count
Bronwyn Scott

MILLS & BOON

Bronwyn Scott is a communications instructor at Pierce College and the proud mother of three wonderful children—one boy and two girls. When she's not teaching or writing, she enjoys playing the piano, travelling—especially to Florence, Italy—and studying history and foreign languages. Readers can stay in touch via Facebook at Facebook.com/bronwynwrites, or on her blog, bronwynswriting.blogspot.com. She loves to hear from readers.

Visit the Author Profile page
at millsandboon.com.au for more titles.

Author Note

The Enterprising Widows series was inspired by the changes occurring in the mid-nineteenth century that allowed women more latitude in how they could live their lives. Emma's story follows the trajectory of many other real-life female champagne entrepreneurs. Up until the twentieth century, champagne was definitely a female-dominated industry, with powerful businesswomen like Barbe-Nicole Clicquot and Louise Pommery leading the way. Like my heroine, Emma, neither of these women inherited a ready-made business. They built their champagne dynasties from the ground up. For an interesting read on women in champagne, check out one of my favourite resources for this story: *The Widow Clicquot* by Tilar J. Mazzeo.

Emma's story is also inspired by the hope of second chances and the tenacity of starting over in the face of great loss and change. Emma and Julien are two sides of the dilemma we face after loss: giving up or going on. Julien has retreated from the world, deciding to give up, while Emma has chosen to go on. Together, they help one another make a beautiful future from the ashes of their pasts.

DEDICATION

For Huckleberry, the sweetest doggy ever
who never forgot his kindness even when his own
early years were not kind to him. I hope the last
six years with our family made up for that rough
beginning. You helped me start this book. I will
finish it without you. The space under my
desk will always be yours.

Prologue

February 5th, 1852

Emma Greyville-Luce was acutely aware she'd survived the night due—quite literally—to the turn of a card. Thanks to whist and a whim, she was sitting in the comfort of Mrs Parnaby's parlour, clutching a warm teacup, a blanket draped about her shoulders, ushering in the chilly February morning *alive*, something several others, including her husband, could not lay claim to. Garrett was dead. Keir was dead. Adam was dead. All three lost to the flood. She should be dead, too.

Her mind whirred nonstop with those two realisations coupled with the horror of the last seven hours and the narrowness of her escape. By the slimmest of margins, she'd evaded the raging torrent that had been the River Holme sweeping down Water Street, angry and rapacious at one o'clock that morning.

One choice made differently and she, Antonia, and Fleur would have been swept away with their husbands, but Emma never could say no to a hand of whist. Thank goodness she hadn't started declining tonight. It would have been easy enough to turn down Mrs Parnaby's invitation to play after supper and take her leave with Garrett. She very nearly had. After all, in seven years of marriage, she'd spent very few nights without him and he'd been ready for bed, citing the need for an early evening because of a morning meeting with the clothiers to discuss a joint venture. That venture was what had brought Garrett and his two friends to Holmfirth. But tonight, Emma had not done as she ought. She'd stayed behind at Mrs Parnaby's and begged Antonia and Fleur to stay with her to make up the foursome needed for whist.

Lady Luck had smiled broadly on her. Emma had just claimed the last trick needed for the rubber when the warning had gone up the street: *'The embankment's breached! The river's in Water Street!'*

Fear had seared through her at the words. Water Street: where they'd rented cottages for the duration of their stay. Water Street: where Garrett, Adam, and Keir had returned to seek their beds hours ago.

The women had raced to Mrs Parnaby's lace-curtained windows and peered futilely into the night. Even at the advantage of their slight elevation, they could see nothing in the dark. But what they couldn't see, they could *hear*. One might have mistaken the water for the howling of wind. It was the most malevolent sound Emma had ever heard; a churning, rushing, swirling, crunching foe she could not see filled the night, everywhere and nowhere all at once.

'We'll be safe here,' Mrs Parnaby had said. 'We're

back far enough from the river and away from the centre of town.' Their hostess had meant to be consoling but, in those panic-filled moments, Emma had not wanted to be safe. She'd wanted to be with Garrett. She'd run for the door, determined to throw herself into the night, to make her way back to Water Street, to Garrett, the river of terror ravaging Holmfirth be damned. It had taken both Antonia and Fleur to pull her from her folly.

'It is too late to warn them,' Fleur had reasoned with characteristically blunt logic, her own face ashen.

'They are strong men, they can take care of themselves,' Antonia had offered with her unequivocal optimism.

'We'll go help once the water has settled and there's less chance of us being another set of people in need of rescue ourselves.' Mrs Parnaby had been all bustling practicality, and Emma had needed to settle for that.

It was the longest night of Emma's life, filled with an uncustomary sense of helplessness for a woman used to being in charge. The morning brought no joy, only a renewal of the fear that had dogged Emma in the hours until dawn. The four women were able to pick their way through the wreckage to the Rose and Crown inn in hopes of lending a hand and hearing news. Emma gasped at the sight of a dead cow mired in the muck and turned her head away, but there was no escape from the devastation.

Morning light hid nothing, disguised nothing. Daylight only served to emphasise how futile any effort to go out sooner would have been. Waters had receded, leaving sucking mud and mangled machinery behind, murderous clues as to just how malevolent the angry waters had been and how strong. The waters that had broken the Bilberry Reservoir and overpowered the embankment had been forceful enough to demolish the mills that lined the river, feeding its fury by devouring machinery and vast quantities of soil.

At the Rose and Crown, the women put themselves to work, serving hot drinks and porridge to those who'd been brought in, wet, exhausted, and as hungry for news of family and loved ones as they were for porridge after a long night of fear, even as new fears began to add to their worries. Many were homeless, many had escaped with only the clothes on their backs. The places they'd worked—the mills—were destroyed. There were no jobs to go back to, no income to collect.

She was lucky, Emma repeated to herself as she served porridge. Other than the things she'd brought with her for the visit, her belongings were safe and dry far south of here in her home in Surrey, Oakwood Manor. Her home was safe. Her belongings were safe. She could leave here. She and Garrett could go home, could leave all of this heartache and devastation as soon as he walked through the door of the Rose and Crown.

Her gaze darted to the door yet again, her mind willing him to walk in as if she could conjure him out of thin air; the dark beard threaded with silver, the broad, bluff build of him draped in his greatcoat, the dark eyes that could melt an honest woman with desire and manage a dishonest man with a stare. She caught Antonia's gaze on her and they exchanged encouraging smiles, trying to lift one another up. Emma told herself no news was good news, especially when the news they were hearing wasn't.

There'd been tales of neighbours watching whole families swept away in the violent current. Near Hollowgate, Aner Bailey had watched his wife and two children carried away while he clung to a timber, he himself pushed downstream to the Turnpike Road. Joseph Hellawell on Scarfold had been rescued from a beam on the top story of his home but his entire family had been trapped below in the bedroom and drowned.

As the morning wore on, hope receded with the waters. Eyewitness accounts were coming in and a clearer understanding of what had happened last night was taking shape. The whole Holme valley had suffered enormous loss. Bodies were being recovered in places miles from Holmfirth in the towns of Mirfield, Armitage Fold, and Honley. Fleur was exceedingly anxious, Emma noted. The colour had not returned to her face and her hand strayed repeatedly to the flat of her belly when she thought no one was looking. Was Fleur expecting? Her husband, Adam, was Garrett's age, in his upper fifties. For him, it would be a late-in-life child. Emma sent up a prayer, *God, let the men be all right.* She'd uttered those words already times beyond count. For a woman who counted everything, that was worrisome.

George Dyson, the coroner, arrived shortly after ten, asking for a word in private. The man looked tired, and she could only imagine the horror he'd seen. These were his neighbours, lifelong friends that were being pulled from the depths of mill races and ponds. Emma gestured nervously for Antonia and Fleur to join her in the Rose and Crown's small private parlour.

She was aware of Antonia gripping her hand as George Dyson cleared his throat, the sound a universal portent of impending bad news. She braced herself, her inner voice whispering, *Be strong, Fleur and Antonia will need you.*

But no amount of bracing could protect her against the devastation of the coroner's words. 'Lady Luce, Mrs Popplewell, Mrs Griffiths, I wish I had better news. I will be blunt. Water Street didn't stand a chance. The river hit it from the front and the side, absolutely obliterating the buildings.' He paused and swallowed hard. 'James Metterick's family, and the Earnshaws, are all gone, their homes destroyed.' Homes that had been next to theirs, Emma thought. The Mettericks and the Earnshaws were the clothiers Garrett was supposed to meet with. Lead began to settle in her stomach and yet there was still a sliver of hope.

'But I heard James Metterick survived,' Emma protested against the news. She'd clung to that piece of news all morning since the moment it had been reported. Metterick was bruised and battered but he was alive. He'd been at his Water Street residence, and he'd survived. Surely, it was possible Garrett had as well…

George Dyson shook his head, his tone gentle. 'We believe the bodies of your husband and his friends have been recovered, Lady Luce. Your husband was found in the Victoria Mill along with others. I *am* sorry.' Emma felt her knees buckle. Mrs Parnaby was there with a chair, helping her to sit and murmuring consolation. But her world was a discordant blur. Somewhere amid her own disbelief and grief she heard Antonia wail, saw her friend sink to her knees. There was a burst of outrage from Fleur followed by plate shattering against the wall. Emma managed to rise, managed to get to Antonia on the floor, and then the three of them were in each other's arms, supporting and comforting one another amid their own grief. How was this possible? Garrett, Keir and Adam, all three of them gone? It was impossible, a bad dream from which she'd awake any moment. Only she didn't.

The bad dream continued. The next hours were surreal. There'd been a need to have them officially identify the bodies and perhaps she'd needed to do it, to have the closure of seeing Garrett one last time, horrible as it was. The bloated, drowned body wasn't her vibrant husband; that man had long since departed the corpse she identified.

George Dyson stood beside her outside the makeshift morgue. 'If it is any consolation, Lady Luce, I don't believe there was much suffering. It would have been fast. The looks frozen on people's faces have been those of confusion and disbelief. They died before they understood what hit them.'

He was trying to be kind, but she was in no mood for it. Some of her usual fire, her usual determination seeped through the numbness that had sustained her since the news. 'Did my husband *look* confused?' Emma snapped. He'd looked fierce, as if he'd battled the river with everything in him. 'My husband is—'

Is. She couldn't use that word any more.

She swallowed back the thickness that settled in her throat, threatening to destroy whatever aplomb she had left. 'My husband was a fighter, the most determined man I've ever known.' Garrett had fought for every success he'd had, climbed his way up an impossible social ladder to earn a baronetcy, and he'd fought for her: Emma Greyville, the gin heiress of England, when his family of grown children from his first marriage had argued vehemently that a newly minted baronet with a fortune could do better than the daughter of a gin magnate. He should aim higher; they'd said to her face when Garrett had announced their engagement. He'd stared down his sons and their wives with a laugh. 'Higher than love? Whatever would that be?'

She'd remember those words always. They were carefully tucked away beside her other memories; how he'd looked upon her with that love on their wedding day, how he'd taken her to France for their honeymoon and shown her the vineyard in Champagne he'd bought her as a wedding gift. The best weeks of her life had been spent at that vineyard. It was their place, their retreat from the world. What she wouldn't give to be there again with Garrett beside her, walking the rows of grapes, sampling vintages.

Tears threatened. She turned from George Dyson and found Fleur and Antonia waiting for her, their own ordeals etched on their faces. They embraced each other once again, holding each other up. 'What do we do now?' Antonia whispered, her face tear-streaked, her earlier optimism gone, replaced with pale despair.

'We go back to Mrs Parnaby's. She has clothes and rooms for us.' Emma could manage to think that far but no farther. Her mind kept running up against one inescapable fact: Garrett was dead. The life they'd built together was gone. The truth was, she didn't *know* what came next and for the moment, she could not rouse herself to care.

Four days later, she was still numb to the realisation. 'We're widows now. Widows before the age of thirty,' Fleur ground out as she paced before Mrs Parnaby's fireplace, anger fuelling her steps and her words as Emma did the math: they'd been widows for ninety-six hours, or five thousand, seven hundred and sixty minutes. Numbers gave her comfort the way anger kept Fleur upright. Fleur had gone out each day to assist in the recovery effort, working until dark, coming home exhausted. Emma had asked her not to go out today, citing that they needed to make plans for departure. The roads were passable now, the rains and the river subsided enough to make travel decent. Her plea had been a bit of subterfuge. They *did* need to talk, but more than that, Emma was worried about Fleur. She was driving herself too hard, not taking time for her grief, but burying it.

'I still can't believe it,' Antonia said softly from her chair by the window. 'I always knew Keir would go before me. With the difference in ages, it was bound to happen. But I thought it would be old age, not like this, not so sudden with no chance to say goodbye.'

Emma nodded, unable to form the words to respond. The three men had been lifelong friends, long before they'd met their wives, navigating London together as newcomers in their twenties and later as established, savvy businessmen: Garrett the canny investor, Adam the intrepid newspaperman, and Keir the emporium magnate. Adam and Keir had already been married when she and Garret wed. She had liked Garrett's friends immediately and she'd liked their wives, women her age, even better. What a group they'd all made—three men in their fifties with their young brides. Now that life was gone. Quite literally washed away. Emma had replayed her final moments with Garrett ceaselessly in her mind—the kiss on his cheek, the whispered 'I love you' as he'd said good-night.

'This is *exactly* what Adam feared would happen,' Fleur exclaimed abruptly from the fireplace. 'It's why Garrett brought him along, to ferret out the truth about the reservoir's engineering.' Emma nodded. Garrett had told her there'd been rumours the reservoir was damaged. Disaster wasn't an issue of if, but when. But nothing was certain and of course the engineers and those responsible weren't likely to confess to construction shortcuts without some manoeuvring. Garrett had not been keen about a joint venture on the mill without knowing for sure what the environmental circumstances were like. His instincts had been unfortunately right.

Emma split her gaze between Antonia and Fleur. 'I think it's time to go. There's nothing more we can do here.' Amid the numbness there was growing aware-ness of all that demanded her attention in the wake of Garrett's passing. There would be paperwork to settle, numbers that would need tallying. Already, her mind was hungering for the peace of the familiar columns. There was Garrett's business affairs to oversee, and there would be his family to deal with. She'd managed to send a note to his sons regarding their father's de-mise but there was a will to be read, and there would be…upheaval. Dealing with his family would be dis-tasteful but it had to be done. The sooner the better. She had no illusions his sons would be kind to her or offer her any more than whatever Garrett had set aside for her. Just the chateau. That was all she wanted, in truth. If they would just let her have that, she would be content. She began to calculate the odds.

Antonia exhaled a long, shaky breath. 'I need to go home as well and see how things stand. Keir was in the midst of restoring an old building in London. He had plans to turn it into a department store, like the ones in France.' Antonia drew another shaky breath. 'I think I will finish it for him. I think it's what I must do, although I'm not sure how. I'll figure it out as I go.' She looked to Fleur. 'Shall we all travel together as far as London? It's a long train ride from West Yorkshire when one is on their own.'

Fleur didn't meet their eyes for a moment and Emma felt her stomach drop. She knew before Fleur spoke she'd refuse. 'No. I think I'll stay and finish the in-vestigation Adam began. There are people to help and justice to serve. People deserve to know if this tragedy was a natural disaster or a manmade one.'

Emma chose her words carefully. 'Do you think that's wise, Fleur? If it is manmade, there will be people who won't appreciate prying, particularly if it's a woman doing it. You should think twice before putting yourself in danger.' Especially if her friend might need to be thinking for two.

'I don't care,' Fleur snapped. 'If Adam died because of carelessness, someone *will* pay for that. I will see to it, and I will see to it that such recklessness isn't allowed to happen again.'

'And Adam's child?' Emma decided to brazen it out. 'Would you be reckless with his child?' She was admittedly a bit jealous that Fleur might have one last piece of Adam while she had nothing of Garrett's. After the will was read and his family had their say, she might have even less. Garrett had been her buffer.

Fleur shook her head, her voice softer when she spoke, the earlier anger absent. 'I do not know if there is a child. It is too soon.' But not too soon to hope, Emma thought privately. Fleur must suspect there was a chance.

'Just be careful, dear friend. I do not want anything to happen to you.' Emma rose and went to her. Antonia joined her and they encircled each other with their arms, their heads bent together.

'We're widows now.' Emma echoed Fleur's words softly.

Ninety-six hours and counting.

There would be enormous change for each of them over the next few months, the loss of their husbands was just the beginning. Widows lost more than husbands. Society did not make life pleasant for those without husbands even in this new, brave world where women were demanding their due. But amid the chaos of change she could depend on two things: the friendship of the women who stood with her now, and the realisation that from here on out nothing in her life would ever be the same again.

Chapter One

February 19th, 1852

Everything depended on the will. Emma literally sat on the edge of her chair in the drawing room of Oakwood, aware that this was her space no longer. She had minutes left as its mistress. She swallowed to dislodge the lump in her throat that formed at the thought. The comfortable room she'd carefully cultivated for herself and Garrett, where they'd spent relaxed evenings entertaining their friends, felt more like an enemy camp on this grey February afternoon than a familiar, comforting space. Her foes had already invaded. Garrett's sons, Robert and Steven, sat alert and watchful on the blue-and-cream-striped upholstery of the matched chairs by the fire, their wives perched nearby on the settee, their avaricious eyes pricing the room and its contents, waiting to strip it bare. The two women reminded her of cats stalking a mouse, bodies wound tight waiting to spring.

There would be little she could do to stop them. She'd

resigned herself to the carnage. The law required she stand by and watch them plunder her life. Robert was the oldest. He'd get the baronetcy and Oakwood. His wife, Estelle—the granddaughter of a viscount—had already made a comment about selling off the items and redecorating. Estelle had not even pretended to be discreet about it, the implication obvious that a gin heiress's tastes were not up to par for a baronet.

The butler appeared at the doorway to the drawing room and cleared his throat. 'Sir Robert.' Robert looked up immediately. He'd taken well to the honorific that now marked his title, a title he'd done nothing to earn except to be born to a man who'd earned it for him. Now Robert would benefit from those efforts. Garrett had never thought of the title as his, but as the family's, something he'd been able to add to the legacy he'd pass on. That was the difference between Garrett and his entitled sons. 'Mr Lake is here. Shall I show him in?'

Robert gave a curt, almost pompous nod. Emma curled her fingers into the depths of the handkerchief she clutched in her lap. So it began. The next few minutes would determine what the shape of her future would look like. Would she live that life of a daughter dependent on her family, once more supported by her father's gin fortune? As a woman of modest means required to live alone and quietly in order to maintain her independence? Or would she have the financial latitude to remake her life somewhere else? Her worry, which had kept her awake several nights in a row since her return from Holmfirth, surged anew, twisting her stomach, making her glad she'd not eaten lunch. Surely, Garrett would not leave her stranded. He'd loved her. One did not abandon those they loved, not even in death. Emma clung doggedly to that hope as assuredly as Aner Bailey had clung to his timber amid the raging waters of the River Holme.

Yet doubt flooded her. Garrett had never spoken to her of arrangements in case of his passing. He'd only been in his fifties and in robust good health. Perhaps he'd felt there was no need and she'd foolishly allowed it. Like Antonia, she'd known theoretically what the reality was in marrying a much older man. But that had been a decade or two away when they'd married. Twenty years had seemed like a lifetime to a twenty-one-year-old bride in the throes of new love. If she had never bargained on losing Garrett to anything other than very old age, perhaps he hadn't either. Perhaps he'd thought he had time—time to say goodbye, time to plan for her.

Stop it, she scolded herself. *You are strong. There is nothing Robert can say or do that can truly hurt you. He is a spoiled boy, pampered by his mother who has grown into a selfish adult.*

Her eyes met Robert's gaze evenly, firmly, as she squared her shoulders while introductions were made and condolences murmured. She'd prefer that Garrett had seen to her protection but she could protect herself. A gin heiress was no sheltered debutante. She'd grown up learning her father's business and staring down women who thought she was less than they for being able to add ledgers and manage accounts, for navigating a man's world.

You faced down a ballroom of catty debutantes when Amelia St James told anyone who would listen the Earl of Redmond was only dancing with you for a peek at your father's fortune.

Whatever happened here, she would be fine on a functional level. Her heart was a different matter, but today was not for emotions, it was for practicalities. She had to survive this before she could start to put herself back together.

Mr Lake took a seat at the centre of the room with Robert on his left and she on his right. He was a spare man with a mop of messy grey hair that had probably started the morning combed back in preparation for the occasion but was already tousled. He wore the decent black suit of the country solicitor, and his eyes were tired as he put on his eyeglasses. Tired but kind perhaps? Sympathetic? Emma tried to read him as he glanced in her direction. She was usually a good judge of character. Her father had relied on that sense over several business dinners with new clients. The question was, what did Mr Lake already know? Had there been no provision for her? Was that why he looked at her with sympathy? The knot in her stomach tied itself tighter. Or perhaps it was empathy because she had to deal with the pompous asses that were Robert and Steven Luce?

Mr Lake efficiently got business under way, perhaps reading the room aright. This was the last task to complete the process of dying and Garrett's sons were eager to get on with living. Their father had been buried yesterday in a ceremony far larger than what Garrett would have preferred but what his sons had demanded. Where Garrett had been a behind the scenes man, his sons were showmen with a flair for the dramatic, something else they'd inherited from their mother, and right now those sons were keen on the world knowing how bereft they were over the loss of their father.

The will was unmistakably Garrett's, skirting the temptations of a flowery introduction and reflections of the lived life. Of course, he hadn't known he was going to die. Still, she didn't think it would have changed. She'd recognise that writing style anywhere; direct, straightforward like the man himself. Even his marriage proposal had been direct, honest if not romantic.

'I've never met anyone like you, Emma. I know it's only been a few weeks, but I want to marry you. I cannot imagine a life without you.'

Like the man himself, his will went straight to the details, bequests and the division of assets. There were no surprises but hearing the words made it no less sad. Robert would have Oakwood and most of its contents, which were both entailed with the baronetcy. The stripping had begun. It wasn't the things she minded losing. It was the memories they represented. That's what she was being deprived of: the right to live among those remembrances. Mr Lake looked up from his reading, eyeing Robert over the top of the documents. 'Lady Luce is to be allowed to claim whatever items she desires from the house.'

'*Dowager* Lady Luce,' Robert corrected, staring at Mr Lake, refusing to look at her. '*My* wife is Lady Luce.' Robert was plundering mercilessly today. She should have expected such callousness. Robert had been jealous when his father had remarried, fearful of sharing his father's love and perhaps more fearful of sharing his father's money and status. After all, his father had given her, a woman of no real standing, a title he himself could not have until his father died. She supposed it stood to reason Robert would take even her name from her—her married name—the name that said she was Garrett's partner.

Mr Lake was not intimidated. He gave Robert a stern look. 'Those are your father's words, Sir Robert.'

'Of course.' Robert's glance flicked in her direction with more disdain than consideration in his dark eyes. 'I am sure we'll come to an agreement. After all, several of Oakwood's unentailed contents are *my* mother's.' Emma met his eyes with the full steel of her own. She was not fooled. His polite words were the barely veiled throwing of a gauntlet. He, who'd not been interested in Oakwood's contents for years, would now use the shield of his mother's memory to argue every unentailed knick-knack, every piece of china, every chair and every picture. He wanted her to beg. But Emma Greyville-Luce begged no one, especially not a man who wanted her on her knees. She'd learned that lesson early at her father's knee. There was money, and then there was gin money, and no number of attempts to do clean gin business could wash away the stain. Society had wanted James Greyville to beg for their acceptance, but her father had refused. A Greyville had nothing to be ashamed of. Now it was Society begging him. She would not beg Robert for a single thing. Instead, she would flank him with Mr Lake in the room as witness.

She gave Robert a hard look, her terms ready. 'I want only the Baccarat glassware, and the chandelier we purchased on our honeymoon in France.' The collection was extensive but it would not beggar the estate of drinking glasses.

'I think that is reasonable,' Mr Lake put in swiftly, using Robert's own argument against him before he could interject. 'Surely, Sir Robert, you have no attachment to that? I can make a note of it today so it's on record.'

Estelle tossed her blond head. 'Let her have it, Robert. It's not even Bohemian crystal. We'll want something with a little more...*lineage* to it.' Emma let the snub go. Baccarat was not old but Garrett, always future-focused, had seen great potential in the French glassblower.

Mr Lake turned to her. 'Is there anything else, Lady Luce?'

'No, nothing other than my personal affects, jewellery and clothes.' She'd resigned herself to leaving much behind in exchange for her pride. She would not haggle with Robert like a fishwife, even if there was artwork and china she could rightly claim beyond the Baccarat. She did not expect Robert and Steven to be grateful though. And they weren't.

'We have an inventory of the family jewels,' Robert began as if they were a ducal family with a vault instead of a family in possession of a baronetcy for a mere ten years.

'I *know* what's on the list.' She cut him off sharply. 'Rest assured, I have no intentions of cheating you out of a single pearl.' It felt good to fight, to feel something, anything, even if it was anger, in her veins again. No wonder Fleur had relied on anger to get her through the early days of their loss. The last of the numbness that had enveloped her since the flood was losing its hold. Estelle gasped at her rudeness as if her own husband hadn't been insulting his father's widow since he'd arrived two days prior and taken up residence with an astonishing sense of entitled permanency.

'Well, so do I,' Robert retorted.

Mr Lake cleared his throat. 'Shall we move on? There are stocks and other assets to go through.' He dangled the carrot of funds and both Steven and Robert bit. The business investments were split between the brothers with the option to share ownership. She'd not expected it to be otherwise, although she'd be lying to herself that she didn't feel a sense of loss at watching her hard work being handed off. She'd helped build those companies as much as the Luce men had, spending her days with the ledgers. She'd been the one to tell Garrett he was being overcharged for his oak wine barrels at the chateau. She was the one who'd set up the dinner that resulted in Garrett winning the shipping contract for a large tea importer. She'd been an active and successful part of Garrett's business life as much as she'd been part of his private life. Still, one could hardly expect a woman to run a shipping empire even in this modern age. A woman at the helm of such a business would likely sink it and such an outcome did not honour Garrett's hard work. Hope whispered: there was one industry a woman might participate in—wine, champagne. If his sons had the British businesses, surely they were satisfied? Surely, Garrett would have saved her something, would have known what she wanted, where she could be successful on her own…?

'Lastly, there is the issue of the chateau in France.' Mr Lake's words had her sitting up stiff and ramrod straight, her body wound with tension. A glance passed between Robert and Steven that made her nervous. Everyone was bracing themselves. For her, this was the moment that decided everything. *Please, please, please…* The word became a litany in her mind.

Mr Lake's gaze was on the papers, inscrutable as he read. '"The chateau near Cumières in France is not part of the entailment and as such it and its lands are left to the care of my beloved wife, Emma Greyville-Luce, in the hopes that it will be a place of remembrance and renewal for her as long as she desires."' The knot in her stomach eased and her eyes smarted with tears. So many words. At last, a little poetry, a little flowery language Garrett-style. This was her husband's idea of a love letter and her heart squeezed. He'd not forgotten her. He'd known how much the chateau had meant to her. He'd not just lavished her generically with his wealth, but he'd given her something that held meaning for her, something she could build with her own efforts. He believed in her.

Mr Lake looked up and Emma did not imagine the satisfaction on his face. '"All accounts and papers associated with the chateau should be placed directly into her possession."'

'No.' Robert's voice cut through the peace that had settled on her.

'Excuse me, Sir Robert?' It was Mr Lake who spoke, his brows arched in perplexity. 'No, what?'

Robert's face was thunderous. 'No, *she* does not get the chateau in France. I will contest this.'

Whatever numbness remained dissolved at this new threat. Fire began to burn slow and sure in her veins. 'Why do you care, Sir Robert?' she said with deliberate challenge in her voice, not waiting for Mr Lake. 'You've never even been there. You know nothing of the wine business.' And she did, or at least she knew the libations business through her father. Selling wine was not much different than selling gin, although producing it was. Like Antonia, she would figure it out as she went.

Mr Lake quietly came to her defence. 'There is nothing to contest, Sir Robert. The chateau is hers.'

'Fine, it's not as if it's a huge money-maker. It barely breaks even. It's an expensive hobby just so my father can import his own wines to his dinner table. I've been telling him to sell it for ages.' Faced with a twin front, Robert settled into his chair, fuming. His gaze landed on her, and Emma braced. Robert had been bested. He needed to save face. Whatever came out of his mouth next would be cruel, designed to hurt. 'Pack up your things, then. If you want that chateau so badly, be gone in the morning. I don't want your fortune-hunting shadow darkening the halls of Oakwood longer than necessary. This is not your home any longer.'

Mr Lake slid Robert a disapproving look and took out a packet of documents. 'These are yours, Lady Luce. You'll find the deed and other papers for the chateau. I will send for my wife to help with your packing. It would be my pleasure to make travel arrangements for you and a pleasure to give you a farewell supper at my home tonight once you've completed packing. You can leave from our place in the morning. There's a coach that departs from the inn for Dover in the morning if that's sufficient. My wife and I can send the Baccarat on later if need be.'

'Mrs Lake's company would be welcome, as would your kind offer.' Emma smiled her gratitude. This was an unexpected kindness. She would not be left here alone to endure Robert's and Steven's glares and the indignities of having every item she packed questioned.

Upstairs in her room, Emma shut the door behind her and allowed herself a deep breath—a breath to steady herself against the emotions of the afternoon, and another breath of relief. It was settled. The chateau was hers. Life was starting again—*her* life was starting again. After fourteen days, five hours, and thirty-six minutes, there was something to look forward to. Although, this was not quite the leave-taking Emma had imagined when she'd pictured departing Oakwood.

In her mind, she'd thought of it as a slow, gradual process, a chance to walk the house, to take out her memories one last time and savour her life here as if it were a fine wine. Instead, Robert's hatred of her had tried to turn 'seeing her off' into 'running her off.'

Perhaps it was better this way. After two weeks of

time standing still, of being trapped in a nightmare comprised of tragedy and the unknown, everything was happening at lightning speed. Within days, barring difficulty with travel and tides, she'd be in Paris. Within the week, she'd be in Cumières. She closed her eyes and leaned back against the door, doing the travel timetables. She whispered to the room she'd once shared with Garrett, 'Thank you, my love.'

Chapter Two

Julien Archambeau had been born to love the land. *La femme la plus difficile qu'un homme puisse aimer.* The most difficult woman a man could love—his *grandpère* would say. And yet Julien knew he'd choose no other, especially on a sharp, clear March morning with rare blue sky above him and the promise of spring lurking in the veins of his beloved vines.

On a morning like this, there was no better place to be but in the vineyards. He squatted between the rows of grape vines and pulled off his thick workman's gloves. He scooped the soil into the palm of his hand, weighing it, then sifting the silt through his fingers, his fingertips recognising the feel of Cumières earth, the sand, the marl, the clay and lignite, the undertones of chalk and limestone, all of it combining to create a soil, Julien was convinced, which existed in only one place on earth, a soil he'd been raised on. Julien didn't think he'd ever had much choice about it. The *terroire* of Cumières, of the Vallee de Marne, of the Montagne de Reims ran through his blood, the product and practice of generations that went back to the days of the Sun King. He stood up and brushed his hands against his work trousers.

Seven generations of Archambeaux had cared for the land, nurtured its crops, loved for it, lived for it, and died for it. When revolution had come, his great-*grandpère* had declared he'd rather lose his head than his land. In the end, he'd lost both, leaving Julien's grandfather and father the task of retrieving the family lands, a task that had only been partially successful. The remainder of that task had fallen to Julien and his Oncle Etienne.

Julien ran a bare hand over the vines bound horizontally across the trellises, looking for signs of 'bleeding'—the leakage of sap that signalled the vines waking up and that budbreak was imminent, that spring was officially here, and the growing season was under way.

There was nothing yet but March had only begun. It was too soon. The grape, like a woman, had its own mysterious time. Grapes and women could be wooed but not rushed. An indefinable instinct told him it would take a few more weeks of sun to see it done. He'd walk the rows again in the early evening before supper, after the vines had spent an afternoon beneath the sun and see if that was still the case. *That* was another Archambeau family ritual. A man must walk his land to know it; every lush curve and plain, every idiosyncrasy— where did water pool? Where was there excessive shade or sun? Any variation would affect the grapes.

He'd been walking the land since he was a boy and the family had been allowed to return to France. At first, he'd walked with Grandpère and Papa, then with just Papa, and now he walked alone. Oncle Etienne seldom walked the land. Grandpère would not approve of Oncle Etienne forsaking the old ways, nor would he approve of Julien's aloneness. Grandpère would say a man his age should have a son to walk the land with him and a wife to walk with him through life. It wasn't that Julien hadn't tried. Clarisse had been all a young man dreamed of and for a brief time the dream had been his. But dreams didn't last.

Julien reached the end of the final row and looked back over the field. *Famille et terre.* Family and land were the only things that mattered if one was an Archambeau. Grandpère would be disappointed to see how little of either the Archambeaux possessed at present. From a great house that had lasted centuries, there were only he and Oncle Etienne now and since Julien's father's death, they'd not won back any more of the old Archambeau lands. Grandpère would turn in his grave to know his grandson was walking another man's land, worrying over another man's grapes when the land had once been Archambeau land. It was not enough for Grandpère to have reclaimed half of what had been lost to the Revolution.

His *grandpère* was not a man for half-measures. Grandpère had counted on Julien's marriage to Clarisse Anouilh, the daughter of the owner, to gain the remainder of the lands, the Archambeau vineyards complete once more. When the betrothal had failed, Grandpère had tried to buy the lands outright but there'd not been enough money. Clarisse's father had sold to an Englishman who fancied the place for his young wife and was prepared to pay any price, besotted fool that he was. The Archambeaux could not compete with a man who had unlimited funds. A reminder, Monsieur Anouilh said, that while the Archambeau name was old, their aristocratic fortune was gone, their funds coming from the trades of shipping and wine these days and their once-esteemed title precarious. The Archambeaux were not what they once were. It had been an absolute snub. Grandpère had been furious.

Julien began the long trek up to the chateau where he'd spend the day checking the cellars and looking over ledgers. By rights and out of loyalty to his *grandpère*, he ought to dislike Sir Garrett Luce, the besotted English baronet. But Sir Garrett Luce had proved astute, interesting, and likeable. Sir Garrett Luce's only flaw was in being an absentee landlord. To his *grandpère*, such a flaw was tantamount to being the eighth deadly sin. A vineyard could not thrive without daily attention.

Grapes didn't grow on their own. Well, they did, but wild grapes did not make for consistent or even good vintages. Grapes had to be tamed and trained for that, curated like fine art, carefully coaxed like a woman to reveal themselves in all their glory. A grape might take three years to come to fruition well enough to harvest it. Grapes took and tried a man's patience. In this case, the patience was his, not Sir Garrett Luce's. Luce's business empire kept him in England most of the year.

As a result, Luce had entrusted the vineyard and the daily oversight of the business to him, his friend and neighbour, unaware of the history that lay between Julien and the land. Luce knew only that Julien and his Oncle Etienne held the property that abutted his. Etienne had felt it was unnecessary to disabuse Luce of the notion, citing the old adage that one could never have too many friends. This friendship might be the way back to possessing the land.

Oncle Etienne believed that Luce would soon tire of the vineyard, especially if it didn't produce a profit, and would want to sell. Who better to take the vineyard off his hands than his neighbour and friend? Until then, they had time to acquire the money needed to purchase the place. It was a delicate dance, his *oncle* said, of keeping Luce interested in the property long enough for them to raise the funds. They didn't want Luce tiring of it too soon before they could purchase it. The land had already slipped away from them once. This time, his *oncle* counselled, they just needed to play a long game. There would be no woman to mess the arrangement up. It would be a straight business transaction between men. And because his heart had been bleeding, and his soul battered over Clarisse, Julien had allowed his *oncle* to have his way.

That had been seven years ago. In the interim, Garrett Luce had named him as proxy, enabling him to live in the chateau in order to be on hand to oversee daily operations and conduct business in his name without much oversight. Oncle Etienne had crowed over the achievement. What an enormous step forward to regaining the land this could be, he'd said. Luce was all but in their pockets, as long as Luce didn't sell until they were financially ready to meet his price. Even then, if they had a good relationship with Luce, his price might be more forgiving. Meanwhile Julien appeased his conscience over the subterfuge with the fact that he genuinely liked Sir Garrett Luce. Luce was not the sort of man who was easily coerced. The odds were shifting in their favour but nothing was guaranteed. All they could do now was wait for him to tire of an overseas property, hope the timing was right and the price was affordable. Grapes took time. Reacquiring the Archambeau lands took time. Meanwhile, at least he got to keep vigil and walk the land. *Le tout en temps utile.* All things in good time.

She'd made good time from Paris. The roads had been dry, a great surprise given the time of year. The north-eastern landscape of France with its rivers and valleys had sped by outside the window of the rented post-chaise. Speed could be bought and she'd happily bought it. Emma wanted nothing more than to be at the chateau, to breathe the fresh country air, and to immerse herself in this new life. Maybe then, the ache within her would subside. That ache had been her constant companion in her month of loss. Who ever thought February could be so long? A month with only twenty-eight days? Usually, it was January that dragged and February flew. But this had been the longest February of her life. Now it was over. As of this morning, it was officially March. Time to begin again.

Yet as much as she wanted the ache to subside, she didn't want it to leave her entirely. To not feel that ache was somehow akin to forgetting Garrett. Mourning was remembering. Hurting was remembering. If she didn't do those things, how would she keep him close? And yet, she had to be stronger than her grief; she could not let that grief weigh her down, make her intransigent. She was not made for inertia. *'Une mille, madame,'* the coachman called down. She looked out the window. One mile until she was…home. Such as it was.

She'd not sent a letter of warning ahead to alert the various stewards Garrett kept on the property to see to its upkeep. There'd been no point. She'd travel as fast as the letter. But she was not expected. There'd be some upheaval upon her arrival and she was sorry for it. She didn't want to make extra work for anyone. Perhaps in this case, she could be excused for her abrupt appearance.

The post-chaise turned a final corner and the groomed parklands of Les Deux Coeurs came into view with their perfectly squared box hedges and the tall oaks that covered the drive to the house. She released a breath she'd been unaware she was holding, relief flooding her. The place looked very much as it had seven years ago when she'd come here as a new bride. Since then, the place had existed for her only on paper in the form of the quarterly reports, and in her mind in the form of memory. Garrett made occasional visits but she'd not returned, staying behind in England to oversee his other interests in his absence. They'd planned to come together this summer, though, to celebrate their seven-year anniversary. There was a vintage he'd put down that would be ready for the occasion. 'I'll celebrate for us, my love,' she whispered.

The chaise halted in the circle before the front door and the coachman helped her down. Emma lifted her veil and tipped her face to the house, to the fading blue sky above it. It had been sunny today. Now blue was bleeding to purple, day and night mixing their colours to produce a gentle violet sky. The dusky light bathed the limestone walls and the green-shuttered windows of the chateau in soft mauve. Lights filtered through the windows from the inside, giving the impression that someone was at home. The scene filled her with a sense of peace. She was glad of the haste if it meant arriving at this magical hour.

The butler, or rather the *maître d'hôtel*...she was in France now...came to the top of the front steps, not quite able to hide the surprise and consternation on his face. Richet was his name. 'Madame Luce.' It was part greeting, part question as he struggled to recognise a woman he hadn't seen in years. His gaze swept past her to the post-chaise, his eyes waiting for Garrett to emerge. Then came the registering of her blacks and veil.

Emma swept up the steps, feeling enormous empathy for the man. He was about to be dealt the double blow of an unexpected guest and the loss of the master of the house. She'd rehearsed the conversation in her head in the hopes that practice would help her get through the announcement without tears. But she wasn't sure she could. It still hurt to say the words out loud. Best to keep it abrupt and direct. 'Richet, Monsieur Luce has died.' She felt her throat tighten. 'I've come to stay. If you could send a few footmen to bring

up my trunks.' She managed a smile that was both com-
miserative and authoritative. She'd learned that it was
easier to cope with the loss if she stayed busy. Others
felt that way, too. When faced with loss, people wanted
to do something, as if that task could ease the pain. She
could see the relief in Richet's eyes at the instruction.

'I will have them brought up right away. Mrs Dormand will have your room readied. Perhaps you'd like
to wait in the drawing room while all is prepared.' He
was already leading the way, already remembering her
French was passable at best. He'd switched into English
that was far better than her French. It had been one of
the reasons Garrett had hired him when he'd bought
the chateau. Garrett had not wanted his bride to feel
the outsider because of a language barrier.

'Thank you, Richet,' Emma said softly. 'I am sorry
to be the bearer of bad news and to descend on you with
no notice. I had little choice in the matter.'

'Bien sur, madame. Ce n'est pas une probleme.' He
fell into his French, flustered for a moment by her kindness and explanation. She'd not meant to discompose
him. She never had got the knack of treating servants
with distance and disdain. She'd grown up with servants, but as a daughter of a businessman the distance
between servants and master was far smaller than in
a noble house.

In the drawing room, she took a seat on a daffodil-
yellow upholstered settee and let her gaze reacquaint
itself with the room. Richet cleared his throat. 'I will
send for tea for you, *madame*, and I will tell Monsieur

Archambeau that you're here. He's just come in from his evening tour of the vineyards.'

Monsieur Archambeau. They would meet at last and she could put a face to the name. Garrett's steward was the only one of the staff she hadn't met in person, although in some ways she'd felt she'd met him on paper over the years in the correspondence he exchanged with Garrett. She had formed an image of him in her head from the thorough reports and meticulously neat, crisp handwriting. In her mind, Monsieur Archambeau was a slender, elegant intellectual, as neatly kept in appearance as his handwriting was on paper; a rational, reliable fellow who perhaps tended towards more reserved behaviours; a man who was respectable and respectful. With luck, they'd have an amicable working relationship.

Richet bowed himself out. A footman came to stir up the fire and Emma made a slow tour of the room, taking in the artwork on the walls, the figurines on tabletops, and the tall empty vases flanking the mantel. All of this was hers. She was safe in a way she'd not been in England. There was comfort in knowing that no one, not Robert or Steven, could take *this* home from her.

She ran a hand over the smooth wood-carved figurine of a dog posed in full trot. This had been one of Garrett's favourite pieces. He'd kept hounds at Oakwood and had loved visiting the kennels. In a world that had been nothing but change in the past weeks, it was a relief to see that this place hadn't changed in seven years. Garrett had bought the place lock, stock, and barrel from a Monsieur Anouilh. The rooms would likely need refreshing to make the place truly hers. But all in good time. For now, there was comfort in the constant and the familiar. She rested her hand on the carving and closed her eyes. For the first time since the flood, she felt as if everything would be all right. At last, she could breathe.

'Madame Luce?' the low tones of a cultured, accented male voice intruded. Somehow, she knew Monsieur Archambeau would sound like that—calm, in control, like his reports. She turned and opened her eyes, prepared to greet the intellectual steward of Les Deux Cœurs, prepared to take the next step into her new life, but that metaphoric next step halted in mid-stride at the sight of the man who stood before her: tall, broad-shouldered, with a labourer's muscled build, and dressed to match in a homespun shirt open at the neck to reveal an indecent expanse of chest, heavy work breeches tucked into dusty boots and dark hair tousled from the elements. Monsieur Archambeau looked as if he *worked* the land he wrote to her husband about.

'Monsieur Archambeau?' She fumbled for words, the mental image in her mind and the reality standing before her scrambling to align themselves in a rare miscue for her. This could not be him and yet who else could it be? She was seldom wrong about people but she was wrong now. There was nothing of the slender intellectual in the rustic farmer who stood before her.

Chapter Three

No. Not even that assessment was right. She knew she was wrong even as she thought it. His eyes ruined it. A rustic farmer would have a humble gaze. There was nothing humble about the slate-blue stare fixed on her at present. This gaze was instead strong and assessing, making no secret that he was taking her measure, making her feel as if she was an intruder. Emma met his gaze with a strong stare of her own, one she hoped hid her own sudden turmoil as she struggled to realign her thoughts.

She extended her hand to him, trying to be friendly, a part of her mind clinging to her earlier hopes of an amicable business relationship with her husband's steward. But this man did not look amicable. He looked stubborn. 'I do not believe you were here when I first visited.' Every fibre of her being screamed a silent warning: If she'd been wrong about this, what else might she be wrong about when it came to Monsieur Archambeau and the chateau? 'You must be my husband's steward. I feel as if I know you from all the correspondence over the years,' which was fast becoming a polite lie. She clearly *didn't* know this man. Her images of him couldn't be further from the reality standing before her, a realisation that both intrigued the natural curiosity in her and unnerved her. What sort of man had her husband left in charge of the chateau?

He took her hand and bent over it, slate eyes holding hers with all the élan of a skilled courtier, at drastic odds with his appearance, a little joke flickering behind his gaze, a joke she suspected was on her. 'I am Monsieur Luce's man of business here, *madame*.' The correction was subtle and it contributed to a growing sense of unease, of being off balance.

Some of her newly acquired sense of peace evaporated. Her usually accurate perception of people had deserted her, leaving her feeling exposed, but she'd gathered her wits enough to be aware of his correction and what it might portend. Not steward, but the man of business. Had he corrected her out of manly pride, wanting to be seen as someone of importance? If so, she would take care to manage his pride in future interactions. It was easy enough to smooth feathers when one was aware they were ruffled. Or had he corrected her because his responsibilities extended beyond sending quarterly reports and overseeing harvests?

If so, had he been appointed to that responsibility by Garrett or had he assumed it for himself, something that was simple enough to do with an absentee landlord? She hoped for the former. Appointed power was easier to amend. The latter was not. It would be more difficult to…dislodge…if necessary. Power was a hard thing to give up and she was deeply curious to discover just how much power Monsieur Archambeau had been given or how much he'd assumed over the years here at the chateau. The potential of the latter was something she'd warned Garrett about when he'd first set up the arrangement. Instinct told her she might have a fight on her hands.

The same lead that had settled in her stomach at the reading of the will settled in her stomach once more. Monsieur Archambeau was an unlooked-for development. She told herself his position didn't matter, it changed nothing, and whatever the arrangement in the past may or may not have been, she would establish new ground rules. 'It seems we'll have much to discuss since I am here now and have every intention of overseeing the vineyards myself.' In other words, she did not need someone to act on her behalf when she was here to do it in person. She'd never been one for subtlety, neither had her father. This place was hers. She would defend it from those who would challenge that both inside its walls and out.

'Perhaps we might exchange news over supper, if you'd care to join me?' Archambeau was all cool smoothness, a veritable wolf in sheep's clothing, or was that worker's clothing? He was undaunted by her sudden appearance or the veiled warning of terminated employment. Did he not believe she would let him go? Did he think she was bluffing or merely meant to put him in his place? Whatever his beliefs, he obviously felt he had the upper hand. She would disabuse him of that soon enough. This was her home. Her vineyards. Her business.

'Are you inviting me to dinner in my own home?' She matched his coolness, his calm.

'Yes, I am.' He did not back down from the challenge. 'We dine at seven. I believe Mrs Dormand has your rooms ready. Shall I show you up?' He was treating her as a guest. She would not cede that ground to him.

'That will be unnecessary. I know the way.' It was the one thing she was certain of in a world that was suddenly filled with the unfamiliar. She smiled to match his politeness. 'I will see you at seven.' That would give her time to realign her thinking. Things were not as she'd anticipated at Les Deux Coeurs. By dinner, she'd be prepared to expect the unexpected.

Seven hells! Emma Luce was *exactly* what he'd expected, only he'd never expected to actually have to meet her. That she was here was a problem, a very large problem he'd have to deal with quickly and decisively. He'd start at dinner, which didn't give him much time. He called for Richet and ordered a bath for his quarters. A smug smile curled on his mouth as he took the stairs. What would Madame Luce think of *that*? Of him *living* in the house? If she were to contest it, he would relish informing her that it was something he and Monsieur Luce had agreed upon so there was always someone on hand. He had as much right as she to live here at present. That would, perhaps, surprise her. And if she thought the rustic farmer from the drawing room would show up at the dinner table, she'd be in for another surprise. If he hadn't been so wrapped up in his own shock at Richet's news, which had been two surprises dropped on him at once—Luce's death *and* his widow's arrival—he might have found some humour in the confusion that had lit her quicksilver eyes. While she'd been what he'd expected, *he* had not been what *she'd* expected, dressed as he was in his working clothes.

Upstairs, Julien divested himself of his dirty garments and slid into the hot water, letting it relax his body and his mind, his thoughts wandering through what he knew about Emma Luce and how best to deal with her. Sir Garrett Luce had once described his wife in glowing terms as a whirlwind, a woman of fortitude and presence. Those were all attributes Julien could appreciate when they belonged to a woman who was on the other side of the Channel, hundreds of miles from here. He appreciated them far less when they were in his drawing room—not that she would think it was *his* drawing room; that much was clear from their conversation.

Presence was a businessman's word for beauty and Emma Luce was certainly that: dark-haired, sharp silver eyes, a lithe figure shown to perfection even in an unadorned black travelling costume. On a woman like her, even mourning attire appeared fashionable. But all of that was a decoy, Julien suspected, for the intelligence housed within. Luce had mentioned his Emma had a 'rare head for business,' a woman full of ideas about how to get goods to the people who wanted them, and how to convince people that they wanted everything.

'Should have been born a man. She'd have made a fortune,' Luce had said once over brandies during one of his visits. Then, the man had winked at him. *'But fortunately for me she was not. I'm quite satisfied that she's a woman.'* He'd mentioned, too, that she came from a business background herself. *'We understand each other,'* Luce had said in the tones of a man well pleased with his marriage.

Julien sank lower in the hot water. He'd envied Luce that, a wife who was his partner *and* his love. Had the man understood such a combination was worth more than any holding in his business empire? It was what he himself had hoped to have with Clarisse. Together, they were going to turn the Archambeau lands into a great wine house known for its *vin mousseux*, its champagne. A house that would aspire to and rival the House of Clicquot, perhaps in time surpass it. The old widow of Clicquot wouldn't live for ever. She was already seventy-five, and everyone knew she was the genius and the mind behind the house. Her family hadn't the same fortitude for the business as they had for spending the profits.

He'd thought Clarisse had wanted those things, too. As the daughter of a self-made man who'd acquired his fortune in the post-Napoleonic world of the Bourbon Restoration, he'd assumed Clarisse would want what he wanted, valued what he valued, that nothing was more important than family and land. All else could be taken away in a moment.

A man had to make himself in this new world. Titles were fickle things. They meant little to Julien. The Archambeaux had lost their title in the Revolution. They'd regained it in 1815 only to lose it again in 1848. There were rumours the title would be restored again but that changed nothing for Julien. Things that could be taken away so easily were not worthy of his pursuit. Land was the only thing that lasted. Not even love could lay claim to that, as Clarisse had proven.

Now Emma Luce's unanticipated arrival threatened the plans he and Oncle Etienne had in place. She couldn't possibly know what she was walking into, nor could she find out, not yet. It was imperative that the running of the vineyards and control of the vineyard finances remained firmly in his hands for the time being. Not only for his plans but for the long-term viability of the vineyards. People trusted him; he had built a reputation for being both an excellent *vigneron* and winemaker. If anyone thought for a moment that he was not at the helm of Les Deux Coeurs or that the place was being run by an Englishwoman, all confidence—which manifested itself in wine orders and financial investment—would be undermined. What did an Englishwoman know of French vineyards? It was a question that must not be asked. And yet, it was a question he was forced to ask himself.

'I am here now and have every intention of overseeing the vineyards myself,' she'd announced, and he'd been glad no one else, not even the servants, had been around to hear her say that. He needed to be sure she never said such a thing to anyone.

Julien held his breath and slid beneath the water for a final dunking. Garrett Luce had picked a hell of a time to die. After seven years of an amicable arrangement that had allowed Julien to quietly assume a liberal free hand, all that was about to change. Whoever thought seven was a lucky number had never met Emma Luce.

Chapter Four

Emma entered the drawing room at the stroke of seven and not a moment earlier. To be early would require extra conversation with Monsieur Archambeau; polite small talk with the understanding that business talk would come later, perhaps at the table, or after. The French did not countenance the mixing of business with pleasure, and nothing was more pleasurable to the French than their food.

'Ah, Madame Luce, there you are, right on time.' Monsieur Archambeau came forward with a smile on his cleanly shaven face. Gone was the dark stubble of earlier, the dusty worker's clothes replaced with dark trousers, jacket, and a blue waistcoat that brought out the slate of his eyes. The dour worker had been replaced with a gallant gentleman. Perhaps he'd decided he'd catch more flies with honey than vinegar. Perhaps *she* ought to be wary of that. He offered her his arm. 'Richet has informed me Petit, our cook, is ready to serve the meal. Shall we go in? I've learned, to my hazard, not to keep Cook's meals waiting.'

So, he was not *all* honey yet. There was still *some* vinegar there. Beneath his smile and low chuckle, she detected a rebuke for having come down with no time to spare for the niceties of small talk. If there was one thing the French valued as much as their food and wine, it was conversation. Her late arrival had cheated him of the latter. He was taking care it did not cheat him of the former. Or perhaps he was reminding her that he'd been here first, been here longer, that he had a relationship with the staff she hadn't seen in seven years. Good Lord, was she going to spend the whole meal analysing everything he said? Turning his words and actions this way and that like a puzzle box? Probably. She'd not lie to herself. Her brain was excited by the possibility of doing *something*, of having new fodder to energise itself with.

'I packed so carefully that unpacking was something of a challenge,' Emma offered by way of polite apology. In truth, she'd lingered purposefully in her chambers, fussing over the unpacking of her trunks to wait out the clock. It had not taken long to change. When one was in mourning there were no decisions to dawdle over and debate: The black gown or the black gown? Mourning took away the feminine joy of selecting the right dress, the right cut and colour, a tool just as much as conversation and charm. In the past, she'd taken great care with her clothes, dressed with purpose. Now that Garrett was gone, she didn't mind the black. She had no one to dress for. The black suited her. It reflected the darkness, the emptiness she still felt. After nearly a month, perhaps those things would be a part of her for ever, going forward. She *did* feel fire; she *did* feel life. The haze of grief had lifted but in its wake the satisfaction, the completion she'd once felt, was missing. Her soul was empty, an intangible hunger gnawing at her, begging to be filled, to be fed. But with what? She hoped the vineyards could help, that being here in France would satisfy the hunger.

She smoothed her skirts, the gesture drawing Monsieur Archambeau's eye and, unexpectedly, his sympathy. 'I am truly sorry about your husband, *madame*. I considered Sir Garrett a friend as well as a business partner,' he offered solemnly, his hard eyes softening. 'You have my sincere condolences. I should have said so earlier.' An apology? That had all her senses on alert. Perhaps he was trying to reposition himself after a less than friendly start. Monsieur Archambeau was *definitely* on his mettle. A man never apologised for anything unless he felt himself entirely in the wrong. Or, unless there was something he wanted—*badly*. She'd wager the latter was the case if he was willing to apologise *and* put on quite the show in his dark evening clothes and excellently tied cravat.

The stern man she'd met upon arrival had been replaced by the most gallant of gentlemen, a transition that Emma thought had been rather seamless, quite natural for him, one that fit him as well as his clothes. That too was cause for caution. A worker with a gentleman's manners was an intriguing and unusual combination. Such a man had angles and facets, depths and agendas. He would not allow himself to be dismissed easily. Indeed, everything about him suggested he did not see himself as an employee to be commanded but as something more. That's what worried her. He saw himself not as a steward but as a partner, perhaps even as the superior business partner. She'd have to help him understand his role otherwise.

He ushered her into the dining room, playing the part of the gentleman to perfection. At the sight of the dining room, her breath caught loud enough to be noticed. She'd not been prepared for this. '*Madame? Is everything all right?*' Monsieur Archambeau solicited with a look of concern.

'I'm fine, it's just that my memories did not do this room justice.' Her memories had dimmed its magnificence and now, seen in person, the room laid overwhelming siege to those memories. It looked exactly as it had when she'd honeymooned as a bride; the beautiful turquoise damask on the walls, the creamy wainscoting that ran from floor to chair railing, the brass sconces set at intervals to illuminate the exquisite artwork, and the massive fireplace with its mantel of carved French oak from the chateau's own forests. The long table, capable of seating twenty, was set for two. A white cloth draped the far end closest to the fire. A heavy multiarmed silver candelabra stood in the centre of the cloth, its flame light glancing off the crystal goblets and elegant white china.

She was vaguely aware of Monsieur Archambeau's hand dropping to the small of her back as he guided her towards the table, of the effortless way he held out her chair and waited for her to arrange her skirts. In the back of her mind, it registered that these were routines he'd performed countless times, routines that came to him as naturally as breathing. They were not routines that came naturally to farmers.

Monsieur Archambeau took his own seat and Richet came forward to pour the wine, a pale gold white that sparked diamond-like in the crystal, while footmen served potato and leek soup in wide, shallow bowls. 'I hope the food is to your liking,' Monsieur Archambeau solicited. 'We'll just have three courses tonight. We were not expecting guests.'

It was a masterful snub, so implicitly done as a piece of self-deprecating apology, one might miss it. But not Emma. She'd weathered the implicit disdain of Society long enough to understand the messages wrapped within messages. *We. Guest.* These were divisive words that indicated who belonged and who was outside the inner circle. She matched his solicitude with a smile. 'The soup is delicious. I will send menus to Cook tomorrow.' Best to establish her authority immediately, starting with the running of the household. 'I'll meet with Mrs Dormand as well and renew our acquaintance.'

The last request seemed to perplex him. A small furrow formed in the space between his dark brows, as if she'd confused him at best, insulted him at worst. 'I assure you that is not necessary. We can certainly see to the care of one guest without her needing to oversee the housework.' He brought to bear all of his French solicitude. 'You should enjoy yourself while you're here; rest, recover. You have had a difficult month, Madame. You have much to think about.'

Truly, he was a splendid actor. If they hadn't got off to such a frigid start, she might have bought into it. A woman must constantly be on guard against such charm when wielded so expertly by a well-dressed and well-mannered man, she thought. Not that she and her broken heart needed such a warning. She was not in the market for such charm or winsomeness. She took a sip of the wine and let herself enjoy the performance before she destroyed it with another smile. 'This is my *home*, Monsieur Archambeau. I do not intend to be a burden, or a guest in my own house. I mean to see to the running of my household.' She did not add *and its lands* again as she had earlier in the drawing room. That would come in time. She hoped it would come by implicit coup instead of explicit, that he would get the message that his time here was coming to an end now that there was a landowner in residence daily. As such, his services were no longer needed. If she needed a steward, she could hire someone who was more amicable.

Another frown deepened the lines between his brows as he feigned perplexity. 'How long do you mean to stay?'

'Permanently, *monsieur*.' He did not like the word *permanently*. If the furrow between his brows deepened any further it would become a chasm. 'This is the property left to me by my husband. His eldest now holds the English estate, as is his right under British entailment law.' She did not begrudge Robert that, only the gloating way by which Robert had grabbed possession. She gave a soft smile designed to communicate graciousness and understanding on her part. 'The new baronet will not want his father's second wife under-foot as he establishes his household.' That was an un-derstated way of putting it, but she'd not make herself vulnerable by telling *monsieur* she had nowhere else to go, that her husband's family had essentially turned her out the moment the will had been read and had been more than happy to see her 'exiled' to France. If they couldn't get their hands on the chateau, they could at least get rid of her.

'Of course, *madame*.' It was noncommittally said as they both smiled at each other over the rims of wine glasses and Emma was not fool enough to believe any-thing was settled, only tabled. Footmen came forward to take the soup bowls and replace them with steam-ing bowls of beef bourguignon. A loaf of bread was set between them, and fresh wine glasses were filled with a rich red, the table laid for the second round as much as for the second course. Round one had been about laying out her situation. It stood to reason that round two ought to be about laying out his. After all, she'd been the one to give out crucial information over soup. They now both knew her plans and expectations. It would be quid pro quo for him to reciprocate, and reciprocation was the foundation of good negotiation.

She speared a piece of the tender meat and waited. That was a tactical mistake. She ought to have guided the conversation more specifically even if it had re-quired a blunt question. He took the opening she of-fered but he did not play by the rules, his voice gentle in the candlelit darkness. 'Sir Garrett and I exchanged

letters at the end of January regarding the spring growing season. He'd not mentioned being in poor health.'
Slate-blue eyes rested on her with empathy. 'I assume
his death was unexpected. If it is too indelicate to ask
or too difficult to discuss, you must tell me and I shall
cease, but I would like to know what happened.'

He was not play-acting now and his request took the
edge off the otherwise sharp evening. They were no
longer two potential foes circling one another, but two
people who shared a common loss, something she'd
not taken time to consider in her haste to protect her
position. But now, here in the intimacy of the dining
room, the belated realisation occurred that Garrett was
common ground between them, as was his loss. She'd
lost a husband. This man, this *stranger*, had lost someone he'd counted as a friend. Where she'd had weeks
to reconcile herself to the loss, he'd had a mere hand-
ful of hours and no details to help his understanding.
Richet would have told him only that Sir Garrett Luce
was dead, and his widow was here. Then they'd been
sprung on one another by mutual surprise, and both
had gone on the defensive.

'I am sorry,' she apologised hastily, 'of course, you'd
want to know.' Perhaps she should have offered the
information sooner. Perhaps she should have not gone
immediately on the defence. Instead, she should have
approached this stranger from a position of softness,
not strength. But in her experience, gentleness was
seldom rewarded and quite often taken advantage of.

'You guess right, it was unexpected.' She took a
sip of wine to steady herself. Even after a month, even

after recounting the horrible events at Holmfirth for Garrett's sons and for her father, it was still difficult to speak of. 'We were in Holmfirth,' which probably meant nothing to Monsieur Archambeau. 'It was business. Garrett was looking at a mill he was interested in investing in. But he'd heard rumours about the dam up-river being unstable. He wasn't going to buy a mill that was likely to be washed away.' She cleared her throat to dislodge the lump forming. 'But it was. There was considerable rain while we were there, and the dam burst. It swept through the street where our lodgings were.' She gave him a meaningful look, pleading with him to understand the implications without her having to say the words.

'Mon Dieu,' Archambeau breathed, automatically reaching for her hand where it lay on the table. 'I am sorry. But you were not there? At the lodgings?'

'No, my friends and I were playing whist.' It still pained her to say that. Perhaps she should have been there, perhaps she should have died with him or she could have saved him. Both were illogical thoughts as Fleur liked to point out, but Emma couldn't get over the feeling of having somehow abandoned Garrett to his fate in exchange for her own selfish survival.

'You were lucky, then.' Archambeau said gently. He gave her a sad smile, releasing her hand. 'We must toast his memory.' He reached for his wine glass and raised it. 'To Sir Garrett Luce, a true and generous friend who will be greatly missed.' The wine glasses chimed against one another, and they drank, the toast leaving her with a surprising sense of rightness. In all the mourning that had taken place, the initial loss in Holmfirth, the funeral in Surrey, there'd been tears and wailing but no toasting and wine. Garrett would have liked more toasts than tears, she thought.

The *plateau de fromage*, the end-of-meal cheese platter, was brought in, featuring a rich Roquefort, a complement of dried fruits and cranberries, and a small pot of honey to drizzle over it. Small glasses were filled with port. 'We farm the honey here on site in our own apiaries.' Archambeau raised the honey dipper over her selection of fruits and drizzled for her. There was no hidden message this time in the use of 'we' as he spoke of the home farm and it seemed to her that the moment to discuss business had long passed. But there was a quietly stunning unintended revelation in this 'we'.

He lives here. The chateau is his home.

It was why he'd been on hand when she'd arrived so late in the day, why there'd been lights in the windows despite no one knowing of her coming, why he'd had evening clothes to change into and a razor for his toilette, why he had such a close relationship with the staff. Perhaps even why he'd felt threatened by her arrival. Should she choose to do so, she would displace him from more than a job.

Should she choose?

Her mind stuttered on the idea. That was a very different thought than the one she'd entered the dining room with. She'd come downstairs determined to establish her position and to disabuse him of any belief that he had a toehold here. Now, one meal later, she was already recanting that position. She shot him a considering look beneath her lashes as she reached for her port. Well, damn him for being a master. For all of her confidence that she was immune to his persuasion, it seemed he'd got exactly what he wanted from supper, and he'd done it by using the oldest trick in the book: making her believe she'd been the one in charge.

She finished her port and rose. 'Please excuse me, Monsieur Archambeau. It's been a long day and I'm tired. I thank you for the meal. Even on short notice, it was the best I've eaten in a while. I will give Cook my compliments tomorrow when I submit the menus. Thank you also for your company. I hope it did not take you away from any plans.'

He set aside his napkin and rose with her. 'It was my pleasure, Madame Luce. I will show you up.'

'It is not necessary,' she began but he interrupted with a soft smile.

'I know, but I will do it anyway. My manners would never forgive me.' She recognised it was a détente of sorts as she took his arm. He accepted her presence, no longer acting as if she were a guest temporarily passing through his life. Perhaps in the sharing of Garrett's loss some of his barriers had come down, too. Or perhaps he could simply be magnanimous in victory because they both knew he'd won the night.

Chapter Five

He had won the night. Now he needed to make good on that reprieve. Garrett Luce was dead. His widow was *here* in Cumières, *in* the chateau, and intending to stay. Julien paced the faded Aubusson carpet that covered most of the floor of his *oncle*'s study at the farmhouse that bordered the chateau's property, his body as unable to still as his mind. After a sleepless night, he'd ridden over as soon as he'd completed his early morning walk of the vineyards.

Even his morning walk, usually a calm, meditative activity, had been disrupted with thoughts of last night. He was still reeling with the news. There was the veil of grief over the loss of Sir Garrett. The loss so sudden and unbelievable, given that he had a letter from Garrett dated just days before his death. He was also reeling from the practical impact of what Garrett's death meant to his plans and position regarding the chateau.

He stopped by a bookcase to finger a globe set on a gold-plated axis. He gave it a gentle spin with his finger. He tinkered with the decorative scales on another shelf, moving the little weights to redistribute the balance. Such fine shelf ornaments for a farmhouse. Oncle Etienne had still been abed when he arrived and was a stickler for his morning routine. He would not deign to receive anyone without being completely dressed and shaved for the day, not even his nephew. Julien would have preferred not to be kept waiting. He'd have been happy to have his *oncle* receive him in his boudoir while he shaved or even if his *oncle* had simply thrown on a dressing robe and come downstairs in *dishabille*. But that was not how Etienne Archambeau conducted himself. He might not live in the family chateau, but he never forgot he was the son of a *comte*, that centuries of nobility ran in his veins. Julien chuckled. As for himself, he was quite the opposite. He didn't stand on ceremony unless he had to. There was no one at the chateau to care how he dressed or when he dressed or even *if* he dressed. He could run around in *dishabille* all day if it suited him. And, honestly, sometimes it did. At least that had been true up until last night. That would have to change now with Madame Luce in residence.

Emma Luce had been something of a revelation; a beautiful woman with sable hair and a cynic's sea-grey eyes that said a man aspired to her at his own peril. It was the type of challenge that would have appealed to Luce, but the cynicism in her eyes surprised him. What did a woman married to Garrett Luce have to be cynical about? The marriage had been a love match. Luce had family from a previous marriage, sons, a fortune. Self-sufficient as he'd been, he had not been required to marry. He'd lavished every extravagance on his young bride. In return, his bride had loved *him*, not his money or the things he could provide. That had been evident last night when she'd talked of her husband. She'd taken the loss hard.

Proof of that had moved him. Moved him right off topic at dinner, in fact. He'd intended dinner to be a chance to stake his claim, to make it clear that he was in charge of the vineyards. He'd not nurtured these vines for years to have a newcomer interrupt and undo his hard work just when results were within his grasp. But instead of business, they'd ended up talking about Garrett and of her plans to stay, which had served his purposes nonetheless in the end. He'd emerged victorious on a technicality. Last night, he'd allowed her to establish that she was not a guest in *his* home but a resident in *hers*. He checked the mantel clock and wondered if she was up already, giving her menus to Petit and meeting with the housekeeper. By extension, if she was *the* resident, what did that make him? The outsider? His response last night had been alarming. He'd been too empathetic by far. From empathy grew attachment. The less he knew about her the more objective he could be. Had he in his empathy allowed her to usurp him, or was there room for two residents?

'Julien, you're up early.' His *oncle* entered the study, pressed and polished in perfectly creased dark blue trousers and jacket, paisley-blue waistcoat and white linen pristine beneath. His cravat was tied with sartorial excellence and his cheek was smooth. His abundant head of sleek silver hair was brushed back from his face, his Archambeau-blue eyes sharp, alert, and yet kind. His *oncle* carried with him an aura of confidence that immediately put one at ease and filled one with the sense that all would be well. It was what he'd come to admire about his *oncle* in the years he'd lived with him in England while he'd gone to school, and what he relied on now that his *grandpère* and papa were gone. Even this morning, the sight and sound of his *oncle* eased the night rumblings of his mind. He'd been right to come.

'I have news, Oncle, and I felt it could not wait.' Rather, *he* could not wait. He wanted his mind to still, he wanted to lay this latest development at his *oncle*'s feet so he could get back to his grapes and his solitude.

His *oncle* raised a silver brow in query, a smile at the ready. 'It must be quite the news indeed to make you leave the chateau.' Julien heard the rebuke. He seldom left the estate. Over the years, after the disaster with Clarisse, he felt more at home with the grapes than he did among people. Oh, he'd not forgotten his manners, but he had less call to use them and he was fine with that. Last night had been the first night in a year he'd had to dust those manners off. 'Come, have breakfast with me while we talk. If I know you, you've been too busy walking the vineyards to have eaten yet.'

Breakfast was a delicious temptation at his *oncle*'s. A man could feast at his breakfast table, really set himself up for the day. All of Oncle Etienne's years in England during the family's exile and then after—all total a sum of sixty-two years of his life—had resulted in a table that catered to his *oncle*'s love of hearty British breakfasts with their eggs and sausages joined with

the traditional French preference for something sim-
pler; croissants and tartines with a cup of coffee or tea.
Today, though, Julien thought a croissant was all his
stomach could handle.

'You're not eating,' his *oncle* commented with a
pointed stare at his mostly empty plate. 'Is it bad news,
then?'

'I'm not sure it's good or bad. At this point, it's only
news, but I fear it does trend towards the bad.' They
took their seats at one end of the table and Julien delivered his news. 'Sir Garrett Luce is dead. He was killed
in a flash flood on a business trip a few weeks ago.'
He watched his *oncle* for a reaction. Luce had been his
friend, not his *oncle*'s. To his *oncle*, Luce was merely
a means to an end. 'Luce's widow arrived last night
at the chateau. She means to take up residence there.'

Oncle Etienne calmly sliced into his sausage and
took a long bite before answering. 'And the vineyards?
Does she mean to take an interest in them?'

'Yes. She declared quite specifically to me last night
that she means to take them over.' She was looking for
a project, something to assuage the loss he'd seen in her
eyes. She was a woman at sea, looking for something
to anchor herself to as she'd once anchored herself to
her husband. It made him wonder what that life had
been like. How had she spent her time? But these were
questions he had to banish from his mind. To know her
would be to invite disclosures, to bring emotions into
the equation. That had not worked well for him in the
past. He'd learned his lesson.

'No one can hear her say that. Her project *cannot* be

the vineyards,' Etienne said with firm finality, coming to the same conclusion Julien had last night. 'We've worked too hard. This a big year for us. The new grapes will be ready for harvest and the vintage we've been counting on goes to bottling. That *vin mousseux* will be the making of us.' They were counting on it. They had their extra funds invested in it. More than extra funds, really. There was his *oncle*'s loan against the farmhouse and the reclaimed vineyards, a loan granted on the collateral of the profits secured from pre-sales of the *vin mousseux*, and Garrett Luce's funds were invested, too, on the strength of Julien's reputation as a *vigneron*. To lose the confidence, financial or otherwise, of their backers at this point would be to court disaster. If they were unable to make payments on the loan they'd taken out last year to buy some additional acreage, they would lose the lands it had taken generations to claim in their play to raise funds to gather the rest. Neither of them had to say anything out loud about what a setback it would be. The expected profit was meant to go towards making Luce an offer for the vineyards, the last hectares of land to complete the restoration of the Archambeau holdings.

'I do not think she will sell any time soon.' Julien addressed the other concern. Even if they raised the money, even if they could continue to control the direction of the vineyards, it would all be for naught if the land could not be acquired.

Etienne nodded thoughtfully. 'That is the least of our concerns. We have choices there. We can convince her the land is not worth anything, that it is draining her coffers. She might part with the vineyards if not the house.' He gave a Gallic shrug. 'It would be a shame not to get the house back, but the land matters more.' The land could be turned to make more money. The house could not.

Julien frowned. 'That persuasion seems unlikely if we have the harvest we anticipate and the success we are looking for from the champagne. We can't sacrifice those things to promote a ruse of low productivity.' To say nothing of how uncomfortable Julien was with the idea of perpetuating a dishonest scheme designed to push someone towards a fabricated belief from which he'd benefit.

'There are other ways.' His *oncle* was undaunted. He spread his hands on the surface of the old oak table. 'Running a chateau and a vineyard is a large undertaking. Grapes are a year-round pursuit, they're a demanding mistress. She may tire of it. I think it's our responsibility to show her how time-consuming it is, especially if she has to make every little decision herself.'

Julien knew what his *oncle* meant: give Madame Luce everything she wanted and then ensure it became too overwhelming so that she'd beg for his intervention, beg for him to take on the responsibilities to the point of wanting to wash her hands of the vineyard completely. He was still sceptical. The strategy seemed mean-spirited.

'Telling people the truth, *showing* them the truth by letting them experience it, is not dishonest, *mon fils*,' Etienne soothed, reading his mind.

'But we haven't been quite truthful, have we? What

if she discovers how liberal we've been in Luce's absence?' Julien had never been entirely comfortable with a few of the decisions he'd made in Luce's absence over the years, like the decision to use Luce's grapes in the Archambeau vintages.

His *oncle* dismissed the concern with a wave of his hand. 'Luce hired you to act as his proxy, to make decisions that could not wait for letters to cross the Channel. You've done nothing but act in the best interest of the estate. You've cost him no money, you've not damaged the estate's reputation. There is nothing to worry about. You were simply doing your job to the best of your ability.' That was not quite true. If he had been doing his job to the *best* of his ability, the estate would have already been producing a profit. He'd merely been maintaining the status quo and making decisions that had been in the best interests of the Archambeaux. In most cases what had been good for the Archambeaux was good for the estate, but there were a few occasions when he'd had to choose and he'd chosen family. Nothing detrimental to the estate of course, just perhaps not a growth opportunity either. For example, he had not entertained offers for surplus grapes even though those offers paid more for them than the Archambeau vineyard did, knowing full well the Archambeau vineyard paid nothing for those grapes.

Oncle Etienne shook his head. 'She's a woman, and a grieving one. She'll have no head for business even if she does decide she's interested. You worry too much.' But his *oncle* hadn't seen her last night, those sharp eyes duelling with him over the rims of wine glasses.

Oncle Etienne always dismissed women, his own wife included, who'd been left behind in England with his son to run the British end of the Archambeau shipping business. Julien did not think Emma Luce would care to be dismissed.

'*Mon fils*, you are looking at these events all wrong. Instead of portending ill omens for us, it could be that this is the break we've been waiting for.' His *oncle* fixed him with the full force of his considering stare. 'Luce is dead, and that is regrettable. I know you liked him. But we could only have bought the vineyard and chateau from him at his whim. We might have waited years for that to happen. We'd already waited seven with no sign of him wanting to sell.' His *oncle* leaned forward, an idea brewing that made his eyes shine. 'But we don't need the widow to sell. You could marry her and claim the estate without us expending a single sou.' His *oncle* grinned. 'In one fell swoop, we'd have everything back.'

'She's in mourning, Oncle. Her husband has just passed. It would be, as the British say, bad form.'

'You don't have to marry her tomorrow. Marry her in the fall after the harvest. We've waited seven years; we can certainly wait seven more months.' His *oncle* scowled, no doubt thinking him a prude. Julien thought of the woman who'd sat across from him at the dinner table last night, whose loss was evident in the way she spoke of her husband, how difficult it had been for her to share the details of his death. He did not think seven months would change that for her. 'Marriage takes two willing partners. She's not emotionally available, not now, not in seven more months.' He knew from how she spoke of her husband last night that she was not envisioning a second marriage in her future.

'These obstacles are nothing, *mon fils*. You make too much of them.' Oncle Etienne gave a wry laugh. 'If she does not think she's *ouvert a l'amour*, then make her open to love, persuade her. You can be very charming when you choose.' Julien frowned and his *oncle* pressed. 'Or is it *you* who is not open to love?'

'I am not open to dishonesty,' Julien retorted sharply. 'Wooing a woman under the pretence of having feelings for her is cruel and devious.' He could not see Emma Luce tolerating such a betrayal. She did not strike him as a woman who forgave easily, or ever forgot. Such perfidious actions would drive a permanent wedge between them *if* she believed him. After last night's rather frosty start, he thought it unlikely she'd believe such a *volte face* on his part.

His *oncle* gave a negligible shrug. 'Fine then, you don't have to *court* her to wed her. This needn't be presented as a whirlwind romance or a love match. Tell her up front it's a marriage of convenience. She's a businesswoman. Convince her it's as convenient for her as it is for you.'

Julien's frown deepened. Usually, he admired his *oncle*'s strategic mind, his ability to look at problems from different angles. But not today. He fixed his *oncle* with a stern stare, a reminder that he was a man of thirty-seven, no longer a boy to be ordered about. 'I am to be bartered in marriage for the Archambeau restoration?'

His *oncle* let out a frustrated sigh. '*Mon Dieu*, Julien,

tu as besoin de te faire pousser un paire. I'd marry her myself, sight unseen, if I wasn't already married.' He gave an impatient wave of his hand. 'You were going to marry Clarisse for the estate. This is no different. It's not as if you're interested in anyone else at the moment.'

Julien bristled at that. What his *oncle* proposed went against his principles. Not even for the Archambeau restoration would he compromise his ethic, nor would he make such a decision that would take someone else at unawares, the full deception not revealed until it was too late to change course. He knew already what Emma Luce would think of such a strategy. 'It *was* different with Clarisse, Oncle. We were in love.'

'*You* were in love,' his *oncle* corrected without empathy. 'It's been seven years, *mon fils*. How much longer are you going to carry that carcass around with you? Clarisse certainly hasn't,' he added pointedly. No. She hadn't. Three months after the broken engagement, Clarisse had married a French politician whose star was rising in powerful circles. It had been an extravagant, very public summer affair at the chateau, her family making no apologies for the speed with which it happened after the dissolution of her engagement to the down-at-heel son of the Comte de Rocroi.

'She has two children now, lives in Paris in a *grande maison*,' his *oncle* persisted. 'She is touted as one of the city's premier hostesses.' His *oncle* raised a brow. 'And what do you have, hiding among your grapes?' He paused and then slapped a palm on the table, indicating that a decision had been made. 'You must come with me. I am meeting with the district growers today.'

Julien groaned. 'Those old men?' There were a thousand things to do at the chateau and any of them were more appealing than lunch with the district's growers, windbags that they were. They'd talk for hours trying to impress each other.

'Yes, *those* old men. They are our friends and our competition. We must keep an eye on them as they keep an eye on us. Charles Tremblay would like nothing better than to see us fail. He'd snatch up the land and we'd never get it back. And if you'd truly like a bit of revenge against Gabriel Anouilh, you need to show him you've moved on from his daughter and that you can acquire that land without him. To that end, it might not be best to mention that Garrett Luce is dead just yet. I don't want the consortium spooking and withdrawing their support.' His *oncle* gave him a stern look. 'The other thing you cannot continue to do, *mon fils*, is hide away and lick your wounds like a whipped cur. You're too young to be a recluse.' Oncle Etienne leaned forward. 'This is *our* year. We will throw a grand summer ball at the chateau in June, just as we've planned, to celebrate the new vintage. We will invite buyers and they will see your genius. It will be a success and I want you there beside me.'

'I am always beside you, Oncle.' Julien reminded him, trying not to take offence. He was the one who grew the grapes, who oversaw the harvests, who decided which vines to prune. Oncle Etienne might be the face of the Archambeau vineyards in their current state today, such as they were—a mid-sized, but high-quality winery—but Julien was the silent brilliance behind the scenes whose effort made those successes possible. It was something he had in common with Garrett Luce, both of them liking to build success backstage instead of on it.

'Publicly, *mon fils*. I know you've been with me, even when you were a schoolboy in England and living with your *tante* and I, you were beside me. But I want everyone to *see* us together. When we reclaim the land and the chateau, I want it to be *our* victory.' Oncle Etienne gave him a fond smile. 'That settles it. You can wash up and change into the spare things you keep here. We'll leave in an hour. The meeting is at Charles Tremblay's. He wants to show off his new carriage horses and his improvements on his stables. Pompous braggart.' His *oncle* rolled his eyes and then gave a sly smile. 'At least he sets a good table for luncheon, *non*? We'll get a taste of that red he's always talking about.'

Julien laughed. Sometimes it was hard to tell if his *oncle* thought the growers' consortium were friends or foes. The line was thin and often crossed and recrossed. Still, there was something comforting about knowing if there was trouble, *real* trouble like blight or drought or, heaven forbid, fire, the other growers would be there to support them. The consortium had celebrated with them when his *grandpère* had bought back the first of the acreage several years ago, some of them having been in the same situation not long before. They'd been there for them when his father had died, supplying them with enough workers to get the harvest in. If Charles Tremblay wanted to brag about his horses, he'd probably earned the right.

'I'll be ready, Oncle. I just need to send a note to Richet and let him know I'll be gone until tomorrow.' He had no illusions about 'lunch' at Tremblay's. The meeting would run well into the evening once they'd eaten and admired the man's stables, drank his wine, and then finally got down to business. They wouldn't be back to the farmhouse until evening, and he wouldn't risk his horse's legs on a pothole in the dark. Better to sleep over and ride home in the daylight. It would be safer, and it would give Madame Luce time to take stock. Perhaps his *oncle* was right. If she could see first-hand the enormity of running the chateau, it may go a long way toward her realising she was no match for it. This way, it would be her decision to step back.

Chapter Six

Richet took a step back from the breakfast table, his note delivered. 'Monsieur Archambeau will be away until tomorrow,' he informed her, making it unnecessary for her to read the note and making it clear that he'd read it before passing it on to her.

She fixed the *maître d'hôtel* with a strong stare. 'Do you make it a habit of reading your mistress's mail before she does?' Or reading it at all. Reading it after her probably wouldn't make things any better. It wasn't his business, regardless.

Richet had the good form to at least *look* scandalised. His brows went up and his long face gave a strong facsimile of shock. 'Absolutely *not, madame. Mon Dieu*, what sort of *maître d'hôtel* do you take me for?'

His disbelief was so creditably done she felt for a moment that she'd been the one in the wrong. 'I thought perhaps it was a French thing?'

Richet drew himself up to his full height, an impressive six feet, almost as tall as Monsieur Archambeau, she thought. 'I only read my mail, *madame*.' He nodded to the note in her hand. 'If you look at the outside, you'll see that it is addressed to me.'

Emma turned the note over, a slow horror dawning as she realised her *faux pas*, and something else, too. 'Monsieur Archambeau left word with you?' But not with her. He'd preferred to tell the *maître d'hôtel* his schedule but not to inform her? It was a most implicit snub. She scanned the note again, looking for a line that indicated Richet was expected to pass the information on to her, but there was nothing. Archambeau had written explicitly to Richet. It was only through Richet's kindness in *choosing* to share the message with her that she knew. Her cheeks flamed with her error. Emma squared her shoulders. 'I owe you an apology. I should not have assumed.' Should not have assumed she couldn't trust her staff's own loyalty. Should not have assumed she'd be treated as an outsider despite Monsieur Archambeau's attempts to do just that last night.

'It is no problem, *madame*.' Richet bowed and left her to finish her breakfast in penitent silence. She needed to do better. Monsieur Archambeau had put her on edge and in doing so, she'd not thought clearly, rationally. These were Garrett's people. People hired by him to see to the running of his home. Her home now. She may not know them the way Monsieur Archambeau did, but she did know Garrett. Garrett meant the chateau to be a place of refuge and recovery, a place to start her life anew. He would not leave her among enemies. Garrett had Richet's loyalty. That meant, she, as Garrett's wife, did, too. Yet Monsieur Archambeau respected Richet.

Of course. It was obvious. Monsieur Archambeau had her so on edge, she'd forgotten one of her father's most fundamental rules: if one wanted to fully understand a situation, one had to look at it from the viewpoints of others, not just one's own. How difficult this must be for Richet, to be torn between the two of them. If she wanted to be upset with anyone, it should be Monsieur Archambeau for snubbing her. She finished her breakfast and set aside her napkin. Well, lesson learned. There was nothing to do but move forward. She would allow this knowledge to inform her upcoming meetings this morning with the housekeeper and with Cook. She would also let it shape her choices. She had today and tomorrow to herself without the risk of Monsieur Archambeau's interference. It was the perfect time to familiarise herself with the house. It occurred to her that though she might have been here before, visiting did not equate with knowledge. To be an effective mistress of her home, she needed to know it. She'd meet with Mrs Dormand and Cook, then she'd change into clothes that would allow her to get to know her home more intimately, another lesson learned from her father.

One day and a whirlwind later, Emma was feeling much more at home. She'd spent the time cleaning, getting to know her new house, and most of all, she'd spent it dreaming of the life she'd create here. It would be a life of acceptance where the origins of her family's fortune didn't matter. Where people would come to her gracious home for tea and cards, garden parties and picnics, and not look down their noses at

her. They would get to know her without her antecedents preceding her.

It was the type of acceptance she'd always dreamed
of, of being part of the district. It was an acceptance
she'd experienced in some small part as Garrett's wife.
There'd been authentic acceptance within Garrett's
circle of friends; Adam and Fleur, Antonia and Keir,
people Garrett trusted with his life. Then there'd been
the verisimilitude of acceptance among those in Society who'd recognised they could not entirely ignore Sir
Garrett and Lady Luce. The Luces had piles of money
and a title. But she and Garrett had been honest with
each other about the foundations of that acceptance.
They could laugh at Society, they could let Society
have its foibles, because they'd had each other. She'd
been alone no longer.

Here, in the middle of the French countryside, it
would be different, and Emma could hardly wait. She
polished silver, imagining the teas she would give,
imagining walking through the gardens, her arm looped
through that of a new friend's as they laughed together.
She rubbed at a smudge on a teapot and laughed at
herself. If she had an Achilles heel it would be sating
her hunger for acceptance in the form of true friend-
ships that weren't contingent on her money or where
it came from. She would prove herself worthy of acceptance on her own merits. She would prove herself
in the wine business. Here, there would be no spoiled
debutantes like Amelia St James to look down at her,
no lords like the Earl of Redmond who flirted with her
money but shunned her behind her back. Yes, here it

would be different. Garrett had given her a fresh start
with his last gift.

Emma hummed to herself, tucking a loose curl underneath her kerchief as she stirred the pot of soup on
the stove. She breathed in the herb-scented steam with
satisfaction. There was nothing like creamy chicken
corn chowder on a cold, damp night, especially when
it was made with barley and garnished with sage and
bacon. Best of all, she'd made it herself. She loved
cooking, an activity her father had encouraged when
she was growing up and one that Garrett had enjoyed
the fruits of on the nights they'd chosen to stay in, just
the two of them. She'd worked on this soup all afternoon, checking it between other sundry chores that had
been self-assigned. Cook had been scandalised at the
suggestion she make her own food, but when Emma
had offered to give Cook the day off to visit her daughter's family and new grandbaby in the village, Cook
had been far more accepting.

People had their pride. One must always be conscious
of that. Mrs Dormand had been wary, too, when Emma
had told her she wanted to do some chores. She'd had
her own degree of scandal when Emma had shown up
in a plain blue work dress and apron, a kerchief on her
head, ready to sort linens and polish silver after a tour of
the house from top to bottom. *'I will not be a tourist in
my own home, Mrs Dormand,'* Emma had said strictly.

When put that way, Mrs Dormand seemed to understand. The best way to know a place was to be a part
of its inner workings. It was also the best way to appreciate a place. Beautiful meals in a candlelit dining

room didn't materialise out of thin air. There were laundresses that ensured the pristine quality of the white cloth, footmen who polished the silver and set the immaculate table, kitchen staff who saw to the cooking and plating of the meal. There were no happy accidents, as her father liked to say. That reminded her, she would need to write to her parents and let them know she'd arrived. They worried about her. In truth, they had not quite understood why she wanted to go to France instead of coming home to them and her family's business. Her father would always see her as his little girl even though she was twenty-seven. That was the main reason she couldn't go home again. She needed to be more. More than her father's bookkeeper, her parents' little girl. It would be her brothers who took over the business when her father retired. Her efforts would gain her naught. She knew her father simply wanted to protect her, but she didn't want to be protected.

Emma dipped a wooden spoon into the pot and tasted the soup. Delicious. She set the spoon aside and began to lay out her supper things on the worktable, a wooden bowl, a board for the bread, the crock of pale country butter. There was a half bottle of red wine left from the previous night and she thought, why not spoil herself in celebration of all she'd accomplished? She'd just set a goblet down beside her plate when she heard boots in the corridor, followed by a raised voice, its tone not unpleasant. 'Richet? Petit?' Monsieur Archambeau was back. Some of her hard-won calm satisfaction faded. But not all of it. She was *not* going to let him put her on edge in her own home.

The door to the kitchen swung open, 'Petit, where is—' His speech halted with his step when he saw her, surprise momentarily stymying him, some of his own casual ebullience evaporating. '*Bon soir*, Madame Luce. What are you doing here? Where is everyone?' The furrow that was all too commonplace on his brow returned as his gaze lingered on her clothes, her kerchief, and the idea that she was in the kitchen while Petit was nowhere to be found.

'I've given Petit the day off to visit her daughter and the others a half day. We've all been working very hard while you've been gone.' She still hadn't quite forgiven him for only informing Richet of his absence.

'You've been working?' He sauntered forward, taking an appreciative sniff. 'Did you make this? It smells good.' *He* smelled good, all cold spring wind and the fresh manly scent of neroli; citrus and bitter orange mixed with spices and honey. The scent gave her pause. The dusty-booted working man she'd met two days ago paid attention to such things? Certainly, the man in evening dress would, but who was the real Monsieur Archambeau? The man in evening dress or the man who'd come in from the land?

'Yes, I like to cook.' She wiped her hands on her apron, trying to remember her lessons; to see things from another's point of view. Where were her manners? 'Would you like to join me?' She couldn't learn about him if she avoided him. She reached for another bowl and glass.

'I wouldn't mind, thank you.' He pulled a stool up to the worktable with ease as if he'd eaten here before, the gesture more reminiscent of a worker than a gentleman. 'Is this what you're drinking?' He held up the bottle of red and shook his head. 'It's all wrong for this soup. It's too heavy. We need a *pinot noir* if we want red wine with chicken, a chardonnay if we want white.' He got off the stool. 'I'll be right back.' He disappeared and returned momentarily carrying a bottle in each hand. 'One white, one red,' he announced and set about uncorking them. 'If you mean to live in France, you'll have to learn your wines, although Richet has an impeccable nose. You can rely on him.'

'He *is* reliable,' Emma said drily. 'He showed me your note. Thanks to him, I knew where you were.' She waited but he said nothing. 'You could have written to me,' she said bluntly. 'You *should* have written to me as well.'

'Why? You knew where I was. I was out conducting estate business with the district growers.' He flashed her a short smile, unbothered by her attempt at censure, and poured her a glass of white. 'Let me show you how to taste. It's all about the three S's: swirl, smell, and sip.' He walked her through the process. 'Now try the red.'

Audacity came naturally to this man. Emma fought the temptation to give vent to her annoyance. An employee that came and went at will? Without so much as a by your leave? She drew a deep breath instead and searched for an alternative explanation for his behaviour. Why would he think to ask permission? The answer was obvious: he'd never had to ask before. Garrett hadn't been here to oversee his activities. Garrett had in fact relied on this man to organise his day as he saw fit, building relationships for the chateau out in the community. She reached for the red and set aside her animosity.

He strode to the cupboard and retrieved another set of goblets. 'Now try the red you selected.' He poured her a small amount and she sipped with a grimace. Archambeau chuckled. 'See, it's too strong. If you want to serve a red wine with a chicken chowder, it's best to have a red with low tannins.'

'I think I prefer the white, after all,' Emma laughed and he poured her a full glass. She ladled the steaming soup into their bowls. He reached for the loaf of bread on the board and began to slice. A sense of calm domesticity permeated the kitchen as they worked, performing the simple tasks of dishing up dinner. It was a different atmosphere than the one that had imbued their supper in the dining room. This was a far friendlier setting. But she was aware that could change on a word, or a tone. *Play nice*, she reminded herself.

'This is good,' he complimented after a spoonful. 'It's very filling and the seasoning is well balanced.' His eyes twinkled. 'Which is unusual for English cooking. It's not known for its careful seasoning.'

He was teasing her, she thought, although there was some truth in it. 'How would you know about English cuisine?' She ventured a little teasing of her own as she tried to get to know this man her husband had hired to represent him.

He reached for a slice of bread and dipped it into the chowder. 'When I turned ten, my *grandpère* and my father agreed to send me to school in England. Trust me, English schoolboys have plenty of experience in unseasoned English cuisine,' he chuckled.

But Emma took the information thoughtfully, trying to imagine Julien Archambeau as a ten-year-old boy sent to England, so far from home. 'You must have been lonely.'

Julien shrugged. 'Not entirely. I had my *oncle*. He stayed on in England for several years after the Terror, after my *grandpère* and father came home. I lived with his family during the holidays, all except summer. There's no crossing the Channel in the winter.' He grinned. 'But summers, I came home.' She could tell from that grin how much coming home had pleased him.

She found the duality of his life intriguing. 'What did your *oncle* do in England?'

'My family has a small, regional, import-export business that is headquartered out of London.' He devoured the bread and took another slice.

There were a thousand questions to follow up that peek into his life but she had no chance. The next question was his. 'Why do you know how to cook? Surely Sir Garrett didn't expect you to do your own cooking?'

'My father was a great believer in a person understanding all the aspects of their lives, from finances to housekeeping and cooking. He taught me and my brothers how to manage money, and he insisted we all know how a big house ran.'

She paused here and sipped her wine as his dark brows went up.

'Yes.' She smiled at his unspoken query. 'Even my brothers learned how a household was run, even though they now have wives who handle that for them. As a result of my father's efforts, though, I am very good at accounting and my brothers understand how to plan a five-course dinner and seating chart for twenty.' She studied him for a moment, watching this register. He was having some difficulty grasping the idea. 'Is it too *bourgeoise* for you?' She was not teasing entirely. The French had strong ideas about classes crossing lines.

'You are a baronet's wife. These are not the skills of a noblewoman,' he said consideringly.

'I was not always.' She shrugged. 'My father was not a nobleman nor was he born to a fortune, although by the time I came along, he had acquired his wealth. But he believed it didn't matter how much money a man had. A man *or* woman still needed skills, still needed to understand all the pieces that made his or her lifestyle possible.' She nodded towards his empty bowl. 'More?'

'Yes, please.' The kitchen had darkened as the evening settled about them. He turned up the wick on the lamp as she refilled their bowls. 'Do you miss your family?'

'I do,' Emma confessed. 'But we write to one another and I would miss my freedom more. I don't think a married woman can ever comfortably return to her childhood home after having a house of her own to run. I would always be in my parents' shadow, always their baby. My mother doesn't need my help and my father especially is very protective of me, probably because I'm the youngest and a girl.' And because gin was a rough industry, socially, politically. Her father had valued her input even as he'd thought to shield her from the rougher aspects of his work.

She could see him think about that for a moment as he poured them another glass, white for her and red for him, each bottle more than half-empty. Goodness, had they drunk so much already? Or had they been at the meal that long? The candles were burning low. 'May I ask what line of work your father is in? I don't think Sir Garrett ever mentioned it.'

'Gin,' she offered smugly, waiting for his reaction. Would he cover his shock with a polite nod and a smile? Would he be outwardly horrified like the ladies and lords of the ton? For a moment she felt as if all her hopes of a new life untainted by her antecedents were held in the balance of his response. Perhaps she'd been wrong to think it could be different here, and yet she *did* hope. Gin wasn't a large French commodity but perhaps he'd lived in England long enough to know about gin and its dubious qualities.

'I know very little of gin.' He smiled over his glass. 'You said it like it's a bad thing, though.' His brow knitted. 'Is it, um, controversial?'

She gave a wry half smile. 'It's political. Gin is something of a social contradiction. It's risen in popularity as a drink among the upper classes and attained a certain level of distinction even as it remains the ruin of the lower classes, although it's nowhere near what it was a hundred years ago. Gin can be cheap, so all classes can afford it. Some employers even use it as part of paying wages, but again, not as often as before. There was a period of time when gin was effectively banned because it was so damaging to the public.' She shook her head, 'But not now. It's better controlled. England isn't selling gin in grocery stalls. Now there are gin palaces.'

He raised an eyebrow in speculation. 'Does *your* father own a gin palace?'

Perhaps this was where he'd become squeamish, and yet the French were notoriously more liberal about such things than the English. She offered her confession meeting him straight in the eye. 'Yes, several of them. Many distilleries do, it's a way to have a guaranteed outlet for the product. My father's are very high-end, though, almost exclusive, with crystal chandeliers and plush red velvet sofas, and polished walnut bars. They are frequented by the same gentlemen who refuse to acknowledge him in public.'

'And his family?' Julien put in.

'Yes, *and* his family. It made my debut tricky to say the least.'

He cocked his head to one side. 'I am trying to imagine you as a debutante, white gown, blue sash and all. Somehow, you seem too smart for that.'

'I was. But it made my disappointment sting no less.' She smiled. 'I shall take your words as a compliment. And now, I must confess, earlier I was trying to imagine *you* as a ten-year-old boy.'

He gave her a mischievous smile. 'Were you successful?'

'Somewhat.' She stared at her wine glass, twirling the stem a bit in her hand. This was nice, talking with him without tension, without wariness. But she needed to be careful. What was she doing, telling a stranger her story? She did not know him well enough, although in this moment she felt that she did. For all of his gruffness, he did have the talent of making someone feel as if they'd known each other far longer. It was the same talent he'd exercised at dinner last night. And they both knew how *that* had turned out.

That ought to be cautionary tale enough to curb her tongue. Who knew what he might do with tonight's information? He might ambush her with it later, or tell others and ruin her chances at a fresh start before she'd even begun. She chose caution and redirected the conversation. 'You know little about gin and I know very little about wine. I don't have your nose for it.' She nodded to the still half-full bottle of red she'd meant to drink with her soup.

'I just drink what someone else puts before me, *but*,' she gave a long pause to emphasise the *but*, 'I do know quite a bit about the marketing and selling of beverages, thanks to my father's business. I watched him take gin and elevate it. I think it would be quite similar to wine. And...' again, she gave another long pause for emphasis, giving him a chance to brace himself '... I want to learn. I want to know what you know. Not just which wines pair well with which foods, but why, and how to make a good wine, how to grow good grapes.' There was so much to know, she was nearly breathless with it.

'Whoa, slow down.' Archambeau held up a hand. 'I've worked with wine all my life. These are things not learned overnight or even in a few weeks, *madame*.'

'I have time,' she insisted. She would not give him a

chance to turn her down or ignore her. 'While you were gone, I got to know the house. Now that you're back, I want to know the vineyards.' She paused. 'That's why my husband hired you, isn't it? Because of your knowledge. Now it's your turn to teach me, to show me what you showed Garrett.'

Speculation moved in his eyes and the evening lost a bit of its pleasure. She almost regretted bringing the subject up. The moment to make her request had seemed perfect with the lamplight and their bellies filled with the comfort of warm food and good wine. But now she wondered if she'd rushed it. What was he thinking behind those blue eyes?

'All right,' he said at last. 'You may have your first lesson tomorrow. I walk the vineyards at six in the morning rain or shine. Dress warmly.' If that was a challenge, she was up for it.

Chapter Seven

She was waiting for him. That was a rarity in itself. Few people ever rose before him. But there she was, looking like a figure from a gothic novel, the dawn-grey vineyards a shadowy backdrop against her dark silhouette swathed in a black cloak, hood up to shield her hair from the morning mist. It leant her an air of intrigue, as if she needed any more of that. She already dominated too much of his thoughts as it was. She'd upended his world when she'd walked into the chateau.

He'd spent the last days trying to mitigate the effects of her presence on his carefully ordered plans only to come home and find her cooking corn chicken chowder and playing the housekeeper in her kerchief and serge. To a rather compelling effect, he admitted. Their meal together had been a striking departure from the tension-filled dinner. Last night's meal had almost been friendly right up until the part where she mentioned her desire to see the vineyards. It had been a reminder that she was closing in, like a relentless tide that crept up on the shore hour by hour, its arrival inevitable.

'*Bon matin*, Madame Luce,' he greeted. 'I am glad to see the early hour did not trouble you and that you've dressed accordingly.' She'd taken his advice in that at least. Beneath her cloak peeped the skirt of the blue serge she'd worn yesterday and sturdy half-boots that would hold up to the dirt of the vineyards. 'We will start here. This section closest to the chateau is where we grow the *pinot meunoir*.' He gestured to the nearest row of grapes and ushered her down the aisle lined with bare vines. 'There's not much to see but soon, though, these vines will sport tight buds, they'll flower in late April and May.' He launched into a treatise on the pruning process as he walked her up and down the rows, then explained the life cycle of the grape. To her credit, she offered no complaint or interruption. Julien stopped at one vine and took out his penknife, making a small nick.

'What are you looking for? Is everything all right?' They were the first words she'd uttered since he'd begun his monologue. Perhaps he *had* succeeded in overwhelming her. Perhaps his *oncle* was right—if she understood the enormity of the task she was undertaking she might rethink her goals. But even as he thought it, part of him rebelled at the idea—the part of him that didn't want her overwhelmed, the part of him that was remembering what it had been like to talk with her across the kitchen worktable while they ate soup and traded stories. In those moments they'd not been enemies.

She leaned forward towards the vine, towards him, the hood of her cloak falling back far enough to reveal the sable sheen of her hair. He caught a brief trace of her scent, the jasmine sambac and orange blossom he'd smelled on her the first night.

He folded the penknife and put it back in his pocket. 'I was looking for sap. It tells us when the grape will enter budburst.'

'And thus, alerting growers the season begins.' She flashed him a smile. 'See, I *was* listening. To *every* word you said, and there were a lot of them.' Her smile turned thoughtful. 'Is it bad there's no sap?'

Julien shook his head, wondering if he should be impressed or distressed by her attention. 'The vines cannot be rushed.' He looked up into the lightening sky. Perhaps there would be sun today. 'If the buds come too early, tricked by a false spring, a frost can kill or stunt them. A grower wants the buds to come when the weather is safe. They have no protection from the frost or the cold.'

'But they do from heat,' she said. 'The leaves offer shade in the summer.'

'Very good,' he complimented. What would Oncle Etienne make of that? Nothing good, he supposed. They wanted her uninterested, not lapping up everything he said. He'd have to try harder to bore her. A carriage pulled into view as they neared the end of the row. 'We'll drive the distance to the next section of vineyard where the chardonnay grapes are grown.' He helped her up and took the seat across from her, stretching out his legs. 'We grow three types of grapes here, the *pinot meunoir* you just saw, the chardonnay, and the *pinot noir*. They are the three grapes that can be used for the *vin mousseux*.' It was a perfect opportunity to launch into a dissertation on the quality of grapes.

She tossed him a smug smile and interrupted his train of thought. The sun *had* come out and she'd pushed her hood back, her face on full display to him, a sharp combination of beauty and intelligence. 'I cannot decide, Monsieur Archambeau, if you are trying to overwhelm me, bore me, or impress me with your extraordinary array of knowledge about vineyards.' Her smile turned smug. 'If your intention is the first or second, it won't work.'

'Most women would have been bored an hour ago.' Most women would not have got out of bed and dressed like a servant in order to tramp through the dirt to look at bare vines.

'I'm not most women, *monsieur*,' she said with all seriousness. Was that a warning? A reminder?

In hindsight, he should have seen it from the beginning. A traditional widow did not travel across the Channel mere weeks after the death of her spouse. A traditional widow did not attempt to take over a business she knew nothing about in a foreign country where her command of the language was no more than adequate. Neither did a woman of title and wealth dabble about in the kitchens making soup and eating at worktables. Yet she had done all these things. His usual attempts at warning off women by boring them to death would not work with her because she was *not* the usual woman. He'd have to try harder. Oncle Etienne would not approve of lacklustre efforts.

Julien crossed his booted legs at the ankles and

opted for a different tack. If one could not fight Madame Luce, one could always join her. 'And the latter? How is that going? Impressed yet?' Some part of him, the manly ego of him, wanted her to be impressed, wanted her to know what she was up against. He was good at what he did. He'd learned his craft well. In the Vallee de Marne, there was no one better when it came to growing and blending the wines.

'Fishing for a compliment, are we, Monsieur Archambeau?' She laughed and the carriage suddenly felt more like last night's dinner table than the sharp edge that had pierced the morning. Perhaps that was their pattern, to start each interaction wary, cautiously relearning one another before relaxing. 'At my peril, I will admit to being dazzled.'

'At your peril? Whatever can be dangerous about that admission?' He should not encourage this line of conversation. It was at his peril, too. An impressed Emma Luce would not be a disinterested party and that was the last thing he and his *oncle* needed.

'All that knowledge piques my curiosity. About you.'

That was *not* where he'd thought the conversation was going. He'd expected her to ask a question about the grapes, to lead him into another dissertation on viniculture. *That* he could handle. He could talk for hours about grapes and wine. Hadn't he proven that already? But he was not accustomed to talking about himself nor did he prefer it. Living alone had its perks in that regard. 'What about me?'

'A person does not come by such a vast compendium of knowledge without some effort. How is it that you

know so much about winemaking and vine-growing?'
She cocked her head and gave him a studious look. 'I
cannot make the pieces fit on my own. Last night you
told me you were schooled in England, a land not known
for its vineyards, I might add.'

'But I was born here, remember? I was raised in
Cumières until I was ten. My *grandpère* lived with us,
or maybe it was us who lived with him.' He offered
a small smile at his joke. 'Grandpère and my father
took me everywhere with them. Even as a small child,
I could not escape learning about the land, the vines.
I rode on my *grandpère*'s shoulders, listening to him
talk to my father. The grapes, the growing cycles, they
were as much a part of me as…' He couldn't quite summon an apt comparison. He couldn't ever remember
not knowing about budburst, or the rhythm of the year.

'As breathing?' she put in quietly. Up front in the
traces, the horse snuffled and whickered in the still-
ness that followed.

'As breathing,' Julien affirmed thoughtfully. It
sounded…right. It also sounded as if she understood
what that meant. 'You say that as if you know what it
means to be attached to something so deeply that it is
part of you.' If she was going to probe, he could probe,
too. He told himself he was asking because it would
help him understand her better, appeal to her better
when the time came, that his question had nothing to
do with him simply wanting to know, or because he
felt drawn to her in a way that had nothing to do with
her possession of his family's land.

She thought for a moment, her gaze dropping to her

hands, for once not piercing him, seeing through him, challenging him. Then she looked up. 'Numbers. I understand them intrinsically the way I understand how to breathe, how to walk. They make sense. They are constant and yet a source of creativity. They can tell me things. Numbers don't lie, they don't hide. They are always themselves.' He should have known then just how much danger he was in. She didn't just understand numbers. She *loved* them. Not unlike himself. He didn't simply understand the land—even Oncle Etienne, who'd spent his adult life in a shipping office, could lay claim knowing the land. No son of Matthieu Archambeau could escape such knowledge. But Oncle Etienne did not love it. To know something and to have a passion for it were not synonymous things. He should have asked her more about her numbers and redirected the conversation but he was not fast enough.

'The pieces still don't fit. Your family has a shipping business. That doesn't seem a place where one would come by agricultural knowledge.'

He needed to tread carefully here. He didn't want her putting too many pieces together. Neither did he want to offer a lie. 'I forget what short memories the English have,' he chuckled. 'During the Terror, my great-*grandpère*, Jean-Pierre, thought it best to protect the family interests. He sent his son's family to London to get them out of harm's way. His son, Matthieu, was an entrepreneurial sort.'

'*Your* grandfather,' she clarified, her grey eyes intent on him, giving the impression of hanging on his every word.

'Yes, my *grandpère*.' He smiled, part of him pleased she was so attentive, part of him worried about what other connections she might make and questions she might ask as a result. 'He knew we needed to find a way to support ourselves in England and he saw a need for shipping, particularly between France and Britain.'

Her eyes narrowed at this. 'While the two countries were at war?' He could see the realisation dawn. She was sharp, he'd give her that. 'By chance, was this "shipping" legal?'

'Well, not at first,' he admitted with a wry grin.

'Your *grandpère*…' she emphasised the French word '…came to England and became a smuggler. Do I have it right?'

He laughed because she was laughing. 'In Grandpère's defence, it was a mutually satisfying community service for all parties. The English had an insatiable desire for French wine despite their politics, and my great-*grandpère* knew several people with wine to sell lying idle in France. With the large legitimate British market gone, wine was languishing in cellars and warehouses thanks to the war. This arrangement satiated British need and kept food on the tables of many Frenchmen.'

'To say nothing of lining your grandfather's pockets.'

'*Bien sur*, it was lucrative enough to turn the Archambeaux legal once the Treaty of Amiens was signed. Now we are a small, respectable, legitimate shipping line, specialising in bringing French wines to British connoisseurs. Most of our shipping these days is done through privately arranged contracts with rich men.' The shipping line had been lucrative enough to eventually allow the Archambeaux, *sans* Oncle Etienne's family, to return to France and start buying back land slowly but surely, when that land became available. 'When it was safe to come back to France, my *grandpère* returned with my father, my mother, and baby me in tow, leaving my *oncle* in Britain to handle the English end of things.'

That was all true as far as it went. There were pieces he was leaving out; that the title of Comte du Rocroi had been restored to the family—something that didn't mean much given the title had been revoked again by law four years ago. He'd left out, too, that his great-*grandpère* had died, losing the chateau and all the lands years before his *grandpère* had been allowed to safely return with other nobles. His *grandpère* had never seen his father again.

'Grandpère taught me about wine. He figured if I was going to help with the shipping business, I ought to know about the product we were exporting.' He gave her a nod. 'Not unlike your father's rationale in teaching his sons and his daughter financial and household management.' Still, not entirely false. Although Grandpère had imagined his grandson would be a *vigneron* of his own grapes by the time he came of age.

The carriage halted at their next destination, forestalling any more of her questions. He came around and helped her down. 'Let me dazzle you some more, *madame*, with these chardonnay grapes. They're used to make a *blanc de blanc*. It's a somewhat new blending and a somewhat new grape for us, but I think the result is divine, it's light and it sparkles. There's a feminine *elan* to it that I think would appeal to women. Rich women, obviously. This could be a wealthy woman's equivalent to her husband's brandy.'

She slanted him a look, her silvery gaze interested. 'Why, Monsieur Archambeau, now you *have* impressed me.' This was followed by a genuine smile that stopped him in his tracks. 'This is the first time I've heard you talk like a businessman and not only a farmer. You have depth, *monsieur*.'

'Does that surprise you?' He slid her a brief, wry smile, feeling quite satisfied with himself because he had pleased her. It was a dangerous feeling.

'It does, most pleasingly,' she answered with a smile of her own, and Julien thought how pleasant it was to be with her like this, without sparring, without competing, without each of them trying to prove themselves. Of course, the sparring and competition *were* necessary. It was how he remembered they were indeed at odds with one another, their wants mutually exclusive. She wanted to run a vineyard he could absolutely not let her get her hands on.

And yet taking a break from being *en garde* was refreshing, enjoyable. It led to interesting thoughts—all purely hypothetical—like, what if they didn't have to be set against one another? What if they didn't have to compete? An idea began to root in his mind. What if there was a way to bring her alongside, to make her feel that she was taking control without really allowing her to do so in a way that undermined his own position?

What if they could be a team? It would be a chance to show her how much she needed him, how indispensable he was to her.

'Are you hungry? I'm famished. I've taken the liberty of packing a picnic breakfast for us.' Perhaps there was a better strategy than any of those posited by his *oncle*. If he and Madame Luce were allies instead of enemies, co-operators instead of competitors, perhaps she would relinquish the lands easily and with the understanding that it was in the land's best interest, because it made *sense*. Because he was born to this life and she wasn't.

Wasn't she? His conscience was an unwelcome intrusion on this sunny morning. *She's been a willing pupil while you prosed on trying to purposely bore her. She is trying to learn.*

And what was he trying to do? For all of his thoughts about bringing her alongside, guilt poked hard at him as he led her back to the carriage. Was he doing this for her benefit or his? What was his motive? Was he trying to steal her inheritance or secure his?

Chapter Eight

Emma stole a look at Archambeau setting out the plates of raspberry jam–filled tartines, her mouth starting to water at the sight of food. Breakfast picnics were something she could get used to, as were the feelings they engendered in her. This morning had turned out to be quite enjoyable. The realisation took her by not entirely pleasant surprise.

Guilt tugged at her. She *was* a having a good time. But should she be? Her husband had been dead a month and here she was laughing, enjoying an outing in the company of another man and thinking she could get used to breakfast picnics. It felt like a betrayal.

Emma settled on the old quilt spread on the ground and cupped her hands around a mug of hot coffee, willing the warmth to ward off the guilt as effectively as it warded off the chill of the morning, but the guilt stayed. What did it mean about her love for Garrett if she found enjoyment so easily, so quickly in the company of another? And yet, to not enjoy the company of another meant to remain alone. Surely Garrett would not want that for her.

'It's not very elegant.' Archambeau gave a self-deprecating shrug as he set out a tray of tartines. 'A farmer's quick meal, nothing more.'

'It's perfect,' she assured him, aware that this fragile peace between them must be handled delicately, explored carefully, encouraged cautiously. He was different out here in the vineyard, not a dour workman doing his chores, but a man who loved the land, whose passion shone through in the transformation of his face when he spoke; it transformed his tone, and it lowered his guard. Once he'd started talking about the grapes she'd had the impression that she was seeing the real man, that the workman and the gentleman at the dinner table were lesser representations of the man who sat across from her on the blanket.

It was that man who offered her the tray of tartines as he gave her a brief overview of the land's history. 'The Romans were growing grapes here long before we were and, the climate willing, grapes will be growing here long after I'm gone.' This, she thought, was the man she'd envisioned behind the thorough reports sent across the Channel. He merely looked different than the image in her mind. He looked *better*. How had she ever thought he ought to be a slender, bookish sort?

He flashed her an uncustomary smile and for an instant her thoughts were arrested by that look. In that moment, he might have been one of his Gallic ancestors walking his land centuries ago. The morning sun slanted through the sky illumining his features, the strong bones of his jaw, the curve of his cheek which softened him when he smiled, as he was now, and lit the slate blue of his gaze so that it matched the newly emergent sky. But it was the sentiment of his words that truly touched her, this idea of a legacy, of building something larger than himself.

Like Garrett.

Everything Garrett did had been motivated by thoughts for his family and what it might become.

'Is something on your mind? You're staring.' Archambeau shifted his position on the blanket, stretching out to his full length, the movement unintentionally making her aware of his maleness.

Guilt pricked again, scolding her: *How dare you be so aware of a man so soon after Garrett's death.*

She pushed the reprimand away. He was barely a foot away from her. Of course she noticed him. How could she not? It was entirely natural. It meant nothing and yet the warm heat in her blood didn't seem to agree.

'You reminded me of Garrett, just then, the way you spoke of a legacy. He always looked to the future. Even his title, which he received later in his life, was not something he thought of for himself, but for his family. He saw it as something that would be handed down generation to generation, something he'd earned.' She cocked her head, thoughtful. 'I think that was why he was so proud of it. He'd earned it. It hadn't been given to him simply because he'd been born into the right family.' She paused, a thought coming to her. The next moment she felt Archambeau's hand on hers, his gaze soft. It was a gesture of concern only, but it was also pleasant, too, in its own right, warm and comforting. Then, she understood. He thought that speaking of Garrett had made her sad.

'I'm fine.' She offered a smile as assurance. 'I just realised that talking of Garrett made me happy.' She was still processing the idea for herself. 'I think this is the first time since his death that I've shared something voluntarily and I didn't break down in tears.' It was the first time sharing about Garrett had actually felt *good*. She pondered that for a moment, staring down at her half-eaten tartine, her words coming slowly, deliberately. 'In the beginning, when it was all new, people would ask about how he died.' She looked up at Archambeau. 'No one wanted to know how he lived.'

'I'm guilty of that, too.' Archambeau gave a dry laugh. 'Even me, I asked you what happened. I'm sorry.' He squeezed her hand and then retreated, taking his hand, his touch away.

'Don't be. It's natural to want to know. It's just difficult to recount.' She absolved him with another smile. She felt the smile falter with confession. 'The truth is, I don't like to think of Garrett's last moments, much less talk about them.' She paused and slid him a considering look. 'Do you suppose that's wrong of me? I wonder if it's selfish to want to push them aside because they are too painful to consider?'

'Perhaps pushing them aside isn't so much a part of ignoring the pain as it is creating an opportunity for healing,' he offered gently. 'One can't heal if they insist on reopening the wound.'

'Perhaps,' she replied noncommittally. It was a nice sentiment, an insightful one, even. But she was too conflicted to believe it entirely. In the dark of night when her demons were at their best inside her head, she thought she didn't like to think about those moments because they reminded her that she'd chosen selfishly that night to stay behind and play cards, and she'd been rewarded—and punished—for her selfishness. She'd survived.

She pleated the corner of the blanket between her fingers. 'The coroner in Holmfirth told me most of the victims died with looks of confusion on their faces, as if they didn't have time to understand what was happening. That was supposed to make me feel better, I guess, this idea that there was no time for pain, for fear. I did not think Garrett looked like that.' She stopped and hazarded a look in Archambeau's direction, suddenly horrified. 'That is too morbid for conversation. I don't know why I said that. I am the one who must apologise now.' Whatever had come over her to make her share such a thing? She'd not discussed that with anyone, not even her family.

'Not at all. You loved your husband and he loved you. He spoke of you glowingly during his visits. You were lucky to have such a marriage, Madame Luce.' His gaze turned inward for a long moment. She sensed his thoughts had moved away from her, towards another time, perhaps another person, another place. She felt her body lean forward in a desire to go to that place with him, to know what thoughts were taking place behind those eyes, craving whatever he might say next.

'I think we must talk about the things we love. Words are to memories as air is to our lungs. Without it we die. Without words, our memories die. The moment we stop talking about them, we surrender them.' He gave one of his self-deprecating smiles. 'Now I am the one who has said too much. I am being fanciful, *madame*. You must pardon me.'

She was still for a moment, taking in his words, taking in the revelation that the rustic farmer-cum-gentleman was also a poet, a philosopher, yet one more side to this enigmatic man. 'No.' She gave him a slow, deliberate smile. 'I do not think I shall pardon you. No offence has been given. In fact, I rather like the idea that words are the breath of dreams. And you are right. Garrett was my dream, although at the time I may not have realised it.' She held out her coffee mug and Archambeau refilled it.

'Tell me, how did the two of you meet?' He set aside his own mug and stretched out along the far side of the quilt, the action drawing her eyes once more to the length of him, the largeness of him. 'Well?' he encouraged, tucking his hands behind his head and giving every sign of a man settling for the duration.

'It's a rather boring story,' she warned, offering him one last chance to opt out, but his blue eyes fixed on her, inviting her to tell him.

He gave a wry smile. 'More boring than a lecture on the growth cycle of grapes? After this morning, I think you owe me a boring story or two to even the scales.'

Julien Archambeau was dangerously charming like this, all smiles and dry humour. The odd thought flitted through her mind: How many other women had spilled their tales to him after such a look? Was there such a woman in his life at present? Not that it mattered. She cleared her throat and gathered her thoughts. 'We met at a political supper in London during the Season. My father was hoping to speak with an MP about some legislation that would affect tariffs on gin. It was all a matter of chance. I was seated next to Garrett. We began talking and the more we talked, the more I felt seen—*truly* seen—by him.'

She smiled, remembering how easy even those early conversations had been. 'Until I met Garrett, men treated me one of two ways: as an heiress they would tolerate and elevate in exchange for my father's money, or as someone they wouldn't even look at, who was tainted because of her father's industry; and the women were worse. Suffice it to say, the girls who came out with me were not particularly friendly.' Even years later, those memories were hard ones to suffer.

'Tell me about it?' Julien asked. 'I can hardly believe a few girls would set you back.'

'Well, not the person I am now. But back then I was bit more naïve than I knew.' She shook her head. 'I really don't want to talk about it. I was foolish and they took advantage of that.' She cringed at the memory.

Julien smiled encouragingly. 'That's all the more reason to tell me then. Does it help to know that once I gave all my allowance at school to keep the upperclassmen from beating me up? English schoolboys don't like French schoolboys, it turns out. It took me a while to learn that paying them only incentivised them to ask for more money, not to stop. The only thing that made them stop was a solid fist to the face.'

'I am sorry you were bullied,' she said sincerely. 'My bully was a viscount's daughter named Amelia St James. I couldn't punch her or pay her but I could spill wine on her dress.'

Julien laughed. 'Now you *have* to tell me.'

She settled on the blanket. 'It all started over the Earl of Redmond, the most eligible catch of the Season. Amelia wanted him and he wanted me, at least that's what I thought. He danced with me every evening, sent flowers every day. I was nineteen and quite swept off my feet. He was handsome and dashing. Then one day, he went further. He took me out driving in his curricle in Hyde Park at peak time. Everyone saw us. It made Amelia into something of a laughingstock. Everyone knew she'd set her cap for him. She couldn't ignore that I held his interest now that he'd driven out with me. She couldn't live with it either. She'd refused two other marriage proposals while she waited for him. She'd go home unwed at the end of the Season at this rate. So, she used the weapons she had. That night, she told anyone and everyone the only reason Redmond was interested was the size of my father's pocketbook.'

'That's awful,' Julien commiserated.

'It was awful but it was also true.' That was the worst part. She should have been more aware. 'My father had made no secret that he meant to have a title for me and he would buy it. I just hadn't believed it. I truly thought Redmond liked me for me. I believed it right up until the moment I confronted him. I asked him to his face if it was true and he could not deny it.'

Julien was quiet for a moment. 'You lost more than a suitor that night.'

She nodded. 'Yes, I'd been betrayed by girls who had acted like my friends, who I'd confided in. Amelia knew how much I thought I'd cared for Redmond. She knew my hopes. In my naïveté I thought I loved Redmond and she dashed those hopes anyway. What sort of friend does that? But she was no friend at all, and she never had been. Neither was Redmond. The whole world I thought I knew was a fiction.'

'But then you found Garrett,' Julien prompted. 'Surely that made up for it?'

Emma smiled. That was how she'd explained it to herself as well, that Amelia's betrayal had been worth it to find real love with a man who *saw* her. 'Garrett and I had that in common. Like my father, he was a self-made man with a fortune, a man other men had to respect because he had money and with that money he'd acquired influence. He understood my experiences because they were his experiences, too.' She smiled. 'For once, I had an ally. He called on me the next day, bringing a beautiful bouquet of spring flowers. By the end of the week, I was falling for him, improbable suitor that he was.' Emma laughed. Now that she'd started talking, she couldn't seem to stop. 'I never thought I'd fall for a man just slightly younger than my father, a man who'd already raised a family. But he didn't seem old, he never seemed old.'

'And now he never will,' Archambeau put in and she nodded.

'I've thought of that.' She offered the confession slowly. It was a somewhat risky idea to voice out loud. 'He died still very much in his prime. Neither he nor I will have to witness the slow deterioration of age stealing him from me. Maybe I am lucky in that regard. I will always be able to remember the best of him.' It wasn't enough to wish him dead, but there was consolation.

Archambeau nodded solemnly. 'My *grandpère* lived into his eighties. Most of his years were good ones. Despite his trials, he was blessed with health, but towards the end he could not do the things he loved in the way he preferred. His world seemed to shrink to the point where his dreams became obsessions. He was not quite the man I remembered growing up with. It was difficult on all of us, especially my father.'

'You were close with your grandfather. I envy you that. I never knew mine on either side. My mother's family cut her off when she married my father and my father had no family to speak of. It was always just us.'

Archambeau gave her a considering look. 'That must have been a lonely way to grow up. My family was always together; my great-*grandpère*, my *grandpère*, my *père*, my *oncle*, my cousin, we were always living with one another in some combination or other.'

'What wondrous chaos that must have been,' Emma laughed and then sobered, remembering other things he'd shared. 'How lonely it must be for you now with them gone.' Perhaps it was harder for him. She couldn't truly miss what she'd never had. She furrowed her brow trying to remember. 'Your *oncle*, is he still in England?' She could not recall what he'd said about that, only that his *oncle* had been in England during his school years.

Archambeau shifted. For comfort? Or because her question made him uneasy? 'My *oncle* is here. He returned in 1845 after my *grandpère* and my father died. My cousin and my *tante* stayed in England to look after that end of the shipping business.'

She nodded, unsure what to say. There was great sadness in those few sentences. 1845 had been a dark year for the Archambeaux. The death of the family patriarch *and* his son in quick succession. More importantly, the death of two men Julien had loved dearly.

We talk about the things we love.

She had not missed the affection that had accompanied his mentions of his *grandpère* and his father. Upheaval had no doubt followed as the family reorganised itself to fill in the gaps left by those deaths. She thought of the family left behind in order for his *oncle* to return. Had that been a sacrifice on his *oncle*'s part? She settled on, 'I'm glad you have your *oncle* at least, Monsieur Archambeau.'

'Julien.' The single word was a gunshot fired into the silence of the morning. 'Perhaps you might consider calling me Julien? Monsieur Archambeau seems so formal at this juncture.'

'Then you must call me Emma,' she replied, trying to understand what his request might mean. She might take it to mean a hundred things. Had he asked because they'd spent a morning together discussing business and pleasure? Because they'd shared stories about those they loved and those stories had left them revealed? Or because they were becoming friends? Did she dare allow that? Friendship would be complicated. Friendship between men and women always was. Friendship between a new widow and a man involved in her business enterprise would be doubly so.

Admittedly, she found herself liking the idea of befriending Julien Archambeau. Far better to have him as a friend than an enemy, especially if they were sharing a roof and a vineyard.

The voice in her head spoke sharply. *Not really sharing. All this is yours. Perhaps he'd like you to forget that. You've not yet fully discovered his role here.*

No, she hadn't. Somehow that kept getting postponed, put off in favour of other things, like walking the vineyard and learning about the grapes.

I need him for that, she told the voice in her head. *I know what I am doing. I must learn the business from him. I'd be a fool to let him go before then.*

Is that what you're doing on the picnic blanket, ogling his legs and swapping stories with your husband only gone a month? Learning the business, is it? The voice in her head was showing no mercy today.

What else would it be? came her rejoinder.

It could be *nothing* else because if it was something else, what did that say about her love for Garrett? It was not the first time she'd reminded herself of that. But it was a troublesome rejoinder because her head refused to treat it as a rhetorical question and let her be. Her mind had answers: it was a friendship that was doomed on all fronts. Men and women couldn't be friends. That wasn't how the world worked. If they liked each other enough to be friends, they were inevitably attracted to each for more than conversation. Secondly, it was a paramount rule in business not to mix the two. At least in England. Perhaps the French felt differently. Her father did not. He'd always preached that friends made the worst business partners, and her father was always right.

'I've enjoyed our picnic, but there is more to see,' Emma began, trying to put the original point of the morning back on track. 'Grapes are only one part of the process. I am eager to see the cellars. I believe they are in caves beneath the house?'

Julien gave her a curt nod, his soft gaze returning to its usual flinty hardness. 'Absolutely. I'd be happy to show you. It will take just a moment for us to be under way.' Within minutes the quilt had been folded up and the hamper stashed beneath the seats of the carriage. All signs of their picnic erased as if they'd never lounged beneath the morning sun, sipping coffee and talking of their families.

If only the consequences of those precious hours could be erased as easily. It was the one idea that floated at the forefront of her thoughts throughout the short carriage ride back to the chateau, all of them coalescing around a single word.

Julien.

He'd asked her to call him Julien. That was one inerasable consequence of the morning picnic. With that single request, objectivity had been stripped away and it could not be restored. She could not unsee the way his face lit when he spoke of the land, of his family. She could not forget the sight of him, long legs outstretched, hands behind his head as he lounged in unabashedly male repose on the quilt, his body open to her study, perhaps entirely unaware of the effect it had on her and the guilt that followed.

In the span of a morning, he'd become a man she did not want to argue against or butt heads with. She did not want to compete for control of the vineyards. She wanted to work with this man, learn from him, but without the risk of ceding control. Was such cooperation possible? Would he be able to see her as an equal? More to the point, even if it was possible, was it something he'd want, too?

The voice in her head was quick to scold, to warn. *Slow down.* But what was there to slow down about? Garrett had trusted Julien for seven years, had left him in charge of what would become her inheritance, her last gift from Garrett. He would not have risked that. If Garrett could trust Julien, by extension, so could she. She was *not* racing towards any impetuous business decisions.

In many ways, these were decisions that had already been put in place. She and Julien just needed to accept them. The more she thought about it, the more she believed Garrett meant for them to work together in some way when the time came. He'd just not planned on it being so soon. Perhaps, if there'd been more time, Garrett would have even forged the link, the expectation between them as the years passed. Garrett meant for Julien to help her. She and Julien just had to see that for themselves, help themselves find their way back to the path Garrett wanted. They'd got off to a poor start, each one more interested in defending themselves than looking at the larger picture. By the time they reached the wine caves beneath the chateau, she was sure of it. Now she just needed him to be sure of it as well.

Chapter Nine

Julien was sure of nothing as he heaved open the heavy oak doors that led to the cellars. He should have postponed the visit to the cellars even if it required making up an excuse, but he'd been loath to part company with Emma, loath to see the picnic end for reasons he was not comfortable explaining to himself. He did not want to like her, but he did. He did not want to empathise with her, but he did. He did not want to be impressed by her, but he was. He'd not wanted to discover anything in common with her, but he had.

That had been the most dangerous of all, sitting on the picnic blanket and listening to her talk about her family, how her father was a man of self-made fortune, who'd raised his children to be self-sufficient, to be tenacious in their independence, to stand up for themselves in a world that would not appreciate their ambition because of their trade or, in her case, her gender. 'Please, be careful on the steps,' Julien instructed, his free hand dropping too easily, too naturally, to the small of her back as he ushered her carefully to the centuries-old staircase.

He held the lantern up, lighting the way. This close, he could smell the scent of her jasmine sambac mixed with the earthy outdoors of the vineyards. It was a sweet torture, letting himself be overwhelmed with the feminine details of her. Was there anything more intoxicating than the scent of a woman? Especially after having been deprived of female company for a spell.

Deprivation was his fault, his own self-imposed choice. He had little to offer a woman these days emotionally or financially. If he was tortured, this was what he got for being alone, for being without a woman for so long. He'd let himself be drawn in by her stories, and now he was paying for his lapse. This was what happened when one let a beautiful woman work her wiles and a man let his imagination run away with him.

The voice in his head teased him. *But you liked her words as much as her scent, you liked the idea that her father had built his business with his own efforts, that she wants to do the same here, that she wants to learn.*

He could admire all of that in theory, even if he could not allow it to occur in practice.

Not without some heavy oversight and guidance.

That was temptation whispering now, trying to carve out a middle ground between what she wanted and what he needed.

Don't be a fool. What he ought to want was for her to remain a nuisance, a disruption to be dismissed and managed. But Emma Luce countered him at every turn. When he attempted to overwhelm her, she became inquisitive. When he attempted to bore her, she became interested. When he attempted to impress her, to awe her, she merely took it in stride as a matter of course.

It was he who had been impressed—impressed by the fortitude of a woman who'd not let herself be beaten down by the pressure of her peers. She'd been relentless today, drawing him out, asking for his stories. When he wanted to give her less, she asked for more, *and* he'd complied, talking about his family, recounting his family history, and she had hung on every word as if they were the most interesting things she'd ever heard.

They reached the bottom of the stairs and the space widened out into a large cavern. 'Stay here while I light a few more lanterns.' He moved around the cave, letting the woodsy smell of oak barrels bring him balance, perspective. Now was not the time to be swayed by a pretty face and an attractive mind. He needed to stay focused on what mattered: his land and family. Whatever feelings or reactions Emma Luce was stirring in him wouldn't last. She was novel, something new in a life that was small and narrow.

'It's enormous!' Her voice, so near, startled him.

He turned to find her standing behind him, her eyes alight with wonder as she took in the cavern. 'I thought I told you to stay put until the lights were lit.' In his shock, his words came out more sternly than intended. 'Do you want to trip and fall? These flagstones are centuries old; I can't account for how even they are.'

'I can see just fine.' She laughed off his concern, her eyes still roving about the space, taking in the shelves loaded with casks and the freestanding triangular stands holding individual bottles. 'It just keeps going and going.'

'The place isn't even full.' Julien couldn't help but show off a bit. 'It could hold eighteen hundred barrels and two hundred thousand bottles if we were at full tilt on production.'

A wide smile took her face and she spun in a slow circle. 'I will see to it that we are. I know my husband didn't focus his complete attention on the chateau, but I mean to change that. I mean to make this place into something grand. Everyone will be wanting wines from Les Deux Coeurs when I'm done with things.'

Behind her grey eyes, Julien could see her dreams were already running miles ahead of reality and it awoke an echoing thrill in him—wasn't that what he also wanted for the chateau? But those dreams also chilled him in their naïveté. It wasn't as simple as she thought. Her dreams had consequences for them both. He could not let those dreams supersede his own. More than that, he could not let her claim them.

'You've only seen the main room.' Julien gestured to an arched doorway. 'This leads down to another subterranean cellar, where the *vin mousseux* is stored.' This cavern was smaller, the three walls lined with casks.

'This place is more isolated, or is *insulated* the word I'm looking for?'

'It's just smaller.' Julien hung the lantern on a peg. 'Both this room and the grand cavern are devoid of an echo because they're so far underground.'

'How far underground?' She began a slow perambulation of the room, stopping to read the labels on the casks.

'Forty feet, not nearly as deep as Taittinger's, but deep enough,' Julien said, citing one of the other champagne houses in the area.

She stopped and faced him for a moment. 'So, everyone has wine caves?'

'Yes.' He leaned against the tall worktable set in the middle of the room, watching her continue her stroll, noting the trail of her fingertips over the oak casks, her touch slow and deliberate, a reflection of her thoughts. He'd give a small fortune to know those thoughts, to know what he was up against. 'Wine caves are a rather serendipitous occurrence.'

He was showing off now, perhaps trying to win back her attention, to see her hang on his every word as she had on the picnic blanket. 'The Romans originally dug these caves as chalk and salt mines around 80 BC. Turns out, they're perfect for storing wine.'

'Are you saying everyone stores their wine like this?' she queried, throwing him a glance over her shoulder.

'Yes. Even Reims town houses have such cellars in their basements. Those who don't naturally have access to such storage build them. Chateaux like this one, though, have been using the Roman cellars for a few centuries now.'

She paused. 'So, you're telling me that people who don't have homes built over old Roman ruins actually replicate them?'

'Yes, and why not? At these depths, the temperatures are cool enough to properly store wine while it ages.

Also, at these depths, we can protect against humidity and invasive sunlight. There is no chance of *gout de lumière* wrecking these bottles.' When she furrowed her brow he translated. 'We call it the "taste of light" or the "light strike",' he explained. 'Any exposure to light can cause it.'

She laughed and he paused, unsure what was so humorous. 'What is it? Is light strike funny?'

'No, it's you, or mainly me. I was wrong about you this morning when I said you either wanted to overwhelm me or bore me.'

'Or impress you,' he reminded her.

'Yes, that too. But it's none of those. You simply can't help it, can you? This pouring out of knowledge. Is there anything you don't know about wine?'

'There's probably very little.'

'And humble, too.' She laughed at his arrogance and he laughed, too, and for a moment they were at ease again, as they had been on the picnic blanket.

'Is my husband's special vintage in here?' She bent down to peer at casks stored on a lower shelf. 'This was the year he was going to reveal it.'

'It's not in a cask. It's bottled, over here.' Julien pushed off the table. 'I'll show you.' That was just the metaphoric bucket of cold water he needed to come to his senses. He was fantasising over a woman who'd recently lost a man she'd loved, a woman who was emotionally and professionally off-limits to him. He'd told his *oncle* as much. So, what the hell was wrong with him? That was a rhetorical question. He didn't need to answer it to know. Oncle Etienne would be disappointed in him. He'd set out to overwhelm her and he'd ended up being the one overwhelmed.

Marry her and claim it all in one fell swoop.

Oncle Etienne's words tempted. What a temptation it was—to marry her and share this life with her, to have the partnership he'd once hoped to find with Clarisse, to experience the partnership Garrett Luce had claimed with her. Perhaps she need never know the motivation, the deception…

Julien stopped his thoughts right there. That was how his *oncle* thought, not him. Shortcuts and easy solutions were dangerous. Such thoughts did his own principles no service and they did Emma even less. She was a smart woman. She would find out. And it would hurt her. He'd heard the undertones of vulnerability on the picnic blanket and in the kitchen when she'd spoken of her past, of how she'd been treated by Society. It had made her tough, but at a cost. He would not be the reason she opened those wounds again. Nor would he be the maker of his own woes, the opener of his own old wounds. She wouldn't be the only one who was hurt. He would not knowingly set himself up for such disappointment.

He joined her at the wooden rack showing her the casks, all neatly lined on the racks that ran the length of the wall each vertical rack twenty bottles high, stretching to the ceiling. 'There are—'

'Two thousand bottles,' she breathed, finishing his sentence, impressing him with the speed of her calculations and their accuracy. 'I'm surprised they're already in bottles.'

'Already? There's no "already" about it. Champagne takes time. It must "rest" at least fifteen months at this point,' he explained patiently. 'This batch started its journey seven years ago. It came from the harvest that fall. It went through fermentation and spent three years in a barrel, it was blended carefully with grapes only from that same year.' He'd insisted on it. Sir Garrett hadn't known better, but Julien did. If this was going to be a special bottling to commemorate an important event, it was going to be done right. 'It's been through second fermentation, through riddling, and now it is finishing its ageing process right on time.'

She trailed her fingers over the bottles. 'Gin is much less complicated. It takes two weeks to make a decent batch of gin. Gin lasts whether it's in an open bottle or not. An open bottle of gin might last a year or more without losing its flavour or potency. Champagne is decidedly more…delicate, more fragile.' She gave a sigh. 'Which makes it a double shame that all these bottles have been bottled for naught.'

Julien cleared his throat and took the plunge. What better way to get his thoughts back on track than to discuss a little business. 'The champagne was meant to be served to guests on the occasion of your seven-year anniversary this year. I believe your husband intended to have most of this shipped back to England after your visit this summer.'

She nodded, her face solemn, and he felt like a cad for bringing up such delicate reminders of her loss. 'Yes, we were going to have a big party at Oakwood.

Garrett had been looking forward to serving this and making party gifts of it for guests.'

'We can still celebrate, if you felt up to it,' Julien began tentatively. He wouldn't push her into doing anything she wasn't ready to do, neither would he allow Oncle Etienne to push her. But he would make the offer and see what happened. There was no harm in that, and in fact there might be a lot of good, he justified. 'We could host an event here at the chateau in June and unveil it as a tribute to him, as a way to celebrate his life.'

It would also be the perfect opportunity for unveiling other vintages, like the one he and his *oncle* were counting on, his new champagne blend. 'If we did it quietly, discreetly, no one would complain. It would be a commemorative beverage put out by the chateau on your behalf.' He paused to let her think before adding, 'You needn't even be at the unveiling if you felt it was too public and too soon.' He was counting on that reasoning having some sway with her. He needed her to keep a low profile at least until after the harvest, solidifying this year's sales with the buyers, which, if received well, would go a long way in smoothing concerns about what was happening at the chateau in regard to any potential change in leadership and the debut of the new vintages. There was no time like the present to have her start thinking about how a widow behaved. Circumspection on her part, would definitely help things on his.

'I love the idea, but I'd want to be there,' she said, her quicksilver eyes coming alive. 'It would be a chance for me to meet the growers' consortium and other im-

portant figures in the local industry.' She brightened at
the prospect of an event. 'Planning an event would be
a good project for me.'

They could agree on that at least. If she was busy
planning an event, she'd have less time and less interest in wanting to see the ledgers, where certain truths
would quickly become self-evident to her. Once they
did, she might be less interested in…him. Unless she
was already on his side. If she thought this event was
her idea, which she would if she was in charge of it, she
might be less likely to feel undermined. *If* they were on
the same side by the time everything was revealed. It
wasn't entirely honest of him, but it was honest enough.
For now.

*Once everything is settled, once the land is safe, I'll
tell her everything*, he vowed.

Until then, it had to be this way. This was perhaps
the best reason of them all he had to curb his fantasies
about the Widow Luce.

He did not see her again until after supper that night,
and that was by accident. He'd not intended to see her
again. He had, in fact, intended to give himself some
distance from her and the potency of their day spent
together. He'd fabricated an excuse to skip dinner and
took a tray in his offices, sending word that he had
correspondence to catch up on after a day in the field.
He'd been careful not to imply that falling behind was
somehow her fault for having put demands on his time,
though, while re-establishing an appropriate business-
like distance between them. It would be a good re-

minder for both of them. Friendly was good; he did need her on his side. But *too* friendly was not and that was what they'd been today, conversing over their families and building empathy.

Despite his best intentions, the fates were against him the moment he walked into the library and saw her sitting before the fire, a glass of brandy at her elbow, a book in her lap, her dark head bent in avid interest as her elegant fingers—fingers he'd spent too much time watching today—turned the pages. She was reading fast and intently.

The soft closing of the door gave him away and she looked up in his direction. 'I am educating myself,' she announced rather happily, holding up the book. 'Chaptal's *Treatise on the Culture of the Vine and the Art of Making Wine*,' she read the rather elaborate title. 'He's got it down, quite literally, to a science. There's even an equation about the relationship between sugar, alcohol, and fermentation.' She smiled, obviously pleased with herself. 'Pretty soon, I'll know as much as you.'

'Science.' He frowned, finding the word displeasing, and strode to the shelves. 'That's the problem with Chaptal. He thinks anyone can make wine if they know the recipe. It takes more than just mixing ingredients. There's a certain *je ne sais quoi* to winemaking that he overlooks.' Julien pulled several tomes from the shelf. 'If you want to read about wines and grapes, read Godinot's *Manner of Cultivating the Vine*, Bidet's *Treatise on the Nature and Culture of the Vine*, perhaps a little of Diderot's encyclopaedia, or the work of your pioneering countryman Christopher Merret.' He piled the teetering pile of books on the side table next to her brandy. That brandy was a subtle reminder that Emma Luce was not a traditional woman.

'I've never met a woman who likes her brandy.'

She grinned and took a swallow. 'That's because you'd never met me.' Her gaze rested on him and softened from her teasing. 'Did you get your letters written?'

His letters? Oh, yes. His little lie to avoid dining together. 'I did, thank you.' He needed to remove himself from the room before he found he was sitting down with his own glass of brandy and engaging in a conversation that might go any direction, all of them dangerous. 'It's been a long day and I want to be up early, if you'll excuse me.'

'Of course.' Did he detect some disappointment in that? Had she wanted him to stay? All the more reason to get out while he had his wits intact. She gestured to the book pile. 'I will read the books. Thank you for the recommendations.'

He left her with a short bow but at the door her voice called him back. 'Julien, thank you for today.' It was softly said, seriously said. He did not doubt she meant it and he wasn't sure he could let such sentiment stand in its entirety for fear it might irrevocably change the balance of their association.

He gave a nonchalant wave to the stack of books and a wry grin. 'You might want to delay your thanks until you're through the reading pile. You might not thank me then.'

Chapter Ten

Emma was thankful for the days that followed. She'd never known days like these. Days that were entirely her own to do with as she liked, to spend as she pleased. And it pleased her to spend them with the books Julien had suggested. The weather cooperated, turning March into a damp, rain-soaked month that was best passed indoors in a comfortable chair pulled near the fire.

Her days took on a rhythm of their own; mornings she would take tea and breakfast in the library, her nose buried in the texts as she busily filled notebooks with information, writing questions lining the margins to ask Julien at dinner. For every one thing she learned, it sparked something new to ask. In the afternoons, she went walking. She visited the cellars, studying the inventory, learning the names and amounts of the wines that made up the chateau's catalogue. She planned the June event, making lists of supplies and jotting down ideas for decorations. Her days were full, but her industriousness was self-assigned. She did what she wanted when it pleased her.

It was one luxury she could not lay claim to during her marriage to Garrett. They were always on the move, always going somewhere to meet someone, to make a deal or close a deal. To inspect a factory or to meet with a banker. She'd liked being included in his projects. Inclusion had led to consultation, and she'd been flattered to be asked for advice, which was often taken. That was flattering, too, to know that she had her husband's respect and his trust.

But she saw now how her time had not been her own. It had been the price of being absorbed entirely into Garrett's life. She'd liked their life, but she was liking this new life of hers, too. She had a chance to discover who *she* was, and who she was becoming. This was an unexpected gift, something she'd not known she wanted.

Women were passed so swiftly from man to man there was seldom time for them to know their own minds. A girl left the schoolroom at eighteen to enter Society with the express purpose of finding a husband so that she could be transferred from a father's responsibility to a husband's. Should that fail, as it had in her case when Garrett died, a girl would return to her family's care once more. But Garrett had freed her from that cycle with this chateau. He'd given her a place where she could be herself, whoever that might be, and it touched her deeply that he'd understood her so well as to recognise her need to be her own person.

Her vision blurred at the thought of her husband's kindness. It was an extraordinary gift he'd left her, but it was also extraordinarily lonely. Was she meant to spend her days alone? To never know the comfort of companionship that she'd known with Garrett? She'd always appreciated him, but in hindsight, she saw how truly rare their marital friendship had been. It set a dilemma for her. How would she find another man to equal Garrett? And if she did, how would she honour the relationship she'd had with Garrett by putting another in his place? Would that diminish Garrett's memory?

She swiped at the tears that stung her eyes and set aside Bidet's treatise. She'd read well past lunch and clearly her thoughts were beginning to wander. Emma moved towards the wide library windows that looked out over the vineyards, noting that the sun had come out from behind the clouds at last. Movement in the vineyard caught her eye. It was Julien, strolling the vines, dressed in his work clothes, a battered hat on his head. Perhaps *strolling* wasn't the right word. Strolling implied a sense of laziness and there wasn't a lazy, idle bone in Julien's body. If her days were her own, his days were ruled by the grapes.

Julien was up with the sun, walking the vineyards each morning, something she knew only because she asked, *not* because she'd witnessed it first-hand. He was up and gone long before she took her breakfast. Their paths would not cross until the afternoons and only if she went to the cellars. His afternoons were spent in his offices there, something she'd discovered on one of her many visits to the wine caves beneath the chateau. He would come out and greet her as she toured the caves, but he never invited her into his space.

She told herself it was because the space was small and cramped and he was a busy man. To prove, one had only to know that he spent his early evenings walking the rows again. She told herself she should not begrudge him his afternoons when she had his evenings.

Supper was fast becoming her favourite time of day at the chateau, the one time of day when their worlds merged, the one time they were together. She enjoyed those evenings more than she probably ought to. She thought he enjoyed them too, although probably not as much as she. After all, she was the one who'd initiated them. She'd sent the first invitation the day following their picnic, on the grounds of wanting to discuss the reading he'd recommended.

She'd started with Diderot's encyclopaedia and read his description of the influence of land on winegrowing, her mind filled with questions prompted by the reading. She wanted to know more. As she read Diderot, the voice in her head became Julien's, reading the entries out loud just as he'd lectured her on the grapes the day of the picnic. She'd read the books but what she really wanted was for Julien to harness the extraordinary amount of knowledge he possessed in that dark, tousled head of his and teach her himself.

Those dinners became the high point of her days. After mornings and afternoons of self-guided learning, the evenings were a time to practice her knowledge. Dinners turned into tastings. She prepared menus that required her to broaden her scope of wine knowledge, to challenge her palate, to become more discerning, all under Julien's guidance. Then, the debates would begin, sometimes at the table, sometimes in the library, where she had her books and notebooks at hand.

They might debate tasting rules: Could someone serve a red wine with fish? Or they might debate wine lore: Did the English really discover champagne first? She rather thought there was decent evidence to suggest that was true. The English had imported still wines and deliberately added sugar to it for fizz. She proudly cited the Christopher Merret treatise in support. But Julien insisted champagne's origins were French even if the process had been codified in England before being refined back in France. It had been a rousing discussion, one that made her smile even now, days later.

But despite those meals followed by those wondrous evening debates, Julien made no further overture to partnership. Each evening the connection between them would surge in the enjoyment of one another's company and her hopes would surge along with it. She would think: perhaps tomorrow would be the day he'd want to discuss the June event, or show her the books, or discuss the business he'd been running for Garrett. But each morning, he was gone from her again, out walking the fields, conducting his business without a thought for her until evening.

Sometimes she felt as if she were living a fairy tale where the princess lived in a lovely chateau of her own, the master of the house only appearing for evening meals to quiz her. She did not carry those stories to their conclusions where, based upon scintillating dinner conversation, the princess fell in love with the ogre despite his looks. Julien's looks were fine—quite handsome when he took the time, and quite appealingly rugged when he did not.

It was his aloofness that she struggled with. If she'd not invited him to supper, would he have ignored her entirely? That gave her pause. Perhaps the mistake was hers. Perhaps she should not wait for an invitation to take part in the day-to-day running of the vineyards. She'd already been waiting several weeks. It was nearly April. How much longer should she wait? There were consequences for not waiting; not waiting would risk the perception that she was shouldering her way into his territory, something he'd been sensitive to since the first night.

It would be far better if he invited her in, which was why she *was* waiting. But at some point, she could wait no longer for him to do the inviting, even if barging in would hurt both their feelings. This was why one did not mix business with pleasure. She had imagined the beginnings of a friendship and had imagined such a friendship entitled her to certain considerations while he clearly did not, indifferent perhaps to whether they spent their evenings together.

She watched him stop to study a vine, then his head bent, leaning against a nearby post, and his broad shoulders sagged. At this distance, he seemed tired, vulnerable, as if the weight he carried had suddenly broken him. The thought taunted her, her mind unable to tolerate the idea of a defeated Julien. Julien was strong and contrary, a stone wall to batter away at endlessly with her ideas and questions.

Was something wrong with the vines? Was there a

blight? That was the word, wasn't it, for grape diseases? Did blights happen before the grapes even blossomed? But there was no time to look through her notebooks. Whatever was happening down there, he wasn't going to face it alone. She took a final look out the window and raced for the stairs, stopping only to grab a shawl. These were her vineyards; she ought to face whatever was down there with him. And it was the perfect time to delicately remind him who was truly in charge.

'Julien!' The sound of her voice startled him into lifting his head. He spun around to see Emma, hatless, pelting towards him, skirts lifted high to show bare legs and half-boots, the ends of her shawl flapping wildly. 'What is it?' She panted breathlessly, her words coming out in a worried rush as she bent, a hand clasped to her waist. 'I saw you from the window.'

'You were watching me?' He smiled, in part because she looked so delightfully mussed compared to the usual perfection of her, the usual control.

'I was looking at the vineyard, you just happened to be in it.' She straightened, her breathing evening out. She shot him a dagger stare with her quicksilver eyes. 'That is beside the point. You looked distressed. What has happened?' Ah, there it was, the sharp tongue, the feistiness he'd become used to over their supper debates. She'd taken to her reading assignments with gusto, ingesting the tomes at an impressive speed and with an even more impressive level of comprehension. She wasn't afraid to test him with her new knowledge.

'But you *were* worried about me.' He couldn't resist one further tease.

Her brows scrunched. She was starting to second-guess her conclusion. 'Are you not in distress? Is something not wrong with the grapes? You bent your head, your shoulders sagged.'

She'd been studying him in detail. Her observations rather stunned him, touched him. When had someone paid that close attention to him? Had a woman ever? Usually, a woman's attention went as far as his title, assuming he was in possession of it. And when he didn't have the title…well, the last four lonely years were proof of how that went. But Emma Luce had watched *him*.

'No, I am not in distress. You could say I am in relief.' He directed her attention to the vine. 'Look, there's sap.' He couldn't stop grinning now that the initial relief had passed and reality had settled. 'Do you remember what that means?' It was his turn to watch her now as she bent towards the vine, her eyes riveted on it.

She flashed her gaze at him, a smile taking over her face as she proudly announced, 'Budburst.' He watched laughter bubble up in her, watched it bring a spark to her eyes, a light to her smile, and he thought he'd not truly seen her alive until this moment. 'It means spring is beginning, the vines are alive,' she quoted him. 'The grapes will start growing.' Her enthusiasm was infectious and rivalled his own. He'd been worried for a week now; budburst had come much later than he'd anticipated. He'd begun to believe something had happened in the winter to kill the vines.

'How wondrous,' she breathed, and he had the sense that she meant so much more than the wonder of the grapes, that the wonder extended to celebrating not only the grapes, but life, and simply being here. Her gaze held his, her smile widened, dominating her features until she shone like a dazzling star. 'We will make wondrous wine this year, Julien, I just know it!'

The moment got the better of them. She was in his arms, her face turned up to his, her arms twined about his neck in what could only be termed as a hug. Emma Luce was *hugging* him, and he was hugging her back. He may even have given her a little spin around in his enthusiasm over the grapes, over her. She laughed up at him, the sound full of life, just before she kissed him, on the cheek of course, an enthusiastic peck of celebration. It felt good. It felt right, and that made it not only wrong, but perilous. How did one come back from this line once it was crossed?

Chapter Eleven

'What shall we discuss tonight?' Julien spoke the usual words as they made their way into the dining room that evening, but she did not miss the forced casualness with which those words were infused. She'd overstepped herself in the vineyard and they'd both felt its effects.

'I thought we might discuss Chaptal now that I've completed reading his treatise, and because you seem to dislike the fellow.' She strove to match his casual tones, strove to set aside what it had felt like to be surrounded by the strength of his embrace, what it had felt like to look up into his face and see another man entirely—a man open to joy. He'd looked younger in those moments. Of course, he was still young, not yet forty.

How old was he? Thirty-five? Thirty-eight? Julien had a rather timeless quality to him. That she was trying to pin down a specific age spoke to her growing curiosity over him on a more personal level, a curiosity that had been piqued the day of the picnic, hearing stories of him as a schoolboy in England.

You think about him too much, came the scold. *Face the evidence. You know his schedule, and you look forward to the evening meal because those debates are with him.*

Early on, she'd told herself he was merely objectively handsome, that she needed to get to know him if she wanted to navigate him, manage him, solve him like a puzzle, and claim the prize of full access to her vineyards.

After weeks of dinners and debates, that was less true now than it once might have been. Now her curiosity was piqued for itself, not for any extrinsic gain. Since the picnic, his appeal had started to shift to something more personal, and today she'd rather spontaneously acted on that shift. She'd like to say it was much to her regret, but that would be a lie. She did *not* regret it even if it left her with complicated emotions. The thrill of being in his arms had been tempered by a sense of guilt, that being in Julien's arms was somehow disloyal to Garrett.

'It's not that I don't like Chaptal,' Julien began after the food had been set down *à la française* so that they could serve themselves from a tureen containing a creamy vichyssoise soup, and a platter of pork loin drizzled in a *poivrade* sauce. The footmen retreated and Julien continued as he served her a plate. 'Chaptal's chemical calculations are a wonder. There's no debating that his formula takes the guess work out of winemaking. A winemaker can reduce his margin of error in the addition of sugar needed to increase the alcohol content to the right levels. It's the consequence of that information being widely disseminated that bothers me.' He shook his head and Emma laughed.

'You don't mind Chaptal's findings, you only mind who gets to be privy to them. What might those *devastating* consequences be? That wine be democratised?' The gentleman in him was showing through tonight.

'What I *mind* is being rendered redundant because everyone has a recipe and no one needs my expertise.'

'But that's not true, though. It would take more than a recipe to make your knowledge obsolete,' she began, but he interrupted.

'Certainly, there's more to winemaking than adding sugar, but people will *think* it's true.' He tapped his temple with a forefinger, his voice taking on an edge of intensity. 'People will *think* they can make their own wine, that *anyone* can make wine. *Alors*, they can, but not everyone can make *good* wine. Too many people making bad wine is not a help for the reputation of the industry.' He stopped to taste a sip of his wine, a chilled chardonnay with oaky notes. 'This was a good choice tonight.' He nodded his approval.

'I chose it myself, although I had Richet approve it,' Emma said calmly, aware that inside her, a warm flame of appreciation had flickered to life at his praise.

Julien held the glass up to the candlelight. 'This is what I'm talking about. A month ago, you had the same access to the wine that you have today, *non*? But you chose a wine that was too heavy, too rich. Despite proper wines being at your disposal, you still chose incorrectly.'

She studied him for a long moment. His usual stoicism was firmly back in place. But perhaps it had been wrestled there with great effort. And she knew better now. The stoicism was a mask for something more, something he tried very hard to hide from the world, from her, from himself. Here was a man who was passionate about his grapes, his wine, but made great efforts to keep that passion under lock and key. Still, it leaked out when he talked of his vines, as it had today when he'd discovered the sap. Why did he try so very hard to be something he was not?

'So, winemaking should be for an elite few?' She gave him a questioning look over the rim of her glass. 'Where is the famed French *égalité* in that?'

Julien turned serious. 'I am no lover of the mob.' Instinctively, she recognised she'd crossed yet another dangerous line. She ought to retreat, ought to seek the safety of Chaptal's fermentation process instead of plunging headlong into French politics. The first rule of good business was never to discuss politics, but it seemed today was a day for breaking rules.

'Why is that? I would think, as a man of your background, that democracy would suit you.'

'My background? What do you know of "my background"?' His slate-blue eyes had become hard flints; his hand had stilled on the stem of his wine glass. Every muscle in his body tensed beneath the fabric of his evening jacket. She had him on the run from something, but what? She'd not meant to corner him any more than she'd meant to kiss him in the vineyard. It was a pattern with them. All sorts of things not meant to happen occurred when they were together: fights when they meant to be friendly, discoveries when they meant to be wary. For two people who prided themselves on control, they didn't seem to have a lot of it when they were together.

If he wanted her to apologise for her statement, he'd be disappointed. 'I meant that as a man who has an obvious love for the land and a talent for it, you must aspire to having your own land as opposed to working another's. Surely, there are better opportunities for a man to be self-made now that the land is not tied up in noble holdings.'

'Opportunities at what price?' The look he gave her was almost a glare. 'I might caution you to not speak about that which you do not fully understand.' He rose, the gesture declaring dinner was over, but she was not ready to let him go, to simply walk away.

'Perhaps we might adjourn to the library, there are other things I want to discuss like the vintage reveal party.' She offered the topic as a peace offering, a promise of détente, a promise that she would take care not to venture into politics again for the moment.

In the library, the conversation did go well for a while. She managed to talk about the event; what they might serve, where they might hold it—perhaps in the gardens. She asked for his input on the guest list and it seemed as if they might end the evening on an amicable note. *Falsely* amicable, if she was being honest.

Emma sipped her brandy, acutely aware of the man who sat in the chair opposite her by the fire. They'd fallen into silence after having exhausted the topic of the wine gala, each of them apparently content to simply be still for a moment. What was going on in his head? Surely, his mind was not as still as his body if her own mind was any measuring stick. Her thoughts were busy debating whether or not she dared bring up the subject of her taking next steps with the vineyard, of asking for an introduction to the growers' consortium. On the one hand, talking about the gala was the perfect conversational entrée for the topic, but on the other, the events earlier today and this evening had fraught their discussion with a sharp edge. When she asked, she didn't want to be turned down. If she was, she'd have to ask again and again until he gave way; the issue would become a battleground. The last thing she needed was more contention between them.

Emma knew how to read a room and she wasn't convinced circumstances were quite right tonight to get a yes from him. And yet, if her entrée to the growers' consortium must go unaddressed, perhaps there were other issues that could not. Not all the tension that simmered beneath their quiet sips of brandy and fireside silence could be attributed to a dinner conversation gone sideways. They might have made their peace with her political remarks but not with the issue of the vineyard. The forced normalcy had still been there when they'd talked of the gala. Julien had been overly polite as he'd poured their drinks, careful to not let his fingers brush hers when he handed her the snifter, and that she noted those nuances was proof that the effects still lingered hours afterwards for both of them.

'Are we not going to talk about it?' she ventured in light tones. 'The kiss in the vineyard?' she offered for clarification.

'It was hardly a kiss.' Julien set aside his brandy and rose, going to the long windows and looking out into the dark, his hands clasped behind his back.

'Then why does it bother you so much?' she challenged, turning in her chair to keep him in sight.

'It doesn't.'

'Yes, it does,' she argued. 'You've not been quite yourself tonight, not that you're ever "quite yourself",' she added as a goad. He had himself on a tight leash at the moment and she wanted to snap his control, make him admit to what he was feeling.

That earned her a growl and a sharp look tossed at her from over his shoulder. 'What is that supposed to mean?'

'Well, since you asked, it means that you work so hard to ignore that you *feel* anything, and yet I think you feel *everything*. Deeply. But you believe you must hide it. Why is that?'

The growl became a harsh chuckle. She recognised the sound. He was going on the offensive. He was the king of the dry chuckle. It was his strategy, his way of dismissing people and topics he didn't want to discuss. She braced. Would his response be denial? Deflection?

'You seem to have spent a lot of time thinking about me while you've been here. Perhaps overthinking. I would not encourage that, although I certainly understand it. We are isolated out here and you are…lonely.' Ah, so it was to be deflection then.

'And you're not?' she challenged. 'You, sir, are lone-liness personified.' She would not sit there and let him patronise her.

He'd overplayed his hand. He'd meant to chase her from the room with his insult, not draw her closer. Julien didn't need to turn from the window to know she was coming for him. Emma Luce would not take being patronised sitting down. He could hear the rustle of her black bombazine skirts, smell the jasmine scent of her as she closed in on him.

'You know nothing about me.' He put up his last defence, hoping to drive her off. It was a lie though, he very much feared that she *did* know him. He'd not meant for that to happen. Oh, she did not know certain things, like he was sometimes a *comte* depending on the government's current attitude towards titles. She didn't know his family had once owned these lands seventy years ago, a legacy that had been built over centuries and stripped away in minutes all for the sake of the mob, for *égalité*. But she did know *him*. She saw his passion, saw his heart, and that scared him. He'd not shown that to anyone since Clarisse. He'd not meant to show it to Emma Luce.

'I could say the same,' came the fierce retort as she took up a position beside him, staring out into the dark-ness, both of them acting like there was something to see. 'What makes you think you know anything about *me*?' She might be surprised there. He watched her when she thought he wasn't looking. He saw the effi-ciency with which the house was run, the quality of the

meals that made their way to the table every night, courtesy of her menus, the extra level of neatness the house
took on under her care. Because he saw how much the
servants enjoyed working for her. Petit sang her praises,
saying how delightful it was to have a mistress who understood the delicacies of cooking. Mrs Dormand appreciated the burden of decision making that was lifted
from her shoulders with a mistress present.

Oh, he knew quite a bit about her and he wished it
made her less likeable. It would be far easier if she'd
hid away in her room, crying her eyes out. But she'd
done none of that. She'd thrown herself into her new
life, her new role, as best she could. That made her
impressive and interesting and absolutely more difficult to manage.

'I know more than you think,' he answered, edging
his voice with a hint of challenge. 'I know that being
alone and being lonely are not the same. I am *alone*.
You are *lonely*.' She could not hide that behind her
constant busyness. It was *because* of that loneliness
that she was a force constantly in motion—reading her
wine books, working with the staff, planning the gala,
walking the cellars, learning her wines. All of it was a
cover for what really plagued her—how to combat her
loneliness. Embrace it and endure, or move on, even
if that meant moving past Garrett Luce's memory?
He wasn't the only one hiding certain truths. Her eyes
flashed with anger and something else—admission
perhaps? Sadness?

'Yes, I miss him,' she confessed. 'It helps to be here.
At Oakwood, I kept expecting to come around a corner

and see him or enter a room and find him in his favourite chair. There were reminders of him everywhere; his clothes in the wardrobes, his toiletries still on the bureau where he'd left them before our trip, everything just waiting for him to come and pick them up again. It was like even our life together was waiting for him to return to it. But not here.'

She drew a deep breath. 'Here, I am free to start again on my own.' She tried for a smile. He could see what it cost her. She was being brave. His heart went out to her and in that moment, he yearned to tell her that he understood, that he knew a little something about starting over without the person you loved. That he knew there was no such thing. There wasn't really a clean slate. The ghosts still followed; the past could never be entirely left behind. No one knew that better than he did. But such a disclosure required he tell her other things; that the woman he'd loved had lived in his family's chateau while three generations of Archambeaux had not.

The Archambeaux had not lived in their home for seventy years. Now he lived here on Garrett Luce's generous sufferance, sharing the residence with the ghosts of his past and his family. That could end. If Emma asked him to leave, if Emma refused to sell, it would all have been for naught. He'd spend his life like his *oncle*—living a stone's throw away from unfulfilled dreams. So, he did what he always did when conversations became too personal, too painful: he deflected.

He softened his tone. 'There's nothing wrong with being lonely, Emma.'

'No, there isn't,' she said staunchly. She pushed back a strand of hair that had come loose. 'It just takes getting used to.' Yes, he could agree to that. Being alone took practice. There was an art to spending all of one's time with one's thoughts without letting those thoughts become overwhelming.

She faced him, giving him a full glimpse of her beauty, her strength. 'Just to be clear though. I did not kiss you because I am lonely.'

'Oh?' He arched a brow, trying to be cool. That was too bad. He could have understood a kiss out of loneliness. Now he'd have to find other explanations and the path those explanations might travel made him uncomfortable. He wasn't sure he wanted to discuss what she called a kiss. If they did, he'd have to admit to his reaction—admit that he'd liked the feel of her in his arms far too much. He'd have to admit that he'd hugged her back, swung her around. That normally, the person he'd have wanted to celebrate budburst with was his *oncle*. But today, the first person he'd wanted to tell was her, and there she'd been, with him in the vineyard at the exact moment he'd wanted her to be there. They'd been reckless and he'd loved it.

He'd thought of nothing else since. He'd been prickly with it, snapping at her at dinner, trying to ignore the intensified awareness that hummed in his blood despite his best efforts these past weeks to keep his distance. The picnic had been a warning and he'd heeded it. But today proved his efforts were for naught. She'd destroyed his defences in moments. 'Do you care to enlighten me, then? Why did you kiss me?'

'To celebrate the good news, to celebrate being here, and for the first time in a while, to celebrate the sheer thrill of being alive in springtime.' The truth of those words shone on her face. 'Because it fit the moment.' She paused, something flickering in her eyes as her gaze held his, something that set undeniable tendrils of desire flaring within him. 'Because I *wanted* to kiss you.'

'I do not think you know what that word really means.' He should not have said that. He should not flirt with disaster. He should put an end to this conversation immediately. He should remind them both there were limits to their association despite the close proximity in which they lived. But he did neither. The distance between them closed. Her gaze became the colour of mist and fog. He traced the fullness of her bottom lip, his gaze dropping to that luscious mouth, his voice husky. 'The English may think that was a kiss, but I assure you, the French do not.'

'What, pray tell, is a kiss then?' Her own voice was reminiscent of smoky brandy, throaty and coy, her teeth nipping at the pad of his thumb as it passed over her lip.

His mouth hovered, a whisper away from hers as he breathed his seduction. 'A kiss is the meeting of mouths, the press of lips, full and open, it is the tangle of tongues, the taste of souls.' He took her mouth in demonstration, the smell of jasmine filling his senses, obliterating all reason, as passion slipped its leash and ran amok.

Chapter Twelve

At the press of his mouth, chaos reigned; want ran like wildfire in her veins, hot and engulfing, her senses splintering like a tree at a lightning strike. Good God, this kiss was desire unchained, and it ignited a rough hunger of her own. She answered with a new fierceness that left her own need naked and known. She knew already that in the aftermath there could be no misinterpreting this kiss, with its unbridled, wild warfare, this duel of mouths, of hands, of bodies. Her hands were in his hair, her teeth tugging at his lip even as his own drifted down to nip at her throat—a throat she'd wantonly exposed, her body begging even as she laid siege to his.

She moaned her madness, her hips pressed hard to his, the physical evidence of his desire unmistakable against her skirts. She wanted, she wanted… The two words thrummed through her with the heat of his kiss, her mind unable to complete the sentence. It was enough to simply want, to let that want rip through her with the intensity of an inferno, devouring reason and anything else that stood in its wake. 'Julien.' She gasped his name, her hands ripped at his immaculately tied cravat and moved onto his coat, his waistcoat, the buttons of his shirt, and each barrier fell before the frantic speed of her hands.

His hands did not reciprocate with such delicacy. He seized the bodice of her gown with two hands and rent, sending buttons scattering while wild laughter welled up her throat. Had anything ever felt so delicious? So freeing? Her chemise and undergarments fared no better. Julien was rabid in his frenzy, and so was she. She wanted to devour him, claim him, as much as her own body cried out for the same.

Claim me. Mark me. Know me. Drag me from the abyss of aloneness. Bring me into the light.

Her breasts were bare in his hands, his head buried between them as he knelt before her, his hands futilely, frustratingly working the string of her pantalettes. He swore and brought his mouth to bear, ripping the string with his teeth, his hands roughly pushing them down, his mouth at her mons. She could feel his breath coming warm and fast against her nether thatch. Desire, honest and raw, surged in her, rising fast, riding her hard. Then he tongued her seam and she thought she'd lose her mind. 'Julien, I can't.' She would fall if he kept this up; her legs had no strength.

'Hold on to me,' came the response, his own desire making him terse. And she did. Her hands dug into his shoulders, nails digging into those muscled depths as his mouth did wicked things to her most private places until release claimed her and her vocabulary was reduced to sounds. How he found the strength to carry her to the fireplace was beyond her, but then, in the moments following that oral decadence a lot of things were beyond her—thought, speech, basic motor functions. And yet, she was by no means sated. Her wildness had only been tempted by his mouth, not tamed.

'How are you?' Julien's voice was a sexy tease, his eyes hot blue flames as he laid her down.

'We are not done yet.' She reached for him, working his elegant evening trousers down past lean hips with quick, adept fingers, freeing his phallus to her gaze. 'You're magnificent.'

He gave a possessive growl, his body fitting unerringly to hers like a puzzle solved. 'I was hoping you'd say that.'

She wrapped her arms about his neck, drawing him down so that the hard length of him pressed against her thigh. 'Don't be gentle, don't be nice. I won't break.' She didn't want to lose the tempo, the heat and the speed that fed the fires of chaos in her, that didn't let her think, only let her feel. If she took time to think she might not like where those thoughts led.

'I was hoping you'd say that, too,' he laughed, low, at her ear. Dear heavens, this man was rough seduction personified and her body was craving it, perhaps even her soul was craving it, needing the ferocity of him, needing the connection with another. It was a potent combination. He entered her hard and swift and she cried out, revelling in the power of the joining. She wrapped her legs tight about his hips, lean and powerful, her own hips rising to meet his.

Please, please, please, please... The words became a gasped litany as her body met his in the old rhythm. *Please* for the pleasure, *please* for the obliteration...just *please*. And then release came, a thunderclap, a powerful storm of its own, its deluge dousing the fire. Passion contained, docilely returning to its leash, chaos caged.

She was vaguely aware of Julien pulling a soft blanket over them, of his warm body curving about hers as they dozed by the fire. She could feel the deep rise and fall of his chest against her back, the strength of his arm as it draped about her, his hand warm and possessive at her hip. This was a new kind of wild heaven, a new kind of wickedness, and it was positively divine. Her pleasure-addled mind flickered to life for a moment. Was it possible something could be both wicked and divine? At present, it didn't matter. But it would. That particular thought was unfortunately already waking up in her mind even as she drifted off to sleep.

The dying fire woke them both shortly after midnight and he draped her in the blanket and took her hand, leading her on a mad dash through the house to her bedroom, stopping once to silence her laughter with a kiss. 'You don't want Richet to hear you, do you?' he chuckled, pressing her to a wall.

She closed her hand around his rising phallus. 'He might hear me, but he'll *see* you.' She had the meagre protection of the blanket, but he had not even that. Julien was striding the midnight halls of the chateau in his altogether.

At her chambers, Julien hesitated. She tugged at his hand. 'Will you stay? Please? We could try something a little slower, perhaps a little more comfortable, like in a bed.'

She gave a laugh and he smiled. 'How can I possibly refuse?'

It was her turn to seduce him, with her mouth, with her touch as she savoured the man in her bed, riding him astride in a slow, grinding trot that teased them both to the edge of exquisite pleasure before she allowed them to claim it. But perhaps the most exquisite pleasure was the one she watched on his face, the way his neck arched, pleasure welling up the muscled column of his throat and taking the form of masculine groans, his eyes going wide, locked on hers as she felt his body clench and prepare inside her. It was her cue to let him go, to take him in her hand at last.

He drew her to him and she tucked herself against his side, her head nestled into the hollow of his shoulder. 'I think this is the wildest, most decadent, divine night I've ever had,' Emma whispered.

'Don't,' Julien breathed into her hair. 'Don't think. There will be time enough for that later.'

She woke much later and knew immediately that he was gone before she even opened her eyes. She could feel the light dawn against her eyelids, could feel the emptiness of the bed, its coolness, the absence of a man's weight. In a practical sense, she understood why he was gone. Her maid would be in to help her dress. Catching the land steward in the mistress's bed would spark all types of rumours, add to that the mistress had only been widowed a short time, and she'd never be able to hold her head up. She'd have scandal attached to her name before she'd even introduced herself to the neighbours.

The last hit her especially hard. She groaned as the reality of the morning settled on her. What had she done? She'd slept with Julien. She'd done wicked things with Julien, behaved decadently with him in ways she'd never behaved with Garrett. More than that, she was supposed to be in mourning. She'd behaved like a hussy. What did that mean? Should she feel riddled with guilt? And if she didn't, should she feel guilty for not feeling guilty enough? It was not her behaviour she felt guilty over. She couldn't care less what Society thought. Society had never done her any favours. The guilt was on Garrett's behalf. Should she feel guilty for moving on so quickly? Or was this exactly what she needed to do *to* move on? Oh, she'd really opened a Pandora's box on this one. What was wrong with her? Why had she acted so impetuously?

She knew what was wrong with her. She *was* lonely. Julien had not been wrong there. She missed Garrett. She missed the simple pleasure of having him present in her day. She'd not realised how much Garrett's touches, a casual touch on the shoulder as he passed her desk, the fifty little conversations they'd have throughout the day, had meant. There was a void in her world that no amount of work could fill. She'd been hungry for a human connection, and not just someone to talk to—after all, she talked to the staff all day. Menus with Mrs Petit, housekeeping items with Mrs Dormand and Richet. But those interactions didn't count. They had to listen to her. They were not her equals. They didn't dare get to know her, disagree with her, probe her secrets.

And Julien should do those things? The voice in her head was quick to point out the flaw. *He is the land steward. Why does he get to be special? Isn't he also an employee of the chateau?*

The explanation was proximity. They spent too much time together. It was an unfortunate but perhaps inevitable situation. She'd been lonely and he'd been there.

Emma cringed at the description and drew the sheets up over her head as if she could block it all out. Was that really all it was? An outlet for her loneliness? A different way to grieve the loss of her husband? Perhaps that was the best explanation she could offer herself. She should leave it at that. And yet, to do so would be to buy into a lie. It had not all been about her last night. She'd not been in it alone. She'd not even been the one to start it. *He* had kissed *her*. Ravenously, like a starved man. She'd not been the only lonely one. They'd been equal participants in what had followed. Dear heavens, it had been rough, uninhibited, and thorough and…new.

Romantic intimacies with Garrett had always been satisfactory, pleasant, comforting, meaningful. No complaints. He'd been a considerate and decent lover. But last night had been beyond any previous experience—both physically in the sense of the things she and Julien had done, but also emotionally in the things she had felt.

Emma blushed at the memories; literally tearing

at Julien's clothes because she could not get at him fast enough, Julien using his mouth to bite through the stubborn string of her pantalettes before using his mouth on her. She'd heard of such things before, but never had she experienced them. Sleeping naked, skin to skin beside the fire afterwards, racing through the house nude, nearly having him against a wall in the hall. It was the stuff of wild fantasies. She'd thrilled to it, and so had he. At some point, it had stopped being about loneliness.

Now she was lying in bed reliving that decadence and comparing Julien to her husband. That did not speak well of her, to compare the two men. What sort of woman did that? Well, she thought she knew the answer to that. The sort of woman who was loose with her favours. By definition, to compare, one must have at least two items to weigh against one another. She'd not ever thought she'd be a woman with more than one lover.

But now you are, came the rejoinder.

She'd not thought to be a lot of things; childless, a widow before the age of thirty, owner of a French vineyard. Alone. Confused.

Get a hold of yourself! her inner voice scolded. *You had a one-night affair with a handsome man, it does not have to mean anything.*

Was that what she wanted? For last night to exist as a moment out of time? An antidote?

She could certainly choose to shape it that way. It would make it easier to ignore. Julien would like that. He'd been fully willing to ignore the kiss in the vineyard until she'd pushed the issue. But she did not think last night could be as easily ignored. Which meant, option two: she had to go on living her life with last night a part of the new reality between her and Julien. There could be no pretending that they hadn't ripped each other's clothes off, seen each other naked, and made mad love in the library and in her bed.

She threw off the covers. It was suddenly too hot to stay underneath them. What did one say to their lover the next morning in those circumstances? Did one simply go downstairs, butter their toast, sip their tea, and ask about plans for the day, and had they read anything interesting in the news?

And, oh, by the way, did we perhaps want to try the library again but in the afternoon with the sun coming through the windows?

Or, *Did you happen to retrieve our clothes from the library floor before the servants were up this morning?*

She rather hoped he had. It would be difficult to explain petticoats and waistcoats and bodice buttons scattered on the floor. She groaned at the thought of one of the footmen or one of the scullery maids who laid the fires finding the detritus of their evening. Emma squeezed her eyes shut. How would she ever face Richet again if he knew? It would be bad enough facing Julien wondering if he regretted it while she recalled everything that had happened. How could she look at him again and not think about last night?

There was the bigger question, too. Was last night one-time only? Or would it happen again? If it was only one time, she might justify it to herself as a bid against loneliness or even an experiment. To repeat it would be to admit to something more. Did she want it to happen again? Did *he*? That came with a host of other questions like: If it did happen again, what would it mean? Where did this lead? She looked up at the ceiling and let out a sigh. Those were only the practical implications. There were more philosophical ones, too.

Why did Julien stir her so deeply when she'd loved Garrett utterly? The guilty dilemma flooded again. Was the speed at which she'd taken a lover unseemly? Or a natural part of the process of moving on? This— all the uncertainty, all the questions—was the price of that one night of pleasure. What had she been thinking? But she knew very well that in the moment, she *hadn't* been thinking—that was the problem. From the moment his eyes had dropped to her mouth and his thumb had stroked her bottom lip, she'd stopped thinking entirely and started feeling. And it had felt good, right up until now.

There was a rap on her door and Emma quickly pulled the covers up. Her maid, Chloe, entered carrying fresh linen. '*Bonjour, madame*. You've slept late, I hope that means you've slept well. The sun is out today. We shall have some pleasant weather at last.' Emma watched Chloe for any tells that she knew what she'd been up to last night and who she'd been up to it with. Chloe was chatty today, but Chloe was always cheerful, always chatty. There was nothing new there. Emma reached for the robe she kept near the bed and started to relax. Perhaps she might be able to keep this…indiscretion…between her, Julien, and her conscience.

'Monsieur Archambeau asked me to relay a mes-sage, *madame*. He wanted me to tell you that he's gone out today.'

'Did he say where?' Emma took a seat at her dress-ing table, letting Chloe brush out her hair.

'No, *madame*, only that he did not know when he'd be back. He said not to wait supper on him.'

She ought to feel relieved. She didn't have to face Julien today. By the time she did see him, she'd have herself together, her mind organised instead of her thoughts flying in a hundred different directions like a heart-struck young girl. But she did not feel the relief she'd expected at this reprieve. She felt disappointment, and dismay. Her mind immediately dissected what it could mean—did he leave because he didn't want to face her? Because he regretted what had happened?

Did he regret it because he'd let his guard down, al-lowed someone to see him at his most vulnerable? Or did he regret it because of what he'd done with her? If it was the former, she could manage it, they could come back from that. But if it was the latter, if it was her, or their actions, he took objection to, that could ruin everything. How would they ever work together then? If she'd known this would be the outcome would she still have done it? If the opportunity arose, would she do it again? She feared the answer would be yes.

Chapter Thirteen

He should not have done it. After a day of brutal exercise in the fields trying to work himself into forgetful exhaustion, that was the conclusion he'd reached. There were, in fact, quite a few things he should not have done. He should not have taunted her, should not have flirted with her, should not have pushed her, because he knew by now that when she was pushed, Emma Luce pushed back. He'd spent all day enumerating his sins. But that had only made the torture worse.

Using the last of the daylight, sunset falling, Julien kicked his horse into a hard gallop along a flat stretch of road that lay between the chateau and his *oncle*'s farmhouse, hoping that if he could ride hard enough he could exorcise the heat from his veins, and convince himself to regret last night, because logically he *ought* to regret it.

But that was only logic talking. He seemed to have little use for such a commodity in the last ten hours and it was a hard sell. He could not persuade any part of him to regret last night. His mind was full of images of her; her hair falling down, the heat in her eyes when she looked at him, the way she'd looked when pleasure claimed her—pleasure *he'd* given her—her back arched, her head thrown back, her hips pressing into his, legs wrapped about him as if she never wanted him to leave her, but of course he had to. He could not spend within her. There were other images, too—her atop him in her bed, riding him like Godiva with her dark hair draped over her breasts.

That had been exquisite. Leaving her bed had been much more difficult than he had anticipated. His body still reverberated with the echoes of their lovemaking, every wild, wonderful minute of it. The ache in his body asking the question *when*? When would they be together again? Not *would* there be a next time—his body had leapt right over any circumspection. His body was not bothered by more sophisticated issues such as the relational implications of last night.

He did not fool himself that he could simply pretend last night had not happened. For one, he did not think Emma would let him treat it so callously, and for another, he did not want to. His body ached for hers, to repeat it. But what would that mean? An affair with Emma Luce? It would have to be hidden. From the servants, for the sake of her reputation, and from his *oncle* for the sake of his. The farmhouse came into view with its green shutters, like the chateau's, and Julien slowed his horse. If his *oncle* saw him racing up the road, he'd know something was wrong. In the yard, Julien dismounted and schooled his features. He must not give away anything. His business with Emma was between him and her, not his *oncle*. His *oncle* had already hinted that intimacies could be strategically used to advance their cause.

That had not sat well with him when his *oncle* had originally introduced the idea, and he liked the idea even less now that he knew her better.

That's because you've become attached, that's what empathy will do for you, his inner voice scolded. *You did not heed your own warnings, your own advice.*

He wanted to dismiss the self-directed scold. Just because he'd slept with her didn't mean he was attached. They were two consenting adults who'd been keen to stave off loneliness. Sex *could* be just sex. Goodness knew he'd tried 'just sex,' trying to find relief, trying to obliterate the pain of the past.

He wasn't doing a good job of selling the argument to himself. In this case there was no 'just sex' about it. It had been physical, and primal, rough and riotous, but emotion had been there bubbling underneath. They'd both been desperately seeking something: belonging, connection, and for a few short hours, they'd found it in each other's arms. He wanted to find it again. With her.

His *oncle* was in his office, sitting behind his desk, poring over reports and ledgers, dressed immaculately, and looking out of place, something that struck him more strongly than usual. His *oncle* dressed well for town, but not for the countryside. His office was also well-appointed with an expensive desk from Paris and all the accoutrements that adorned his bookshelves— the scales, the globe, the leather-spined books with the gold gilt letters that came from a Paris bookseller monthly. This was an office to rival a noble's town house. It was not an estate office of a man who lived in a country gentleman's farmhouse. But his *oncle* had never aspired to be a simple country gentleman, had he? His life, all sixty-two years of it, had been dedicated to the pursuit of something larger—restoring the Comte du Rocroi's land.

His *oncle* looked up and smiled. 'Julien, welcome. You are in time for supper. It will take no time at all to set an extra place.'

Dinner was a pleasant affair; one could always count on eating well at the farmhouse, breakfast or supper. Perhaps eating a little too well. Only a nobleman ate like his *oncle*. They talked of the weather and of local news in the neighbourhood, making a two-hour meal of it, which alternately soothed and chafed at Julien's nerves. It was not until they'd adjourned back to his *oncle*'s office that there was a shift to business.

'I suspect you haven't just come to catch up on the news. You've come to tell me something.' His slate-blue eyes, so like Julien's own, twinkled, and Julien froze. How did his *oncle* know? Then he remembered. The other news.

'Yes, we've got budburst. The vines are showing. Another season is under way.' That's what had started everything yesterday. Julien took his usual seat across from his *oncle*. Budburst seemed a lifetime ago, and far less significant than what had followed, a sure sign that logic had deserted him. When had anything been more important than the vines? 'Now we just need to hope the winter weather is gone for good. I don't want a cold snap bringing a frost and killing us off before we truly get under way. And your vines here? Are they showing?'

'*Our* vines, you mean,' his *oncle* corrected. 'Yes, buds showed a couple days ago. It took them long enough this year. They're as unpredictable as a woman.' He chuckled. 'Speaking of which, how is the situation over there? Has Madame Luce given up on her fantasies of being a vineyard manager?'

Emma. He'd not thought of her as Madame Luce for quite a while now, not since their picnic. 'No, in fact, just the opposite. She's become an ardent student of viniculture.'

His *oncle* scoffed at the idea. 'Assign her some hard reading like Merret's treatise. The science will put her to sleep. Have her read Chaptal.'

'I *did* assign those.' Julien took a bit of satisfaction in informing his *oncle*. 'She devoured them and she debates me nightly. Ask her who invented champagne at your own peril.'

His *oncle* arched a white brow, catching his slip. 'Then, I'd say you are not trying hard enough. The goal was to make her disinterested in the process, not to have her become intrigued by it.' He gave a sly look. 'But perhaps if you debate nightly, her interest isn't so much in the wine as in the instructor? Perhaps she wants to impress you?'

Julien took refuge in chagrin. 'She is a woman in mourning. I doubt she even looks at a man with such thoughts.' But she'd looked at him with want and desire last night. He'd not let himself contemplate how much of that want and desire was for him and how much was a want and desire to assuage her loneliness. Had she simply used him? Could he blame her when he had used her for his own needs as well? And yet, somehow in the riot of passion, they'd transcended those needs.

His *oncle* gave a shrug, unconvinced. 'Well, *I* won't debate with you. Perhaps an invitation to the chateau might be in order? I could come to dinner and discuss the wine gala with her. I do admit to some curiosity about this woman who seeks to unseat us.'

'She doesn't seek to unseat us,' Julien corrected swiftly. His *oncle* was being hyperbolic. 'She just wants what is hers, what her husband has left her.' He realised as he said the words that he believed them. The resentment he'd felt upon her arrival over a month ago was absent. How had that happened? *When* had that happened? Last night or before? How long had he felt that way?

His *oncle* was silent for a long while, his gaze fixed unblinkingly on him. 'Oh, my, *mon fils*, she's really got her hooks into you if she's got you thinking about throwing away the family legacy. No woman should come before your family,' he cautioned. 'A woman is nothing but trouble. You should know that by now.'

'It's her chateau, Oncle.'

'It's your inheritance, it's what your great-*grandpère* lost his head for, what your *grandpère* lived in exile for, what he and your father came back for, what you were raised for. We have all lived for this moment, invested for this moment, and now it's up to you to see it through.' He waved a beringed hand. 'I am an old

man. But you are the Comte, you are the next generation.' If his *oncle* was trying to make him feel guilty,
he was doing an excellent job. When had he moved
away from his old dreams?

His *oncle* sighed. 'Maybe it is easy for you to care
less because you live in the chateau every day, surrounded by our family's artefacts—the art collection,
the furniture that's been acquired over the centuries.
You can pretend it is yours. I have never lived there.'

'It is not truly mine either. It has not been ours for
seventy years.' Julien gritted his teeth. He would not
be made to feel guilty about not wanting to steal a
woman's inheritance from her. Nor would he allow
himself to feel as if he were betraying a man who'd
been like a second father to him. He and his *oncle*
had always been on the same side, always shared the
same ambitions.

But today, he felt caught between his *oncle* and
Emma and it was not necessarily his *oncle* he wanted
to favour. The Archambeau dream seemed too expensive if it cost Emma her home. And yet, such a thought
disconcerted him greatly. Was he really willing to protect Emma from his *oncle* at the expense of not restoring Archambeau land? What end did that serve? What
did he get from playing Emma's hero? What would he
be left with? An alienated *oncle*, a lost family dream,
and quite possibly hurt by a woman yet again if he let
himself keep falling.

His *oncle* smiled. 'Ah, to be young again, *mon fils*,
and to feel spring running through my veins, blood
pounding, and a woman to share it with. You think I

don't know how you feel, but I do. Take my advice, even though you are not in the mood to hear it. If she's got your blood boiling, marry her, have it all—the woman, the land, the house.'

'It's not like that, Oncle.' Julien prepared to make the old arguments about dishonesty and the morality of such a strategy, realising even as he did that he was making the arguments for different reasons than before. He had decided to defend Emma. His arguments now were not so much for him but for her—to protect her. Every lie he told his *oncle* was told to protect what had happened between them last night. 'As I said when you first suggested it, it is the dishonesty that I cannot countenance.' This time, it was not the dishonesty of his feelings, but using those feelings to lead her down a dubious path. He cared for her; he did not want to use his caring to trap her.

'But is it still dishonest? It is only dishonest if you feel nothing for her, *if* you lie to her about those feelings. I know in the beginning, that was your worry, but now it seems that perhaps there *is* feeling between the two of you.' His *oncle* had a serpent's own tongue.

Julien scoffed. '*If* that were true, do you think she'd believe in those feelings once she found out all I stood to gain? She would never believe it was love alone that motivated me and I would have no way to prove to her otherwise.' He shook his head. He was uncomfortable even naming that feeling. *Was* it love that he felt? That seemed a rather strong, rather incautious word for a one-night affair. 'You surprise me, Oncle. You of all people know that love is a fiction, simply a name we give to an emotion. It only exists because we call it out of thin air.'

'I didn't call it love. I called it "feelings". I said only that now you have them, whereas before you didn't. It solves your concern over duplicity. It doesn't matter if you or I believe in love or not. It only matters if *she* does. If she does, she will believe you.' It was entirely obvious to his *oncle*. But Julien did not think it was that simple.

'I think you forget she has already had a great love in her life. She will be hesitant to believe she gets to have two.' Last night had nothing to do with love. Other emotions perhaps, but not love. 'She is not in love with me any more than I am with her. One night does not require marriage especially when one is a widow.' And she was a smart widow. She knew how the world worked. She had lived in that world, been on the receiving end of its cruelty. She would not let her guard down easily. She *would* question his motives. What would he say then? It was a deuce of a dilemma he was faced with. In the beginning, he'd been concerned because the strategy required false feelings. Now he was worried because it didn't. His feelings had become very real, real enough to want to protect her at the expense of his own gain.

His *oncle* laughed when he might have been angry at his nephew's stubbornness. 'Ah, Julien. You don't have to say anything about what happens at the chateau. I have eyes. You look like a stag in rut, worn, ragged, and hungry for more. I am a patient man, *mon fils*, and I believe in you. Go home, watch your grapes grow and sort it all out. Strike while the iron is hot because when it cools, she may not find you as attractive.'

There was a fearful wisdom in that, Julien thought as he swung up on his horse a few minutes later and set off for home. He'd not fooled his *oncle*. He'd not even fooled himself into thinking one night with Emma wouldn't lead to another. All he could think of on the way home was how quickly he wanted to reach her, to lose himself in the passion, to let the hunger obliterate his dilemma. She would not thank him for it if she knew his motivation in seeking her out was to drown his conflicting thoughts. If she discovered the truth of him and his connection to the land, she would think the worst even though it wasn't true: that he'd manipulated her for the benefit of his own inheritance at the expense of her own. Love words, even spoken in truth, would not be compelling enough then. The question was, how would he convince her otherwise if she discovered the truth? Did he really think his secrets would keep for ever?

The moment she left the chateau, she would learn he was a *comte*. Whether or not the French government *du jour* recognised his title or not, his family's nobility went back to the fifteenth century. If she learned about the title, it stood to reason she would learn about the land and that her inheritance only existed because his family had lost theirs. It was not a matter of if but how long he would have before she knew. Before she'd want to make herself known to the neighbourhood. Already she was asking questions about the consortium, already planning the June gala. But he didn't think he had until June.

He ought to be the one to tell her, but he did not relish the idea of it. Still, if he didn't tell her, there were plenty of people who would. Everyone around here knew the Archambeau story, knew about the tragic love story, the Archambeau-Anouilh feud that followed, and the broken-hearted, defeated death of his father. If he didn't tell her, someone would let something slip in passing and pique her curiosity or tell her outright. That decided it—he couldn't let her leave the chateau without him to gatekeep, to make sure no one let anything slip until he had his chance to tell her. But not yet. Not before the passion between them had its chance. He wanted a little more time before he had to risk what it was that lay between them with the truth. He spurred his horse as hard as he dared in the darkness and headed for home, for Emma.

Emma took a tray in the library for dinner with the intention of continuing her reading. She was trying to get through a brief overview of a history of *vignerons* in the Champagne region, written in English. She'd found it lurking on the shelves and wondered if it had been one of Garrett's purchases in an attempt to learn more about the property and industry he'd bought into. Two pages in, she was ready to admit defeat. Not because the treatise was too difficult to follow, but because she'd chosen poorly. This had been a mistake, dining in the library without Julien, with no one to talk to, or argue with, with nothing to distract her from reliving last night in the room where it all happened, from reminders of exactly why her body was deliciously sore and her mind sorely exercised with the emotional implications.

Each ache reminded her of Julien and those reminders prompted questions: Where was he? What was he doing right now? Was he on his way home? Or was he immersed in business with people she hadn't had the chance to meet yet, the passion of the previous night already taking a back seat to his precious grapes and the impending growing season? Surely not, and yet his absence was indicative of how much last night had disconcerted him, perhaps left him with the same questions it had left her. Had it also left him with the same wants as well? She might not have arrived at all the answers today, but she had come to a place where she would not let herself feel guilty about the passion, about the need to feel something with another.

These were not the only dilemmas on her mind. Another dilemma mingled with the interpersonal, reminding her that in bedding Julien, she'd conflated business and pleasure. In an attempt to distract herself from Julien's absence and her tendency to overthink last night, she'd gone down to Julien's office in the wine caves thinking to retrieve the accounts. After all, now that she had a basic grasp on the winemaking process, it was time for her to turn her attentions to the books.

It was something of a surprise to realise she'd been here several weeks and hadn't once looked at the vineyard accounts. To be fair, she'd had a lot of other things to sort through: household accounts, the accounts of the home farm, and the various other budgets that supported the running of the chateau. But now, it was time. Only it wasn't. When she'd reached Julien's office, she found it locked and a key nowhere in sight. She'd made a mental note to ask Julien about getting the ledgers, adding it to the other mental note to ask Julien about meeting the members of the consortium. If she remembered correctly, they'd met at the beginning of March near the time of her arrival. If so, they'd be meeting again very soon. It would be the perfect time to introduce herself and take up her place among them.

So much to do, so much to talk to Julien about. But not tonight. Tonight, there were other things to think about. Emma sighed and curled into the deep seat of the chair. If indeed she had thought of taking a lover, this would have been rather sooner than she'd imagined it would be, but she was certain Garrett would not begrudge her. He'd want her to carry on, to claim her happiness. She closed her eyes and let the warmth of the fire bathe her, let the memories of what they'd done in front of that fire flood her mind and lull her to sleep.

'*Ma cherie*, wake up and make love with me,' Julien's words, followed by the gentle, inviting buss of his lips against hers, woke her shortly before eleven. 'What were you dreaming of, *ma cherie*?'

She smiled up at him, her body coming alive from its slumber. 'You, what else would I be dreaming of?'

'Let's go upstairs and make some of those dreams come true.' He kissed her, long and slow, making her wonder if going upstairs was really their best option.

The fireplace wasn't a terrible choice, as they'd proven last night.

'Only some?' she teased, her body warming to memories of the pleasure and wanting to repeat it more than her mind wanted to offer caution.

'Well, if we made them all come true tonight, what would we do tomorrow?' He reached for her then, scooping her up in his arms, and carried her to bed.

Chapter Fourteen

If she'd thought the prior night had been an anomaly brought on by the heat of a fight and the excitement of a challenge realised, or that such bone-shattering love-making only existed as a moment out of time, not to be repeated, tonight was proving otherwise. One did not need rough, ravenous sex to claim the luxury of a shuddering climax. One apparently only needed Julien to carry them to bed to put one on the path.

'A proper bed and a proper night tonight,' Julien murmured in muted tones that sent a delicious thrill of anticipation down her spine.

'Not too proper, I hope.' She felt the mattress take his weight as he sat beside her.

'No, but perhaps gentler.' He raised her hand to his lips. 'Tonight, I want to notice everything about you, everything that I missed last night.'

'And if I want the same?' she murmured, playing along with this rather sophisticated flirtation of his.

'Then you shall have it.' He stepped away from the bed, his gaze intent on her, a reminder she ought to take care with what she wished for. That gaze alone was burning her alive, raising her desire to a fever pitch, and this was just the beginning.

He shrugged out of his long riding coat and she realised belatedly that he still wore his outerwear. He'd come straight to her in the library, not stopping to even take off his coat. He'd been thinking of her, wanting her. The knowledge that he'd come to her primed for passion carried its own thrill and whittled away her doubts. He wanted *her*, not the madness—the person, not the emotion.

This was all for her, this wicked, decadent show of masculinity revealed. He drew his shirt over his head and her breath sucked involuntarily at the sight of his sculpted torso exposed in the soft flicker of firelight. She had a sudden urge to run her hands over the planes of his skin.

'Later, *ma cherie*.' He gave a low laugh, reading her thoughts. Her face had become glass. 'This is for your eyes only. Later will be for your hands, your mouth if you would like, and we'll both enjoy that very much.' His hands dropped to the waist of his trousers and her eyes dropped with them. Whoever thought a man could not be a temptress—or was that *tempter*, her riveted brain could not decide the right word—did not know Julien.

His trousers dropped and he gave them a gentle kick aside with a flick of his foot. He was all bare now, all for her. She'd thought him gorgeous last night, thought she'd seen quite a bit of him, that she'd paid attention. But it was nothing compared to now, to seeing the manly sculpture of him, the carved definition of his upper arms, the chiselled symmetry of his abdomen, the squared angles of his iliac girdle, tapering downward, leading the eye to the magnificence of his phallus jutting upward, the divine architecture of man on perfect display. 'I doubt Michelangelo could have done better,' she breathed.

He came to the bed and for a moment her heart leapt and she reached for him. But he laughed, drawing her up to her feet. 'It's your turn now, *ma cherie*. Shall I instruct?' He took her vacated place on the bed, lying on his side, a leg propping up a hand dangling dangerously near his erect phallus. She had sudden, erotic visions of him pleasuring himself as she undressed. Perhaps he meant to—perhaps that was part of this feast for the eyes.

His hand wrapped about his phallus and gave an experimental stroke. 'Would you like that, *ma cherie*? Would you like to watch?'

She blushed, her body prickling with an embarrassed, wanton heat. 'How did you know?'

He laughed. 'You give yourself away too easily tonight. Every thought is written on your face.' He dropped his voice. 'I love it. I want to know what you want.'

She moved to him and disengaged his hand, pushing it gently aside, taking him in her hand instead. 'I want it and I don't want it. If you spend yourself now, I will have to wait that much longer for you to spend yourself for me.'

He leaned forward and nipped at her neck. 'You're a

selfish minx, and a tease, too. I thought you were supposed to be getting undressed.'

'You expect me to be able to concentrate on undressing when you're putting on quite a show just lying there?' she scolded. She lifted a leg, resting it on the chair near the bed, and pulled back her skirts to reveal a stockinged expanse of long, slim leg. Then she began to roll.

She was killing him with her slow seduction. Women wore too many damn clothes, especially English women. Julien bit back a groan as she finished with her stockings and instead of releasing her skirts, she moved to her hair, taking out one pin at a time. Vixen! She was going to make him pay in anticipation for every inch of skin revealed and he was loving every moment of this exquisite, seductive torment. But what he was loving more was Emma's confidence in her sexuality. He had had a taste of that last night when she'd taken the lead in their lovemaking, riding him astride. Tonight was yet another course in the feast that was Emma Luce's sensuality and he meant to see that they both ate their fill.

At last, she discarded her dress, a plain, dark work dress that buttoned up the front. She'd not dressed for dinner and he gave a silent thanks for that. There'd not be layers upon layers of petticoats and fancy corsetry beneath a work dress. He did not think he could have withstood an elaborate siege to his senses tonight. He'd been aroused before he'd even reached home. That arousal had only ratcheted at the sight of her drowsing in the chair. Coming to this room, watching her watching him remove his clothes, had done nothing to diminish it. Now he was flagrantly rock-hard on her bed, and she was teasing him with every button.

At last, the dress fell from her body and the firelight played with the thin fabric of her chemise and pantalettes, outlining the high, full curve of her breasts, hinting at pebbled nipples beneath the linen, lining the flat plane of her belly between her hips, the trimness of her waist. Emma Luce was a woman who kept herself in good shape. Over her head went the chemise and the pantalettes fell with far less resistance than last night, no teeth ripping required.

He went to her then, when the last garment fell, to hell with his self-imposed rules about no touching. That part of the game was over now. He wanted his hands all over her, wanted to scoop her breasts into his palms, to feel the weight of them in his palms, wanted his mouth on them, his tongue on her skin, tasting the salt and jasmine of her.

She wanted it too. There was no demur from her when he picked her up and carried her back to the bed; no cries of unfair play when he laid siege to her body with his mouth. She begged just the once, dragging him over her, and he complied. There was nowhere he'd rather be than inside her, pushing them both towards that incredible place they'd discovered last night.

'Help me get us there,' he whispered, his mouth against her throat. Her legs closed around his hips, her hips rising to meet his own in welcome. He felt the sweet clench of her muscles squeezing around him, the silken slide of her channel as his phallus entered. A soft moan escaped him, a sound to mirror the relief that came with being inside her. The fanciful notion swept him that somehow when he was with her, he was home, that there was a completion he could find nowhere else, with no one else. It was nonsense, but it fit the moment and he didn't challenge it, he went with it, followed it, gave himself over to it as their bodies picked up the rhythm. It was slower than last night. There was a poignancy to this lovemaking, his body aware of every nuance from the rise and fall of her hips, to the little adjustments of her body to accommodate his, to the catch in her breath as her body gathered itself.

He lost himself in the prelude to climax. They were in a world of their own making, a world they were building moment by moment, a world where there was no time nor room to think about the vineyards, about his *oncle*, about his secrets. There was only the two of them, only their pleasure. Nothing else mattered. Nothing else existed. Climax took him like a thunderclap, sudden and strong, a cacophony of the senses that overwhelmed him. He let himself be overcome, carried along the current of release. Peace would come later. For now, he let himself revel in the unbridled explosion of pleasure coursing through him and her.

If a man could climax twice in succession, watching Emma claim her pleasure would have sent him over the edge yet again. She met her pleasure head-on, eyes wide open as it took her, and tonight there was a special sense of manly pride in knowing he'd given this to her, that it wasn't a product of the night, of unleashed emotions out of control. Tonight, everything they'd done had been by deliberate choice and still the ending had been spectacular.

Peace came, the hard current of climax releasing him into a quiet pond where he could float. With her. He gathered her to him. She made a soft sound in her throat, her head resting in the hollow of his shoulder, a place that seemed uniquely made for her. This was what had haunted his day. This was what had brought him home tonight.

'This is new for me,' she whispered after a long while, her words an intimate confession in the dark.

'What is?' he felt compelled to ask, although he could guess, with some trepidation, where the conversation might go. He'd had widows as lovers before. There was always that moment of comparison, that brief glimpse into the marital bed and how their husbands had failed them by contrast. He'd rather not have that moment with Emma. Garrett had been a friend. But more than that, he wanted this to be just between himself and Emma. He wanted no intruders.

'Being reckless, letting myself be overwhelmed, caught up in the moment.' Her answer surprised him. 'I never thought…' Her voice trailed off. 'I never thought a lot of things,' she started again. 'I never thought I'd be a widow before I was thirty. Never thought I'd be facing so much of my life without Garrett, without a family of my own. I thought there'd be plenty of time.'

That was not what he'd expected to hear. He ran an idle hand down her arm in a gentle caress. 'Do you feel guilty?' He hoped not. It would taint the pleasure and he didn't want that for either of them. If she felt guilty, he would feel guilty, too.

'No. I've squared my conscience with that. There is no shame in seeking comfort or consolation.' She sighed. 'May I be completely, bluntly honest with you?'

'Yes,' he said solemnly. 'Please do.'

'It is the overwhelming pleasure I am having trouble countenancing. I had not thought to feel that way so soon, or to feel the pleasure so deeply with someone else.' She paused here and worried her lip. 'If I am being truthful, it's not just that I felt the pleasure deeply, but that I felt it *more* deeply.' She gave a long exhale and Julien waited, patient. He could guess what she wanted to say, but he would not say it for her. It was something she needed to say for herself.

'That's where the guilt comes from: feeling with a stranger what I did not feel with my own husband whom I loved with all my heart. Or at least thought I did.' Her gaze met his. 'What does it mean about the quality of my love if I found pleasure so soon with another? It is something of a surprise to me to be swept so entirely away by someone I didn't know a month ago, and I don't know where it leads or what it will accomplish, and all of that unnerves me.'

Of course it would. The pleasure, the planning, the purpose—or lack of purpose—in their lovemaking. She was a planner and Garrett had been all that was good and stable, the personification of reliability. But what was happening between them bore none of those trademarks. 'Is it any consolation to know I don't know where this leads either?' Julien offered. If she needed the consolation of promises, or the reassurance of a future together, he could give her neither. They were not his to share with any surety. All he could give her was the moment. At some point in the future, she would turn from him. She would hate him, feel betrayed by him. Perhaps these moments would offset the depth of that hurt, unintended as it was, when it came. Perhaps she would know that he'd not meant to hurt her.

She sighed and drew a circle around his nipple with the tip of her finger. 'When one is married, one takes a lot for granted without realising it, because imagining anything else is too horrifying. I assumed Garrett would always be there for a long time because anything else was unthinkable. A stable marriage blinds one to the reality that nothing is guaranteed; not for tomorrow, not a year from now. We had dreams and we never thought we wouldn't get to them.' He felt her smile against his chest. 'But this is hardly seemly conversation for bed. I'm sorry.'

'No, it's the perfect place. This is our cocoon, our safe place,' Julien assured her.

'What about you? What are your dreams, Julien? Has there been anyone?'

No intruders. He didn't want anyone here but the two of them. 'There was someone, a long time ago. We did not have the same dreams. She needed more than I could give her.' Let that be a warning to Emma. He had his limits. She couldn't say he hadn't said so.

'She broke your heart?' He could hear chagrin on his behalf rising in Emma's voice and it touched him that she sought to be his champion. Then she quieted. 'I'm sorry, Julien. I am sure you didn't deserve it.'

'Are you though? How do you know I didn't deserve it?' he teased lightly. 'I'm argumentative, and stubborn, according to you.'

'And don't forget contradictory,' Emma added. She rolled to her side and fumbled in the drawer of the bedside table.

'What are you doing? Come back.' He reached for her, not wanting the idyll to be over. There were hours yet before dawn and he wanted to spend every one of them right here.

'I'm still here. I haven't left. Now, roll over. You promised me I could touch you, later. Now it's later.' He watched, entranced, as she poured oil from a vial into the palm of her hand and blew on it, warming it. 'I've wanted to give you a massage ever since you took your shirt off. Lie still and let me.'

It was the most decadent proposal he'd likely ever receive. He rolled onto his stomach and felt the weight of her across his buttocks as she straddled him, felt the warmth of the oil, then the competence of her hands as they rubbed the oil into his skin, into muscles he hadn't realised were tired until she kneaded them into relaxed submission. This was heaven, to be here with her in the dark. Something deep in his soul cried out, wanting this for as long as it could last.

Over the next weeks, that one thought sprang constant in his mind. If spring could last for ever, he would be the happiest of men. Spring was the perfect season—

a season of hope, a season full of potential, all things were possible. There was promise everywhere Julien looked—the land promised renewal after a long winter: trees with leaves, fields of green, flowers in bloom. Overhead, the skies were blue with the promise of mild weather, warmer weather, to come, the vineyards burgeoned with the buds of new grapes. It would be May soon, there would be leaves and flowers on the grape vines, the buds of April having blossomed.

He spent his days in anticipation of that. He showed Emma how to trim out unneeded growth, how to structure the buds so that they produced quality grapes. These were heady days, filled with walking the vineyards with Emma beside him, showing her the work of raising grapes. There were picnics aplenty, sitting on the south-facing slopes of the vineyards, making love in the afternoon sun, telling stories, learning one another. He told her stories of attending school in England. He loved listening to her talk of her family, of her brothers; he railed on her behalf when she talked of her miserable debut in London and how the other girls would have nothing to do with her because of her father's 'dirty' money.

In the evenings, he loved to pull a stool up to the kitchen worktable and watch her as she cooked. Petit had acquired several nights off in order for them to have the kitchen to themselves. He treasured those meals prepared by Emma and eaten at the kitchen table. And always the lovemaking. No honeymoon could have been finer. But like with all honeymoons, he was acutely aware there would be an end. The gala was drawing closer and he could not keep her here at the chateau for ever. But out there, beyond the chateau walls, his secrets waited to destroy his happiness one more time. One more day, he told himself each morning, and then the next. One more day, before all of this unravelled and Emma learned the truth. One more day before it would all end. The only question was how and when.

Chapter Fifteen

When it ended, he was naked on a picnic blanket caught quite literally with his trousers down, Emma lying beside him drawing her circles on his chest while the early May sun beat down on them. 'I've had a note,' she began in drowsy tones. 'From Widow Clicquot. She's invited us to tea at Boursault.' It was said so casually, Julien did not at first grasp the full import. 'Well, she's invited me, but I assumed it would be fine to have you come along. *Would* you like to come? I didn't stop to think that you might be too busy here with the grapes.'

He didn't hear the last. His brain had finally caught up with the implications. Dear God, Emma was going to have tea with the Queen of Reims. The widow knew everyone and everything, and that boded ill for him. He levered up on his elbows, the sudden movement dislodging Emma rather abruptly. 'Why did she invite you for tea?' How had this connection come about? He certainly hadn't prompted it.

Emma looked bewildered. 'I wrote to her last week

to introduce myself and to let her know we would be holding a gala in June. She is a living legend. I figured if I was going to run my own vineyard I needed to know her.'

Julien felt his gut clench. He tried to keep the panic out of his voice and only partially succeeded. 'Is that what you told her, that you were running the vineyard?' Good God, if the Widow told Edouard Werle, her business partner and currently the Mayor of Reims, and if he told any one of the consortium, it could lay waste to his plans. That was just the beginning of the damage, what one wrong word could do to business. That wasn't counting what one wrong word could do to him, to them and the relationship they were starting to build. It would annihilate them.

'Julien, what's wrong? I just wrote to her and told her I was new to the chateau at Cumières, that I was newly widowed, that my husband had left the chateau to me, and that I was interested in learning about wine.' Two little creases formed in the space between the slender arches of her brows. 'Is it because she's the competition? Is that why you're upset? I can't figure you French out sometimes. One moment the consortium is a council of your friends and the next it's a cabal of competitors.' She gave a light laugh. He had to be careful not to overreact.

'It is a competitive business first and foremost,' he reminded her. 'Clicquot-Werle is so far above the rest of us, they aren't really the competition. We just compete amongst ourselves. I once saw their cellars in Reims.

They have cranes to lift the barrels up to the bottling rooms. We have three presses, but they have eight.'

'Perhaps *we* should have eight,' Emma hypothesised.

'We don't dominate the Russian market,' Julien pointed out, reaching for his trousers. 'Her champagne does.'

Emma laid back down on the blanket and looked up at the sky. 'We need to dominate a market. What about the British market? Surely with the Season and all the balls and parties there's room to expand.'

Julien frowned. 'Not even the big houses sell more than a few thousand bottles a year to Britain.' He tried to tease, 'The English are too busy drinking your father's gin.'

'Do you wonder why that is? It seems to me that you should do some research. Why is it that the Russian court consumes thousands upon thousands of bottles each year but the British do not? Is it the taste? If so, what about the taste? Can we cater to that taste with a particular blend? For instance, is it too sweet for the British? The Russians love sweet things, but the English are more of a savoury people, wouldn't you say? They like their beef and gravies.'

She kept saying *we*. It was an intoxicating and dangerous little word. It conjured up all sorts of fantasies of what it would be like to build a champagne empire with her. To teach her all he knew about the grapes and the growing, the blending and the bottling. All she had to do was give him the land. *Marry her.* His *oncle*'s grand strategy echoed in his mind, taking on a different tone than when his *oncle* had first floated the idea.

It was no less palatable than it had been the first time, but it was becoming shockingly more tempting and harder to resist. Perhaps because it was less dishonest than it had been in the beginning. To seduce her, to feign love for her in order to trick her into marriage all so that he could claim the property through her, had smacked of dishonesty—a dishonesty of feelings, and a dishonesty of agenda. He would not entertain such an idea. But now the idea wasn't based entirely in dishonesty. His feelings would not be a lie. He cared for her. He wouldn't be feigning his desire. That part of it was honest. Getting the vineyards back was a benefit by association. Would she ever believe though that that wasn't his primary motivation?

You're going to lose her in the end. She'll hate you if she thought you married her for the vineyards. But she's going to hate you anyway when she finds out you've been dishonest about who you are and what your purpose is here—that you want the chateau and the lands for yourself. You don't have to lose the vineyard, too.

'Julien, are you even listening to me?' Emma punched him on the arm, a playful scold. 'I'm rolling out a whole new marketing plan for us and you're somewhere else. I'm going to write to my father and see if he can investigate reactions to champagne for us. I was also thinking, we could set my brother Gabriel up as an agent of sorts. He already travels for my father, selling gin. Why not have him travel with our champagne? We can send him cases for sampling and he can meet with all the hostesses in London, at least get their feedback about the taste. He could also go to restaurants. Why limit oneself to just private parties?'

Us. We. It was too much. 'You are aware that Garrett was not turning a profit here. You act as if this place were a growing concern.'

'Because he was not serious. This was a hobby to him. He loved having his vintage shipped to him, to tell everyone the wine on the table for the evening was from his own vineyards. That's all he wanted it for. Now we could really make something of the place. You've kept everything in immaculate shape. You just need a marketer, and that's me. I might not know as much about grapes as you do, but I do know how to sell things. With your guidance, I am sure I can put this place on the map, so to speak.' She sat up and reached for his hand. 'But I *will* need your guidance. I can't do it without you, you needn't worry. I need you to introduce me to the consortium, to be my liaison with them until I'm more familiar.'

The way she talked was everything he'd ever dreamed of, what he'd wanted with Clarisse. A partner by his side. But he had to tread carefully here. They weren't partners. He owned nothing here. She talked as if they were equals but they were not, for so many reasons. And yet, beneath the sun on a picnic blanket, or lying in her bed in the dark of night, they were equals for a short time when they made love. He was desperate to hang on to that, desperate to appease both his *oncle* and her without hurting either of them.

He pulled on his shirt and she made a pout. 'I miss you already, Julien,' she teased. 'I like you better naked.' She pulled him down beside her. She smelled of jasmine and sunlight. 'Shall I tell the Widow we'll accept her invitation?'

'Yes.' He would go and be on hand for damage control, if needed. There was always a chance the Widow would be discreet and not bring up anything personal. He might survive the interview. The Widow was a businesswoman first and foremost. Perhaps she would not stray too far from that.

'And the others? Shall I invite them individually to the chateau or shall I expect to meet them at the next consortium gathering, which should be fairly soon. They meet the first part of each month, yes?'

His *oncle* would say he wasn't doing a very good job of distracting her. Perhaps he'd put his shirt on too quickly, after all. He leaned over and tendered a soft kiss. 'You have a lot on your mind today, Em. Should I do something about that?'

She looked up at him with clear grey eyes. 'The note from Madame Clicquot was a reminder that I can't just sit around watching grapes grow. I've been idle too long.'

He made a playful grimace. 'That is not an endorsement of my skills. I shall have to try harder to keep you entertained.' He dropped a kiss to the column of her throat. He nipped and she laughed but she also batted him away. 'No, seriously, Julien. I've been decadently lazy. It's not that I haven't enjoyed these past weeks. But there's work to be done. Do you realise I've been here two months and I haven't left the estate? I haven't met anyone. I haven't minded it, but if I remain a recluse any longer people will think I'm rude.'

'They will think you're an English widow in mourning. They will understand.' Julien took refuge in the old argument. 'No one expects you to be entertaining.' He still wasn't sure how her presence would impact the gala. The event he and his *oncle* were counting on was exciting in its possibilities as well as frightening. There was so much that could go wrong.

'I'm a businesswoman. The vineyard business never rests, as you've told me. I cannot be idle in the spring. I must prepare for the harvest, for the marketing that comes afterwards.' She cocked her head, smiling at him, unaware of how much her conversation unnerved him, of how much her words were bringing everything to a head. 'I think if I were to ask you when the busiest time of year is, you would tell me spring through the harvest. But I would tell you the hard work is autumn through spring, getting our bottles into the hands of clients.'

Julien tried one last time to dissuade her, although he was already recognising it solved nothing, only delayed the inevitable. 'You cannot be her. You cannot be Madame Clicquot. I have to be honest with you, *ma cherie*, if you're thinking to replicate her personal trajectory to the top of the champagne industry, it cannot be done any longer.'

'What do you mean by that, Julien? Do you doubt me?' He hated seeing the smile fade from her face, the spark in her eye turn to something harder. But she had to be told the truth for her own good.

Be honest, it's for your own good, too. His conscience stabbed hard. *You have a stake in this. Don't you dare forget about that.*

'Don't be angry, Emma, because I am willing to point out some not inconsiderable truths to you,' he replied hotly. There was a long silence, he could almost feel her bristling beside him, then he felt the tension ease from her, felt her eyes upon him. A look of apology passed between them. They'd both behaved badly, quick to snap, quick to temper. While it made for good lovemaking, it also made difficult conversations that much harder.

'All I mean, Emma, is that the times and politics are against you in a way they were not against her. One could argue that she was successful because she slipped through the cracks and succeeded when no one was looking.' It was in fact an argument his *grandpère* had repeated from his father, Julien's great-grandfather, who had indeed been a contemporary of the Widow. Champagne was a tight knit region, Julien explained to Emma. Everyone from Epernay to Cumières knew everyone, and for a long while there were no outsiders. The industrial revolution that had swept Britain and parts of France had been slow in coming here. That, too, had worked in the Widow's favour.

'If anything,' Julien concluded, 'the coming of industrialisation has not freed women, at least not middle and upper-class women. It has done just the opposite. Those women are expected now, more than ever, to occupy the private sphere of the home. It is the one distinction that sets them apart from their lower-class working girl counterparts. Those girls must earn their bread.'

'Like the distinction of a gentlemen, hmm?' Emma replied languidly, but he was not fooled by it. There would be a sharp barb nestled in her response. 'The only thing that defines a gentleman is that he does not work for his income. Others do the work for him.' That barb hit rather too close to home for Julien, and in ways that she would not have meant to target.

'Yes, I suppose so. So, you see, as Lady Luce, the wife of a baronet, you cannot possibly dabble in trade or business.'

'But as the daughter of a gin merchant?' she countered easily. 'Perhaps then I might.'

Julien frowned. 'Not even then. You're an heiress in that regard. Be honest. Is your father leaving the running of his gin company to you?' They both knew the answer already. The company would go to her brothers when her father retired. They both knew as well that even now, her mother was not involved in the day-to-day running of the business. Her mother's role was to throw lavish parties and help sweet-talk politicians, but nothing beyond that. 'Don't hate me because I'm right, Emma.'

Oh, no, he thought sardonically, *there will be plenty more and much better reasons to hate me, just wait.*

'I see.' Emma gave him a hard final look and jumped up from the picnic blanket. She brushed at her skirt, her voice calm. 'You're not as much like Garrett as I thought. He was never intimidated by my ideas.'

'Since when has disagreement been a sign of intimidation?' He got to his feet. His temper was starting to rise again. 'I have offered you my opinion because I respect you. I am *not* intimidated by you. If I was, do you think I'd tell you things I know you don't want to hear?'

'Yes, I think you might.' Her grey eyes flashed. Emma Luce in a temper was as formidable a sight to behold as Emma in a passion. 'It would depend on your motives.'

'What would those be? I can't think of a single thing I'd gain by making you angry at me.' Julien made sure his voice was well infused with just how ridiculous he thought the assertion was. There was a long pause and for a moment Julien was hopeful that the pause meant she saw the flaw in her reasoning. But when she spoke, it was with calm, measured tones and chilling words.

'I can. To keep me in the dark.' She gave him a hard look before turning to walk away.

That barb hit too close to home. 'About what, Emma? What do you think I'm hiding?'

'I don't know. Something.' She paused before spearing him with a stare. 'I notice that you don't plead denial. That says a great deal, that my worries aren't baseless, after all.' She did leave him then, striding away to begin the long trek home.

'Emma, wait!' he called after her. 'We're too far from the house. We'll drive back together. I'll have the picnic things cleared up quickly. Just wait.'

She turned back long enough to say, 'I have been waiting and I'm done with that now. I'll walk back. I need time to think, and so do you.'

Every fibre of his being urged him to go after her.

No good could come of Emma being left alone too long with her thoughts. She would imagine all sorts of perfidious things. But what would he say? Were there any words, any arguments that could make things better? He shook out the blanket and folded it, watching her retreat into the distance. This was not going well at all. He would not be able to contain her much longer. Nor did he want to, and that was as much a problem as anything else.

He loved her ideas, loved her desire to engage in the business of winemaking and selling. But those were the very things that kept him and his *oncle* from their dream. If she were to succeed, she'd have no motive to sell. And if she were to fail, he and his *oncle* didn't have the funds yet to make an offer on the place. Julien climbed into the gig and gave a desultory cluck to the horse. Everything had been going so well until she'd come along, and now his quiet world, a world that hadn't made him happy but at least had been a world he understood, was on fire. She was burning him from the inside out. At this rate, he'd be nothing but ash when she was done with him.

Chapter Sixteen

She was done with waiting. Emma strode through the fields that abutted the road, her steps wide, her pace angry. She was angry with herself, angry with Julien. She'd waited because she'd wanted to. She'd chosen this affair over pushing forward with the vineyards, all the while knowing deep down that the two were not mutually compatible, that it *would* come to a choice. She could not have both.

She'd not expected, though, that it would come to a head over an invitation to tea. She'd actually expected a very different reaction from him. She'd thought he'd be excited about the initiative she'd taken and about the doors this invitation could open. But he'd reacted as if it were the worst possible thing she could have done.

Emma picked up a stick and swatted at the tall grasses as she walked. A few bumblebees buzzed in irritation at the disruption. Julien's reaction was proof that she didn't know him as well as she liked to believe. She'd felt they'd grown close over the past weeks. They'd told each other stories of their childhoods, of their families. They'd made love exotically, erotically, on picnic blankets, before fireplaces, even once on the kitchen worktable after a homemade supper. She'd never known the depths of pleasure that she knew in Julien's arms. Surely such pleasure could not be feigned or fabricated without there being genuine feeling, sincere caring for one another.

She knew that was true on her part, which was why this current impasse cut at her so deeply. She liked Julien, perhaps more than liked him. It was hard to use the word *love* so soon after losing Garrett, mostly because she'd not expected to ever fall in love again. But here Julien was, showing her a different passion than the love she'd shared with Garrett, showing her that a person might have more than one meaningful relationship in their lifetime. And yet, there was a price for that. He was not Garrett. She'd keenly felt that today.

Julien had not supported her today. It had all been subtly done. Someone less aware might not have even noticed, but she had. He'd looked for any opportunity to undermine her ideas, and her ambition. She'd not understood it. Didn't he see that her success with the vineyard was his success as well? She heard her father's voice in her head: *It's never just one thing.*

Businesses or relationships didn't succeed or fail because of one single incident. Some might say they'd won or lost a fortune on the turn of a card, but it was never that clear-cut. There was always something underneath, something that preceded the watershed event. The quarrel today had been that—a watershed event—

bringing to the fore issues that had existed from the beginning between her and Julien, issues that she'd not bothered to resolve. Mainly, the issue of who was in charge here. That had been between them from the start. Julien was still trying to be in charge.

Emma made a list in her head of all that she'd not yet done since arriving: she'd not seen the books; she'd not met the consortium; she'd not driven around to the various domains and introduced herself; she'd not gone into Reims and connected with the bankers. Ideally, these were things Julien should have helped facilitate. But he'd never once offered. It prompted questions she didn't want to ask: Had he deliberately blinded her? Kept her here? Distracted her on purpose? Was there something he didn't want her to know? Without her in the open meeting neighbours and the growers' consortium he could maintain the illusion of being in charge. And she'd let him. In hindsight, she could see the pattern. Each time they'd got close to issues of her being in charge, he'd found ways to divert the conversation with a story, with an argument, with sex. And she'd allowed that, too. She'd chosen to pursue the pleasure he offered.

The chateau came into view, its majestic turreted wings and steep skyline demanding her attention. This was Garrett's gift to her. She needed to be worthy of it. That would require taking a stand against Julien if he continued to block her way forward. It would mean letting him go as a lover.

You knew it would end, her conscience taunted.

Had it been worth it? To fill the loneliness, to experience something new? To remind herself she was alive? These were no small things. But now it was time to move forward with or without Julien. If he was a man who could not support a woman's success, then she was better off without him. But that didn't stop the idea from hurting.

He was in the cellars when she returned, in the room he claimed as his office. The door stood open. The only time the space was unlocked was when he was in it. It had not struck her as odd at first, but it did now. *Was* there a reason he kept it locked when there was essentially just the two of them here? Field workers were not up to the chateau and the house servants could be trusted implicitly. Keeping it locked meant she had to ask him for access to the room and to all the room contained even though the room and its contents were technically hers.

Julien looked up from the desk that was crammed inside; it wasn't a large space. It seemed more like a closet hollowed out from the cave walls. There were no windows, just the desk, a chair, and shelves lined with books and ledgers. He also looked crammed inside, a man too big for the space. His eyes met hers, his brow lifting in challenge, in question, as if to say, *You're in my space, what do you want?*

'I would like to see the books from the last seven years.' She was pleased her words came out cool and polite. 'Please have someone bring them to the library right away.' What could he say to that except yes? They both knew he had no grounds on which to refuse her. This was her house, her books, her right.

'Would you like me to join you?' he answered her with equally polite tones. 'I would be glad to show you the books.' They both knew that was a lie. If he'd been glad to show them to her he would have done so already. The fact that he'd not voluntarily offered to show them to her weeks ago when she'd first arrived, coupled with the recent reality that he hadn't pled denial when she'd accused him of hiding something this afternoon, hung palpable between them, gilding the interaction with an air of suspicion.

'No, thank you. I will let you know if I have questions.' She wanted to see the books with her own eyes and form her own opinions first without seeing them through whatever lens Julien might want her to view them through. The idea that she could potentially not trust that lens made her stomach clench. She did not want to believe that but she *must* consider it.

The books were waiting for her on the long library reading table when she arrived after a short detour to her chambers to change from the picnic. She'd traded her outdoor clothes for a loose gown of dark blue. It wasn't quite black but she wasn't seeing anyone, and she wanted to be comfortable. It was going to be a long night and likely an uncomfortable one. Soon she would know if Julien was hiding anything from her, or she'd know she owed him an apology for her thinly veiled accusation this afternoon. If she was wrong, would he forgive her? She'd attacked his honour. Even so, she'd prefer to be wrong than to discover some perfidy on his part. If there were lies, it meant there were also other, difficult, realisations she'd have to face as well and she'd rather not, especially when they'd all rotate around the knowledge that she had been duped.

There was something wrong with the books. This was the only conclusion Emma could come to after running through all seven years twice. The books were not complicated: money in, money out, and this was not a busy chateau dealing with countless exports, just one man's delight in having wine from his own property. She did not think she'd overlooked anything. But two problems were staring her in the face.

First, there weren't enough grapes accounted for. The chateau had more acreage than there were grapes being recorded. Second, Julien wasn't drawing a salary. Not once in seven years had any money been paid to him and yet Garrett had always talked of having hired him. Hired people were paid. Other wages not attached to the household budget were recorded here—like the payments made to the grape picking crews that came through every harvest.

An awful fear took root in her stomach as she stared at the ledgers. Had Julien stolen from Garrett? Was that what he was trying to keep her from discovering? It would be impossible to know how much he'd taken. Had he also taken the grapes and sold them, pocketing the profits? It would be so easy to do without someone here to oversee the overseer.

And yet it felt wrong. A man like Julien, who loved the land, who spoke of this place with such passion for it, would not steal from it. People didn't steal from those they loved. She couldn't stop her mind fast enough. What did that mean for them? Nothing good. Emma left the table and began to pace. Whatever was happening here, he'd not felt enough for her to tell her. Why was she so surprised by that? She'd been betrayed by so-called friends before and Julien had at least left her plenty of hints. She should have been on alert for that pattern to repeat itself since the day he'd left word with Richet about his whereabouts but not bothered to share them with her.

Her mind might understand those conclusions but her heart did not like them. It refused to believe she was that inconsequential to Julien, that he could be so callous. She glanced at the clock on the mantel. It was just after eleven. She'd worked through supper and well into the evening. It was late but not too late. How would she ever sleep tonight? She'd been angry and hurt when she'd started the process, and now she was angrier still, her hurt magnified by what might very well be a truth she could no longer hide from. There was nothing so embarrassing as self-delusion. Especially when it wasn't the first time. She was supposed to have learned her lesson.

There's no time like the present.

She wasn't going to sleep. She might as well put her questions to him. Ask him about the missing grapes and the non-existent salary. She would see his true colours. She made for the stairs. This time of night, he'd be in his room—a room that was actually guest chambers. Quite nice quarters for someone who worked for the chateau. No attic room or below stairs dormitory for him. Garrett had treated him like a king with those rooms.

Or did Garrett know? Perhaps Julien had self-assigned those rooms because there was no one to gainsay him?

Oh, how she hated such negative thoughts. Even more, she hated that sometimes they were necessary. One didn't get ahead in the world by walking around with blinders on.

She halted at the door to Julien's room. Suddenly, knocking on the door became a litmus test. If he was worried about what she'd find in the ledgers, how could he be asleep? He'd be awake, concerned. Surely, that boded better? Only a man who didn't care would be able to sleep after the quarrel they'd had. She rapped on the door and waited.

'Come.' Relief flooded through her. He was awake. It was a sign of concern, a sign that perhaps the quarrel had left him restless and dissatisfied, too. Perhaps it was also a sign that all might not be lost.

Emma stepped into the room. It was a distinctly masculine space. Tall leather wing-backed chairs were set before the fire. Julien occupied one of them, dressed in banyan and trousers. The banyan gaped open, exposing a glimpse of his torso. He was such a handsome man. Just this afternoon they'd been… No. She must set aside such thoughts. Until she got to the bottom of this, there could be no more of *that*.

'I have questions. I didn't want to wait until morning.'

'So, you've come for a bedtime story.' Julien's eyes

were like glacier shards as he watched her progress. She took the empty chair, feeling the coldness of his gaze.

She cut right to it. 'Were you stealing from my husband?'

'Why would you think that?' His fingers played with the stem of the brandy snifter on the table beside him.

'Because there is no record of your salary in those books.'

'And that makes me a thief?' He was unbearably aloof. He was making her do all the conversational work here. But what had she expected? That he would be in tears, begging her forgiveness, on his knees declaring undying devotion for her? There she went again, conflating business with pleasure, assuming that he cared for her and that caring would spill over to how he treated her as a business partner. She had to stay resolute.

'It makes you dishonest. We can start with that and go from there.'

It hurt to look at her, to see the stony shards her eyes had become, a gaze that had so recently looked on him as if he were the focal point of her world. He wanted *that* Emma back. He wanted to be on a picnic blanket with her, touching her, smelling her, talking to her, listening to her spin impossible dreams. He wanted to feel alive, the way he felt when he was with her, as if he could conquer the world, as if the world had not beaten him down but instead had marched him towards this moment.

Julien reached for his glass and took a swallow to give himself something to do besides watch her. He'd known she'd come. She was a woman who didn't like to wait. That she'd waited this long to make her discoveries was something of a miracle. He'd had plenty of time to come up with explanations and he had nothing except the truth to offer her. He did not think the truth would go over well. But if she was going to hate him, it would be for the truth, not a lie.

'The truth might not suit you. Are you sure you want it?' He poured some brandy into the spare glass and pushed it her way. 'You'll need this.' He let her take a swallow before he started. 'I am not stealing from you and I never stole from Sir Garrett. I do not draw a salary because I do not take a monetary wage from the estate, although your husband did offer me one.'

He gave her a moment to digest that, her sharp brain working. 'The grapes,' she breathed. 'There is a certain quantity of grapes missing each year.' She paused. 'You took your pay in grapes?'

'And in investment in wine futures—the predicted sale of upcoming vintages,' he supplied.

'Is that why the estate doesn't appear to be making money on the wines? Because the profit is paid to you after Garrett breaks even and gets his money back?'

'Yes. Of course, I roll quite a bit of my profit back into the estate. You could say I'm something of a shareholder. Garrett and I treated the estate like a joint venture. He put up the money, I put up the time and effort. It's been an experiment, we started small. Like you, he wanted to study the industry before he fully committed.'

She nodded. 'This year was important to him. That

seven-year vintage was to be a turning point for him.'
A turning point for them all. He'd hoped to increase
his level of investment in the estate and then in a couple years make an offer for it with his profits from the
estate and his other venture with Oncle Etienne. 'And
the grapes?'

Julien to a deep breath. 'My Oncle Etienne and I
blend the grapes with the grapes on his property to
make a *couteau champenois*, but we need the *pinot noir*
grapes from here. We don't have enough of our own currently.' Because his *oncle* had not been able to acquire
the *pinot noir* vineyards yet.

She seemed to give that some thought. 'That works
for now, but what happens when the chateau is up to
full bottle production and needs its grapes for itself?'
He'd hoped to own the chateau by then. 'The wine must
be very good then for you to live off the proceeds.' He
could see her running the numbers in her head.

'The *couteau champenois* is good, more importantly
it is becoming somewhat rare. People aren't in want of
the "red champagne" like they used to be. It's for an
exclusive club of wine drinkers.' Who paid large sums
for the bottles, an example of how important it was to
control supply and demand.

She was silent, gathering her thoughts. 'Those are
not damning things, Julien. I do believe they're true,
as far as they go. But they don't go far enough. They
make me wonder why a land steward would eschew an
income and choose to invest in the estate he works for.'
She took a thoughtful swallow of her brandy and stared

into the fire. 'These are not the actions of a land steward, are they, Julien?'

'I am very entrepreneurial.'

She gave a hard laugh. 'My husband may have believed that but I don't. Nothing about you has added up since the first day. You were nothing like what I expected.'

'You were *exactly* how I imagined you.' Julien poured a half glass.

'You were part farmer but only part because your manners were too fine. That made you a gentleman.' She was getting close now and Julien tensed with the knowledge of it. Any moment now she'd make the more difficult of the two connections and then the other would follow.

'Gentlemen don't earn money, it's what sets them apart.' She reprised the discussion from the picnic before spearing him with a look and a verdict. 'Julien Archambeau, are you a gentleman? Is that why you wouldn't take a wage from my husband?'

'A man has his pride, Emma.' It was untrue. He and his *oncle* made enough money from the *couteau champenois* to keep themselves afloat, and his *oncle* had the funds from their small shipping company, although much of that was kept in savings for the day when they could buy the rest of the vineyard. Still, he wasn't about to take coin for work. The Archambeaux had not sunk so low as to take wages for working their own land. It was all right for his *oncle* to have the shipping money—he was a second son. He'd always been expected to make his way in the world. But Julien's father had been the Comte. The title might mean nothing now, but there was pride.

She was studying him again. 'You would do all this work—walking the land, pruning, harvesting, all to attain some grapes?' She was prodding, prompting, and prying. Her instincts were telling her it didn't make sense, didn't quite add up. He could see her mind working. 'There's only one reason a person would make such a commitment to a place and that is attachment, love.' She fixed him with her stare and he met his fate bravely. 'Julien, tell me the truth. Did this chateau once belong to you?'

Chapter Seventeen

She sat frozen in place by her own revelation, disbelief and shock rolling through her even as her mind acknowledged that it made sense. The manners, the haughtiness of him, his willingness to challenge her, unlike any servant she'd ever encountered. The next question naturally asserted itself. 'Who are you, Julien?'

'The Archambeaux were gifted this land by the king in 1455.' Julien's voice was quiet in the dimness as he calmly delivered his *coup*.

'Then there must be a title that goes with it.' She would not let him sneak any detail past her, although her stomach was starting to tighten.

'Comte. Comte du Rocroi. But it doesn't matter any more. Titles come and go in this new France. Did you know they were suspended again four years ago? If a new government is voted in this year, there's rumour titles will be restored once again.' He shrugged. 'Not that it would mean anything. It would most likely just be the restoration of hereditary titles, which our family's is,' he added. He gave a sardonic smile. '*Et voila*,

I am the Comte again.' This was followed by a harsh chuckle. 'No privileges though, just the words. Just the title.' She recognised he was trying to mitigate the revelation, and her heart, most regrettably, warmed to it, prompting her to wonder even now—was he trying to protect her?

'The purported land steward is a French *comte*.' She repeated the words, starting to feel silly now. All the things she'd accused him of seemed ridiculous.

'As I said, it doesn't matter. Titles are meaningless now in France. We lost the title in the Revolution and then we lost the land when my great-*grandpère* lost his head. Great-Grandpère sent his son, Matthieu, my *grandpère*, and my father, who was only an infant, to the safety of England, as I've mentioned before. But when the decree went out that all emigres must return in order for their families to keep their lands, my great-*grandpère* refused to bring his son home. He knew it wasn't safe. It cost him everything.'

'But when it *was* safe,' Emma picked up the story. She knew this part to some degree from what he'd shared during one of their many long, lazy afternoons. She spoke slowly, piecing it together. 'Your grandfather returned, leaving his younger son behind in England to continue running the now legitimate shipping company. But he had nothing to return home to. The lands had gone to someone else by then.'

'Titles were restored by the Bourbons so he had that to come home to. He established a second branch of our shipping business in Calais. He began saving his profits and making enquiries. It took time. The land had been broken up and it was owned by several different people. Once my grandfather was able to secure one of our old parcels, one with a house on it, we moved to Cumières and left the shipping office in capable hands. I was still quite young when we came here. Cumières is the only home I know. All I know of the time in Calais is in the stories my father told me. I grew up walking the land beside them, learning from them.'

'Until you were ten,' she prompted when Julien fell silent.

'Yes. It was hard to leave. I didn't want to go but Grandpère insisted that I have a foot in both worlds. He wanted me to learn the shipping business from my *oncle*. Just in case, he said. France was unreliable. The Revolution changed my *grandpère*. He lived with the knowledge that his country had killed his father, taken our family's property, forced him into exile not knowing if it would ever be safe to return. For a man who loved the land, it was a heavy fate. He lived with a strong sense of betrayal and distrust after that. Land and family were all a man could rely on, he would tell me.' The little boy he'd been had learned those lessons well, perhaps better than he thought, Emma mused. Julien kept his cards very close to his chest, as Garrett might say. People knew only what Julien wanted them to know. She was starting to see his omissions not as lies but as protection. Unnecessary protection, perhaps. He could trust her.

'As you know, I spent my winter holidays with my *oncle*. The trip to Cumières was too long to undertake for Christmas and the Channel too unpredictable. But

I had the summers here. I looked forward to those all year long.' There was a hint of a smile on his lips and a softness to his gaze, as if the words had conjured memories of fairer times. This Julien was irresistible, and he was dangerous to her resolve. Some of the fight went out of her. The longer he talked, the harder it was to remember why she was angry.

Her father's lesson came to her again: *Everything has two sides*. Perhaps she would have been less angry with Julien, perhaps they would be in bed right now if she'd applied her father's lesson sooner. The explanation was so simple. Julien didn't draw a salary because he was a gentleman, because he couldn't let go of that part of himself, of what his family had been. There was nothing nefarious about that or about the missing grapes.

'I am sorry for all your family has suffered,' Emma said quietly, aware that she'd have to do better than that for an apology. She had reparations to make. Julien wasn't the villain here. But quite possibly, she was. It had not gone unnoticed, although Julien had delicately not mentioned it, that she was now the owner of a piece of his estate, a very large piece, including a home that had been in his family for centuries before it was taken away. 'Julien, am I the enemy?' She didn't want it to be true. If it was true, why befriend her? Why teach her? Why make her his lover? These were implications she'd so far avoided pursuing because they led down unpleasant paths.

'Why would you think that?' His tone was more guarded now and she sensed he was trying to protect them both by evading her question. But she could not let it go.

'I am living in your house. *Your* house, *your* land is my inheritance from my husband.' How it must gall him to be the caretaker of this beautiful land and yet have no legal rights to it, to make decisions regarding its future. The only rights he had were given to him by Garrett to act as his man of business. With such freedom to act, perhaps it had become easy for Julien to pretend the place *was* his in all ways that mattered. Until she'd shown up. 'You must resent me.' How ironic that she'd feared being the one who would be betrayed in all this, when it was really Julien who was the one betrayed—by his country and in some ways by her and Garrett, albeit unintentionally.

'I don't resent you. Just the situation,' Julien said quietly. 'You had nothing to do with the circumstances.'

'I am part of those circumstances now, though, and I *do* affect them simply by being here, by having my own ambitions.' She thought about that for a long moment—something didn't seem right. There was another piece still missing. 'Julien, did you not try to buy the place from Monsieur Anouilh?' This place had been available seven years ago. Had it been a lack of funds? Chateaux and land didn't come cheaply, but surely they might have applied for a loan in Reims, especially if they already had some land established. They would have had collateral and a shipping firm to vouch for their solvency.

Julien gave a bitter laugh. 'We tried. Monsieur Anouilh refused to sell to us.'

He paused and she prompted, 'There's more, I sense it. I can handle it. It seems odd that a Frenchman would choose a foreigner over a neighbour.'

He shot her a swift glance before returning his gaze to the fire. 'Garrett outbid us. His pockets were endlessly deep and he was determined to have the place for his new bride.' For her. Her heart sank even as Julien tried to pass it off. 'Your husband had no idea of our history with the place. He didn't know us or anything about the property.'

'You never told him? You let him hire you thinking that you were just a convenient neighbour to watch over the property while he was away.' She was trying to figure out if she thought that was dishonourable behaviour or not.

His gaze turned to her and lingered. 'You think it was somehow a lie to not tell him, don't you? But what could I do? This was the only way I could get close to the land, to take care of it. Then, Garrett offered me rooms here. My *oncle* and I decided it would do for a time.'

'Until you could make an offer to Garrett? Hoping perhaps he'd run out of enthusiasm for a place so far away?' Never guessing that Garrett would never let go of it, that the place had been consigned to his bride as part of her widow's portion. How it must have stung when she'd walked in, upending Julien's long-held hopes.

Julien nodded. 'That was the plan. We realised we'd need more money to make an offer to Garrett. He'd paid more than the place was worth but he didn't care.

He had money to burn. We'd have to at least match that amount when the time came. But meanwhile I could take care of the land and make sure it would be fruitful when another chance came.'

'But I came instead,' Emma put in.

'Do you really want me to say it, Emma? Yes, you were somewhat of a wrinkle in those plans.' The wrinkle being she was not interested in selling. She was interested in staying. She had nowhere else to go that allowed her the freedom and independence she was used to, the chance to build something of her own.

Guilt swamped her against her better judgement. She was now part of an untenable situation for Julien, for his *oncle*. *She* stood in the way of the family dream to restore the Archambeau lands and legacy, generations of work. She had no intention to sell. Surely, Julien must know that by now. There was no way he could get his hands on the land as long as she owned it and she *would* own it unless circumstances changed. Unless...

One of her father's lessons: *If something seems impossible in one environment, change the environment.* Julien could change the environment. He could chase her away, make things so unbearable for her that she would sell. That strategy seemed unlikely at this point given the time he'd spent coaching her on viniculture. Although, she wondered in retrospect if it was merely a failed strategy. Had he in truth been trying to overwhelm her with all the books, the long walks filling her with knowledge, and she'd thwarted his attempts? If that failed, there was another option even less savoury.

He *could* marry her. The land would become his upon marriage. She felt sick to her stomach. Was that why he'd taken her to bed? When all else failed, seduce it out of her? No. She would not believe it of him. She'd kissed him first. He'd been a complete gentleman right up until that day in the vineyard. He'd made no inappropriate overtures.

'Emma, say something. You've been silent too long and I can see your mind working.' Julien's low voice interrupted her thoughts.

'That's just it. I don't know what to say.' Emma rose. Anything she said now would be driven by emotion and confusion. She would regret it come morning. 'I think it's best that I leave now.' She needed to be somewhere he was not, somewhere she could think without those slate-blue eyes on her, where she wasn't driven to subjective empathy for this man. 'I have tea with the Widow tomorrow. You needn't come. I can manage it on my own.' Then, to restore a touch of the professional to a conversation that had begun that way and then severely veered off course, as so many of their conversations did, she added, 'Thank you for your time. Be assured, I will not make a habit of importuning you at such a late hour.'

That was too bad, he'd like to be importuned by her at this hour quite frequently, but for different reasons than awkward, secret-spilling conversations. Julien slumped in his chair after the door shut behind her. Now she knew. As predicted, the knowing had been disastrous. She wanted nothing to do with him beyond what she needed for the vineyards now. If she wasn't so inexperienced and in need of his expertise, he had no doubt she'd have asked him to leave. He'd not been dishonest with her, but he had not been truthful either about his attachment to this place. Should he have been? Would things be different if he'd told her from the start?

He stared at his empty brandy glass and debated a third glass. No. Another drink would not make it better. He feared nothing could. His family's legacy of loss had made him hard-bitten. He'd inherited quite a lot of his grandfather in that regard. He might have shaken that off if it hadn't been for Clarisse's betrayal, which had resulted in a broken heart and the loss of the land. His grandfather had been right. You could trust no one, and no one should be entrusted with the things you hold dear—one's heart, one's family, one's land. These precious items must be protected, locked away. He'd lost his heart to Clarisse, and his father had died of a broken heart over the double disappointment, defeated after a life of striving. How much more proof did he need?

And yet.

Those two simple words reminded him of his stupidity. And yet he knew all this and he'd still managed to lose his detachment when it came to Emma Luce. Julien ran a hand through his hair and let out a sigh. She'd done a number on him with her voracious appetite for knowledge, her intoxicating idiosyncrasies—he didn't think his mind would ever quite erase the pictures of her in the kitchen, rolling out dough with a smudge of flour on her cheek, or stirring a pot and bending over it with her eyes shut, sniffing it. He'd never had a woman cook for him before. Clarisse wouldn't be caught near the kitchens.

The two women couldn't be more different. Clarisse, blonde and diminutive, who loved to shop, who'd never worked a day in her life or known how to. How he'd loved pleasing her with a trinket or sweet. He'd lived for the sound of her laughter; the sparkle of her smile turned his direction in a crowded room. She'd been surrounded by beaux but she always found her way to his side—the young handsome heir to the Comte du Rocroi. He'd been a good dancer in those days. She'd loved that about him and his kisses, too. He'd not minded it had been hard to keep up with her tastes on his limited funds.

Emma was pleased with quieter pleasures. She'd immersed herself in the chateau, buried herself in reading, took delight in debating him where Clarisse had no interest in disagreeing with him. That would have required a discussion of things she had no knowledge of or desire to learn about. Whenever he'd talked about the grapes she'd laugh and say he sounded like a farmer. And of course, sounding like a farmer was definitely a bad thing according to Clarisse. She would teasingly remind him that a future *comte* didn't prune vines and walk the land in dusty boots. There would be servants to do all that for him once they married. She'd been keen to remind him of that, too. He'd have to start living like a *comte* after they wed.

Their marriage would never have worked. He would

have been unhappy within months. But he would have had his land. Oncle Etienne would have been happy. As soon as Julien produced a son in that marriage, the universe would be righted. The Archambeau line would inherit the chateau and all the vineyards between the chateau and his *oncle*'s farmhouse, the damage of the Revolution undone, the family avenged. No sacrifice, not even Julien's happiness or integrity, was too much to ask for when it came to *famille et terre*. Only he'd not understood it that way at the time.

He was different now, too. The young man who believed in love, who was hungry for a taste of it, was gone. He was approaching middle age, jaded and used to being alone, used to disappointment. He was not used to getting what he wanted. It always slipped away in the end. He and Emma had never stood a chance. He was too ruined. Ruined by a broken heart, ruined by a family legacy that was on the brink of becoming poisonous. It had defined four generations of Archambeau males, been the sole driving purpose of their lives. Now it had cost him Emma, a woman he had…feelings… for. He didn't dare call it falling in love. That was for fools. But he had feelings for her. Together, they might have made a passionate partnership—they might have built something remarkable if they'd had the luxury of a clean slate between them. That was gone now. Perhaps it had never existed.

He closed his eyes, leaning back in his chair, the wicked thought coming to him: At what point did a dream become a nightmare? At what point was he entitled to live his own life? To set his wants over those of his family? And if he could do those things, what would that life look like? He'd lived with the Archambeau legacy for so long he wasn't sure if he could live outside it.

Chapter Eighteen

It was the first time she'd been outside the estate since her arrival and the day couldn't be more different. The carriage top was down, the sun was on her face, and the countryside was in bloom, a far cry from the closed carriage she'd arrived in, the landscape as barren, as grey, as her mood. Grief had been her constant companion in those days. And yet her mood today was not as light as it might have been.

She was making the five-mile journey to Boursault by herself, without Julien beside her. The visit should have brought her great joy. What a thrill it was to meet the great champagne widow, Madame Clicquot, but that thrill was lessened by the tension between her and Julien. Last night's revelations had clarified some tensions but instilled new ones.

As a result, she'd not slept well, dozing off only at dawn for what turned out to be a dream-plagued nap. She probably looked like a hag between her black widow's garb, pale face, and dark circles beneath her eyes. This was not the sort of drama she was used to over a man. She and Garrett had never fought, never kept secrets, not even in the beginning when they'd been trying so hard to impress each other as new couples do. With Julien she was out of her depth. It was a new and uncomfortable experience.

She liked being in charge, liked knowing what came next. With Julien she did not know. Now, when she ought to be focused on the Widow and making a good impression, all she could think about was Julien. What was so terrible about what he'd done? He'd done nothing illegal. She'd come to the conclusion that what grieved her the most was simply that she hadn't known, that he hadn't felt he could tell her. He could take her to bed but he couldn't tell her who he really was or about his family's association with the estate.

Because it would have altered everything.

But why not after they'd begun the affair, when, surely, he was more certain of her? She had no answers for that, at least not answers she liked.

The Chateau Boursault came into view and Emma cleared her mind, focusing on the details of the building with its squared wings on either end and the rounded turrets, the steeply pitched roof, all done in the neo-renaissance style, and then there were the windows—so many windows! She began to count them to put herself at ease. She'd got to twenty when the carriage stopped in front of the steps leading up to the white six-panelled door. The place was magnificent and her first thought was that she wished Julien was here to see it with her.

She was expected and shown into the entrance, her

heels tapping on polished parquet flooring. The foyer was a room unto itself and decorated accordingly with a nod to Italianate styling. Columns set into the walls framed trompe l'oeil murals. A crystal chandelier hung from the ceiling, reminiscent of her own. This chateau was a palace, an homage to elegance. But it wasn't as old as Julien's. Where his had the patina of centuries, this one was new, barely lived in for two years. *Julien's.* She needed to be careful with that word. Was she really thinking of the chateau as his? That boded ill if she was already mentally ceding it to him. It echoed back to her earlier fear that perhaps he saw marriage as a way forward if he could not get what he wanted through business avenues. If she'd not had that revelation, would she have fallen for his ploy? Had she been that close? A footman led her through a series of interconnecting rooms to a small sitting room that overlooked the back gardens. The glass doors were open to let in the fresh breeze and Madame Clicquot was already there.

'Madame Luce, welcome. Forgive me if I don't get up. Age and my bones don't always agree with me.'

'Please, I would not have you bother on my account.' Emma crossed the room and helped herself to the chair adjacent to Madame Clicquot's. Seventy-five was indeed an august age and in ways the woman looked it. She had the double chin of a life well-fed if not well-lived, and Emma thought there was a resoluteness in the set of her jaw that came from perhaps the accumulated fatigue of carrying on, perhaps too often carrying on alone. Especially when there were burdens to be borne. Would she look like that at seventy-five? Worn

and shaped by the pressures of her world? The aloneness of it? It was a sobering thought. But everything
came with a price. Just different prices.

'Am I not what you expected?' The woman's eyes
were shrewd. Whatever fatigue Emma might have detected was absent from her gaze. Her speech was certainly direct.

'I did not know *what* to expect. Thank you for receiving me. I am new to the area and I am desperate to
learn everything I can.' Emma smiled. 'And desperate
to meet you because you are a legend.'

'Hmmph.' Madame scoffed at that. 'Or was it that
you wanted to meet because we are alike? You see
some similarity between us? Both of us widowed at
twenty-seven, trying to make something out of nothing? Like you, the wine was a side business for my
family when Francois and I married. It was still a side
business, really, when he died.' A maid brought in an
enormous silver tea tray and set it down between them.
Emma moved to do the honours.

'How do you find the Chateau?' she asked with a
gimlet eye as Emma passed her a teacup painted with
delicate sprigs of lavender. 'It has a ridiculous name, it
should be a *domaine*. You should think about renaming
it,' Madame hinted broadly. 'Nothing says Englishman
like a poorly named vineyard. Aside from that though,
your husband was a good sort. I met him once. I *am*
sorry for your loss.'

'Thank you.' Emma sipped her own tea. 'I wanted
to ask you about your *vendangenoir* and your presses.'

It was a good enough question to set Madame off

on her favourite subject, champagne. One question led to another, which led to a second pot of tea and another plate of cakes. The woman was impressive. Emma could have listened to her talk all day but it was clear the older woman was tiring. Emma immediately felt some guilt over that. She'd been enjoying herself so much. 'I must apologise for keeping you so long.' Emma set down her teacup as a hallway clock chimed five. Dear Lord, she'd been here two hours!

'Nonsense, I've enjoyed it immensely. There are not many women to talk with about the industry these days.' She waved a plump hand. 'In the old days, when I first began, there were several female *vignerons*.' She paused. 'Do you know the term? A *vigneron* is a grape-grower, someone who grows grapes expressly for wine. There were even women who blended the wines. Many of them widows who had to see to themselves. They took over their husbands' businesses and with success in most cases. But these days, there's no room for a woman unless she's already in position.' Madame gave her a strong look. 'I don't envy you trying to break into the business these days. There's machinery to think of now. Which of the new inventions can we use that will make the process efficient while still maintaining the integrity of being hand-crafted? It is a delicate balance to consider.'

And yet the House of Clicquot managed to turn out thousands of bottles a year. Emma thought industrialisation hadn't stumped Madame at all. But perhaps it hadn't been maximised to its fullest. Emma leaned forward. This was her moment to impress the Widow, to give back a piece of knowledge for all the woman had given her this afternoon. 'Industrialisation is not only changing how we can produce wine but also the markets it can reach. With railroads, we can reach far more potential customers without having to contact them directly. Right now, we need agents to represent the products to a select few. But with railroads, we can connect with people faster and farther. There's already a railroad in Epernay, more will be coming. I think the future is in labelling. The right kind of label can market a product as well as any agent. My father is in the gin business in England, and he's already using that technique to good success.'

'Is that so? We have labels already,' Madame countered.

'But are they labels as recognisable as the product? As if the label were its own product, one might say. Maybe not just a label with words on it, but a label with a picture of something people could associate with the product. A grape vine, the silhouette of a chateau, a glass, anything as long as it's a consistent image the buyer can count on seeing.'

'It's a very interesting idea. What does Monsieur Archambeau think about it?' Her eyes sharpened and she laughed. 'You did not think you'd escape today without us talking about Julien Archambeau? I'm surprised he didn't come with you.' And a little disappointed, too, Emma thought.

'He's busy with the grapes,' Emma improvised.

Madame lifted a brow. 'He's always busy. Too busy for a man his age. He needs to get out and meet people.

By people, I mean he needs to meet women. A handsome man should be married. Oh, I see I've shocked you. Age has nothing to do with appreciating a fine figure of a man. I've known the Archambeaux for ages. My family knew his back before the Revolution. Of course, Julien wasn't around then, but our families knew one another. My family wasn't noble so the Revolution posed a lesser threat to us and my father knew how to play the right sides. But it destroyed the Archambeaux. Matthieu, that's Julien's grandfather, never got over it. Etienne carries the family torch now.' She offered a stern look, 'I'm sure you know your chateau used to be theirs. Seventy years ago, to be sure. But French memories are long and they carry a grudge.'

'Yes, I know,' Emma said tersely, but it occurred to her that she just barely knew. The news was not even twenty-four hours old. Was this what Julien feared about tea with Madame Clicquot? That the old woman would unpack his family history without his permission?

'You'd best watch yourself. Julien is a persuasive man. I'm surprised he hasn't married you already. That's one sure way to put the chateau back into Archambeau hands.'

The old woman, legend or not, was outside the pale with that comment. 'I lost my husband only a couple months ago. I am not looking to remarry.'

'Well, one doesn't need to marry to enjoy the pleasures of Julien Archambeau,' the widow said sagely. 'But it does put one on the path towards marriage, just thinking of having him all to oneself for a lifetime.' Emma hoped her face didn't give her away. Did the widow guess that she'd already succumbed to Julien's charms? What an embarrassingly easy conquest she'd been.

'All I'm saying, *ma cherie*, is to watch yourself, if you don't mean to marry again. He was willing to marry for the chateau once before. There's no reason to think he wouldn't try to marry for it again, especially if there's no other way to get it.'

'Marry for it?' She stopped the widow in mid-story. 'He said he had his heart broken once.'

'Oh, indeed he did.' The widow shifted in her seat, settling her plump form in for a good telling. 'Seven years ago, before the government suspended titles yet again, he was the son of the Comte in those days. He was engaged to Clarisse Anouilh. Her dowry was the chateau and its vineyards. But her father broke the engagement off. He found someone better for his ambitions. Hers, too, truth be told. She never would have satisfied Julien. She was pretty enough, but she was a girl. Julien was a man and he needed, still needs, a partner, not a pretty doll.'

Emma barely heard the last of the widow's opinion on Clarisse Anouilh. What a stupid fool she'd been. Now she had her answers, her real answers. What hadn't made sense last night became clear. She rose. 'I must take my leave, Madame. Thank you again for your time and your…insights.'

'It was nothing. I wish you all the success over there.'

Emma nodded and departed, thankful for the footman who saw her back through the warren of rooms to her carriage. Her mind was too full of other things to spend any energy on how to find her way back through the house.

By the time she reached home, she was furious. Furious with herself for having been duped and furious with Julien. How dare he sit there last night playing the wounded victim against her accusations while he'd been using her all along, manipulating her into getting what he wanted, which wasn't her after all—a thought that was a bit lowering—but the chateau. He'd offered himself in marriage once before in order to get his land. She could no longer pretend he wasn't above doing so again. Last night she'd not been willing to believe it of him, but Madame's revelation about Clarisse Anouilh was incontrovertible proof.

'Where is he?' she ground out, breezing past a stunned Richet.

'In the cellars, *madame. Madame*, there's been a delivery for you—'

'Not now.' She shook her head and was off down the long stairs to the wine caves. Good. The cellars were soundproof. That suited her. There were things she needed to say to Julien she didn't want anyone else to hear.

He heard her coming before he saw her. There was the loud thud of a heavy oak door shutting, as if it had been heaved to with considerable, rapid force. Then there'd been the sound of her feet on the flagstones, staccato clips. If anger had a stride, that would be it.

That damn tea was today. Something had apparently gone wrong. That worried him. One did not upset Widow Clicquot without reaping consequences. He should have gone. He could have at least smoothed things over. He did not need a boycott of his wines.

She stormed into his little nook of an office, eyes bright, face flushed, hair coming down from beneath the little hat she wore. She'd be magnificent if she wasn't aiming all her ire at him. She slammed her reticule down on his desk with a solid crack. 'You used sex to seduce the chateau out from under me. You rotten bastard!'

'Slow down, Emma. What are you talking about?' Julien said carefully, easing back from the desk lest he become a casualty of her anger. He scanned the desk-top, thankful to note he'd put away the letter opener. He didn't fancy a stabbing.

'I am talking about Clarisse Anouilh. You were going to marry her for the chateau! Save yourself a pile of money. Why buy the place outright when you can just marry for it? It was only when that didn't work out that you tried to buy the place.'

Julien held up his hands. 'It was arranged by my father and her father. It was meant to be an alliance. Our ancient name in exchange for the return of our lands.' He paused. 'If it's any consolation, I did care for her and it broke my heart when her father called off the engagement. Does that make you feel better, to know I didn't come out on top?'

'It does not change the fact that you were going to try that ploy again with me when it became clear I was not going to sell.' There was the tiniest of cracks to her voice, that's when he heard it. She wasn't just angry. She was hurt and he had hurt her. The sheen in her eyes was tears and he did not want a single tear to fall, did not want to be the reason Emma Luce cried.

She faced him across his desk, her features stark with loathing. 'The two questions I asked myself all the way home were how could I have been so stupid to let myself fall for a man I barely knew, and how could you be so cruel? Julien, I trusted you with my grief, my stories, my hopes, my wants, my passion, I gave myself over to you entirely in ways I'd not given myself to anyone, not even Garrett. You exploited every last piece of me.'

Could someone *feel* ashen? Julien felt as though if he looked in a mirror in that moment he would look pale, entirely drained of life. 'Such a man would be a despicable creature indeed. But that creature is not me, Emma.' Against his better wisdom, he came around the desk and knelt before her, reaching for her hands, desperate to touch her, to comfort her. He wanted nothing so much as to take her in his arms and kiss away her doubts. But she snatched her hands from his.

'Don't you dare touch me again. That's what started this trouble.'

That was unfair. 'You started it, in the vineyard,' he shot back and immediately regretted it. He rose and went back to his seat. 'That is not why I made love to you, Emma,' he said in slow, patient tones. 'I did not make love to you out of pity or to manipulate your grief or to lead you down the path of a whirlwind marriage.'

'Those are the only reasons that make sense.' Emma glared at him, anger the only thing keeping those shiny tears of hers at bay. 'You hardly knew me and it all happened so fast. I should have seen the signs, should have known better.'

Julien interrupted, overriding her with his words. 'I made love to you because you are the most intelligent, irritating, beautiful, capable, interesting, and stubborn woman I've ever met. And if given the chance, I would make love to you again and again and again because you challenge me, you've brought me back to life. And I don't want to go back. I need you, Emma. You've turned my life upside down, but it will never be right side up again without you.'

Her face registered shock and disbelief. 'That is conveniently the perfect fallback position. You can deny the "strategy" while still advancing your cause. That is rich. You've lied about who you were, you've hidden information from me about the chateau and your history with it, you tried to distract me from meeting people in the area and announcing my presence. At this point, why should I believe anything you have to say?'

'Because I love you. Because I didn't want you to be hurt, to feel that somehow what happened between us was no different than what you'd experienced with Redmond. All of this was to protect *you*.' He made the confession with a new confidence. He did love her. It was entirely true even if he had not named it to himself until this moment. And in this moment, he felt powerful and yet vulnerable. What would she do with his confession? Would she throw it back in his face or would she embrace it and open a path for them? He hoped for the latter but braced for the former. His Emma was a fighter.

She rose. 'No, you don't get to say that.' Ah, so she was going to fight. 'I've been in love before, with a *good* man, and *this* is not what love feels like. Love does not hurt; love does not tie one's stomach into knots. Love does not make a person decide between two things they care about deeply.' Her quicksilver eyes flashed with deep emotion and her jaw clenched, her words tight and terse as if she could barely restrain herself long enough to civilly grind them out before she left the room. So, it was to be a two-fronted battle, Julien thought. She was fighting him and a past she couldn't quite let go of.

Chapter Nineteen

Julien loved her. The thought followed her all the way upstairs to her chamber, unwilling to be kept out by her door. She could leave the room but she could not leave the thought. Emma pressed her head to the door. How dare he say those words when he knew she'd been made a fool of in love before and when he knew how difficult it would be for her to believe them. How did she dare *believe* them? How could she when she knew what he stood to gain? Did he think her naïve? Willing to take a handsome man at his word? Worst of all, how dare her heart side with him when it ought to know better.

But could you do it? Could you love Julien? came the whisper.

To love Julien in return would be an enormous leap of faith across a wide chasm filled with doubting fingers that reached up from her past to clutch at her at every opportunity. Once more, she was the one with the money, the property. How could she be sure Julien saw beyond that? Or even wanted to see beyond that? How could she be sure that he saw *her*? The answer was, she couldn't be. To love Julien would be a true act of blind faith, both in him and in her own intuition. Such an act had not been required in loving Garrett. There'd been no risk, no cost, just reward. It had made her choice easy. This choice was not easy.

There were so many reasons not to make it. It was too soon; it was too good to be true. Men used her for money. She should not expect Julien to be different when he openly had so much to gain. But she wanted him to be different. Her heart wanted a reason to believe, a reason to leap, and that was a dangerous place to be. 'Whose side are you on? You are supposed to be on my side,' she muttered to her traitorous heart as she got ready for bed, acutely aware that she need not sleep alone tonight—that too was her choice.

'Who side are you on these days?' Oncle Etienne's tone was sharp and scolding, the same tone he'd used when Julien and his cousin were eleven and had been caught with the brandy at the Christmas party. It was all Julien could do to not feel eleven again now as they strode the Archambeau vineyards. It was perhaps a warning to him just how angry his *oncle* was that they were outside walking the land, something his *oncle* usually left to his workers. He suspected they were walking the land now in order for his *oncle* to make a point. Although Julien was not certain what point that was. The summons had been sudden and unexpected.

'Are there any sides, Oncle? I'm afraid you have me at a disadvantage.' Perhaps word of his quarrel with Emma had reached his *oncle*'s ears. No one would have

actually heard the quarrel but the icy atmosphere at
the chateau the last few days would hardly leave anyone in doubt there'd been a split between them. In the
evenings, the dining room was dark. There were no
more elegant meals that lasted hours. No more retreats
to the library to finish those discussions. Emma had
been sure to keep her distance. She'd not come out to
the vineyards when she knew he was walking, or down
to the cellars when he was in the office, and he'd felt
the absence of her keenly.

'There's our side, *mon fils*. I feel as if you've forgotten that.' His *oncle*'s tone relented slightly as he clapped
a fatherly hand on Julien's shoulder. 'I thought you had
Luce's widow under control.'

The thought of controlling Emma was almost laughable. 'She's not a woman to be manipulated. She's too
smart for that,' Julien cautioned. Despite the words
she'd flung at him and the things she thought of him,
he felt compelled to protect her. He might not be
her enemy, his intentions had been honourable, but
his *oncle* would do anything to regain the lands. His
oncle was more than capable of doing the things Emma
had accused *him* of doing. That was the difference,
he realised, between him and his *oncle*. He'd always
admired his *oncle*'s business sense. His *oncle* ran a
successful regional shipping company, he had acquired
some of the Archambeau lands, but Julien had never
seen the cost of that up front like he was seeing it now.

'Your widow went to visit *the* widow at Boursault
earlier this week.' His *oncle* slid him a sideways look.
'Without you in attendance.'

'She asked me not to come,' Julien replied simply. 'I cannot keep her captive at the estate.'

'You should have been with her to control the conversation,' his *oncle* chided. Silently, Julien agreed. If he'd gone, perhaps he could have prevented the widow from spilling the tale of his engagement to Clarisse, from suggesting to Emma that he was the sort of man who'd sell himself in marriage for an estate. He'd taken a gamble there, thinking the women would limit themselves to business only instead of making his personal history a primary topic of conversation. But that wasn't something that would have upset his *oncle*. Something else had happened as a result of the visit.

His *oncle* stopped to study a vine. 'Everything bloomed a little later than expected but it's making up for lost time. I think we might have an early harvest.' He smiled and Julien felt the tension that had been building between them ease. Whatever happened, they had the grapes between them—the grapes kept them together. 'The old widow told her agent and the agent told Charles Tremblay, who has made it his business to share with everyone he can find, that Madame Luce is at the reins of the estate, that she's running the vineyard. A woman, and an outsider, is at the helm of the chateau, not Julien Archambeau, a man who implicitly had everyone's trust and subsequently their money.' That was the rumour they'd feared the most, the idea getting out that Julien was no longer in charge.

'Her being in charge doesn't affect what's already in production there. She won't even have a harvest to call her own until next year, and there won't be a vintage that can be attributed to her management for a few years yet.' Julien tried to soften the blow. 'If you're worried about the consortium, we can reassure them of that.'

'And your position there? Is that guaranteed?' came the pointed question.

'I do not know,' Julien answered truthfully. He would have felt more secure in the position if his *oncle* had asked this question last week. This week he wasn't so sure. 'She's not asked me to leave.'

'But she might?' His *oncle* sounded worried. 'You have to be indispensable to her, Julien. She has to be made to see that her success relies on keeping you there.' His *oncle* shook his head. 'I don't like it, Julien. Our fates are too intertwined with hers. She has us trapped. If we support her and help her succeed, help her retain the good faith of the consortium, then she will not sell and we are no closer to getting those lands back than we were seven years ago. But if she asks you to leave, and tries to go it on her own, she'll ruin the land, and if we ever get it back, it will be a mess to rebuild the chateau's reputation from there. But the latter is a future concern. I am more concerned with the immediate fallout from the Widow's gossip. We are losing money, *mon fils*.'

'What?' Julien straightened from his examination of the vines. 'Why?'

'Can you really not guess? A few of the consortium members who'd bought futures on our *couteau champenois* have asked for their money back. They are concerned about the grapes that come from the chateau if you are no longer the one making decisions over there. I suspect once word gets around people have asked to pull out, others will want to do the same.' That would be devastating. They'd put all they had into expanding the production of the highly sought after *couteau champenois*. 'There's more. I received this just this morning.' His *oncle* reached into his coat pocket and withdrew a letter. He passed it to Julien. 'It's from the Growers' Consortium Bank, the one that holds the loan we took out for the acreage we were able to buy back last year. They are concerned that the "changes in our circumstances" make us a high risk. They want to foreclose on the loan.'

Julien stared at the letter. He knew what foreclosure meant. If they didn't pay the loan in full, the farmhouse, the vineyard which they'd put up as collateral, would be lost. He handed the letter back to his *oncle*. 'Can we pay it?'

'If we bankrupt ourselves. It would take everything we've got. We would have to use the funds we'd set aside so far for buying the chateau. We'll have to dip into them already to return the money on the futures. In short, it will take all of our reserves.' Which meant it would take years to put money aside for the chateau—again. It also meant a significant setback in their ability to run their own vineyard.

'But our vineyards would still function because I'd be there. We could slowly rebuild, find a new source for the grapes in the *couteau champenois*. Tremblay's been wanting in on that and his grapes are good.' Julien spoke slowly, thinking out loud. He didn't want to believe it, but it was possible Tremblay had started the rumour on purpose to force them to turn to him as a source for the grapes.

His *oncle* nodded and let out a sigh. 'It is what I was thinking as well. Pay the damn loan, scale back production to what we can afford, perhaps support the vineyard from funds from the shipping company until our coffers are restored and create a new partnership for the *couteau champenois*. But dammit, Julien. We'll lose the chateau. We won't have the lands back in my lifetime.'

For the first time, Julien saw true age in his *oncle*'s face. There were wrinkles and lines, a bit of sagging at the jaw. 'Oncle, perhaps what we have is enough. There's the farmhouse, and there's the land we do have. It was Archambeau land before and now it is again, because of your efforts and my father's efforts.' Today, his *oncle* looked defeated, a warrior who'd fought his whole life for an unattainable goal, but also a man who'd been so set on his dream that he hadn't enjoyed what was right in front of him. Julien thought there was a cautionary tale in that for him. Would this be him at sixty-two? Alone, obsessed? Oncle Etienne looked like a successful man on the outside, but he'd given up so much, including his marriage, compromised so much, and each compromise asked for another and another.

'I made *mon père* a promise on his deathbed.' Oncle Etienne shook his head. 'Do not give up now, *mon fils*. We must stay strong. I think the way forward is to distance ourselves from Madame Luce. The consortium will come around if we show we're good for the money and that we'll support them, not an outsider.' He gave a shrug. 'Who knows, once she has no place with them, she might give up, and perhaps the consortium would help us buy the chateau as a reward for *our* good faith.'

Julien's blood chilled. His *oncle* meant to drive her out. If his *oncle* couldn't have the chateau, he wasn't going to allow her to have it either. 'Mutually assured disappointment, then?' Julien asked.

'Unless you marry her?' his *oncle* asked, too hopefully for it to be taken as a joke.

'I don't think there's any chance of that,' Julien said. Even if their latest quarrel hadn't taken away some hope of that, this latest conversation did. Refusing to marry her was a sort of protection for her. If he married her now, no matter what his own motives, he'd be his *oncle*'s puppet. That would create a shadow over their marriage before it started and Julien did not think it was a shadow that could be overcome even with time. Emma would question every decision about the vineyard. Was this decision for the good of them or his *oncle*? It would destroy them. She would doubt the truth of his feelings and that would destroy *her*, to say nothing what it would do to *him*. Trust was everything to her. She'd given it once and been betrayed.

His *oncle* gave him a final clap on the shoulder. 'Well, that settles it then. The consortium meets tomorrow. We'll announce our decision there and you can find the right time to tell Emma Luce you'll be leaving her to devote yourself full-time to your family enterprise.' He drew a deep breath. 'I feel better already, *mon fils*. I knew talking to you would help me organise my thoughts. With luck, Widow Luce will have been nothing but a small detour in the road to our success.'

Julien offered a tight smile and wished he could say he felt the same. But no, that wasn't quite right. He didn't want to wish Emma gone from his life. He didn't want to leave the chateau. He'd spent seven years of his life managing those vineyards with the hope they'd be his someday. Maybe one day they still would be.

He said goodbye to his *oncle* and made the ride home, taking the long route so he could think. Did he tell Emma about the consortium meeting? It was the monthly meeting, and as the head of the vineyards she was entitled to a spot among them. She should have been invited once Madame Clicquot had let the news circulate that she was in residence and planning to work. There'd been plenty of time to send her an invitation this past week. That they hadn't was further proof they meant to ignore her, shun her for being an outsider. She was a woman and English. Julien reasoned this was perhaps not much different than the reception she'd received when she'd made her debut in London. His heart had gone out to the young girl she'd been and the courage it must have taken to keep showing up even when she was obviously unwanted. That pattern was about to repeat itself.

It was clear, too, that his *oncle* knew she wasn't invited and he was expecting Julien to keep the secret. He was not to tell her. That was the dilemma he chose to focus on as he rode home. Did he tell Emma? It felt unfair and dishonourable to decide her fate without giving her a chance to defend herself. The consortium was casting her out without even meeting her, judging without even hearing her brilliant ideas for the future of marketing wines. These were ideas that all of them could benefit from. One didn't need to be a *vigneron* or an expert blender to be a good marketer. She would be an asset to them if they would give her a chance.

Why the hell did he care so much? She'd made it clear what she thought of him. She stood in the way of his family attaining their ancestral lands. He ought to want to see her pack up and leave, to have things go back to how they'd been with Sir Garrett—a few letters a year and a yearly visit to check in. But he found it was the last thing he wanted. What he wanted was for her to stay and fight. If he kept this meeting from her, it would be one more thing she could add to the list of sins against him, one more secret he'd kept. It would prove that he was everything she thought he was.

If he told her, she would go to the meeting and his *oncle* would know he'd chosen her side. The cost of that would be great. To lose his *oncle*'s trust, his *oncle*'s pride in him, was no small thing to Julien. His *oncle* was all the family he had left here. He'd hardly seen his cousin and aunt after he'd left England. By contrast, what did he gain by telling Emma that would be worth that? Would she thank him for telling her about a meeting meant to drive her from Cumières? Would she understand what this act would cost him? Would it be enough to earn her respect? Her trust? Her love?

Does it matter? his conscience whispered. *Does it matter what you gain or lose? You need to do the right thing regardless of cost. She did not ask for this. She did not ask to be thrown into the midst of your family drama. All she did was come here to heal and start a new life, a new life that your* oncle *and the consortium want to make impossible. She has no ally but you. You say you love her—is keeping the meeting a secret how you show the woman you love that you care for her, even if she doesn't love you back?*

Emma's last words to him whispered. *'I've known the love of a good man, and this isn't how love feels.'* Damn, but he hated it when she was right. He left his horse at the stable and went to find her, his decision made.

He didn't have to look far; she was in the foyer giving directions to footmen busy with ladders and pulleys hoisting a gigantic crystal chandelier. 'What is this?' For the first time in days, Julien felt a smile creep across his face.

She turned and her own smile faded at the sight of him. That hurt. She'd not forgiven him yet. 'My crystal arrived. I hadn't had time to get the chandelier up yet. But I definitely wanted it up for the gala.' He wondered if the pronouns were intentional. *I wanted.* A reminder that she was in charge here. This was her home. The gala was her event. 'It's only three weeks away.' Julien wondered if after tomorrow there would even *be* a gala. If there was, would he be invited? Would he even be a part of her life come June? His heart cracked a little further at the thought of being sent into exile, from this place, from her.

'It's beautiful.' Julien raised his gaze to the chandelier being slowly lifted.

'We bought it on our honeymoon from Baccarat.

Garrett was impressed with his work. It's not old, of course. His son's wife thought it too nouveau for Oakwood Manor. She always hated it. But Garrett thought—'

Julien didn't want to hear any more about Garrett. Garrett, the good man she'd been married to, the man who knew what love was. 'Let me help,' he interrupted, taking the stairs two at a time to assist with the pulleys.

The chandelier had granted him a reprieve, one last opportunity to rethink his decision, but at last the big chandelier was securely in place and everyone had a moment to come ooh and aah over it. The servants scattered, talking excitedly, and the footmen removed their ladders. Julien could put off his conversation no longer. 'May I have a word, Emma.' She gave him a cold quirk of her dark brow at the familiarity, but he refused to call her Madame Luce, refused to take a step backwards. They'd been lovers, and if it were up to him they'd be lovers still—more than lovers.

'You may say anything you like. I trust the grapes are progressing well. It looks greener and greener out there every day,' she said crisply, politely.

'In private,' Julien replied when it became clear she meant to have this conversation in the foyer where anyone could hear. 'Perhaps in the sitting room.' He gestured to the room closest to the foyer.

Once inside, he closed the door. 'I have some news. It is not pleasant but I thought you should know. The growers' consortium is meeting tomorrow. You should be there.' He'd done it. The secret was out. His *oncle*'s trust in him broken.

'Of course I should be there.' Emma's response was tart. 'I should have a seat on the board as one of the larger growers in the area.'

'There are other reasons you should be there. They mean to shut you down. Not literally,' he explained, 'they just mean to make it impossible for you to carry on without their support, support they plan to withhold.' He watched Emma stoically take in the news. Was this how she'd looked when she'd learned about Garrett? Staunch, pale, the only sign of distress being the clench of her hands in her lap, her knuckles white.

'On what grounds? They've never even met me,' she countered.

'You're an outsider and you're in the way of the goals of some consortium members,' he admitted plainly, although it hurt to do so, hurt to see the betrayal in her eyes.

'I suppose by that you mean you and your *oncle*.'

'My *oncle* is the one leading the charge, you might say.' Then he added, 'My *oncle* is losing money. Madame Clicquot let it drop that you were at the reins here and now some of his—our—investors with the *couteau champenois* want to pull out due to a lack of confidence,' he explained briefly.

She fixed him with one of her grey stares. 'I suppose I could make it all right though if I agreed to marry one of the consortium. That might restore their confidence in what was happening here.'

'No, not at all.' In all of his imaginings he'd never once thought of that, of applying public pressure in order to attain her hand. 'Why would you think that?'

'Because I can think of no other reason why you'd tell me about a meeting I wasn't invited to and at which men will attempt to decide my fate. I am either to marry and become acceptable through my husband's reputation, or I am to be pushed out because my own is lacking. Either way, you win. You get what you want.' She glared at him, 'Don't celebrate too soon, though, because I don't go down without a fight.'

He wanted to yell that he didn't want a fight, that all of this was for her, that he'd taken a huge risk in telling her, that he'd jeopardised his relationship with his *oncle* for *her*. He wanted to grab her by the arms and look into her eyes and tell her that what he wanted was her, that he didn't give a damn about the chateau. Not any more, not when he'd seen the cost, not when it meant losing her. But Julien did none of those things. She'd made it clear she would not believe his words. He could only hope she'd believe his actions. He'd unburdened himself completely. Would she understand what this would cost him when she showed up at the meeting tomorrow? Because she would be there. He knew Emma Luce and she could not be in possession of this information and stay away.

Chapter Twenty

Emma exited her carriage and smoothed her skirts, taking in the landscape So, this was the Archambeau farmhouse and the ancient Archambeau land. It commanded a view of the Marne in the distance, and it was neatly kept, hectares filled with rows of grapes spreading around the house in all directions. Even the drive was lined with grapes. One had to go past them to reach the house.

The drive was full of carriages, and grooms walked the horses of those who'd chosen to ride instead of drive on this glorious May day. She was definitely in the right place. Or the wrong place, depending on how one looked at it. She'd come here to confront those who would keep her down and lock her out. It was a place where she was not wanted and yet after what Julien had told her last night, how could she not come? She had yet to decide how she felt about Julien's disclosure. Had it been done as a bid to win back her trust? Or had it been bait to a trap? Did he want her to come because he knew the odds of her succeeding here were slim? Had he told her as a way of setting her up to fail once and for all?

She didn't want to believe it, but she had learned the hard way about the costs of naïveté. She may not want to believe it, but she had to consider it. The reality was she was walking into a den of her enemies, and yet she could not stay away. From the house, the camaraderie of low voices spilled out, punctuated by male laughter and chuckles, a subtle reminder that she was outnumbered here and in uncertain territory.

Well, she'd been outnumbered before by the likes of Amelia St James and her wicked coterie. But she'd triumphed. She'd risen above their pettiness. She'd been the one to make a love match with Garrett Luce and when Amelia and the others had looked down their unwed noses at the two of them the following year, Garrett had been willing to bulldog anyone who was out of line.

Emma walked towards the house, making sure to lift her head and square her shoulders. Today, she was on her own. She'd have to be her own bulldog. She couldn't even count on Julien. What could she expect from him? Would he support her? Why should he support her after the way she'd spoken to him on the last two occasions? She'd been rough with him, blunt and honest, but she did not regret the words. They needed to be said. If they weren't, they would fester.

He told you about the meeting, her conscience prompted. *That counts for something. He said he loved you. Those are not easy words for a man like him. Love has hurt him, too.*

She still hadn't quite processed that. The argument that had kept her up all night swirled relentlessly in her head one more time, as if she had not just considered it. Why tell her about the meeting? After her harsh words, he owed her nothing, unless he wanted her there so he could press his marital suit, turn her failure to his triumph.

Or maybe he is trying to prove his words. He loves you. Why would you think he'd pressure you when he's never once spoken of marriage to you?

Technically, it was a fairly large leap to marriage. She and Julien had never spoken of the future during their affair. They'd lived in the present. It was Madame Clicquot who'd brought up his previous engagement and what had been involved, who'd warned that perhaps Julien was leading her down a path that ended at the altar. And Emma had ran with that. Because it made sense. Because it answered the question: Why would he want her? Because he wanted the land and she was the key.

Inside, Emma handed her straw hat to the footman. A footman? At a farmhouse? She wondered if Etienne Archambeau lived so well or if the footman had been brought in by the consortium for the occasion. She opted to believe the latter. '*Madame*, everyone has already eaten,' he began, unnerved by her arrival. She was not on his guest list.

'I am aware.' She smiled at him to put him at ease. She'd arrived late on purpose, in part because it was a good strategy—she wanted to take them by surprise—and in part on principle. Jesus might have eaten with

Judas but she wasn't that magnanimous. She could not stomach the thought of sitting down for a meal among those who would persecute her, see her destroyed. 'If you could just show me where they are?'

The hired footman directed her to the dining room where the men were gathered around a long, old, oak table, set at odds with heavy silver and china containing the residue of lunch while a few continued to peck at leftovers.

She stopped in the doorway and raised her voice to be heard above the din of male conversation. 'Good afternoon, gentlemen.' Conversation stopped, forks dropped along with jaws, and the room went preternaturally still. She found Julien at the table and allowed herself a quick glance, careful not to risk too much for either of them. Perhaps Julien wouldn't appreciate the glance here in front of his friends and colleagues. She wasn't sure what she expected to see in those cool blue eyes of his. Strength? Support? She saw a glimmer of both, although she knew she didn't deserve it, not from him. They were ill-fated lovers, caught in an impossible situation.

A silver-haired gentleman rose. 'Madame Luce, I presume?' He was all gracious manners and had blue eyes like Julien's. 'We weren't expecting you.' He found an empty chair and pulled it up to the table.

'You should have been.' She swept the table with her gaze, including everyone in the scold. 'I am the owner of the vineyards at the chateau.' She smiled to indicate she'd be candid but friendly for as long as she could. They needn't be enemies. 'But I am here now.

By good fortune, I found out about the meeting, so no harm done,' she said cheerily. 'I believe the business meeting is about to begin?' She was rewarded with the man at the head of the table—Etienne perhaps— shifting uneasily in his chair, the table remaining silent. Julien had been right. They did mean to see her deposed. She decided to help them out. It would be the last favour she'd do them. 'I see, gentlemen. I *am* the business meeting. Well, let me start the conversation. It has come to my attention that there is some concern about my ability to run the vineyards at the chateau.' She'd spent quite a while last night thinking through her position. How she might establish her own credibility while also shoring up Julien's losses. 'I want to allay those concerns by letting you know that while I will be overseeing marketing and many of the back-end aspects of the business, Julien Archambeau will remain at the helm of the agricultural and blending aspects. You all respect his reputation, so there should be no doubt about the quality of wine that will continue to be produced at the chateau.' It was a difficult concession for her to make. She'd debated it hotly with herself all night. But she would not allow her business to suffer for the sake of her personal feelings. She would have to find her way past that. The chateau needed Julien.

A man at the end of the table cleared his throat. '*Madame*, allow me to introduce myself. I'm Charles Tremblay. I own Domaine Arnaud, my wife's property, but I understood that Monsieur Archambeau would be working exclusively at his family's vineyards.' He shot a look at Etienne Archambeau, apparently waiting for Etienne to confirm it. She shot a look at Julien. Was that true? Her whole solution hinged on having him with her.

But why would he stay when you have accused him of terrible things? Did you really think he had nowhere else to go?

The silence stretched out at the table, all eyes turning towards Etienne. She might have overplayed her hand, unwittingly. It was a dangerous thing putting a man on the spot where he felt cornered in front of other men whose admiration he needed. Cornered men and animals were dangerous, unpredictable creatures. She'd cornered Julien, too, she realised. Her eyes darted to where he sat, his eyes cool and calculating, directed at his *oncle*. Why didn't he speak up? His hesitation was telling. Why wouldn't he defend her?

Because he knows you want to defend yourself.

But she couldn't defend herself at present. While it did not suit her to give in, sometimes one could talk too much and make a situation worse. A good cook knew it paid to let the stew simmer before stirring the pot. That was the case here. There was nothing she could do or say in this moment that would make things better.

Etienne looked at his nephew. 'Apparently, Madame Luce has not heard the news. Perhaps you'd be so good as to tell her about your plans.' Her stomach tightened. Etienne seemed so sure of himself, as if Julien's answer was obvious, a foregone conclusion.

Julien spoke. 'I think this is a matter better settled in private.' The last of her hope—her fight—faded. It meant Julien had already chosen. He was truly gone from her now in all ways. Her gamble, her trust in Julien to save her business, and in turn her independence, was lost. He'd sided against her. She felt as if her insides were ripping her apart, so complete was her sense of betrayal. She had a choice: she could stay here and be further humiliated as a woman who didn't even know what her own employee was doing, or she could gracefully exit.

'I see, gentlemen. Perhaps you'd prefer to complete all your discussions in private. I give you good day, and I look forward to your decisions.'

She managed to exit before tears threatened, before the dam of her reserve broke. She'd half expected— or was that half wanted?—Julien to come after her. But what would he say? Why would he suddenly have words when he'd had none in that room? He could not fix this. Nor did she think he *wanted* to fix this. He'd done nothing but shoot steely blue daggers at his *oncle*, but that had amounted to nothing in the end. Dear Lord, she'd almost believed him when he'd said he loved her. She'd been so close. So close to nearly being his fool, just as she'd been Redmond's all those years ago. She'd be thankful for this reprieve later, but right now it hurt like a knife stuck in her gut.

She did not allow herself to cry until she was in the safety of her carriage. She couldn't fight every front, the biases of the past with the injustices of her present. It was all the same—*they* were all the same. She managed to give the command for home before the sobs welled up. She let them come. Amid the noise of horses and the road, no one would hear her cry. The sobs racked her, loud and body-shaking, shattering the temple of her resolve. In some ways Julien's betrayal was worse than Redmond's. He'd known she'd been hurt before and in the same way. He'd not hesitated to poke at the wound, to re-create the betrayal and humiliation of the past. All for his own gain. For his damned vineyards. And she'd nearly fallen for it.

The truth was, she had no ally here, no true friend. How she missed Fleur and Antonia. But they had their own troubles. They could not come to her. *But you could go to them*, the temptation whispered. Leave. Go back to England. Sometimes retreat was the best option for self-preservation. She'd never felt so desolate in her life. She had wagered on love—on Julien's love—and she had lost. Perhaps, in her gut, that same gut where the metaphoric knife was still stabbing her, she'd known what would happen. She'd just needed to show up today at that meeting to see it in order to believe it.

A smart strategist knew when a game was unwinnable. She could not change those men's minds, not without Julien. They did not want her here. She could run the chateau from afar, a *laissez-faire* owner as Garrett had been. But that didn't help Julien.

Why should you help him?

He'd not stood up for her.

He is in an impossible situation, her heart whispered. *How can you ask a man to choose between his family and a woman he's just met? Some might say you were never meant to have this place, that you are the interloper, the one in the wrong.*

It was a thought she'd had since the night Julien had told her everything. That she and Garrett were the interlopers here, they were the aberration. She ought to return the chateau to its rightful owner and restore the historic line. That Julien stayed to work for another owner, knowing it was rightfully his, proved his love for the land like she'd never know it. It was the right thing to do even though it put her at an enormous disadvantage. She had money, though. Garrett had left her well provided for. She could find a place of her own in England and start over or participate in the family business. There was always room for her there even if there was no future.

Perhaps the chateau had served its purpose. She'd got over her grief; she'd learned that she could feel again. Perhaps that was all it was meant to do and now it was time to move on, to go back, healed, strong, and ready to write herself a new chapter in life. She thought of the words from Garrett's will, that this was to be a place of rest and recovery for as long as she desired it. There was no pressure to hold on to the place, to make it a family estate like Oakwood Manor. Perhaps she'd been too grandiose in her idea to run the vineyard. She'd recovered. She'd explored passion. It was time to go. Julien had made his choices and now she'd made hers. Once a decision was made, it was best to act on it immediately. She would start packing at once. For the first time since she and Julien had quarrelled, she felt better, stronger. This was the path forward. She was sure of it.

* * *

The heavy tread of boots sounded in the hall, followed by a low curse and the apologies of two footmen she'd just sent down with a trunk. Emma straightened from her folding. That would be Julien—she'd recognise that voice anywhere. Perhaps she wasn't the only one packing. She'd have preferred to have left without any goodbyes. She'd hoped he'd have the decency not to kick her when she was down.

'Emma, what is going on?' Julien burst into the room, sending the maids scattering. 'Yesterday I come home to find you hoisting a chandelier and today I come home to find you packing trunks.' He looked as if he'd ridden hard. His dark hair was wind-blown, much as it had been the first night he'd stood in the drawing room, dusty boots on an expensive carpet.

'I've decided to do some travelling. I am going to visit my family in England. I may stay awhile if I'm having a good time.'

'You mean you're leaving,' Julien paraphrased. 'One meeting with the growers and you're leaving? Are you going to let them drive you off so easily? What happened to fighting?'

She set aside the nightgown in her hand and faced him. 'It's not just one meeting, is it? My father taught me when there's a problem or even a success, there's not just one reason for it. I am not wanted here. You have made that plain. I am an interloper here, and an outsider. I have hurt your business with the consortium by laying claim to what was mine by law. I did not realise that until yesterday when you told me about the lost funds. I am truly sorry for causing you financial hardship. But it is not in me to pretend to be something that I'm not. I cannot take a secondary role here, if I were to stay, and I don't think I can. You warned me that the days of a woman heading a Champagne house were fading. The consortium showed me that today. They have no confidence in me without you. Even if I could make it on my own, I will not be given the chance.'

'Emma, stop,' Julien interrupted with a rough shake of his head. 'That's what I came to tell you. You *do* have me. I choose *you*.' Even as desolate as she was, as empty as she was, the words stunned her. How could she even think about believing them? They were the perfect words, the words that made everything all right. She simply couldn't believe them. They were illogical against the backdrop of the afternoon.

'But your *oncle*? What about working for the family vineyard?' she started with the practical contradiction. He couldn't choose her. Julien confused her. Just when she thought she understood him, he showed her something different.

He gave another shake of his head. 'I told the consortium if they insisted on making me choose, I would choose you. I told them you were brilliant, that you had ideas for marketing the wines that were exciting, that took advantage of this new world we live in.'

'Your *oncle* couldn't have been pleased. You would have made him look like a fool.' She was still trying to wrap her head around what had happened and what she thought about it. She couldn't let herself believe; she couldn't set herself up for loss again. There was no reason to believe him, no precedent. When others had had to choose between her and themselves, they'd not thought twice about choosing themselves. Amelia, Redmond, Garret's family. Garrett had chosen her but it had not cost him anything.

'That's why I wanted to have the discussion in private. I wanted to find a way to help him save face.' He reached for her hands and she let him take them against her better judgement. Touching was dangerous. 'I could not go along with his plans any further, not when they were so malevolently aimed at you. It was unfair. His dream is not worth the cost of yours.'

Emma swallowed hard, her mind working against her heart, trying not to be swept away by the emotion of his words.

He'd chosen her.

This was new, but his motives weren't. Of course, the cynic in her argued, *He chose you because you hold the chateau.* 'And what of your dream, Julien?' she countered softly. She didn't want to argue any more, but she had to know.

'My dream is not the chateau. It is you. I can't say anyone was happy about the decision I made, except me. I want to be here with you, although it won't be easy. People are not happy with me or with you at the moment. They may take that unhappiness out on us in sales.'

'Only locals.' Her mind was coming alive with the impact of what this meant. Julien was staying. She could produce wines. 'Britain is a vastly unexplored market, no one there will care about the local politics of Cumières.' But then she slowed her mind. She was getting ahead of herself. 'I can't let you give up your family because of me. I will not be a wedge driven between you and your *oncle*.'

'He's done that on his own,' Julien offered, his eyes softening. She disengaged her hands and stepped back. This changed very little between them, in truth. It did not change the fact that she was living in his house. That her dreams would only be achieved at the loss of his. That any way forward would always be shrouded in doubt for them. Just like the betrayal in England had cost her more than a suitor, this betrayal had cost her that carefully rebuilt trust. She needed distance.

'Perhaps it would be best if I returned to England and ran things from there in the fashion Garrett did. Maybe out of sight and out of mind will help with rapprochement between you and the consortium.' At least she'd be leaving on better terms with him. At a distance, she'd be better protected, too, from the natural seduction of him. There would be no chance for Julien to woo the chateau from her, or for them to reignite the affair between them, which seemed a very real possibility from the look in his eyes. But reigniting the affair would also be done under a cloud of doubt about intentions, and that doubt would always be between them now.

'Leave? Three weeks before the gala? I can't possibly manage it without you.' There was genuine panic in Julien's voice. 'Besides, you just hung the chandelier.' He smiled and if the situation had been less fraught, she would have laughed. Instead, she had to stand firm.

'Perhaps this isn't the best time for a gala. Besides,

I doubt anyone would come with the way things are at present,' she conceded. She'd had so much fun planning it and she'd been looking forward to it. It was to have been a debut of sorts for her.

'I don't know about that. Your guest list was very impressive, as is the list of respondents. Nearly everyone you've invited is coming.' That list had been full of clients invited from all over Europe to come and taste the wines, especially the special one Garrett had put up seven years ago and the *couteau champenois*. They'd hoped to have a lot of orders come out of the gala.

'The growers won't come.'

'That's where I think you're wrong.' There was a spark of mischief in his eyes. 'I offered them a chance to show their wines as well if they attended. Now our guests can taste not just our wines, but all the wines of the region. I may even have suggested a tasting competition with judges and a prize in each category.'

'That's brilliant,' she said carefully, letting the idea roll over her in a slow wave. 'Why, you might make a decent marketer yet.'

He smiled warmly. 'I was taught by the best.' She made her decision. It couldn't hurt to stay another few weeks. It didn't mean she had to stay for ever. If the gala failed, then Julien could see first-hand what they were up against and he might agree that it was best she returned to England.

'All right then, I will stay until the gala, and then we'll decide from there.' Only time would tell which of them was right, and her heart desperately hoped it wouldn't be her, even as she realised it probably would be. She could not love a man she couldn't trust. How could she trust another when she couldn't even trust herself? Her world and her emotions at present were fragile like fine crystal and liable to shatter at any moment.

Chapter Twenty-One

'This is the infamous Baccarat?' Julien's tones cut sharply through her thoughts as she unpacked the crystal in the dining room. She'd been too lost in memories to hear him approach. She looked up, startled, nearly dropping a glass.

'Yes, nearly all of it. I just have this box to open.' She tracked him with her eyes as he made a slow perambulation around the table. She'd not seen him since the day of the growers' meeting when she'd tried to leave, the day they'd struck their bargain and she'd agreed to stay for the gala. He'd made himself scarce in the interim, perhaps understanding she needed time, space.

'Thank goodness,' Julien chuckled, stopping to pick up a goblet and holding it to the light. 'We're out of space on the dining room table. The collection is rather impressive.' It was indeed. Six glasses deep and rows that ran the length of the table.

'It's rather large,' she amended. 'Garrett insisted we buy everything in the set. I don't think there's a type of glassware not accounted for here. There are sherry glasses, brandy snifters, cordial glasses, water goblets and some I don't even know what they're for. I did not think it was *all* necessary but Garrett said I could give it to my daughter someday when she wed.' She gave a sad smile. 'But now, it shall be mine for ever.'

She watched Julien's long fingers still on a flute. 'Garrett wanted more children? At his age?' Julien's brow furrowed in a gesture she was far too familiar with.

'Yes, daughters if he could manage it.' She gave a shrug. She didn't want to talk about it: more hopes and dreams dashed. 'I'm afraid all of this unpacking has made me a bit maudlin. Happy memories mixed with the sad.'

'You wanted children, too?' Julien pressed, not taking her hint.

She nodded. 'Yes, but we do not always get what we want. I settle myself with being an aunt to my oldest brother's children.' She should not ask but suddenly she couldn't help herself. 'And you? Did you want children?'

He set down the flute. 'Once I did. I have not thought on it for a long time. There seemed to be no point.' His eyes lingered on her for an extended moment and she felt herself grow hot. No. She did not like the unspoken implication in his words that somehow he, who had not imagined children for years, could imagine them with her. The breach of trust was still too raw for her, the reconciliation still too new, and their peace too temporary. Perhaps that was when she'd first realised she would indeed be leaving no matter how the gala went. If she did not, her life would be filled with moments of temptation like this, glimpses into what could be, and she would not be able to resist them for ever. To stay would be to capitulate, to set herself up for disappointment after disappointment.

Julien smiled, breaking the moment. He picked up the flute and reached for a *coupe*. 'Do you know the difference between the two of these?'

She shook her head. 'There is no difference. They are both used for Champagne.'

Julien grinned. 'They are, but that's where you are wrong.' He gestured for a footman. 'Bring up a bottle of the forty-eight.' He winked at her. 'I'll explain while we wait. The flute is long and narrow. It allows the champagne to remain bubbly, fizzy, if you will, longer. It also allows the champagne to hold on to its scent, its aroma, longer. I think a serious taster would always choose to drink from a flute.' He set it down and held the coupe aloft. 'But a coupe is sexy.' His eyes were dark, his voice low. Emma braced herself. Julien *would* try.

'The coupe is wider, it holds more, but it trades quantity for quality. The wide bowl allows the fizz and the aromas to escape more quickly. The champagne doesn't retain its properties for as long.'

'How is that sexy?' Emma knew she shouldn't ask but she couldn't help it, she was drawn in by those eyes, by that voice.

He gave a wicked grin. 'Haven't you heard the story? A coupe is cut to be the size of Marie Antoinette's breasts. Her left breast, particularly.' There was a glint in his eye.

'No, that is not true,' she contested with a laugh, forgetting to be on her guard, forgetting that Julien was a master of seduction.

'You're probably right,' he chuckled. 'There are coupes that date prior to Marie Antoinette. But it makes a damn good story, and it's tempting, isn't it? To see if the glass fits?'

'Sort of like a naughty version of Cinderella's shoe?' She couldn't help the rejoinder.

'Well, yes, now that you mention it. Can you imagine the prince going about the kingdom with a coupe to fit over all the ladies' breasts? Quite the social visit that would have been.' Oh, he was wicked. She'd never look at a coupe the same way again.

The footman returned with the bottle and Julien poured. 'Try it in the flute first, and then let some sit in the coupe for a little while.' His eyes were hot on her, their message clear. He'd gladly take this sipping foray into a less public arena.

She shook her head. 'Julien, I can't,' she said softly, and he nodded as if he understood even as he regretted her answer.

He lifted his glass. 'There is no hurry, Emma. I will wait for you and in the waiting I will prove my worth. We have time, all the time we need.'

She raised her glass to his and she did not correct him. Time was her enemy. If she waited long enough she would fall for him again. This afternoon proved it. She would leave the night of the gala and she would not give him a chance to say goodbye because she could not risk being talked out of leaving again. For her, time had run out.

* * *

Time had been on his side right up until the night of the gala. Julien adjusted his cuffs for the umpteenth time as he waited for Emma to come downstairs. Everything was ready, even the weather. Outdoors in the gardens, a lovely June evening was under way: lanterns were lit, the fountains were burbling, the musicians were playing. The judges' dais had been set up and draped in white bunting. Beyond the gardens a sunset was turning the sky purple over the vineyards. There were even guests, with more arriving in the drive. He could hear the carriage wheels on the gravel. All that was needed was the evening's host and hostess.

There she was. Emma appeared at the top of the stairs, and his breath caught. For the occasion, she'd set aside wearing black and had opted for something more in line with half-mourning to complement the evening, a gown of soft grey silk. The gown was simplicity itself. It was not overdone with trimmings and bows, just a product of good tailoring, and it fit her to perfection. Jet earbobs hung discreetly at her ears and an ivory cameo on onyx hung with a black silk ribbon was at her neck, both pieces of jewellery a tribute to her mourning. It was tastefully done.

'I've never seen grey look so beautiful on someone before.' He bowed as she descended the stairs, his eyes noting how the dress flowed over each curve and plane of her. The last three weeks had been a special torture, working side by side with her, and yet not being able to touch her, to renew the spark that kindled so easily between them. She was not ready for that. She was still learning whether or not she could trust him. He bent over her hand, adorned in a long grey silk glove that reached her elbow and matched her gown.

'It's not just grey, Julien,' she teased. 'It's *gris de perle*.' Ah, the colour used to describe the mixing of black and white grapes.

'You've been reading the old wine manuals in the library,' he teased back. It felt good to tease with her again, to laugh. He wondered how far her goodwill extended. He was nervous tonight on several accounts; he wanted the event to go well, he wanted everyone to get sales offers in the hopes his goodwill with this event would smooth over his desertion of his *oncle*, he wanted his wines to show well at the tasting, but most of all, he wanted Emma to stay. He had only one trick up his sleeve left for that. If it should fail…well, he wouldn't think on that.

'Did anyone show up?' Emma whispered, taking his arm, and he realised she was as nervous as he. He wondered if it was for the same reasons.

'Yes, you cynic. The garden is filling up with guests. I am told Madame Clicquot has just arrived. She agreed to judge the blind tasting.'

'So, everyone has come to watch Rome burn?'

'Have faith, Emma. The consortium is interested in money and profit. If we can help enhance theirs, all will be forgiven rather quickly,' Julien assured her, and he hoped he was right. 'Tonight, we are going to greet our guests, we're going to laugh and dance and drink champagne as if all is right with the world.'

And for a while, all *was* right. Julien could not recall

a more perfect night, sipping ice cold champagne and dancing beneath the stars with the woman he loved. He'd not danced in ages and the feeling of Emma in his arms as they turned about the outdoor dance floor was intoxicating in a way that transcended the bubbles of champagne. She'd been surprised to find he was an accomplished dancer and he teased her mercilessly about it.

The blind tasting was scheduled at eleven and they eagerly lined up with the other guests to hear the results. The *couteau champenois* won a blue rosette, which he let his *oncle* claim on his own, Etienne basking in the applause. Some of the Archambeau wines took a few other second- and third-place ribbons, which also pleased his *oncle*. Then came the sparkling wines, the champagnes, and Julien felt his nerves ratchet up. Emma's grip on his arm tightened. Garrett's special vintage was in this category. Les Voyage des Noces, Garrett had wanted it called. The Honeymoon. Julien had taken special care with it, knowing how important it was to his friend.

There were several in the category, and it seemed to take for ever before the tasting was done. Madame Clicquot and the other two judges set aside their score sheets and Charles Tremblay, who'd offered to act as the facilitator of the tasting ceremonies, began to read the prizes. Julien's heart sank as the list went on. They'd not taken fourth or third, or second. He was beginning to think the great experiment had failed. 'This last wine has been described by the judges as bringing a new taste to champagne, it is crisp, sweet, and yet sharp. Like new love itself, as suggested by its name. Our winner is Les Voyage des Noces.'

'You did it,' Emma whispered beside him, and he understood that her nerves had been for *him*, that she'd cared because he cared, because he wanted it so badly for her, for them. He hugged her tight, not caring what anyone might think, or what *she* might think. In that moment he only wanted to share this victory with her. He felt her arms go about his neck, and she was hugging him and crying. 'Go on, go get that ribbon, you deserve it.' On stage, there were congratulations and hand shaking, and there was the expectation of a speech from him, which he made short work of, but when he made his way off the dais into the crowd, Emma was gone.

Julien told himself not to panic. She might have gone to deal with some detail of the party. A champagne supper to celebrate the victors was to be laid at midnight. He went to the kitchens but Petit had not seen her. He checked the retiring rooms but she was not there either. That was when real panic came to him. He stopped a footman on the stairs. 'Have you seen Madame Luce?'

'Yes, she just went out to the carriages in front.'

Julien began to run. He knew with a bone-deep surety she meant to leave, to slip away now that she'd honoured her end of the deal. She'd stayed until the gala.

But everything had gone so well. Why would she leave now? How would he find her amid the line of carriages? It was her dress that gave her away. The *gris de perle* caught the moonlight, her foot lifted to enter, shining in the dark at the last carriage in the row, one that was easily positioned to leave without alerting all the others. 'Emma!' he called, his voice laced with panic. If she got in and decided to make a dash for it, he had no hope of running her down in dancing shoes.

'Julien, please. Go back inside and celebrate your victory.' She was calm, as if she were just going into town on a short errand.

'Why are you doing this? There is no reason to leave, the evening is a success. Madame Clicquot has given you validation. No one dares gainsay us now.'

She put a gentle hand on his arm. 'It is you who received the validation. Your wines won. This is your world, Julien.' She was too calm. This was not a spontaneous decision and that chilled him. All night she'd been saying goodbye while he'd been hoping for more, for a second chance, for a new beginning.

'You were going to leave all along,' he accused in low tones.

She nodded. 'I cannot take you away from your family and I cannot pretend that this can only be a business relationship for me. If I stay, I will not be able to resist your charm, Julien, and that is a dangerous place to be when you're the woman who is keeping the man she cares for from his inheritance. I could never marry you and not wonder how much of your affections are for me and how much are for the estate. That shadow would always be there.'

'No, it wouldn't. I can make that shadow go away. When I told you that I chose you, I meant it. I chose you, not the estate or the vineyards, or the Archambeau legacy. That way lies poison. I see it eating my *oncle* alive. If you want to give this place up, sell it to someone else, that's fine. We can start somewhere new. Or…' He reached into his coat pocket. This was his last hope and it had to work. 'I will sign this agreement as part of our marriage contract.' He passed it to her and gave her a moment to read it, wanting her to see it with her own eyes.

She looked up, astonishment in her gaze. 'You are signing away your husbandly rights to the chateau?'

'Yes, I am giving up all claim to it through marriage. It must remain yours. I do not know of any other way to convince you of that.'

'You would give up your dream for me?' She put out a hand to the carriage side to steady herself.

'I've already told you, you're my dream. I am giving up nothing. I am gaining everything.' He reached a hand out to smooth back a strand of hair. 'You've brought me back to life, Emma. I was dead inside before you came. And now, I want to live and live and live but I can't do it without you. Will you stay as my wife?' A slow tear rolled down her face. He brushed it away with the pad of his thumb. 'Emma, what is it?'

She sniffed. 'I didn't think a person could find happiness twice in a lifetime.' She gave a shaky breath. 'But I have and I hardly know what to do with it. Do I dare believe in it?'

'If I can dare it, you can dare it. Will you say yes, Emma?' His world, his entire being hinged on this.

She nodded and he swept her into his arms for a kiss it seemed he'd waited a lifetime for. *This* was what love felt like. It was not hard or angry or ravenous like some of their other kisses, but it was consuming all the same.

'What do you propose we do now, Monsieur Archambeau?'

'We turn this gala into an engagement celebration. I want everyone to know right away.' She smiled up at him and he was acutely aware that he'd only survived the night because she loved him.

Epilogue

Late spring, 1858

'Papa! Papa! Pick me up! I want to go riding on your shoulders.' Sturdy three-year-old legs pelted towards Julien, arms outstretched. He turned from the vines with a wide grin at the sight of his son.

He assumed a teasingly stern stance. 'What do we say when we want something, Matthieu-Philippe?'

'*S'il vous plait?* Please may I have a ride on your shoulders?' dark-haired Matthieu-Philippe amended eagerly, quicksilver eyes—like his mother's—dancing with the thrill of being outdoors and quite possibly out from under his nanny's strict, watchful eye.

Julien picked him up, giving him a twirl before settling him on his shoulders. He revelled in the solid, well-fed toddler weight of his son, in knowing this exuberant little boy was his. His to love, his to nurture, his to teach. The days of Matthieu-Philippe riding on his *père*'s shoulders would come to an end, sooner rather than later if the boy kept growing at this rate.

He would miss them; the gentle tug of pudgy fingers in his hair, the giggles when Julien would bounce him up and down. Julien would savour these days for as long as he could. But there was consolation in knowing that the days of walking beside him would begin.

Julien smiled at the thought. At last, he had a son to walk the land with him. A son named for both Julien's *grandpère* and *père*. A son who had his mother's eyes and energy, and his father's passion for the land. Matthieu-Philippe gave a tug. 'Père, how are the grapes this morning?'

'Why don't you see for yourself.' Julien bent low, letting the little boy study the vines.

'They're green. They've got buds!' the boy exclaimed, bouncing a bit on Julien's shoulders.

'They're growing,' Julien affirmed, his gaze drifting from the vines to the end of the row, caught by a movement. His smile widened at the sight of his wife. Someone else was growing, too. One could see the prominence of a six-months-pregnant belly when she stood in profile as she was now. Julien's heart swelled at the thought of another baby, another child to love in a few months. It would arrive just in time for the harvest. But if anyone could handle harvest season and a newborn all at once, it was Emma. His wife was indefatigable.

He loved her more now, six years after their wedding, than he had that beautiful summer afternoon in the vineyard when they'd said their vows before family and friends in an intimate service at home. Although, at the time, he'd not thought it possible to love her more. He'd been the happiest of bridegrooms. That happiness had only grown apace with their grapes. She'd become his partner in all things, or was it that he'd become hers? They'd added three new presses to their production line, they were bottling double the amount of wine they'd bottled six years ago, and sales were up.

She'd been right about the British market. It was definitely an unpicked plum. Emma's brother Gabriel had played an indispensable role in helping promote their champagne in England. Even now, they were experimenting with a *blanc de blanc* blend of sparkling wine designed with the British palate in mind. But more than her business sense, he treasured *her*. She was the heart of their home, keeping the house running, raising their son, running their business. Loving him. Even when he was stubborn and intractable, which he often was. They still quarrelled on occasion, but at the end of each day one thing remained constant: she was his heart.

Julien waved to her and she came to meet them, a picnic basket at her side. He balanced Matthieu-Philippe with one hand and took the basket from her with the other and a scold. 'You should not be lugging around something so heavy, *ma cherie.*'

She laughed at his concern. 'I won't start waddling until next month, I have some time to enjoy walking yet.'

He kissed her cheek. 'I love it when you waddle. I think it's adorable.' Julien nodded to her belly. 'How is our little *enfant* this fine day?'

Emma covered her belly with a hand. 'Stubborn like his father and just as insistent. He's been kicking since sunrise.' She stifled a yawn.

'Ah, that's why you were up early.' Julien led them

to a grassy area at the end of the row and set Matthieu-Philippe down. 'Help me with the blanket, *mon fils*,' he instructed. 'Mama is to rest. We will wait on her for luncheon. She is not to lift a finger.' Matthieu-Philippe giggled and thought it was a great game to unpack the picnic hamper. This was the life he'd dreamed of, Julien thought. To eat lunch on a blanket in one's own vineyard, his son and his wife beside him. Nothing could be finer.

Nothing could be finer than a vineyard picnic, even if one was six months pregnant with a mule kicking inside. Emma's eyes caught Julien's and she smiled. He was thinking the same. She could tell by the way he looked at her, his slate-blue eyes soft with a special tenderness he reserved just for her and their son. She was not sure she'd done anything to deserve finding such happiness twice in her lifetime. But she was thankful for it every day.

She had loved Garrett, fiercely, devotedly. She did not doubt that love now. She'd learned there were different kinds of love, that she could love Garrett and Julien, and that love would be different for each because they were different. That loving one did not demean the love she had for the other. Emma watched her handsome husband lay out the picnic and wondered if Garrett had known they might suit. That if anything happened to him, that Julien would be there in some capacity as a friend, perhaps to see her through? Had Garrett imagined something more for them? If so, she loved him all the more for it.

'What is it, *ma cherie*? You look contemplative.' Julien passed her a plate with a ham sandwich on it and a mug of lemonade. The only thing she didn't like about pregnancy was not being able to drink champagne.

'I'm just happy, that's all.' She smiled. 'Your *oncle* sent a note this morning. He'll be joining us for dinner. We can celebrate his birthday.' She knew it pleased Julien that the rift between him and his *oncle* had healed. It had not been easy and it had taken the birth of their son to really bring Etienne around, but it had happened. Etienne was her family now, too. She wanted that family to be whole.

Julien's eyes glinted mischievously. 'He'll be gloating about that new award his wine has won. He'll be insufferable.'

'He's earned it. I am happy for him. He can win all the awards he wants for the *champenois* as long as he leaves the champagne to us,' she laughed and then sobered. 'We'll have to be at our best though. I hear rumour there's a new widow looking to head her family's champagne house. Madame Pomeroy.'

Julien stretched out on the blanket. 'I'm not worried. I've got the best widow in town.'

She gave him a soft look. With Julien, she was home in all the ways that mattered. Gone were the days when she struggled against betrayal, struggled to find acceptance. She'd found it here with him. 'Here's to another good year, Julien Archambeau, and to my liaison with my Champagne Count. *Famille et terre tout les temps.*'

* * * * *

HISTORICAL

Your romantic escape to the past.

Available Next Month

Duke For The Penniless Widow Christine Merrill
Spinster With A Scandalous Past Sadie King

....

Miss Georgina's Marriage Dilemma Eva Shepherd
Wedded To His Enemy Debutante Samantha Hastings

Keep reading for an excerpt of
STOLEN BY THE VIKING
by Michelle Willingham — find this story
in the *Her Untamed Warrior* anthology.

Prologue

The kingdom of Maerr, Norway—ad 874

It was the morning of his wedding. Although most men would have welcomed the day, Alarr Sigurdsson had the sense that something was not right. The shadowed harvest moon last night had promised an ill omen, and the wise woman had cautioned him to delay the marriage.

Alarr had ignored the *volva*, for he was not a man who believed in curses or evil omens. The union would bring a strong alliance for his tribe. He had known Gilla Vigmarrsdottir since they were children, and she always had a smile and was even-tempered. She was not beautiful in the traditional way, but that didn't matter. Her kindness made him amenable to the match. His father, Sigurd, had negotiated for her bride price, and the *mundr* was high, demonstrating their family's wealth.

'Are you ready to be chained into the bonds of marriage?' his half-brother Danr teased. 'Or do you think Gilla has fled?'

He didn't rise to Danr's bait. 'She will be there.'

Alarr had worn his best tunic, adorned with silver-braided trim along the hem, and dark hose. His black cloak hung over his shoulders, but it was the absence of his weapons that bothered him most. His mother had asked him to leave them behind, claiming that they would only offend the gods. It was an unusual request, and one that made him uneasy, given all the foreign guests.

Her beliefs did not mean he intended to remain defenceless, however. During the wedding, he would receive a ceremonial sword from Gilla as a gift, and at least he would have that. Weapons were a part of him, and he took comfort in a balanced blade. He felt more comfortable fighting than joining in a conversation.

It was strange being the centre of attention, for he had two brothers and two half-brothers. As the second-born, Alarr was accustomed to being overlooked and ignored, a fact that usually allowed him to retreat into solitude and train for warfare. The intense physical exertion brought a strange sense of peace within him. While he practised with a blade, he didn't have to compete with anyone, save himself. And now that he had earned his status as a fighter, the men respected him. No one challenged him, and he had confidence that he could win any battle he fought.

Not that Sigurd had ever noticed.

Although his father tried to behave as if they had no enemies, Alarr was no fool. There was an air of restlessness brewing among the tribes. He had visited several neighbouring *jarls* and had overheard the whispers of rebellion. Yet, his father did not want to believe it.

Danr shot him a sidelong grin. 'Are you afraid of losing your innocence this night?' With that, Alarr swung his fist, and Danr ducked, laughing. 'I hope she is gentle with you, Brother.'

'Be silent, unless you want me to cut out your tongue,' he threatened. But both knew it was an idle threat. His half-brother was never serious, and he often made jests. Fair-haired and blue-eyed, all the women were fascinated by the man, and Danr was only too willing to accept their offerings. Alarr knew that his half-brother would find his way into a woman's bed this night.

The scent of roasting meat lingered in the air, and both cattle and sheep had been slaughtered for the wedding feast. Sigurd had invited the leaders of neighbouring tribes, as well as their daughters. Undoubtedly, he would be trying to arrange future weddings to advance his own position. Although Sigurd was a petty king, it was never enough for him. He hungered for more status and greater power.

Alarr walked towards his father's longhouse and found Sigurd waiting there. The older man had a satisfied expression on his face, though he was wearing only a simple woollen tunic and hose. His hair was greying, with threads of white mingled in his beard and hair. Even so, there was not a trace of weakness upon the man. His body was a warrior's, lean and strong. Sigurd had bested many men in combat, even at his advanced age. 'Are you ready?'

Alarr nodded, and they walked alongside one another in silence. Outside their settlement, his ancestors were buried within the Barrow. The graves of former warriors—his grandsire and those who had died before him—were waiting. There, Alarr would dig up a sword from one of the burial mounds. The weapon would become his, forged with the knowledge of his forebears, to be given to his firstborn son.

After a quarter-hour of walking in silence, Sigurd paused at the base of the Barrow and gestured for Alarr to choose. He was glad of it, for he already knew whose sword he wanted.

He climbed to the top of the Barrow and stopped in front of the grave that belonged to his uncle, who had died only a year ago, in battle. Hafr had trained him in sword fighting from the moment Alarr was strong enough to lift a weapon. There was no one else whose sword he wanted more.

He and his father dug alongside one another until they reached the possessions belonging to Hafr. Alarr tried to dispel the sense of foreboding that lingered while he respected the ashes of his uncle. The sword had been carefully wrapped in leather, and Alarr took it, uncovering the weapon. The iron glinted in the morning light, but it would need to be cleaned and sharpened.

'Do you wish to take the sword?' Sigurd asked quietly.

'I do.'

His father then reached out to seize the weapon. Once he had given it over, Sigurd regarded him. 'Much is expected of you with this marriage. Our kingdom of Maerr has risen to great power, and we need to strengthen our ties with the other *jarls*. You must conceive a son with Gilla immediately and ensure that our alliance is strong.' He wrapped the sword in the leather once more and set it aside. 'Perhaps my brother's wisdom and strength will be yours, now that you have his sword.'

Alarr gave a nod, though he didn't believe it. He wanted the sword because it gave him a tangible memory of his uncle. Hafr had been more of a father to him than Sigurd, whether he'd known it or not. Alarr had spent most of his life trying to gain Sigurd's approval, to little avail.

They reburied the ashes of his uncle, along with Hafr's worldly possessions, before returning to the settlement. Alarr walked towards the bathhouse, for it was time for the purification ritual. He had not seen Gilla since her arrival, but he had seen several of her kinsmen and a few others he didn't recognise.

When he entered the bathhouse, the heat struck him instantly. Steam rose up within the air from heated stones set inside basins of water. Wooden benches were placed at intervals, along with several drying cloths.

Alarr stripped off his clothing and saw that three of his brothers were waiting. His youngest brother Sandulf was there, along with his older brother, Brandt, and their half-brother Rurik, Danr's twin. Unlike Danr, Rurik was dark-haired and quiet. In many ways, Alarr found it easier to talk with Rurik. They trained together often, and he considered the man a close friend, as well as a brother. Their youngest brother, Sandulf, had a thirst to prove himself. He had dark-blond hair and blue eyes and had nearly put adolescence behind him. Even so, Alarr didn't like the thought of his brother fighting in battle. Sandulf lacked the reflexes, though he'd trained hard. He feared that only experience would help the young man gain the knowledge he needed now.

'Whose sword did you choose?' Sandulf asked.

'Hafr's,' Alarr answered. At his answer, Rurik met his gaze and gave a silent nod of approval. His brother had also been close to Hafr, since Sigurd had distanced himself from his bastard sons.

Alarr strode towards the wooden trough containing heated water. He began the purification ritual, pouring the warmed water over his body with a wooden bowl and scrubbing off the dirt with soap. As he did, Brandt remarked in a low voice, 'There are many strangers among the guests. Did you notice?'

'I did,' Alarr answered. 'But then, our tribe is well known across the North. It's not uncommon. And we know that Sigurd wants to make other marriage alliances.' He sent a pointed look towards Rurik, which his half-brother ignored.

Even so, Brandt looked uneasy. 'He's endangering our tribe by bringing in warriors we don't know. Some were from Éireann.'

The island was several days' journey across the sea. Sigurd had travelled there, years ago, and had brought back a concubine. She had given birth to Rurik and Danr a few months after her arrival and had never returned home, even after Sigurd set her aside. Although Saorla had died years ago, this was the first time any visitors had come from Éireann. Alarr wondered if there was some connection between the visitors and his half-brothers.

Regardless, he saw little choice but to let the foreigners witness the marriage. 'They are already here now. We cannot deny them our hospitality.' With a shrug, he added, 'Sigurd likely invited them in the hopes of wedding one of their daughters to Rurik or Danr.'

'Possibly.' Brandt thought a moment. 'We cannot deny them a place to stay, but we can deny them the right to bring in weapons. We will say it is to abide by our mother's wishes.'

It was a reasonable request, and Alarr answered, 'I will see to it.' He reached for his clothing and got dressed.

'Wait a moment.' Brandt approached and held out a leather pouch. 'A gift for your wedding.' Alarr opened it and found a bronze necklace threaded with small pendants shaped like hammers. It was a visible reminder of Thor, a blessing from his older brother.

He stood so Brandt could help him put it on. Then Alarr looked back at his brothers, unable to cast off the sense that something was not right at all. Perhaps it was the unknown warriors, or perhaps it was the knowledge that he would be married this day.

A sudden premonition pricked at him, that he would not marry Gilla, as they had planned. Alarr knew not why, but the hair on the back of his arms stood up, and he could not set aside his uncertainty. He tried to dispel the restlessness in anticipation of the wedding. Like as not, every bridegroom had those feelings.

Sandulf trailed behind him. 'May I join you, Alarr?'

He shrugged. 'If you wish. But we are only exchanging the *mundr* and Gilla's dowry. You may want to wait.' The wedding activities would last most of the day, and there were enough witnesses without needing Sandulf there. 'You could return when we make the sacrifices to the gods. That part is more interesting.'

His brother nodded. 'All right. And in the meantime, I can watch over our guests and learn if any of them are a threat.'

'Good.' He understood his youngest brother's desire

to be useful, and it might be a wise idea to keep a close watch over the visitors.

Alarr departed the bathhouse and watched as his brothers went on their way. Brandt joined him as he approached the centre of the settlement. His older brother said little, but his face transformed when he spied his heavily pregnant wife, Ingrid. There was a moment of understanding that passed between them, along with joy. Alarr wondered if he would ever look upon Gilla's face in that way when she was about to bear a child.

'It won't be long now,' he said to Brandt. 'You'll be a father.'

Brandt nodded, and there was no denying his happiness. 'Ingrid thinks it's a boy from what the *volva* told her, I hope they are right.'

Alarr walked alongside his brother until he reached Sigurd and Gilla's father. It was time to discuss the bride price and dowry. But before they could begin, they were interrupted by his mother. She hurried forward and whispered quietly to Brandt, whose face tightened. Then he gave a nod.

'I must go,' he said to Alarr. 'There is a disturbance with tribes gathering to the north. I should be back later tonight for the wedding feast, but I've been asked to intervene and prevent bloodshed, if possible. I am sorry, but it cannot wait.'

Alarr inclined his head, wondering if this was the ill omen the *volva* had spoken of. It also struck him that his mother had spoken to Brandt and not to him or to her husband. She did not like Sigurd, but then again, it was possible that the king already knew and had ordered Brandt to go in his stead. Sigurd's presence at the wedding was necessary.

'Do not go alone,' Alarr warned his brother.

'Rurik will accompany me, along with a few other men,' Brandt promised. His gaze fixed upon his wife, who was walking towards the other women, and his features softened. 'I will return as soon as I can.'

'Go then,' Alarr said. 'And return this night for the feasting.' He clapped Brandt on the back before turning his attention back to the negotiations.

Sigurd was already bargaining with Vigmarr as the two exchanged the dowry and *mundr*. Since they had already agreed upon the bride price, it was hardly more than a symbol of the union to come.

Alarr saw Gilla standing behind her father. She wore a green woollen gown with golden brooches at her shoulders. Her dark hair hung below her shoulders, and upon her head, she wore a bridal crown made of woven straw, intertwined with flowers. Her smile was warm and welcoming, though she appeared slightly nervous.

Beside her, the *volva* was preparing the ritual sacrifice to the gods. The wise woman began chanting in the old language, supplications for blessings. Several of the guests began to draw closer to bear witness, and the scent of smoke mingled with the fresh tang of blood. The slain boar was offered up to Freyr, and the *volva* took a fir branch and dipped it into the boar's blood. She then made the sign of the hammer, blessing them with the sacrificial blood, as well as the other wedding guests.

Although Gilla appeared amused by the ritual, the sight of sprinkled blood upon her face and hair made Alarr uneasy. He watched as the wise woman then sprinkled the boar's blood on each of the guests. But instead of the guests revering the offering, there seemed to be an unspoken message passing among several of the warriors. Alarr could not shake the feeling that this was an omen of bloodshed to come.

Let my brothers be safe, he prayed to the gods. *Let them come back alive.*

Alarr watched the men, his attention caught by the tall Irish king. He didn't know if Feann MacPherson had come as an invited guest, or whether he had arrived of his own choice. It might be that he wanted an alliance or a wedding for his daughter, if he had one. The king wore a woollen cloak, and there were no visible weapons. Yet the man had a thin scar along his cheek, evidence of an earlier battle. His dark hair was threaded with grey, but there was a lean strength to him.

When he saw Alarr staring, his expression tightened before it fixed upon Sigurd. The hard look was not of a man who wanted an alliance—it was of a man itching for a fight.

Someone needed to alert the guards, but Alarr could not leave in the midst of the ceremony. He searched for a glimpse of Danr or Sandulf, but they were nowhere to be found. He only saw his aunt nearby, and she could do nothing.

You're overreacting, he tried to tell himself. But no matter how he tried to dismiss his suspicions, his instincts remained on alert. He could not interrupt the ceremony, for it would only humiliate his bride. This was meant to be a day of celebration, and Gilla's smile was bright as she looked at him.

She was a kind woman, and as he returned her smile, he forced his thoughts back to the wedding. Friendship was a solid foundation for their union, and he inwardly vowed that he would try to make this marriage a good one.

He stood before her, and Sigurd brought the sword of Hafr that they had dug from his uncle's grave. Alarr presented it to Gilla, saying, 'Take this sword as a gift from my ancestors. It shall become the sword of our firstborn son.'

She accepted the weapon and then turned to her father to present their own gift of another sword. 'Take this sword for your own.'

The blade had good balance, and he tested the edge, noting its sharpness. Gilla knew of his love for sword-fighting, and she had chosen a weapon of quality. It was a good exchange, and he approved of her choice.

Alarr placed the ring for Gilla upon the hilt of the sword, and was about to offer it, when he caught a sudden movement among the guests. Feann cast off his dark cloak and unsheathed a sword from where it had been strapped between his shoulder blades. His men joined him, their own weapons revealed. The visible threat made their intentions clear.

Sigurd's face turned thunderous at the insult, and he started to reach for Alarr's sword.

He handed the weapon to his father and commanded, 'Take Gilla to the longhouse and guard her.' The last thing they needed was his father's hot-headed fighting. 'Vigmarr and I will settle this.'

He took back his uncle's sword from Gilla, and her face turned stricken when she murmured, 'Be safe.'

His father heeded his instructions and took Gilla with him, along with a few other men. His aunt joined them, running with her skirts clenched in her hands. He heard his mother scream as she fled towards another longhouse in the opposite direction. Only when the women were gone did Alarr breathe easier.

It was a mistake. Chaos erupted among the guests as his men hurried towards the longhouse where they had stored their weapons. King Feann uttered a command in Irish, and his men surged forward, cutting down anyone in their path.

Alarr ran hard, and iron struck iron as his weapon met an enemy's blade. He let the familiar battle rage flow through him, and his uncle's sword bit through flesh, striking down his attacker. The weapon was strong, imbued with the spirt of his ancestor. Alarr swung at another man, and he glimpsed another warrior behind him. He sidestepped and caught the man in the throat before he slashed the stomach of his other assailant.

The volva *was right*, he thought. *It was an ill omen.*

Already, he could see the slain bodies of his kinsmen as more men charged forward in the fight. Alarr searched for his brothers, but there was no sign of Sandulf or Danr. By the gods, he hoped they were safe. If only Brandt and Rurik had been here, they could have driven off their enemies. He caught one of his kinsmen and ordered, 'Take a horse and ride north as hard as you can. Find Brandt and Rurik and bring them back.' The man obeyed, running hard towards the stables.

A strange calm passed over him with the knowledge that he would likely die this day. The shouts of kinsmen echoed amid the clang of weapons, only to be cut short when they died. The Irish king started to run towards the longhouse, but Alarr cut him off, swinging his sword hard. The older man caught his balance and held his weapon against the iron.

threw open the doors, and Sandulf staggered out. Four other men emerged from a different door, and Alarr struggled to his knees. He spied the slain bodies of his father... Gilla... Vigmarr and his wife...

His stomach lurched, and Alarr turned his gaze back to the sky, hating the gods for what they had done. A lone raven circled the clouds, and he could only lie in his own blood while his enemies cut down the remaining wedding guests and returned to their ships.

In the dirt beside him, he saw the familiar glint of a golden brooch.

Feann paused a moment. 'Stay out of this, boy. The fight isn't yours. Sigurd has gone too far, and he will pay for his crimes.'

'This is my wedding, so the fight *is* mine,' Alarr countered. He swung his weapon, and the king blocked his blow. 'And I am not a boy.' He was beginning to re-alise that Feann had travelled seeking vengeance, and his intent was to slaughter Sigurd. But what crimes was he talking about?

They sparred against one another, the king toying with him. Alarr struck hard, intending to stop the man. But with every blow, he grew aware that Feann was stalling, drawing out the fight. It was then that he saw men surrounding the longhouse where his father was protecting his bride. Gilla's father, Vigmarr, was fight-ing back, trying to defend them.

And then Alarr caught the unmistakable scent of smoke and fire.

He renewed his attack, slashing with his sword as he fought to find a weakness. Feann parried each blow, and when the screams of the women broke through, Alarr jerked his attention back to the longhouse.

A slashing pain struck him in the calves, and he saw the king withdraw a bloody blade, just before his legs collapsed beneath him. Alarr met the man's gaze, waiting for the killing blow. Instead, Feann's expres-sion remained grim as he wiped his blade. 'If you're wise, boy, you'll stay on the ground.' Then he strode towards the longhouse.

Alarr tried to rise, but the agonizing pain kept his legs from supporting him. He called out to his men to attack and defend the longhouse. But a moment later, he watched in horror as the fire raged hotter. Someone